"What fun it is to visit my favorite fishing spots, not in a guide-boat but in a wonderful murder mystery."
                    —Henry Winkler, author of *I've Never Met an Idiot on the River*

"Two chapters in and you know you are in for an interesting read . . . Each scene is set up with a fisherman's patience, with the wind, water, and wildlife of Montana becoming as important as the human characters we follow. . . . *The Royal Wulff Murders* should be on any outdoorsman's reading list."   —*Suspense Magazine*

"Keith McCafferty's *The Royal Wulff Murders* is the mystery fly anglers have been waiting for. Finally, an author who knows the crucial difference between 2X and 4X tippet! But it's not just the fishing details that make this novel so enjoyable: it's the rich characters, the robust sense of humor, a sadly topical plot, and a writing style that is as gin-clear as a Montana trout stream." —Paul Doiron, author of *Trespasser* and *The Poacher's Son*

"*Wulff* is fun . . . with sharp dialogue between characters . . . [and] fishing scenes that read right . . . [McCafferty is] *Field & Stream's* survival editor, and that savvy shows in subtle and satisfying ways."
                    —*Fly Rod and Reel* (online)

"A muscular, original first novel. McCafferty is one of the country's most convincing writers on survival and life in the wilderness, and this mystery is an impressive foray into fiction—taut, often highly amusing, filled with memorable characters like the lady sheriff and the former private eye who paints and fly fishes—and it's a real page-turner."
                    —Nick Lyons, author of *My Secret Fishing Life*

"The last time I fished the Madison River it was high, fast, and dirty—words that come to mind for parts of McCafferty's tangy debut mystery. But there are also episodes of angling wonder and Montana beauty, rendered in prose so gorgeous they make this book a truly rare catch, the page-turner that doubles as a poetic meditation."
                    —Mark Kingwell, author of *Catch and Release: Trout Fishing and the Meaning of Life*

The Gray Ghost Murders

"This is a truly wonderful read. In an old and crowded field, Keith has created characters fresh, quirky, and yet utterly believable, then stirred them into a mystery that unfolds with grace and humor against a setting of stunning beauty and danger. Stranahan, the fisherman sleuth, breaks free of the old clichés and delights with his humanity, vulnerability, and love of cats. Yes, cats. Keith has written a book that speaks to women and men regardless of color or background. The only downside of this book is that we must wait a year for the next one."

—Nevada Barr, *New York Times* bestselling author
of the Anna Pigeon mysteries

"McCafferty skillfully weaves Big Sky color, humor, and even romance (in the form of Sean's stunning new girlfriend, Martinique, who's bankrolling veterinary school by working as a bikini barista) into the suspenseful plot as it gallops toward a white-knuckle . . . climax."

—*Publishers Weekly*

"Think big-city CSI teams have it tough? Their examinations of crime scenes are hardly ever interrupted by a grizzly bear like the one that sends Deputy Harold Little Feather to the hospital. . . . Irresistible."

—*Kirkus Reviews*

"You'll find yourself obsessed with the story . . . due to McCafferty's hilarious, spot-on depiction of rural politics (starring a female sheriff, a latte-making love interest, and a fishing buddy), which proves that small western towns are as rich . . . as any world capital."

—*Oprah's Book Club 2.0* (5 Addictive New Mysteries We Can't Put Down)

Dead Man's Fancy

"McCafferty knows his country and his characters, who have a comfortable, lived-in feel and yet shine as individuals. . . . [His] understated prose deserves to be savored." —*Kirkus Reviews*

"McCafferty's beautifully written third mystery . . . The complex, multilayered story smoothly switches from one character to another."

—*Publishers Weekly* (starred review)

"*Dead Man's Fancy* breathes new life into the mystery genre with its unique milieu and . . . loveable characters." —*Salt Water Sportsman*

"McCafferty's third series entry lassos up a range of topics—wolf reintroduction, wilderness living and survival, animal rights—that are uncovered through his protagonists' meticulous sleuthing."

—*Library Journal*

A PENGUIN MYSTERY

DEAD MAN'S FANCY

Keith McCafferty is the award-winning survival and outdoor skills editor of *Field & Stream* and the author of *The Royal Wulff Murders* and *The Gray Ghost Murders*. A two-time National Magazine Award finalist, he has written articles for publications as diverse as *Fly Fisherman* magazine and the *Chicago Tribune* and on subjects ranging from trout to tigers. He lives with his wife in Bozeman, Montana. *Dead Man's Fancy* is his third novel in the Sean Stranahan series.

Keith encourages you to visit him at keithmccafferty.com

DEAD MAN'S FANCY

Keith McCafferty

—A SEAN STRANAHAN MYSTERY—

PENGUIN BOOKS

PENGUIN BOOKS
Published by the Penguin Group
Penguin Group (USA) LLC
375 Hudson Street
New York, New York 10014

USA | Canada | UK | Ireland | Australia | New Zealand | India | South Africa | China
penguin.com
A Penguin Random House Company

First published in the United States of America by Viking Penguin,
a member of Penguin Group (USA) LLC, 2014
Published in Penguin Books 2015

THE LIBRARY OF CONGRESS HAS CATALOGED THE HARDCOVER EDITION AS FOLLOWS:
McCafferty, Keith.
    Dead man's fancy : a Sean Stranahan mystery / Keith McCafferty.
        pages   cm
    ISBN 978-0-670-01469-9 (hc.)
    ISBN 978-0-14-312613-3 (pbk.)
    1. Private investigators—Fiction.   2. Policewomen—Fiction.   3. Fly fishing—Fiction.   4. Fishing
guides—Fiction.   5. Missing persons—Fiction.   6. Animal rights activists—Fiction.   I. Title.
    PS3613.C334D43 2014
    813'.6—dc23
    2013036804

Printed in the United States of America
10   9   8   7   6   5   4   3   2

Set in Warnock with Zemestro display
Designed by Carla Bolte

For my brother, Kevin

"All stories are about wolves. All worth repeating, that is. Anything else is sentimental drivel."

—Margaret Atwood, *The Blind Assassin*

"If you have a sister and she dies, do you stop saying you have one? Or are you always a sister, even when the other half of the equation is gone?"

—Jodi Picoult, *My Sister's Keeper*

ACKNOWLEDGMENTS

Like many who toil in the murky profession of building words into books or, as writers may privately dare to think of it, turning lead into gold, I work in the dark. Much as I'd like to be able to consult Charles Dickens regarding a plot twist or summon F. Scott Fitzgerald's advice about a turn of phrase, it's just me shining the light, digging with the pick. Some nights, many nights, the gold I mine is fool's gold that floats to the surface and is washed away the next morning; other nights, better nights, it glitters from the bedrock upon which the story is built.

In this manner of working I have never flattered myself as being much different from anyone else. The acknowledgment sections of a few novels to the contrary—so many mentions that one would believe producing a book is a collaboration requiring the manpower of the Normandy Invasion—writing remains a solitary, constantly humbling affair that comes down to one person aspiring to unearth fundamental human truths, or at least tell a compelling story, while stringing together lies summoned from the ether. There's a measure of irony in the fact that one shuts the door on his fellow man in order to write about him, but recognizing the predicament you have put yourself in doesn't seem to alleviate the difficulties.

Those who are truly important in a writer's development belong to a short list indeed, at the top of which is the person who bestows upon him or her the magic of the written word. In my case that is my mother, Beverly McCafferty, whose voice, as she read aloud to me a children's book about a little snake titled *Slim Green*, is among my very first memories. Then came the writers whose books first compelled me to turn the pages myself. They include Mark Twain, Sir Arthur Conan Doyle, and Jim Corbett. I was nine years old when our car broke down and I found myself with two hours to read in a Denver public library, where I chose a story called "The Talla Des Man-eater" in *The Temple Tiger and More Man-eaters of Kumaon*. I opened the book wanting to lead a life of adventure. I closed it wanting to write about it. Rounding out the most important influences are those people who provide the necessary support for the realization of the writer's dream, and so are not among the well-wishers from afar (nice as it is to have them), but loved ones who not only share the infrequent celebration, but far too often suffer the doubts and fear of failure that plague all writers. My wife, Gail Schontzler, who also is my first and most trusted editor, deserves all the credit for keeping body and soul together.

On the professional side of the ledger, I wish to recognize my literary agent, Dominick Abel, as well as the team at Viking/Penguin who help me polish, publish and promote the final effort. They include Kathryn Court, Tara Singh, Scott Cohen, Beena Kamlani, Mary-Margaret Callahan and Rebecca Lang. Independent bookstore owners remain crucial to bringing writers to the attention of the reading public. None has been more helpful to me than Barbara Peters at the Poisoned Pen in Scottsdale, Arizona, and Ariana Paliobagis at the Country Bookshelf in Bozeman, Montana. I'd also like to thank Hurricane Isaac, which caused an electrical outage in New Orleans that led to Nevada Barr picking up my second novel, *The Gray Ghost Murders*, to while away a few powerless hours. For her irreverence and encouragement, both personally and professionally, I'm grateful. *Dead Man's Fancy* demanded I have a thorough understanding of the wolf reintroduction effort in the Rockies and its ramifications for those who live among these great predators. Many thanks to all those I have interviewed over the past several years, on both sides of this controversial issue. In particular I'd like to recognize Montana Fish, Wildlife and Parks biologists Julie Cunningham, Justin Gude and Ken Hamlin, and wolf specialist Mike Ross. Special thanks to Robert Millage.

There are winter days in Montana when the office feels cold even with a wood fire and I need more warmth than Rhett, my adopted feral cat, can provide. On these mornings I bicycle through the snow on studded tires to Wild Joe's Coffee Shop, where baristas Marissa Grinestaff, Jenalyn Lorilla, Adam Golder, Corissa Hannemann and Melissa Hoard, along with writer pal Sarah Grigg, make me feel at home, and a little less lonely in a lonely line of work.

Finally, there are the remarkable individuals who inspire my best effort simply because I look up to them in life and don't dare let them down. These include my children, Jessie and Thomas McCafferty, my brother, Kevin McCafferty, and my life-long friend, Karen Basil. And my aunt Jackie Bailie—matchmaker, dog boarder, and doctor of dubious mail-order degrees—who mended spiritually broken children with a wave of her fairy godmother wand, or, when the body needed more succor than a seventy-year-old woman wearing a prom dress and face glitter could provide, passed herself off as a physician and cajoled specialists into seeing patients they otherwise would never have seen.

"You're just whirring away in there, aren't you?" Jackie once told a little boy whose thoughts were so jumbled he found it hard to talk. "Some day you'll be a writer, and I will say I knew you when."

DEAD MAN'S FANCY

CHAPTER ONE

Where Trees Grow Close Together

At the sound, Martha Ettinger glanced from the trail, the brim of her hat rising to uncover the early stars. In the foredistance loomed the indigo silhouette of Papoose Mountain. Crooked fingers of pines groped toward the peaks and it was from one of those forests the howl had risen, a deep, sustained note haunted by a higher harmonic that now stirred to song other voices, the lament of the pack dying away to leave her in silence, feeling the beating of her heart.

"What was that, Marth?"

"What do you think it was?" She touched Petal's ribs and pulled alongside her deputy's mount, a gelded chestnut walker that had her Appaloosa by four hands.

"I thought I heard wolves."

"In the Madison Valley? What are the odds?"

"Actually they're pretty fair, you listen to the ranchers' bellyaching."

Ettinger switched off her headlamp. "It's called irony, Walt. Of course there are wolves in Montana. Anybody has ears can tell you that."

"Well, I never heard one before."

"Really?"

"Not that I could be sure of."

Martha was asking herself how you could mistake a wolf's howl when three drawn-out notes drifted down from the basin, the first wolf joined by one whose voice was pitched higher, the third higher yet, the chorus recalling to Martha the Inuit folktale of a mother who couldn't find food to feed her children, her wailing becoming howls until she turned into a wolf herself. She told Walt while the horses blew from the climb.

He made a sound like *puh.* "That story don't make no sense 't all," he said.

"That's why it's called folklore. Come on, we're here for a reason if you haven't forgot."

"I haven't, but you ask me, that young woman isn't missing because her horse bolted and stranded her on the mountain, she's missing 'cause she swapped the saddle for the pommel. Mark my words, she'll show up tomorrow with a bowlegged walk account a' too much cowboy lovin'."

"I'd agree with you if it wasn't for the likeliest cowboy calling our number."

"You want to bet a dinner on it? Bison meat loaf at Ted's Montana Grill if she's shacked with a fella, frog food at Cafe Provence she turns up lost."

"I don't bet when a person's life could be at stake, but if I had a mind to that's one I'd hope to lose. I wouldn't want to be up there with those lobos serenading my tender flesh." She clucked to Petal, just one side of her mouth moving, and the horses clopped up the trail into the basin.

———

The call had come in three hours after Judy Woodruff took over the second-shift dispatch. Sunset seemed premature to call out the troops for a dude-ranch naturalist slash fly-fishing guide who'd failed to show for a planning meeting with the activities director only an hour before, but the wrangler telling the story of the woman's disappearance was telling it priority backward. When he mentioned that her absence at the meeting prompted him to check the paddock where he found her horse standing outside the rails, riderless and sweated through its blanket, Judy didn't wait for elaboration but immediately patched him through to Sheriff's Sergeant Warren Jarrett. Jarrett reached Martha Ettinger at her home.

"You call up the hasty team?" she said.

"Sure. She's hurt serious, you don't want to lose time on something like this. My guess is she got bucked and they'll find her before we mount up. The wrangler's heading up there to backtrack the trail she was taking. He'll have an hour start on us. No reason for you to come, but I've known you long enough to know you might rather."

Ettinger stuck her head outside her back door and whistled sharply to round up Goldie, her Australian shepherd. She said, "That's the Culpepper place on Papoose, right? Do they have a sign? I seem to remember making a wrong turn six, seven years ago when old Ollie tickled his tonsils with the barrel of his Winchester."

"Yeah, well the widow's got it clear marked. A gate big enough for Paul Bunyan to yoke his ox. But just in case you don't pick it up in the headlights, I'll drop off a traffic cone with a reflective strip."

Martha had picked up Walter Hess in town and filled him in on the drive up the valley. The missing woman—she was twenty-five, named Nanika Martinelli—had taken advantage of ranch policy encouraging the help to participate in trail rides if there was a mount available, and being midway through September, there had been. The wrangler had led his party of yahoos on a standard afternoon outing, a twelve-mile loop trail skirting Lionhead Mountain, when Martinelli pulled alongside to say she was taking the long way back on a branch trail that cupped the headwall of Papoose Basin. The trail added six miles and would get her back to the ranch in about an hour and half. Martinelli being an experienced horsewoman who had soloed before, the wrangler just reminded her to check Boregard's shoes for rocks before sponging and brushing him down.

It struck Ettinger as careless to allow someone to ride off into the wilderness alone, no matter how competent she was sitting saddle. A dude outfit like the Culpepper's held its breath anytime a guest hung a fingernail or hooked himself with a trout fly. Even if Martinelli had signed on the dotted line of the liability clause, it opened the barn door for a lawsuit about as wide as you could push it. But without details it was hard to speculate.

Jason Kent, the incident commander of search and rescue, sat at the communications desk he'd set up in a corner of one of the ranch's unoccupied guest cabins. "Martha, Walt." No handshakes, the big sandy-haired man with the farmer's tan glanced up at them—Walter Hess, thin, hawk faced, about five ten, Ettinger an inch shorter, solidly built with curly auburn hair, startling blue eyes that were spiderveined from strain and a broad face that was handsome rather than pretty. Kent indicated to Ettinger to bring him a stick of kindling from the stack beside the stone fireplace. He took the stick in his left hand, the one with two missing fingers, swiveled his chair and tapped the topo map he'd pinned to the wall.

"This is the trail Martinelli said she was going to take after leaving the party. It switchbacks up the north side of the basin, contours under the headwall for a mile and a half, then switchbacks down the south side. We have riders going up both legs. The wrangler had an hour start on us, so if she went spurs over stirrups up there, he should have found her by now. But Bucky, Bucky Anderson's the ranch manager, said the young fella saddled up in a rush, went off half-cocked and has no way of contacting us or vice versa."

Martha's smile was sour. "I know Bucky. We share blood on my father's side. Last I heard he was going to marry lady Culpepper herself, see ranch life from the top rung of the ladder."

"Like my dad used to tell me," Kent said. "Son, you can marry more money in five minutes than you can make in a lifetime."

"Where is Bucky? I'd like to talk to him before Walt and I ride up there."

Kent shook his head. "I told him you'd want a word, but he's bullheaded and couldn't wait. Reminds me of somebody else I know." He briefly met Martha's eyes. "Anyway, Bucky knows that country better than anyone. He left a half hour ago, I put him up the south side, the wrangler went up the north. Warren Jarrett's coordinating the containment. We have riders here, here and here. As you can see, we drew the circle pretty big. Plus we have ATVs on the 26 A and B trails. If she's conscious, it would be darned hard for her not to know people are out looking. In case she tried to find her way back on foot, we're going to build bonfires at the trail junctions and shoot off strobes. She doesn't show by morning, Karl Radcliffe will take his Piper Cub up and I'll organize a ground search."

"Where should Walt and I go?"

"By the time you get somebody to round up mounts . . ." He ran a hand through his crew cut. "Steep country, unfamiliar horses, riding in the dark, I don't have to tell you that's the paraplegic's trifecta."

"I trailered Petal and Big Mike," Martha said. "We can be saddled in fifteen minutes."

"You buy another horse?"

"I'm pasturing Big Mike for a friend. He's bombproof and he's got good feet. Walt shouldn't have any trouble."

"I can see it isn't worth arguing." Kent stared at the map and nodded to himself. "You could do worse than go off trail"—he tapped the stick—"directly up the main fork of Papoose. Say that young woman got bucked up along the headwall; if she panicked, she might take a shortcut down through the bottom of the basin. Bucky says there's an elk trail skirts the south side of the creek. But you know elk trails, they go a ways and then they don't. You might get turned around a time or two. Find yourself in a jackpot, just build a fire and hunker down. I'm not drawing anyone off the search to look for a sheriff and a county mountie who ought to be able to take care of themselves."

Martha grunted. "Thanks for the vote of confidence, Jase."

Kent shrugged. He handed her a printout with the description of the missing woman and tapped a few keys on his laptop, inserting Martha and Walt's route into the search grid. "That's all," he said without looking up. "Just leave a crumb trail and check back on the hour."

———

"You sure you know where we are? I thought Jase said the south side of the creek."

Reining Petal to a stop, Martha dug her GPS out of her jacket pocket and touched a button to illuminate the liquid crystal display. "We *are* on the south side. But we're on the north side of a creek, too. The problem is there's three forks, four if you count the intermittent. I can't be sure which one he was talking about."

She raised her eyes to the triangle of timber that covered the basin. The gloom of the thickets, eerie under a haloed half moon, was fissured by darker lines marking the tributaries of Papoose Creek. Looking at the map, it seemed to Martha that they had the bases covered. But by god, the country was big. You could hide a herd of cattle in it.

"What's that, Walt?" She hadn't been listening.

"It's going to be blacker than a witch's snatch in there."

Martha grunted. "And one would know that . . . how?"

"Just saying," Walt said, "I don't know what we're going to accomplish riding around in the dark. Hell, we haven't even reached the trees and we're already lost."

"Not lost, just considering the route. You don't have to consider with me. I know you're not as comfortable sitting on critters as I am."

"No, if you think we're following the right path, I'm right behind you."

As they climbed into the pines, it was the right path—Ettinger was sure of it. She was less so a half mile later, having to choose when the path forked, and forked again to cross the left-hand creek, the trees leaning in so that she and Walt had to dismount and attach rope leads to the halters. Martha saw immediately that Big Mike was head shy around Walt, who was decent enough with his boots in the stirrups, but leading a horse along an elk trail was a different matter. He was on the wrong side of the horse, for one thing. Martha coached him but Big Mike had Walt's number, and after balking changed tactics and started crowding him.

"Don't let him barge you," Martha said. "When he gets too close, just push him on the shoulder." Walt stepped closer and when the horse's left forefoot came down, it came down on the toe of Walt's buffalo hide Tony Lama.

"Jesus, son of Mary!" he shouted, going over backward. The horse snorted and reared. Martha jumped for the lead, got it before it tangled in the brush and, gripping the rope in her right fist, stuck her elbow into the horses' neck to keep it close. She held tight rein and stayed in Big Mike's face until he calmed. "We just about had ourselves a rodeo," she said.

"I can hear it squishing, Marth." Walt had pushed himself to a sitting position. "My god, it's like my foot's on fire."

"Then you better get that boot off before it swells." She waited for her heart rate to come down and blew out a long breath.

"This is my fault," she said. "We had no business leading horses in here, even if you were the whisperer himself."

The bloody sock gleamed in Walt's headlamp. "I shoulda' stayed in Chicago," he said. "I'd a' been safer on the street."

"And leave me with no one to insult? Nah, the county needs a man who knows the street. There's more of them in Montana than there used to be, you may have noticed."

"This isn't the street. Jeez, do you think it's broke?"

"Can you wiggle it?"

Walt winced, the skin around his eyes fissuring in Martha's headlamp. He nodded. "I think he just got the tip. I bet I'll lose the nail, though." After a moment of silence, he managed a wry smile. "'I think I just got the tip.' That's something my ex-wife was fond of say-ing. She was a regular comedienne, Lydia was."

"I'd say you were lucky enough. Big Mike only weighs about twelve hundred pounds . . ." She stopped, tilting her head to listen. She brought a hand up to worry her jaw.

"Is it the wolves again? I don't care what they say about 'em never attacking. Just thinking about Little Bo Peep out here wandering around in the dark. It gives me the willies. Why—"

"No. Ssshh. It sounded like a whinny." She tapped at her GPS.

"What are you doing?"

"Checking to see if we're close enough to the headwall to hear one of the searcher's horses. We're," she waited, "a mile, no, mile and a half from where the trail comes closest. In this timber, I don't think we'd hear a horse that far away."

"Maybe it's that wrangler's horse. Maybe he saw something that took him off the trail."

"Maybe. Let's just sit and listen."

But a pall had fallen over the wilderness, and she sat in silence ex-cept for the assorted groans coming from the direction of Walt's sil-houette. The minutes ticked by. "What now?" Walt said finally. "I can probably sit the saddle but I don't know about hobbling out to where it's open enough to mount up. You could keep going, Marth."

She shook her head. "I'd keep pushing if there was something to push toward. No, we'll check in with IC and then I'll water the horses down at the creek. They're ground-tie trained, but if they get wind of the wolves I'm afraid they'll bolt, so what we'll do is run a high line between a couple trees and tether them to the line. Then build up a fire, keep it going. If that girl wandered down into the basin, she might spot it and come in."

Martha unholstered her radio. The crackling as she turned the volume knob brought a short snort from Petal and she immediately dialed it down to listen, to see if she'd hear the horse she'd thought she'd heard earlier. Horses that want company talk. It was logical that one separated from its rider would neigh, especially if it heard another horse. But the wilderness was silent.

Jason Kent's voice was broken but audible. He'd been following the crumb trail from Martha's GPS on his computer screen. Bad luck about Walt's foot. He agreed that where they were was as good a place as any to spend the night. Nothing to report on the search except that Harold Little Feather, after following the trail the wrangler had taken, had met up with Bucky Anderson on the headwall. They'd heard the wolves howl, too, but of the woman they'd seen nothing. Nor had they bumped into the wrangler.

"So now we're looking for two people could be in trouble. Citizens want to help, but all they do is make my job harder." He sounded tired. To Martha, Jason always sounded tired. She told him about maybe hearing a horse in the distance. The radio went silent and Martha could picture the incident commander sipping coffee from his paper cup. "All the more reason for you to stay put." He said he'd put out the word to the searchers and signed off.

Martha rigged the tarp she'd packed in a saddle bag; it was the time of year when once a week you'd wake up to see the high elevation forests dusted white. An hour later, lying on a rough saddle blanket that smelled of horse with Walt snoring beside her, Martha heard the long, drawn out bugle of an elk. The voice was faint, floating into the basin on the cold sink of night air, and in the light flicker from the fire, she saw Petal cock her ears. But the bugle was not joined by a rival bull, and after a while Petal relaxed her vigilance and Martha felt sleep coming as the fire hissed from the first snowflakes.

CHAPTER TWO

Hard as Bone

When she awoke, it was so light that Martha thought it was dawn. She pulled up her jacket cuff to glance at the luminous hands of her watch. Three a.m. It was just the diffuse light of the moon reflecting off the snow. She unbuttoned the waist of her pants to take the pressure off her bladder. Walt was still snoring, a line of blown snow in the center crease of the hat tilted over his face. The man could sleep through anything. Still, he was, at least marginally, a human being and she would not rather have been alone.

"Oh, quit stalling," she muttered.

She shuffled off behind the trees. Her face relaxed as she relieved herself. Men on a search, they just unzipped; they could care less she was standing ten feet away. She'd commented on it once to Harold Little Feather, that time when they were hunting elk in the Badger-Two Medicine. He told her that in uniform she was just one of the guys. "It's respect. That's the way I'd look at it." Then he'd shuffled a few feet away and pissed on the campfire coals. Martha shook her head. *Harold.* She kicked pine needle duff over the lance her urine had cut in the snow and went to check on the horses.

"Hey girl. It'll be light in a jiff now," she said, coming around the trees and then abruptly stopping. Directly in front of her, a little to the left of the two horses, a bulky shape loomed, blacking out a section of forest. For a second Martha thought it was a moose. But of course it couldn't be a moose; Petal and Big Mike would have gone crazy. Then she heard the nicker and knew the horse that she'd heard earlier had followed its nose into camp. Martha started talking in a low voice and immediately the horse advanced, extending its neck. Martha rubbed her fist under its eye. It was a gelded quarter horse, a bay with a cropped mane and irregular forehead star.

"Where did you come from?"

She switched on the low beam of her headlamp and ran it across the saddle. A braided lead rope was neatly coiled and secured to a D-ring ahead of the left fender, indicating the rider probably hadn't dismounted before separating from the horse. *Thrown?* Martha added a stop to the high line so the quarter horse couldn't trample into Petal or Big Mike, clipped the lead to the halter and considered the sky. She went back to the shelter and buckled on her duty belt. She thought of waking Walt, but what was the point? He couldn't go where she was going. And she *was* going, for the moon was showing only because it had found a hole in the clouds. It could snow again at any time, and the tracks the horse had left would be erased.

In the skiff, the impressions of the horseshoes were sharp sided. Martha backtracked them down to the creek, across and up and then a quarter mile farther to the north, down and across another creek. From there she backtracked the horse steadily upslope, her lungs straining and her legs quaking from the buildup of lactic acid. She had reached an open park some thousand feet or so below the escarpment. Snow was deeper here, the tracks pockmarks without definition. It had still been snowing when the horse reached this point, but had quit shortly after it entered the tree belt. Martha's smile was grim, for she understood that the window of opportunity to discover why and where the horse had separated from it rider was closing. She was now deciphering the trail of a horse whose tracks had been filling in as soon as they were made, and the higher she climbed, the more snow would have accumulated. She could be left knowing the end of the story without its beginning.

Martha turned to look at the roll of forest through which she'd been climbing. The camp was marked by smoke that was visible as a ghostlike smudge over the trees. No stars, just the hazy half aureole of moon and the mountain deathly still in the grip of night. She shuddered and placed two fingers to the side of her throat, searching for her pulse. Strong and steady.

"Get a grip, Martha," she said out loud. "You're the sheriff of Hyalite County."

When she picked up the track, her professional mask was firmly in place. But there was no longer a trail to follow. The tracks had disappeared. She cast upward and found where the horse's hooves had cut furrows, kicking up dirt. When a horse is at full gallop, there is an interval in its gait when all four hooves are in the air, resulting in gaps in its stride. Martha understood this horse's tracks had disappeared for twenty feet not because they were filled with snow, but because the horse had been plunging down the face of the mountain. A startled horse can run a long way—she had once witnessed a packhorse scared by a grizzly bear run at least a quarter mile across a scree slope before falling over a cliff—but most mountain horses had the sense to settle to a trot fairly quickly. She felt she had to be close to the place where the horse had panicked, where logic dictated it had bucked its rider.

Two hundred yards up the slope, a patch of timber made a black blot against the satin hump of the mountain. The horse had come from the direction of the trees, but as Martha continued to climb, the tracks became less distinct and then disappeared completely. She ran her front teeth across her chapped lower lip. "Don't give up, Martha," she muttered under her breath. She switched off her headlamp, which had gradually been dimming, and reached for the Carnivore tracking light holstered on her utility belt. The light had a two-position switch. In the tracking mode, a cluster of red and blue LED bulbs were activated to highlight the color red. A spot of blood would seemingly jump off the ground and appear to suspend in midair. In its normal mode, it was a simple flashlight, but the five lumen xenon bulb threw a much more powerful beam than her headlamp. Martha switched the light on in the normal mode and cast it on the trees. She had not been able to backtrack the horse for the last fifteen minutes, but had evidently followed the course of its flight precisely, for the snow at the lower end of the timber was littered with pine boughs that the horse had snapped in its panic.

She paused to catch her breath. For the first time since leaving camp, she found herself reluctant to follow the trail. Instinctively, she sought the leather strap that secured her sidearm in its holster. She withdrew the Ruger .357 magnum, felt its reassuring heaviness and replaced it in the holster, leaving the strap unsnapped. Stepping cautiously, she entered the trees and began to backtrack the trail of branch litter. She had climbed perhaps thirty yards and was still in the thicket when she noted a place where the horse's hooves had dug in sharply, kicking up dirt. She swept the cone of light back and forth, illuminating a small opening to her left. Her eyes were drawn to what appeared to be a section of log and as she stepped toward it, not looking at the ground, she slipped on a branch under the snow and fell heavily.

Going down with the light tight in her right fist, she jammed the hand to stop her fall, inadvertently switching the button to the tracking mode. She felt her breath catch. Before her, the circular opening in the trees appeared to be dusted pink, the snow pushed up into irregularly spaced moguls. It was as if someone had spilled dozens of weakly flavored cherry snow cones, ranging in size from baseballs to beach balls. Martha stood and tentatively toed the snow under her boot. Immediately, it shone with brilliant crimson dots that appeared to levitate a few inches above the ground. It was blood. She knew then that it was all blood. Because it had been sifted over, the color did not jump into the air but rather pulsed from beneath the snow. The effect was startling, the forest floor all around her appeared to be radioactive with a diffused neon glow.

Her nostrils flared at the iron metal scent. "Oh, shit," she said under her breath. She rested her thumb on the hammer of the revolver. Again, her attention was drawn to the log. She turned her eyes from it and then back; something was ticking at her brain. Why wasn't it covered with the snow that blanketed the other downfall? She took a step toward it, she took another, she stopped. She knew it wasn't a log.

In the eerie pinkish light, the man appeared younger than she'd thought he'd be. With his innocent, almost serene expression, he looked little more than a boy who had laid down and fallen asleep with his eyes open. Or at least his right eye, for his face was tilted to the side. She was so focused on the face that for a moment she did not notice that his posture, his body bent backward, was caused by the bulk of what he was lying on top of. She felt the hairs lift at the back of her neck. A sharp pain pulsed behind her eyes. She shook her head to clear it. It was not a mound of snow, as she had first thought. The young man was draped over the eviscerated rib cage and front quarters of an elk carcass.

Martha thought of the wolves she and Walt had heard earlier. But if the elk was a wolf kill, where were the tracks? And the man, had he died from head trauma or from spinal fracture when the horse bucked him and he fell onto the carcass? She swept the Carnivore light over his body, the LEDs reacting to a large stain of blood in the area of the groin. Though she could see no obvious sign of injury, the fabric under the waistband of the man's jeans was tented up, as if a stick were protruding. Martha's smile was sour. If Walt was here, he'd make a comment, say something about the man going out with a hard-on, dying happy. "Humpff."

She bent down, then jerked back up as her gorge rose. She swallowed bile, steeled herself and gingerly unsnapped the man's jeans. She worked the zipper down and pulled the fabric over the protrusion. It looked like a sharpened stick had stabbed upward into the man's back and punctured the lower abdomen, from which it protruded four or five inches. Martha touched the object with the back of her fingernail. Hard as bone.

She turned her back on the body and drew out her radio.

"What do you have, Martha?" Jason Kent's voice had some gravel in it after relaying messages all night.

"I found the wrangler. His horse wandered into camp and I backtracked him to where he got thrown. He's dead."

Kent told her to stay where she was. He'd relay her coordinates to Harold, who was the searcher closest to her, up on the headwall.

"So you figure he died in the fall?"

"That was my first thought, but I don't know, Jase. He has an elk antler sticking out of his gut."

"Maybe you better tell me about it."

"I'll tell you about it. But right now I got to throw up."

She made it to the edge of the timber before heaving. She grabbed a handful of snow to wash her mouth out, found that her hands were trembling and sat down on a log that actually was a log. She felt empty inside, but the bad taste was gone, replaced by something else, not exactly a taste but more of an odor that exuded from her body. It was the odor of fear. She'd smelled it before when she found herself on a heartless breast of snow in wilderness, felt the dread gathering in the limbs of the trees. The scream that came from her lungs, she couldn't believe she'd made it. *God help me*, she thought. But it was real. It had to be. For the wolves had heard. The first one answered from a long way off. The second was closer.

CHAPTER THREE

Reading the White Book

When Martha saw a light flicker up the mountainside, she switched the beam of the tracking light on and off a few times. She waited until her signal was answered, then her eyes fell to the revolver in her lap. She fingered the latch to swing out the cylinder, removed one cartridge and replaced the cylinder so that the hammer rested over the empty chamber. She holstered the revolver.

Harold was riding his paint. He dismounted and pulled his braid out from under the collar of his jacket. Martha made room for him on the log. She breathed in Harold's odor that wasn't sweat exactly, but dark and organic. Familiar. They had shared more than logs before, before Harold took back up with his ex-wife.

"Aren't you going to tie off your horse?" she said after a short silence.

"Only white people lose their horses." And after another stretch of silence: "I see you're packing the Ruger again."

"I can shoot it. I can't shoot those damned semi-autos. Besides," she said, "I'm a Western sheriff, I have to look the part."

"Got to please your public, famous woman like yourself."

Martha grunted. It had been more than a year since she'd shot a U.S. congressman in these mountains some twenty miles to the north, the congressman a murderer and the shooting cleared by a coroner's inquest, but no one had ever looked at her the same way since. Nor had Martha looked at herself the same way.

"Those wolves did some talking tonight, didn't they?" she said. "I thought one of them was going to walk right in on me a while back."

She put nonchalance into her voice, but felt her heart beat waiting for Harold's reply, wondering if he'd heard her screams a half hour earlier.

"My understanding was FWP wiped out that Black Butte Pack," Harold said. "Back when they got into the cattle that last time. Looks like a new one moved in."

He wouldn't say if he had heard, Martha thought.

"You want a piece of corn cake?" Harold was unfolding a square of wax paper on his knee. Martha told herself to let him get around to it in his own time. Talking about anything other than what brought two people together under unusual circumstances was a trait shared by many westerners, but perfected to an art form by Native Americans. Harold retrieved a thermos of tea from a saddle-bag and they sat in easy silence, trading sips from the screw-on plastic cup.

"You make good tea," Martha said. "What is it?"

"Whatever was in the cupboard at my sister's. Why don't you tell me what you saw tonight, starting with that horse wandering into your camp?"

"Did Jason tell you about the guy with the elk antler sticking out of his gut?"

"He did. I can smell the blood. But we'll be able to read the white book a whole lot better in an hour or so. Just muddy up tracks if we go in now."

So she told him, omitting only the scream. Harold refolded the wax paper and put it in his jacket pocket. "Couple things," he said. "Did you notice any other tracks besides the horse's? Wolf? Human?"

Martha said no, but that didn't mean they weren't there. Once her light registered the blood bath, her attention had centered on the body.

Harold nodded. It was gradually growing light. Martha could see the barred blue grouse feather that Harold wore in his braid flutter in the wind.

"Okay, last question. Did you circle around to see where the horse entered this stand of trees?"

Again, the answer was no.

"Then that's the first thing we'll do. I need to know if the horse was already running, which means something up above spooked him, or if he was walking. If he was walking, then what made him bolt was the kill. Horse coming from upwind, he could have stumbled right into the blood before it registered. Things go sideways in a hurry when a horse smells blood."

———

"Reading the white book" was an expression that Harold had picked up from his grandfather, who'd taught him to track on the escarpments of the front range that bordered the Blackfeet reservation. It was the skill of deciphering stories written in snow, the pages turning as each animal went about the business of his day. Who came here, what was his name, whom did he fear, in whose teeth did he die? In early autumn, many pages in the white book were blank, while others were written in a disappearing ink, for the snow came and the snow went, often in the same day. When Harold and Martha circled the trees to find where the horse had entered them, Harold figured he had several hours before the snow melted and the book shut. He examined Martha's boot tread so he could identify it and told her to follow two steps behind, placing her boots exactly in his own tracks.

The horse had entered the copse of pines at the upper northeast corner, where the trees were sparsest. Harold pointed with a stick. The pockmarks were spaced at regular intervals, faint scoops in the vanilla swirl.

"He was walking, huh?" Martha said, and cursed herself for commenting on the obvious. Notwithstanding the personal baggage of their relationship, she always felt inadequate following Harold while he tracked. He didn't suffer fools and was disinclined to honor any but intelligent questions with an answer.

She followed him down into the thicket. Harold pointed again. "See where he crow-hopped?" The horse had kicked up dirt over the snow where it jumped. "And here, here's where the rider bailed." He was pointing to two narrow impressions—the snow-covered tracks of a man. "He landed on his feet." Harold's voice was matter-of-fact. "Good horseman."

Martha felt the quick tremor of a vein in her neck. She rubbed at it and put her hands on her hips. The corners of her mouth turned down. "If he was bucked off here, how does he end up on the sharp end of an antler yonder down the hill?"

A momentary tightening of his cheeks was Harold's only response. He tucked his braid under his jacket collar and pushed through the wall of branches. As Martha followed him, she watched where his stick tapped the snow, but if there were tracks she couldn't see them. When they reached the edge of the clearing, Harold motioned to Martha to stay put while he conducted a perimeter search and disappeared into the trees. Martha squatted twenty feet from the elk carcass. It didn't look as ominous in the dawn. The face of the wrangler was hidden by the bulk of the elk and most of the blood was at a remove under the snow. *I should be tired*, she told herself. Instead, she found herself snapping her fingers, sending Harold telepathic signals to hurry.

Harold was back. He drew his belt knife before squatting next to her and whittled a stick into a toothpick. It shifted around as he worked it with his teeth.

Martha fought her impulse to break the silence. And lost. "What's the book tell us?"

Harold spit out the stick. "The pack that took down the bull is four, maybe five strong. They've probably been feeding on it couple days, hanging about the vicinity. They left just after it started snowing."

"I didn't see any wolf tracks."

"You wouldn't. They're more shadows than anything physical."

"Did the wrangler spook them when he rode in? Maybe that's why the horse bucked."

"No, I'd say the wolves left about an hour before the wrangler got here. But it wasn't just the wrangler. There were two others."

"Two?" Martha felt the breath slowly leave her lungs. Her lower ribs pressed against the muscles of her abdomen.

"They came in an hour or so after the snow started and it was snowing for a couple hours after they left, so we're talking dents. You look close, half the dents are about two inches longer than the others. And neither has a square heel. Wrangler's boot has a square heel. That tells me two other people were here."

"Were they together?"

"Same time frame, but I don't think so. The wrangler, we know he came on horseback. He stumbled into the opening from above. Call him person one. Person two came on foot from the timber flank there"—he pointed with his stick to the south—"ninety-degree angle to the route the wrangler took. Left the same way. His track's wider than the wrangler's track. The smaller track, person three, came in from the north, opposite direction from person two. Also on foot. Also left on his backtrack. Spacing says he was running on the way out. Tripped and fell down once, down below in the trees. Running blind, down timber all around, no more sense than the horse."

"Or a woman." Martha scratched the soft skin under her chin. "You said the third set of tracks are shorter. Why couldn't they be a woman's? That's who's missing on this godforsaken mountain."

"Could be at that. Make sense if she came onto the scene, saw him dead like this."

"I damn near bolted myself."

"No, Martha, you didn't. You just walked out to the edge of the trees where I found you and threw up and kicked some snow over it."

"Damned white book," she muttered under her breath. "Any idea where number two and three came from?"

Harold shook his head. "Once you get in the open, the tracks are windblown. Odd thing, though. There's a drag mark near the elk carcass, a little dirt kicked up. Like someone dragging a heavy branch. Hard to tell with the snow cover."

Martha fingered the point-and-shoot in her breast pocket.

Harold shook his head. "Pictures will just wash out, all that light bouncing off the snow."

"I know that. I'm not taking pictures of the tracks. This is just my way of telling you to finish up so I can take the scene photos. If you haven't noticed, there's a man over there who's cooling down to room temperature and he has an antler sticking out of him that's long enough to hang a hat on."

"That's what I miss about you, Martha."

"What?"

"Oh, just you being you."

"That was your choice, Harold."

"My wife had something to say about it."

"Your ex-wife."

Harold looked away. Martha felt her shoulders sag.

"I'm sorry," she said. "What's going on with you and Lou Anne, it's none of my business. Except . . ." All right, she told herself, I'm just going to say it. "I don't know, you and me, I thought we had something. I keep asking myself what I did to screw it up."

"You didn't do anything. Lou Anne and I have known each other since we were kids. She's my people. She's got a problem with depression; she wanted to talk about it. I thought I could deal with it without getting involved, and I couldn't. I wasn't going to be two-timing you.

You mean too much for me to be anything but honest." He swept his arm, encompassing the opening in the trees, the pines beyond, putting on their colors as the country came awake. "All this, there's no place I'd rather be than working a story in the snow with you looking over my shoulder, tapping your foot and telling me to get off Indian time."

"Yeah," Martha said drily. "We ought to do this more often, get together on a mountain drenched in blood."

Suddenly she *was* tired, her voice was tired, everything about her was tired. "I better radio Walt," she said. "He'll be waking up to three horses and wondering where the hell I am."

"Don't bother. I spotted him when I was searching the perimeter. He's following your tracks, humping it about as fast as a Scotsman reaching for the check." Harold got his feet. "I'm going to need some time here alone. Keep him out of my kitchen. Same if Bucky Anderson shows up. Jason radioed him the coordinates same as me. He should have been here." He reached into his jacket pocket and brought out an apple, took a quarter of it in one bite and handed it to Martha. "Give it to Snow. Mind your fingers."

Now he's telling me how to feed a horse, she thought.

Back on the open mountainside, she clucked to the paint. "Hey there, Jerry Old Snow," she said, and offered him the apple on the flat of her hand. She could see Walt coming up from below and waved her hat to draw his attention.

"Walt, I'm sorry about this. I should have called in earlier," she said as she stepped down the slope. She could hear his labored breathing and held out a hand, but he waved her off. "I made it this far. Point of pride to finish the climb."

"Jesus, you're leaking blood." She wiped the snow off the log so he could sit at the lower end. "Let me see the damage."

He held up his left foot. He'd cut the toe off the boot. The sock was torn and his big toe curled out like a plum.

"I thought I heard a scream 'bout fifty minutes ago," he said. "I was on your track already, but after that I come fast as I could."

"Those were just the wolves."

"Then there must have been a werewolf with 'em 'cause it sure sounded human."

Martha felt a wave of emotion. For all his faults, Walt was the most devoted to her of anyone on the force. She could count on him having her back, even if it meant showing himself in a disadvantageous light. The fact that they had nothing in common beyond the job and that she betrayed her exasperation with him on a daily basis made no inroads on his loyalty. She poured him the last of the tea.

"Jase fill you in?"

He took a sip and nodded. "I take it that wrangler's got himself impaled on an elk antler."

Martha grunted. "Or maybe he had help."

Walt frowned. "What makes you think that?"

"Harold says there were two other people here last night. He's working out the tracks."

"Speaking of the red man," Walt said.

Harold had materialized at the edge of the trees. He inclined his head for them to follow. "I've tracked lung-shot elk that didn't leave a blood trail as heavy as yours, Walt," he said, the words tossed over his shoulder. "We finish up here, I can build us a fire and cauterize that toe."

"Say what?" Walt said.

"I said I got a clean, sharp blade. I can take that toe off, once we're done here."

"Funny," Walt said. He hopped to follow Martha into the trees.

"Oh Jesus." Martha sucked a lungful of air as she looked at the wrangler's body.

"You didn't notice last night?" Harold said.

Martha shook her head. "I couldn't see this part of his face. What do you think? There was a fight?"

"I don't know. You get punched in the side of the head, this is what it looks like, like Walt's big toe there. But snow would tell me if someone was knocked to the ground, and the bruising looks more than a few hours old. Something else." He pointed to an ankle-high cut in the leather of the man's right cowboy boot. The cut looked fresh, the leather lighter in color at the edges where it was sliced.

"Maybe when he bailed, his horse stepped on him," Martha said. "Like Big Mike stepped on Walt."

"Maybe." Harold's voice sounded doubtful.

"Hurt like the dickens if it did." Walt was nodding his head. "That's a trophy elk, I ever saw one. Look at the length of those G4 tines."

Martha gave him a withering look. "We got a man twisting on the spit and that's all you have to say, it's a big bull?"

"Score three-sixty, maybe three-seventy. What do you think, Harold?"

"At least," Harold said. "You look at the brow tines, good length on the main beams, hardly any points subtracted for asymmetry, he's maybe not Boone and Crockett but the Montana record book for sure."

Martha looked from one to the other. "Let's . . . focus . . . here."

They stood in silence over the body. Martha's fingers reached for the pulse in her neck. Harold crossed his hands over his belt buckle.

"That G4," Walt said, "They don't call it the sword point for nothing, do they?"

CHAPTER FOUR

Long Story Short

It would be a stretch to call it a house. But then, Martha Ettinger thought, it would be a stretch to characterize the man who sat behind a feather-blown fly-tying bench on the porch a home owner. Until this summer, Sam Meslik had lived in a dilapidated trailer on three acres of cottonwood bottomland bordering Hyalite Creek. Dirt poor but land rich, he'd turned a dime on the place when a Kern County orange grove owner, looking for a place he could put his feet up for six weeks each summer and worry about something other than water rights and migrant labor, made him an offer he couldn't refuse. Sam had immediately parlayed his windfall into this place on a bank overlooking the Madison River.

"Is that beast of yours going to stay where he belongs?"

"You mean old Killer here?" Sam reached down to pat the broad head of the giant Airedale mix—"half terrier, half Hound of the Baskervilles," as Sam liked to say—that was lying at his feet. "Why he wouldn't hurt a mosquito."

"Uh-huh." Martha stepped out of the Jeep. She placed her hands on her hips and took in the shack, it was a shack, it said so in crudely painted letters above the porch: Fly Shack. Took in the dilapidated barn from Septembers when ranch owners traded their straw Stetsons for felts and brought the cattle down from the high pasture, instead of handing the reins to the ranch manager and packing the family off to Carmel. She glanced at Meslik's trailered drift boat with a leaping rainbow trout painted on the bow. The bumper sticker on the back window of the old Nissan 4 X 4 read, I Don't Care if You Flyfish.

The fishing guide folded his hands under the fly-tying table.

"Tain't riverfront," he said, "but I got the trespass rights." He jutted his chin toward the ribbon of current under the high bank. "I still have to use developed boat ramps for my ClackaCraft, but Stranny can slip his raft in right down there by the willows. Gives us an option no other guide outfit has on this part of the Mad.

"So where is Sean?"

"He's on a fish-a-bout. I thought you two were like that." Sam held two fingers pressed together. "Now that you're neighbors and all."

"We haven't been keeping in regular touch. What's a fish-a-bout?

"It's like a fisherman's take on a walkabout. You jump in the truck and take off fishing without knowing where you're going. You know what I saw him do the Fourth of July? We were float tubing Henry's Lake for the damsel fly hatch, right there where I got shot a couple years ago, and when we pull up on shore, Sean takes off his fly vest and finds he got water in the pockets and it's shorted out his cell. I say these things are like Jesus after the cross, bury it in rice and it'll resurrect. And he says, 'Or I can do this.' He sidearms the phone across the lake like a kid skipping a stone. Got a good half dozen bounces. You been inside that tipi? He's got it fixed pretty nice."

Martha nodded. "Be a hell of a place to spend the winter, though he says he's determined."

"That's something we agree on. So what I can do for you, Sheriff?"

"Do you mind if I sit? I've been up all night."

"Be my guest."

He indicated a folding camp chair. "You know, you're just the woman I wanted to see," he said.

Martha sat down, one eye on the Airedale. She arched her eyebrows. "How's that?"

"I'm called Rainbow Sam, right? It's on my drift boat, it's on my card, it's like my business name. I even got a line of flies I tie and market here from the shop. 'Rainbow Sam's Skinny Minnows.'"

"Um-hmm." Martha examined the slim marabou fly clasped in the jaws of the tying vise bolted to the table.

"Well, this fishing guide works out of the Kingfisher, he's going around calling himself Cutthroat Bob. Like cutthroat trout. And he's got long hair like me. And . . . and the fucker's selling a fly out of the shop he calls 'Cutthroat Bob's Busty Baitfish.' Isn't that, like, copyright infringement? Can you do something about it?"

"I don't think so, no." She put her hands behind her head and took in the dead soldiers on the table. "Isn't it a little early to be knocking them back?"

Sam smiled, showing the Vs ground into the enamel of his front teeth, a result of nipping monofilament leader tippets instead of using clippers. "I got women problems," he said.

"Tell me about your women problems."

"I can't see how you'd be interested."

"Then why did you put your hands under the table when I drove up."

He looked hard at her, then deliberately brought his hands up and folded them amid the scattered feathers. Like everything else about Sam Meslik, the hands were oversized, the backs matted with hair. Sean Stranahan had told her that he'd seen Sam remove the skull ring from his pinkie and pass a quarter through it. She saw that the knuckles on his right hand were scraped, the one at the base of the middle finger was grotesquely swollen.

"There were witnesses," he said. "I was defending myself."

She waited.

Sam shrugged. "I was in the Silver Dollar, cowboy comes through the door, says I been six-inching his girl. I tell him redo the math and maybe we'll talk. Add a few inches. He takes a swing, I put him down." He took a pull from a bottle of Moose Drool. "Long story short."

"This would be when?"

"Night before last."

"Were you?"

"Greasing the Robusto? Number one, Nicki wasn't his girlfriend. You can ask her. Number two, it was none of his business."

"You didn't answer my question."

"You don't like me much, do you, Sheriff?"

"No, I like you well enough. I just have a hard time believing you're for real. I think you're so far into this persona you've created that you don't know who you are. You're one of those people who can't draw the line between fact and fiction. My jail's full of them. For the life of me, I can't see what Sean sees in you."

"And I can't see what he sees in you. That makes us even."

"Back to this woman you fought over. You called her Nicki."

"Short for Nanika. He fought over her, not me. Nicki worked for me this summer, did some guiding, kept the shop open while I was on the river. She didn't have any place to stay, so I let her crash in the barn. It doesn't look like a hell of a lot from the outside, but the guy I bought it from plumbed it and it's got running water." He spread his hands. "It's good digs unless the roof collapses. I've been staying on a cot in the shack, but this winter I plan to beam the barn up, put in a woodstove and move in myself."

"Why would this guy think you were, ah, six-inching her, as he put it?"

"Maybe because she'd lived here this summer. I don't know what Nicki told him. We haven't been buckle to buckle since mid-July. Anyway, it was a long time before he met her."

"So you did sleep with her?"

Sam shrugged.

Martha mimicked him and waited.

"Is your own love life that boring? You ought to take off your badge and draw one down once in a while. I've heard sex is good for middle-aged women, keeps their juices flowing."

"Humor me."

"There isn't much to tell." He shifted his shoulders, the big slabs of muscle rippling under his T-shirt, the sun pegged and the day warming. Already, the mantle of snow on the distant ridges had all but melted.

"You ever hear of the Fly Fishing Venus?" Sam said.

"I can't say I have."

"Really? *Fly Angler* ran a picture a couple years ago. Ennis paper did a piece on her in July."

"Enlighten me."

"She guided out of a fly shop on the Kootenai. Most fisher chicks, they couldn't catch their tit in a wringer if they were churning ice cream and providing the milk. But Nicki was a good angler. They called her the Venus 'cause she has this hair that's like one of the seven wonders of the world. Sort of a copper waterfall. She's every fly fisherman's wet dream."

Sam fished another beer out of a cooler. He knocked the cap off against the edge of the table and held the neck with two fingers while foam ran down the sides.

"Anyway, I'm sitting right here second week of June, up she drives on a beater mountain bike, got a fly rod case strapped to the frame, a pack on her back, pedaled all the way from Libby. Said it took her ten days. Told me she was a fishing guide looking for work. 'Course I knew who she was right away, she's halfway famous, but it was a high-water spring and I didn't see how I could afford to hire her, at least not until the river dropped into shape. Hell, I'd just moved in myself. I hadn't even opened the shop. She said if I gave her room and board, she'd help me start the business. Gave me the number of the fly shop she'd worked for on the Kootenai. I called it. The guy said she'd suck in clients like a vacuum cleaner."

"And you decided to let her stay."

"I told her I'd sleep on it. She let me know she'd help me sleep on it." Sam smiled, showing the Vs. "Mama didn't raise an idiot. But we're talking high maintenance. I managed to get her out of my system before I ended up snake bit as that cowboy."

"But you stayed friends?"

"Sure. It was a business arrangement. She had a head for numbers and there were clients who took one look at her, one look at me, and wanted her on the pins. I let her use my old drift boat and took a cut off the top.

"Where's that boat now?"

"She's got it at the dude ranch. I told her she's free to use it until the season ends."

"Why did she leave you to work at the ranch?"

"After Labor Day, the guide business starts to die down. She figured she could make more money at the ranch and I encouraged her. But that job will peter out end of October. I don't know where she'll go once winter sets in, maybe back to Libby."

"That's where she's from originally?"

"Nicki's sort of vague about the past."

"Uh-huh. Let's talk about the cowboy. What's his name?"

"Grady Cole. He's a wrangler at the ranch. Probably got her the job. But I didn't learn that 'til after. When he came into the Dollar, I'd never seen him before in my life."

"And after the fight, when did you see him again?"

Sam began to speak. Then a look came over his face. The creases between his unibrow deepened. His tongue pressed between his lips, tasting the corners of his beard. He abruptly stood up, his chair scraping across the floorboards of the porch.

"What aren't you telling me?" he said.

Martha said, "Sit down, Sam. Just tell me about the fight."

For a long moment, Sam looked at her. She could see the gears grind. Then his face relaxed and he sat back down. "Hey, I don't have anything to hide," he said. "The dude called me out. I didn't want to fight him, the guy's half my size, but he started swinging. What could I do? I waited 'til he got up to his knees. I'd just hit him the once, just the once. He was okay, I figured. There were a few guys came out to gander, but they went back inside. A half hour later I started feeling pretty bad about it and went out the back door and found him sitting there in the alley. I offered him a beer. I can see he's been crying and I say 'What the fuck, buddy?' But Nicki, she must have cast a spell. And the thing is, all she gave him was a sniff. He ends up getting clocked and for what, the hope she'll kiss him someday? With all those rich broads at the ranch . . ." Sam shook his head. "He's got women leaving a snail trail on the saddle every time he helps them out of the stirrups, broads who don't think they've got their money's worth until they milk the wrangler, and he's as blind to it as the one-eyed monster. I told him to forget about Nicki, take what's shaking at him and go to college and make something of himself."

"Aren't we the counselor," Martha said.

Sam picked up his beer bottle and looked critically at it. They sat in silence, Martha watching Sam's blank expression. For the most part she had him figured as a no-filter guy. The second a thought formed in his head, it was out of his mouth. But he'd held back information from her before.

"So is this about Nicki? Is she okay?"

"I wouldn't know, Sam. Nobody's seen her since yesterday

afternoon. She rode into the sunset and her horse came back without her. There's a manhunt up on Papoose Mountain."

"What did he do?" Martha saw the color come into Sam's face. "Did he hurt her?"

"Grady? I doubt it." She got to her feet and looked down at him. "He's too dead to do anybody much harm. But then that's something you might be able to tell me about. I got all day."

CHAPTER FIVE

The River of No Return

At nightfall, Sean Stranahan took his coffeepot and walked the steep, rooted path down to the gravel bar. Upstream, the river was a rope of pulsing phosphorescence, but at his feet the thin water seemed not to move. He played the pencil beam of his flashlight over the current, trying to picture the great seafaring trout called steelhead, lanterns to one another as they ascended the current on their migration from the Pacific.

Earlier that evening, he had sent a fly tied from the dyed feathers of a marabou stork into the elbow of water at the head of a riffle, and a steelhead, attracted by the pulsating orange hackle fibers, or perhaps by the shimmering mylar tinsel, had taken the fly in a quick turn. It had nearly yanked the rod out of his hands before rocketing to midriver to jump, a yard of silver muscle twisting into the air, bulking against the darkness of the pines. Twenty minutes later, when Sean had finally been able to lead the fish close enough to extend a hand, the steelhead had turned with disdainful grandeur just out of reach, its broad tail slapping water onto his face. It had bulled back into the current, keeping him in that place where all fishermen want to be just a little while longer.

Stranahan squatted down to dip the kettle and set it aside. He dug his left hand into the coat of the mixed-eyed sheltie that had followed him from the campsite. "Time for dinner, Choti," he said. "Trip's almost over." But he was in no hurry to break the spell the river had cast, and man and dog sat side by side as he played the flashlight beam over the water, through the smoke that had risen over its surface. He wasn't sure what he was looking for, but he had been looking at water in this way since he was a child. After a while he shut the light off and just listened, internalizing the sound of the current until it was no longer the river he was listening to, but the rhythm of his heart.

———

"Where are you?"

Stranahan had to smile. No hello, no how are you. Pure Martha.

"Ah, it's called the River of No Return. I just hiked out of the canyon."

"Well how soon can you return from it?"

"Good morning to you, too, Martha. I called to say hi and see if my tipi was still standing. I didn't know you'd missed me so much."

"I didn't, but we could use another set of eyes on the ground and you can read sign better than anyone except Harold. See . . ."

As he listened, Stranahan trapped the handset between his ear and his shoulder and used both hands to dig into his pants pockets for more quarters. By the time Martha drew a breath he'd run out of change. He gave her the number taped to the pay phone's instruction card and tapped his boot on the porch of Mother Chukor's Cafe, one of two remaining businesses in the ghost town of Shoup. The other was a general store with gravity fed gas pumps under a hanging sculpture of a steelhead drinking a cup of coffee.

"I know Sam," Sean said, picking up at the first ring. "Whatever else he might be guilty of, he didn't kill that wrangler. He's got a heart, it's just buried beneath a couple hundred pounds of bluster."

"Yeah, and he's got a big fist that's imprinted on a dead man's face. I'm heading to the morgue in about an hour. We'll see what Doc says about it. So how soon can that old heap of yours get here?"

"I'm not sure I'm done fishing yet."

"You're done fishing."

"In that case, six hours. Maybe by nightfall."

"Then you're not going to do us any good today. You know how these things go. The first forty-eight hours are critical. This is day three, it was Tuesday this happened. Let me think a second. Okay, here's what you do. The missing woman's name is Nanika Martinelli, goes by Nicki. Her ranch application lists an address outside Libby. Worked for a fly shop called Hook and Hackle. I want you to drive up there and learn what you can. I'll clear it with the sheriff so you can search the residence."

"What about Sam?"

"What about him? If he's innocent, then you'd be doing him a favor to find out the truth. I don't see a conflict of interest."

"So does this mean you're hiring me?"

"I'm still hoping she's going to walk off the mountain. But if she doesn't, then yes, a couple days 'til we get this straightened out. It isn't your day rate, but look at the company you keep."

"I'll still want to talk to Sam."

"Call him from the road. And when you get back to Bridger, do *me* a favor. Buy a cell phone and resist the impulse to throw it in the drink. This is the twenty-first century."

CHAPTER SIX

Death by G4

"How's the ticker?"

"Ticking." Doc Hanson rolled his shoulders and twisted his neck from side to side. "I've been up to my elbows in gore all morning. Darned thing is, I knew the table was set too low and didn't reset it, didn't want to spend the time. Now my back's in spasm and I'll pay for it the next twenty hours."

"If you don't want to talk about your heart," Martha said, "I'm not going to make you."

"Four months. That's how long it's been since the stent, but I can't seem to carry on a conversation five minutes before the subject comes up."

"Then excuse me for caring, Doc."

"Martha, it's not you. What sticks in my craw are people who are friends of my wife, women who've never carried on a serious conservation with me, asking me about my feelings. How do I feel about coming close to death? How has it changed me? I'll tell *you* how it's changed me, what I don't tell *them*." His voice became matter-of-fact. "About once a week, two in the morning, I wake up and listen to my heart. Any twinge in the chest wall, any tremor of the intercostal muscles, I dwell on it. Elizabeth's a foot away and I listen to her breathe awhile. Then I move the dog and get up and go into the kitchen and pour myself a glass of milk. I have a bucket list under a refrigerator magnet and fiddle with it, prioritizing. I'd like to hike up to the Chinese Wall in the Bob Marshall Wilderness before I pass. That one's at the top, because you have to be in shape. I'd like to see that Grand Staircase Escalante Monument in Utah. And I'd like to canoe the Smith River again, right here in Montana. But you know what I really want to do. I'd like to bring a few days back and live them over again. I figure a man has about six days in his life that are as good as it gets. The day when I was catcher for the All Stars and made the play at the plate that sent us to the regionals, a day in the Mekong when I pulled my best friend out of a firefight where he'd gotten blown up and got him on the chopper. I found I had courage that day. It wasn't happiness so much as every cell in my body was alive. And God bless Elizabeth, but I'd like to relive a night up in the U.P. when I was in med school at Michigan and made love with Vicki Pendergrass under the northern lights. Right there on a blanket on the shore of Lake Superior."

"I bet that one isn't written on the list."

"No. That one stays up here." He tapped his temple. Hanson pulled his glasses down on his nose and looked at Martha. "What is it about us? We get together a few days a year, if that, and I tell you all my secrets and you tell me something, anyway. How's that happen? And then each time, we say we should get together for dinner and share something other than a body on an examining table, then we don't. How's that come about?"

"I don't know, Bob. Maybe we're afraid that if we meet somewhere else, we won't have anything to talk about."

"I truly doubt that."

Martha inclined her head. "What do you say we have a look at him?"

Hanson compressed his lips under his bristly salt-and-pepper mustache and nodded. He led her over to the steel examining table and pulled the sheet down. The skull had been sawn horizontally to reveal the brain pan.

"I read your report," Hanson said. "The facial bruising is consistent with the blow you described. See the dark blue color of it, almost purple? That means the red blood cells have begun to break down. It tells me the blow occurred approximately twenty-four hours before the man's death. A CAT scan revealed no evidence of concussion. Was the man knocked out?"

"Witnesses said he went down and stayed down, but wasn't knocked out."

Hanson nodded.

Martha set her hands on her hips. "Could the blow have affected comprehension or his stability twenty-four hours later?"

"You mean, could he have fallen onto the elk antler accidentally, as a result of being punched by Sam Meslik the night before?" He answered his own question with a thoughtful nod. "Brain trauma manifests in many ways, instability is common. But in this case there is no physical measure of impairment."

"What if he reinjured his brain when he jumped off his horse? Harold says the man came out of the stirrups when his horse bolted and that he landed on his feet. If his brain was already traumatized, could jarring it compound the damage so that he'd more or less pass out and lose his footing?"

Hanson frowned, then nodded. "It's possible. It's why you don't send a football player who's suffered a concussion back into a game or allow a fighter who was knocked unconscious back into the ring a week later. But I think you're on the wrong track."

"No, I'm just eliminating. So it leaves being pushed so he fell on the antler, or did he just trip over his own feet?"

"Let's let the evidence talk before we speculate." Hanson pulled the sheet down to the line of the man's pubic hair, exposing the gaping wound. The skin was darkly reddened in a softball-sized area surrounding the puncture.

"Okay, Doc. I'll bite. What does the evidence say?"

Hanson's voice assumed a professorial tone. "Typically, one would suspect that head trauma or spinal injury was at least an ancillary cause of death. In a fall, that's the most likely scenario. But that is not the case here. This man died from massive blood loss from a rupture of the common iliac artery, where it is formed by the junction of the external and internal iliac arteries. The antler tine was the sole cause of this poor man's death, the G4 to be precise."

"I heard Walt refer to it by that designation. What's it mean?"

"G is the section of the Boone and Crockett Club scoring sheet relating to the length of antler tines. Over time, it became convenient for scorers who judged big-game heads to simply refer to the tines as G1, G2, and so on. On a typical six-point bull, the G4 is the fourth from the bottom, usually the longest tine on the antler."

"I didn't think you were a hunter."

"I'm not. I was given a lesson by Julie McGregor. She's the game biologist who examined the elk. The head's over in the FWP barn. The length of this particular tine was forty-six centimeters, or just over eighteen inches. It entered through the skin of the back, punctured the thoracolumbar fascia and the internal oblique muscle before punching through the body cavity—that smell is from the ruptured small intestine—and came out through the lower right quadrant of the abdomen, with approximately seventeen centimeters protruding. The abdominal depth is twenty-three centimeters, a little less. He was impaled on the lower section of the tine, more or less wedged down against the base, where the tine reaches its greatest circumference. The puncture wound is nearly eleven centimeters in circumference at the entry point, tapering to just under seven centimeters where it exited the abdomen; that's one hell of a big hole. I'd estimate he died within five minutes."

"Hmm." Martha steepled her fingers so that her forefingers rested against her nose, with her thumbs under her chin.

"You look lost in prayer, Martha."

Ettinger didn't answer. She took her hands from her face. "You're a strong guy, Bob. What if you were to throw me down on an antler tine like the one that skewered this guy? Would I be impaled the way he was?"

"That's the question I posed to Julie when she showed me the head of the bull. She said she'd check it out with Wilkerson."

"Ouija Board Gigi?"

He nodded.

"Why don't I know about this?" Martha's brow furrowed. "I knew when we stole her from Custer County that she was the best CSI in the state. I didn't know she'd bypass chain of command and go cowgirl three weeks into the job."

"That's something you'll have to take up with her." Hanson glanced at the bird call clock on the wall. "You go over to the barn before the chickadee sings, you should catch her. Julie said they'd be conducting their experiments at three o'clock."

"Then we're done here?"

"Almost. You asked me to look at the right ankle, where you thought he could have been stepped on by his horse."

Martha nodded. "His boot was cut. I was looking for a reason he'd stumble and fall onto the elk."

Hanson drew the sheet back over the head and went to the other end of the table. He pulled the sheet to expose the feet. Ettinger stared at the ugly line of bruise over the instep.

"You see there's a corresponding contusion on the outside of the ankle," Hanson said.

Martha pursed her lips. "If it was made by the horse, the injury would be curved, like a horseshoe. Right?"

"You'd think."

"Looks like he stepped in a coyote trap."

"That's what Wilkerson said, too. She said Julie had leghold traps of various sizes in the barn and they were going to see if one matched. If a trap was set by the elk carcass for the wolves and he accidentally stepped onto the pan, then you have a logical reason for him falling onto the antler."

"So Wilkerson's seen the body?"

"She was here just before you."

Ettinger drummed the fingers of her right hand on the edge of the table.

Hanson shrugged. "She made an appointment. She went through channels."

"Not my channel."

"Can I give you a piece of advice?"

"What? I can see you're going to, anyway."

"Don't be too hard on her for taking the initiative. This county's grown twenty percent in the last three years. Bigger population, bigger department, bigger workload. You can't micromanage like before. I know it irks you not to have your finger in the gravy, but you've got a good team with Walt taking on undersheriff duty and now Wilkerson, you couldn't ask for better technical support. I'm right if you think about it."

Ettinger pulled off her blue latex gloves and dropped them in a wastebasket. "You're right. I need to delegate more. It's just, I don't know, a couple nights ago up on the mountain, I felt like a fifth wheel with Jason Kent running SAR and Harold taking over the crime scene, if that's what it turns out to be."

"Do I have to remind you who found the body?"

Ettinger grunted, conceding the point. "It's just that something happened up there, I don't want to get into it, but it shouldn't have. It *wouldn't* have a few years ago. I lost control for a couple minutes." She closed her eyes, could hear her scream echoing off the rock walls of Papoose Basin. "I seem to be full of doubts these days, not just professionally."

Hanson nodded. "Twenty years ago I went through something

similar. It's called a midlife crisis. If you're like me, you'll work through more than one of them. I seem to be at the onset of one right now."

"Thanks for pointing that out to me."

"You're welcome. You know how I feel about you. I—"

Ettinger held up her hand. "I know. You love me for all my warts and graces. I still think you stole that line from somebody."

Hanson shook his head. "I'm an original, Martha."

She was going to say something wry, something that would put Doc Hanson, the old walrus, in his place, when the chickadee on the clock said its name.

———

The Fish, Wildlife & Parks barn was wishful thinking—not a barn at all, but a Quonset hut constructed of corrugated galvanized steel, hollow as the empty half of a tin can it resembled. Flick a BB against the wall and it echoed like a gunshot in a limestone canyon. Ettinger heard the voices before she entered, could see two figures at the far end of the building.

"Let's raise the ladder to ten feet and try the mule deer again." It was Georgeanne Wilkerson, whose breathy, conspiratorial voice was hard to mistake. She tended to speak as if she were in cahoots with you, planning to rob the Bridger Federal Savings and Loan.

"O . . . kaaaay." Julie McGregor, the Region Three wolf and elk biologist, had adopted the same breathy expansion, full of mystery and derring-do.

Ettinger set her hands on her hips and watched as McGregor took the two forelegs of a field-dressed mule deer buck while Wilkerson held onto the rear legs. They lifted the deer and began to ascend twin ladders that faced sides over the severed head of a bull elk.

"High enough?"

"Let's do a couple more steps."

"Okay, okay," McGregor said, blowing like a weightlifter. "On three. One, two, three."

The mule deer fell through space. The squishing thud that reverberated through the barn was followed by a moment of dead silence. Then a peal of laughter rang off the steel walls. Martha could see two tines of an elk antler poking up through the rib cage of the deer.

"Whoa! That was way cool." McGregor tossed her head, her mop of hair flying. Wilkerson was laughing so hard she started to cough. The women climbed down from the ladders and high-fived each other over the carcasses.

Martha thought *When did everyone get so young?* She cleared her throat. "Ahem." The laughter died down as she approached.

"We were just having a bit of fun," Wilkerson said, still out of breath. She was a pear-shaped brunette, not unattractive, but with a blotchy indoor complexion and small hands that flitted like bats. Her glasses magnified her eyes, giving her a permanently startled expression.

"And you, Miss McGregor, you were having fun, too, it appears."

The biologist, dressed in a khaki shirt embossed with the head of a grizzly bear over Department of Fish, Wildlife & Parks, blew back an errant strand of hair that had fallen across her nose. Freckle-faced tomboy to the core, she was a fair-skinned towhead with crinkly eyes that had seen a lot of weather. *Where the hell are her hips?* Martha thought.

McGregor looked down at the mule deer, the elk antlers skewered through it like the tines of a giant fork. "There's been a couple fellas I wouldn't mind dropping onto a sharp G4," she said. McGregor glanced sidelong at Wilkerson, immediately initiating another round of laughter.

Ettinger, recalling Doc Hanson's wisdom, told herself to stay calm. She offered a grudging smile. "I suppose I could say the same about my first husband," she admitted. "And the second, come to think of it." Her eyes went from one to the other. "So what's this little experiment prove?"

"We were just seeing how far you had to drop a deer before it got stuck on the antler," Wilkerson said. "You know, instead of bouncing off." She dug into her shirt pocket and produced a notebook. "I started to do some calculations in the lab, but it's hard because of the variables. You have to take into account mass, weight and profile of the victim, the size and configuration of the antler tine, drag coefficient and velocity at impact, how much force it takes to impale through skin, fascia, organs and then skin again . . ." She shook her head, her eyes swimming. "If Doc had a John Doe in the drawer it would be perfect, but Julie said she had some confiscated game we could use and this mule deer dresses out around one-seventy, which is approximately the same weight as the victim. Of course it's minus the guts, which throws a wrench into the equation, but I thought I'd learn more here than with the calculus."

"So what's the verdict?"

Wilkerson cocked her head. "Even with a skinned deer dropped from two meters we didn't have penetration, that's with an impact velocity of twelve point three miles per hour, so it's clear that he didn't fall onto the elk and impale himself. Certainly not to a depth of forty-six centimeters; I'm sorry to be trading back and forth on measures, but we use imperial for velocity and metric for most everything else. Should I call you Sheriff?"

"Everybody calls me Martha. So what you're saying is he had help."

"I'm saying that he could not have been impaled by simply falling onto the antler tine. Considering the mass, the tine itself, which looks sharp but is technically blunt, puncturing the involved tissues would take at least forty-five Newtons of pressure. He didn't reach impact velocity sufficient for that to happen. Also, that's not factoring in the give, for lack of a better term. The antlers weren't set in cement. They would absorb some of the impact before the skin punctured."

"If you were called as an expert witness in a court of law—"

"Then it would still be my opinion, but if you're asking if a defense attorney could find another CSI who would contradict my finding, he could. You can hire a forensic analyst who'll tell you a man died of snakebite after you've dug a forty-four slug out of his heart."

"So somebody pushed him against the antlers."

"Or he fell. Then he was pushed."

"Maybe he was pancaked," McGregor said. "Like in wrestling. You grab the guy chest to chest and fall on him. That would drive the antler in for sure."

Martha fingered her chin. "Would it take a strong man to do that?"

"Well, you've got the downward pressure," Wilkerson said, "and then there's the weight behind the pressure, that's the same thing, really. I don't know. I'll have a better answer after doing the math, but offhand I'd say it would take a good-sized person."

"Could someone my size do it?" Martha was a solid one forty.

"I'd guess at least your size."

"Mmm. So what exactly were you trying to accomplish by dropping dead animals from ten feet in the air?"

"At that point, we were just interested to see what happens."

"Yeah," McGregor chimed in. "Once you start dropping deer onto antler tines, it's hard to stop." She looked at Wilkerson, her eyes dancing. The two were on the verge of being girls again. Martha resisted the temptation to roll her eyes.

She walked out into the hard sunshine. She put on her polarized fishing glasses, her expression sober behind the mirrored lenses, and brusquely walked halfway to the Jeep Cherokee before realizing she hadn't asked about the bruises on the victim's ankles. For a victim was what he was, contradictory expert witnesses notwithstanding. What was it Walt had said about the G4? "They don't call it the sword point for nothing." Wilkerson was leaving by the same door Ettinger had and Martha, walking back, snapped her fingers and cocked her hand like a gun, pointing the CSI back into the barn.

CHAPTER SEVEN

Death Town

Libby, Montana, it would later occur to Stranahan, was a town of never agains. Yawning trucks with hoods that would never close again. Boarded-up houses with doors that would never open again. Boats that would never again see water, rusting on trailers with tires that would never roll again. It had once been called God's Corner, an elbow-shaped town of under three thousand souls on the south bank of the Kootenai River, its western flank presided over by the imperious peaks of the Cabinet Mountains. By the time Sean Stranahan passed the giant eagle sculpture at the junction of Highway 2 and Mineral Avenue, Libby, Montana, had earned the distinction of being the deadliest Superfund site in U.S. history, asbestos clouds from a vermiculite mine having sifted like fairy dust into the lungs of its residents, insinuating wormlike fibers into their pulmonary systems and killing an estimated four hundred people. It was known, simply, as Death Town.

The sheriff's department was opposite the VFW, catty-corner from a smoke shop with a service window where two pickups waited behind a paint-peeled sedan, autumn in the air, the exhaust hanging low over the gravel drive-through. Stranahan ran a comb through his hair and walked into the sheriff's office, which was fronted by a man with heavy jowls who regarded him through bulletproof glass. Stranahan was directed to a chair, where he idly leafed through an old *Golf Digest* with Phil Mickelson on the cover, the man in black smiling like he'd swallowed a canary.

He heard a door open and glanced up into what could have been his father's face, had his father lived to be older, angular and darkly complected, with graying temples bracing midnight hair swept to the side. It was a manly, old-fashioned face, one that belonged in a black-and-white movie, looked into with longing by a platinum blonde. The fact that it could be his own face in twenty years didn't register.

He followed the Lincoln County sheriff into his office; they shook hands. Sean repeated the man's name, Carter Monroe, so he would remember it and briefly ran his eyes around the room. A glassy-eyed mount of a bull elk presided over an oak desk, the only furniture that wasn't green office steel. Under the elk was a row of framed photographs of girls' softball teams.

"One of them must be your daughter," Stranahan said.

"She's the one with the blue bat in the center frame." Monroe had a husky smoker's voice, but Stranahan didn't see an ashtray, nor the giveaway thinning of fabric where a cigarette pack customarily rode a shirt pocket.

"How long have you been coaching?" Stranahan had noted the sheriff squatting front row left in each photo, the girls growing taller, filling out their uniforms, while he just looked older.

"Seven years," he said. "Past tense. My Jenny graduates UM with a master's in counseling next spring, she'll get a job God knows where. My wife's gone six months now, bless her. I'm up for reelection. If I lose I don't know what I'll do with myself. If I win . . . well, I'm not so sure about that, either."

"I lost my mother last year," Stranahan said. "When they die you see them all broken apart, but in time they become young again, you remember the best that they were. It'll come. Family's everything, isn't it?"

The sheriff let out a long breath and held Sean's eyes, then looked away. "It certainly is," he said softly.

The fact was if you asked Sean Stranahan, he would say he was

unaware of his effect on people, the way he disarmed nearly everyone with his forthcoming nature. Casual acquaintance came so naturally that he seldom paused to consider that it was anything but
ordinary to exchange hellos with a passing fisherman and take the
confession of his infidelities a half hour later, or converse with this
man who looked like his father in a way that brought a sheen to the
man's eyes ten minutes after they'd shaken hands. Never meeting a
stranger was a Western trait, and Stranahan had grown up in the East
where people conducted business with skins of reserve so thick that
you had to peel them like an orange. In that regard, moving to the
Rockies had been like coming home. His personality was a form of natural grace, like throwing a baseball, but a weapon for all that. Stranahan was not entirely ingenuous; he knew he could extract more
information with a smile than most men could with a cocked .38.

Carter Monroe briefly shook his head, as if to clear it. "So if you'll
take a seat, here's what I have for you." He picked up a piece of paper
from his desk. "The house is off Kaniksu Mountain Road about ten
miles south of town. Belonged to Nanika Martinelli's father. Old Alfonso passed last year."

He studied the paper. "Alfonso Martinelli," he recited. "Born in
Saint Véran in France, moved to the Morice River valley in British
Columbia in the seventies. Commercial fisherman, trapper, carpenter, jack of northern trades. Moved a number of years later to a place
near Kamloops, worked the southern part of the province as a
wolfer." He looked up. "My understanding is that's just what it
sounds like; he killed wolves. Packed up his traps and came here
about eight years ago. Hired on as an animal damage control specialist for the U.S. Fish & Wildlife Service. They liaison, if that's the
right word, with our own FWP to eliminate predators that kill livestock. Cougars, bears, coyotes, and wolves, of course. We've got
wolves here like no tomorrow."

Monroe squared the paper and looked up. "He was a recluse. I'm told the place stank to high heaven from pelts and home-brew wolf lure and the like, though he was law abiding. I never had the occasion to knock on the door. People called him Fonzo or the Fonz, after the character in the TV show. Maybe you're too young to remember."

Stranahan said he remembered. "I thought you said he was a recluse. Somebody called the Fonz doesn't sound like a recluse."

"I did, didn't I? Alfonso had a strained relationship with his daughter. She was a hellion, rebelled against everything he stood for. When they reconciled, he came out of his shell, you saw a different man." He caught Sean's eyes. "That doesn't surprise me. Nicki was on the track team with my Jenny senior year. All I can say is the mother must have been a stunner. She didn't get her looks or that hair from him. And she sure as hell didn't get his personality. You hear about people who walk into a room and the room changes? Nicki changed a room. Put her in any group of people and she just bubbled to the top. I called her a hellion but that was a wrong choice of words. More like an innocent with a strong sense of purpose. Everyone was drawn to her.

"Anyway, Alfonso, when he lost his job, or quit, or whatever derailed him from the federal gravy train, he started a handyman service—I'll Do Most Anything. I used to see him driving around, shuttling cars for the rafting companies and fly shops."

Stranahan's head came up fractionally. "Nicki worked for a place called Hook & Hackle."

Monroe nodded. "The Fly Fishing Venus. The owner of the shop had the bow painted with a mermaid with red hair. She gave her old man a new lease on life, so says just about everyone I talked to, but I already told you that." He frowned. "I'm repeating myself."

Stranahan said, "Was there anyone in Nicki's life, a boyfriend, girlfriend, who might be able to tell me something about her?"

"Last I heard she was seeing the guy who owned the fly shop. His name's Robert Kelly. Look, all I did after Sheriff Ettinger gave me the heads up was boot the computer and punch numbers into a phone. There's more digging to be done if someone wants to dig. Nicki was arrested twice for disturbing the peace, demonstrating against the mine. Fairly innocent stuff, though I can't say that about some of the people she associated with. I'd be happy to help, but anything extracurricular, you'd want to coordinate with me, this is my jurisdiction." He waited for Stranahan to acknowledge with a nod. "Just what is it you do, Sean?"

"I'm an artist and a fishing guide, but I used to be a private investigator and still am, in a small way. I liaison, if that is the right word, with the Hyalite County sheriff's office. What I'd like to do today, with your permission, is drop in at that fly shop and then have a look at the cabin before it gets dark."

"That isn't a problem, although to my knowledge there hasn't been anyone living on the premises since Alfonso French-kissed his revolver on Memorial Day weekend."

"So he committed suicide?"

Monroe nodded. "He suffered from asbestos poisoning, cancerous mesothelioma to be exact. I don't blame him for taking matters into his own hand."

"That's from breathing asbestos into the lungs, right?"

"It is. Unfortunately I'm an expert on the subject. It's what took my Mary Ellen. If you asked me even a couple months ago, I would have a hard time talking about it."

"I'm sorry," Stranahan said.

"No, it's okay. You distance yourself from these things, or time distances you, I don't know which. You keep breathing, anyway. The story with asbestos is the fibers irritate your lungs and make scar tissue. Then plaque builds up around the fibers. What it does is choke you; you can't get enough air. You walk around town, you'll see people dragging their canisters of oxygen. That's called asbestosis. I have it to the degree that I can't hunt elk anymore and talk like I swallowed a jar of buckshot. The worst-case scenario is cancer develops and you hike out to the wood pile like Alfonso did." He made a gun of his hand and dropped the hammer, pointing his index finger at his mouth. "It was Nicki who made the call. By the time I got there, she was holding him in her lap, just soaked in blood. She was beside herself, kept telling me how she should have seen it coming and it was all her fault."

"What did she mean?"

"It was just crazy talk." Stranahan heard a change come into his voice. "People assume a lot of blame when loved ones die." He pressed his lips together and briefly looked away. "When my wife got the diagnosis, I beat myself up pretty bad. We weren't from here, came sight unseen for the job. That reporter from the *Seattle Post-Intelligencer* who blew the whistle on Zonolite Mountain, what W. R. Grace and company were putting into our good, clean air, those stories were just coming out. I could have got Mary Ellen out of here, she might be alive today. But she was a nurse and wanted to stay and I was loyal to the town." His voice trailed away.

"Why don't you leave now?"

"Because it wouldn't matter. All of us who breathed the stuff, we're like ticking bombs. I could hide under a rock in Africa for the next five years and the big C would know right where to find me. Or I could die drinking kava in Fiji on my ninetieth birthday. Knock wood." He rapped his knuckles against the desktop. "Anyway, they say the risk of accumulating more fibers is slim; it only took a five hundred mil cleanup. That's what they say. Besides, I love this town, and I love the Kootenai. There's good people here, and I say that as someone who deals with the dark side of human nature. I just wish we could climb out of this goddamned recession and the county could pony up for another deputy."

He looked askance at Stranahan. "I ought to warn you, it's Appalachia West up along that Kaniksu Mountain Road. We call it the

Boneyard because it's where a lot of hunters toss game carcasses. It's a checkerboard ownership, private and Forest Service, about a dozen houses strung along the creek. We've shut down one meth lab and another could have popped up, so keep your nose in the air. Shouldn't be anyone at the Martinelli place, but you never know. If it smells like a hospital ward or wet diapers, just walk away."

"You wouldn't have a key to the door, would you?"

"No, but anyone with ingenuity ought to be able to find a way inside. Here," he lifted his hip to extract his wallet, "I'm going to give you a card with my private number on it. Anybody asks why you're poking around, call and I'll put them straight."

Stranahan said thanks and took the card. He thought of his cell phone, skipping like a basalt stone across the surface of Henry's Lake. He really was going to have to get another one.

Monroe stood up. "Sheriff Ettinger told me if you didn't show up today, it was either because that heap you're driving died or else you were up to your waist in a steelhead river. You want to float the Kootenai tomorrow morning? Seven a.m.? I could have you off the river by eleven. What is it, seven hours to Bridger? You'd be home before dark."

Stranahan thought about it, "Why not?"

"Where are you staying tonight?"

Stranahan asked if there was a campground along the river.

"There's one right at the put-in. I'll come by and collect you in the morning. Here, I'm going to draw you a map." He scribbled on a legal pad and tore out the sheet and handed it over. "You don't hesitate to call that number now."

————

The Hook & Hackle, on the north bank of the Kootenai River, was everything Rainbow Sam's Fly Shack wasn't. For starters it wasn't a shack, but a neat, two-story clapboard with twin trailered Clacka-Crafts in a gravel swing-through drive. He entered the shop, which could have been any of fifty fly shops in Big Sky country—a picket fence of fly rods, gleaming bar-stock aluminum reels, bins stocked with every variety of fur- and feather-clad hooks, custom teardrop landing nets, logo hats—right down to the obligatory Labrador snoozing on a throw rug. Stranahan exchanged nods with the man behind the counter and bent down to pat the broad head of the Lab.

"Does she hunt?" he asked without standing up.

"Does she hunt? You come into my shop and first thing you do is insult my dog?" Stranahan looked up. He was a big man with an outdoor complexion, a high wattage smile at the center of a doorknob-style beard and brown eyes in the pale ovals of skin where his sunglasses would rest.

"First time to the Kootenai? I can offer you the off-season rate if you're looking for a guided float. I know this river better than anyone."

"Thanks, but I'm fishing tomorrow with Carter Monroe."

"That's the name of our sheriff."

Stranahan nodded. "It's why I'm here, actually. He's assisting the Hyalite County sheriff's office with the search for a woman who went missing in the Madison Range a couple days ago.

The man was nodding. "Nicki. I read about it. I sure hope she's okay."

"So do we." Stranahan waited.

"I don't know what to tell you. She worked here right up until this summer." He counted on his fingers—"Four seasons." He raised his eyebrows. "The newspaper says she was working at a dude ranch. One of the wranglers looking for her fell on a dead elk and got an antler through his gut. That's a hell of a way to go."

"It is. I'm up here trying to collect some background information."

"They don't suspect her of having anything to do with that man's death, do they? That wouldn't be the Nicki I know."

"Not as far as I'm aware. Who was the Nicki you knew?"

"A . . . good . . . kid." The brown eyes had become hard. "Who did you say you were? I didn't catch the name."

"Stranahan. Sean Stranahan." He extended his hand, which the man took after a moment's hesitation. "I work for Sheriff Ettinger in Bridger."

"Robert Kelly," the man said. His eyes relaxed. "It's just that you're not the first person who's come here looking. A guy was asking questions about her at the start of the summer, after her dad passed."

"What can you tell me about him?"

"He rode a motorcycle. About your size and build. Younger. Had these little cornflower blue earrings. Long hair. Wore a leather vest unzipped, man had chest hair like a brown bear. But his face was almost delicate, not handsome, but beautiful. Like the *David*. The sculpture." He tilted his chin in an approximation of the pose. "I'm as hetero as the next guy, but I'm not ashamed to say I was attracted. Not in a sexual way but like a mouse mesmerized by a snake." He crooked two fingers and jabbed them like fangs. "He had a rawhide shoelace with a pendant about the size of a silver dollar that he wore around his neck. An embossed wolf, facing forward like it was looking at you. It had garnet stones for eyes. I made a comment about it, just to say something, the way you do, and he said 'The wolf is my brother.' Not like a hippie would say it, 'The wolf is my bro, man,' but matter of fact. Like you'd say 'I got a sister from Poughkeepsie.'"

"What can you remember about the motorcycle?"

He shook his head. "I don't know bikes that well. High exhaust, like an off-road bike. I think it had a red gas tank."

"Montana plates?"

"Maybe. Nothing registered. I might have noticed if it was out of state. He had a girl with him. She sure as hell registered."

"Oh?"

"They were riding tandem. Just a bitty thing, short black hair, had sort of a scrunched-up face. A pixie doll. But she had eyes, I'm not kidding you, they were the color of a Bloody Mary. More orange than red. You felt like if you were in a room, she'd get up on the mantel and crouch down, stare at you like a cat. A very strong vibe. Never said a word, though. He did the talking."

"What did he say?"

"Said he was a friend of Nicki's, wanted to know if she still worked for me. I told him she'd left town but he was persistent—where did she go, did I have a number. His questions were . . . direct. Polite but distant, cold. Like he wasn't going to let you see anything but the mask. When he saw he wasn't getting anywhere, they left."

"Did you see them again?"

"No, but I had a feeling, you know, that maybe there was something up with Nicki. Maybe she hadn't left town like she'd said. I thought if she was at her dad's old place, I should warn her about this guy. So I drove over there and someone had broken a window and trashed the place. I figured it was him. I mean, who else? It wouldn't have been hard to find the address. A lot of people knew Nicki. Just like it was common knowledge she worked for me. Some wrong impressions about that."

"So she wasn't your girlfriend?" Stranahan kept his voice casual.

"The sheriff tell you that? Well, he's wrong. I'm a married man."

Stranahan nodded agreeably. "I know for some men that wouldn't be the same as an answer."

"It is when you're talking to me." A glitter came into his eyes. "A lot of guys, they leave the door open. They say they'll be faithful, but all it takes is someone to put her foot in the crack. Not me. The door shut the day I took the vows."

"But Nicki did live here?"

"She lived with her old man. I never saw her in the winter, she went up to B.C. a lot with her dad, but during the busiest fishing months she stayed upstairs here, just more convenient. Sometimes Alfonso would drop by after work. We'd grill burgers on the porch. He was okay then, nobody knew he had the cancer. That man, he'd been a trapper, run sled dogs, survived two bush plane crashes. He was sort of hard to understand, but he could tell you stories."

"How did Nicki work out?"

"Best move I ever made was hiring her. Most guys, they wander around the shop with their hands in their pockets, maybe buy a few bugs. Nicki would shake that hair of hers, they'd walk out with an Orvis fly rod." He licked his thumb and imitated someone peeling bills off a wad of cash. "Clients gave her hundred-dollar tips. You're blessed with her DNA, you learn how to use it."

"And she used it."

"Sure she did. It was her idea to paint a mermaid on the boat. But she would deflect the attention if someone mentioned her looks. I remember when the photographer from *Fly Angler* came here to take her picture, she said, 'You ought to see my sister, she's much prettier than me.'"

Stranahan inched his head up. "I didn't know she had a sister."

"Neither did I until then. Nicki told me she was older. Lived in B.C. I guess she didn't make the move when the old man came to the States, but they visited her every winter."

"We might have to get in touch with next of kin. Do you know how to contact her?"

"All I know is Nicki called her Asena. She said there was a wolf in folklore named Asena."

"Really?"

"Yeah. You know, Nicki herself was big into wolves. Anything environmental. She demonstrated against the vermiculite mine, got herself arrested. I know because it was on the application she gave me."

"Did she ever say what she planned to do after her dad died?"

"She asked me who to contact to put antifreeze in the pipes, so I knew she was going away. Once she said something about opening a fishing lodge with her sister, up on one of the Skeena tributaries. Up where she was from. But I got the impression that was down the road, a someday kind of thing."

"When's the last time you heard from her?"

"Not since the memorial, not directly. A fly shop owner on the Madison called for a reference, so I take it she went down there.

Stranahan nodded. "Sam Meslik. He's a friend of mine."

"Yeah, that's the one. So, did she go to work for him?"

"She guided for him this summer, before she worked at the dude ranch. She stayed in a barn on the property.

He nodded. "Same kind of set-up she had with me. So," he cocked his head, "this friend of yours, was the door open, or closed?"

"Open."

"Then maybe he's the one you should be talking to."

CHAPTER EIGHT

Love Potion #29

It was a Montana Stranahan had passed through but had never spent much time in, a rural hodgepodge of unzoned, anything goes, fly the flag, gun rack in your truck Montana—trailer homes with crude additions, automobile graveyards, Support Our Troops bumper stickers, tool shed businesses that had sold nothing but dreams for forty years. At a crossroads, a defunct bookmobile sat on its rims in the evening gloom, skull and crossbones spray painted over the rust with a sign in pink letters—METH—NOT EVEN ONCE.

Stranahan downshifted as the road climbed into solid timber, switchbacking toward a low saddle that marked the watershed. He was looking for a black mailbox stenciled with Martinelli, found it and switched off the Land Cruiser. A No Hunting, No Trespassing sign swung from the center of the chain blocking the dirt access road, the metal punctuated with bullet holes. Stranahan stepped over it, then turned around and went back to the mailbox. It was empty. As he tapped his fingernails against the metal, his eyes were drawn to a smear of white in a drainage ditch. A bone? One of many. The ditch was littered with them, deer skulls with the antlers sawn off, hooves connected to strings of bones, scapulas growing moss. They looked surreal in the dimming light. Between the bones of a rib cage protruded a piece of paper. Stranahan climbed down into the ditch, still muddy from the last rain. It was an envelope from the power company, dated in June. He found more mail, an advertising flyer for tires with a July expiration date, a Lincoln County phonebook, and an NRA propaganda missive—all addressed to Alfonso

Martinelli. The only opened piece of mail was a padded Scripts prescriptions envelope postmarked June 15 that Stranahan suspected had held pills. Though it had obviously rained within the past few days, none of the envelopes were swollen by moisture.

Stranahan patted Choti's head—"Better stay here, girl"—got a flashlight and a bear spray canister from the Land Cruiser—he had never owned a gun—and started hiking down the drive, still thinking about the mail. Scattering it seemed a careless act and he tried not to read too much into it beyond the obvious fact that someone had been here quite recently. But stealing pills, what did that mean? Martinelli had suffered from cancer. It was reasonable to assume he'd been on pain medication. So had the same person who raided the mailbox pocketed a vial of Vicodin? Maybe not, he thought. Someone could have opened that envelope at any time over the summer and taken the pills, then put the envelope back into the mailbox. Stranahan watched a garter snake slide like a silk ribbon from one side of the drive to the other. He tried not to read too much into that, either.

Stranahan had proceeded a couple hundred yards, still without seeing the house, when the road bent sharply and dipped toward a creek. What he was looking for were boot prints and he found them at the ford, cutting across old tire tracks. Nothing looked at all new, but then anyone who wanted to approach the cabin unseen, for that's what it was, a one-story log home that he could now see in the distance, would not use the two-track, but bushwhack through the pines. Fat chance of finding a track there, though he suspected Harold Little Feather would say otherwise. Sean had witnessed Harold not only track men across what looked like trackless ground but also tell you the weight of the person who'd passed. "Like you, running a pair of soft hackles through an inside river bend," he could hear Harold saying, "you've done it so many times you can picture the flies, damn near will a trout into hitting. Same thing with tracking, except the earth is my river. Ground's just a little more reluctant to tell a story when it's hard. Like a woman not sure about taking off her clothes. You got to sweet talk her a little."

Well, Harold wasn't here.

You're stalling, Stranahan told himself. He strode briskly down the track and up the steps onto a porch of unfinished pine boards. One of the two front windows was boarded from the outside. He rapped sharply on the screen door. Silence.

Stranahan tried the door. It creaked open on unoiled hinges. A shaft of twilight striped the floor, the light swarming with dust particles. Stranahan's eyes fell on the floorboards, which were coated with dust and showed, as clearly as if they were cut with glass, the imprints of shoe soles. He fitted the elastic strap of his headlamp around his forehead and switched it on. The tracks indicated an aggressive tread with the outside heels smudged from mild pronation. Stranahan wore a ten and a half. He placed a foot beside one of the tracks. Quite a bit smaller. He opened the door all the way to let in what was left of the light and saw that the tracks were everywhere floorboards were exposed.

The beam of his flashlight bobbing before him, he followed the intruder's tracks into every room, feeling his chest expand as he opened the doors, his thumb on the safety tab of the pepper spray. It was a small dwelling with Victor traps placed in the corners of the rooms, scenes of minor tragedy marked by skeletal mice with intact tails. Robert Kelly had said he'd restored some order to the chaos, putting papers back in the desk, organizing the furniture. Stranahan figured he'd been the one who boarded up the window, as well. That had been nearly four months ago. In his brief tour, Stranahan saw no disarray beyond an unmade bed in what he took to be Nicki's old room, from the odds and ends of clothing hanging in an armoire.

Stranahan opened the slatted cover of the desk to look for a piece of paper to sketch the footprints before they were obliterated by his own. Had he heard something, or was it just the rollered slats rubbing against each other? No, he'd heard something, but then maybe it was nothing. Wood talked to itself sometimes. Still, a little more exploration was advisable. The bedroom he'd identified as Nicki's was closest to the living area and he shone his light into it. Crumpled sheets on a mattress and bedspring set on the floor, two pillows without pillowcases. The room had been drywalled and painted, showing rectangular patches of lighter color where paintings or photos had been removed. In the armoire stood cracked cowgirl boots embroidered with roses. Stranahan opened the drawers in a fiberboard bureau. He found some frayed jeans in a size eight, a denim shirt with pearl snaps, the seams shot, and a tie-dyed T-shirt. That and a few pieces of underwear told him nothing beyond that Nicki was a substantial woman who wore a 36C cup underwire and stood five eight or so. About the same size as Martha Ettinger, he thought.

Stranahan found himself standing at the foot of the bed, feeling fatigued. When he'd heard the sound his heart rate had come up, but he was in a wash of inertia now and sat down on the bed, his butt coming up against something hard under the covers. It was a book, the light revealing a cover with a wolf howling at the moon. *Killer or Kindred Spirit?: The Lore and Allure of the Wolf,* by Barbara Barr. In the other bedroom, which he assumed to be Nicki's father's, the bedstand had been littered with Louis L'Amour paperbacks, old dime novels of a West that never was. He opened the wolf book and found that it was scholarly and densely written. Nicki's?

Suddenly it bothered him, not the book so much as the bed. Why would someone shutting a house down for an indefinite period as Nicki had leave everything shipshape but her bed. And if the reason it looked unmade was because the man on the motorcycle had mussed it looking for something, why hadn't the fly shop owner at least pulled the comforter over it?

Stranahan itched at his ten-day beard as he walked toward the back of the house. Alfonso's room was dominated by a gun case, no guns but there was a workbench with a reloading press and two shelves with gear—powder tins, primer packets, unprimed brass and die sets for a half dozen rifle and pistol calibers. The press held a brass cartridge case in a bullet-seating die, poured three-quarters full of powder. Beside the press were a half dozen cast-lead bullets ready to be seated and three already loaded into cases. Without really thinking about it, Stranahan pocketed a couple of the bullets. He turned his attention to the far end of the bench. More tools—a firebrick, an acetylene torch setup for melting metal, bullet molds. He reached his hand into his pocket and rolled the heavy chunks of lead with his fingers. The man had been a serious hand loader, but considering his profession, that was unremarkable. What was odd was that the table looked to have been abandoned in the middle of a reloading session. It didn't add up, the way the unmade bed didn't add up.

A worm of fear twisted in Stranahan's gut. There had been a sound; he'd been a fool to dismiss it. *But he'd checked all the rooms, hadn't he?* Unholstering the pepper spray, he went back to the living room. Mountain cabins often included unfinished cellars accessed by trapdoors. Near the desk was an Indian print area rug and Stranahan bent over to pull one end back. "What do you know," he muttered. The door was there, with a circular iron latch recessed into the wood. Stranahan flipped it up. Rough-hewn wood steps descended into darkness, and as he peered down, he felt rather than heard the floorboards creak behind him. Spinning around, his headlamp came off and spun across the floor, its beam glancing up to reveal the ceiling shadow of a distorted human figure, a chimera with a head that seemed to swarm with snakes. He felt searing pain at the back of his head and a light began to flicker behind his eyes, ticking like the blank tape at the beginning of an old movie reel. The square hole in the floor started to shake. It seemed to take forever to fall and he felt the bullets hard against his fingers as he landed on his hand. His head hit and bounced up. The light flashed into brilliance, then raced to a point and flickered out.

In his amateur boxing career, which ended with Stranahan outpointed in the finals of the Silver Mittens Tournament in Lowell, Massachusetts, a match that nearly twenty years later he still believed in his heart that he'd won, he had never been knocked out. Now he knew what it was like to come to from a blow, with his brain seeming to shift sludgelike in his skull. He reached behind his head and his hand came away wet.

The darkness was absolute. A moldy organic smell invaded his nostrils. He spoke into the blackness and got no response. His voice didn't seem to belong to him, and the sound made his head hurt. He finally withdrew the hand cramped in his pocket. He flexed his fingers. No bones seemed to be broken. The act gave him a thought, but the thought floated out of his consciousness. Some time later, it could have been a minute or an hour, he had the thought again and reached into his jeans' pocket to retrieve his key ring, which had a small Swiss Army knife with a press-and-hold light. Stranahan clamped it between his teeth.

It was a root cellar. He rose cautiously to his feet, for the cabin floor had protruding nails and he couldn't stand straight without spiking his head. He shone the single LED. The room was about six feet by ten feet with sets of shelves against both long walls. The shelves were lined with Mason jars sealed in wax. Beets, jams, onions, kokanee salmon—French spellings with dates that went back about eight years. At the back of the room were a half dozen plastic gallon containers with pressure locks. He brought the light closer. Potion L'Amour #29. Love potion? He had no idea what to make of it.

At the other end of the cellar were the rough timber stairs leading to the trapdoor. He remembered that the door had no lock, but was unsurprised to find it had no give, either, even after pounding up at it with a piece of two-by-four he found on the earthen floor. No doubt whoever had knocked him into the root cellar had pulled something heavy over the door. The desk was handy and would have done the trick. There remained digging his way out, but with what? Besides a few odd boards left over from the construction of the shelves, there were the stairs themselves, which were studded with rusty nails. He might be able to pry up a step. A dull metallic glint caught his eye. The cellar was shallower at this end and he had to bend over to peer behind the steps. Hanging from stout ceiling hooks were a dozen or so leghold traps with large, offset jaws. Some had teeth. In a box were a jumble of smaller traps. He removed the largest trap from the hooks. Etched into the pan was the number 4½ under "S. New-house." A stout drag chain ended in pronged hooks that would dig into the ground to keep an animal from carrying the trap away. Sean knew something about traps, having long ago befriended a woods-man who was his grandfather's neighbor in the Berkshire Moun-tains. The old man, whom everyone called Smithy, had shown the young boy how to set a trap by depressing the springs and pinning the toggle sear to the pan. Sean remembered setting one off with a stick and jumping backward when the jaws snapped shut.

Stranahan carried the trap to the east-facing wall, where two three-inch diameter PVC pipes with shut-off valves protruded into the cellar at chest height. He jammed the jaws of the trap into the wall. A few bits of earth crumbled and dropped away. Again. A little more. In ten minutes his arms ached and he'd dug out no more earth than would fill a coffee can. Hot spots on his palms promised blis-ters if he kept at it. He sat back, shone his light on the trap and won-dered what he'd been using for brains. The pronged grappling hook at the end of the drag chain was comfortable to hold and he began to dig with it, first taking his shirt off and wrapping it around his hand to reduce friction. It was slow going, but an intermittent stream of moldy earth pouring out of the wall assured him of progress. The irony of using a trap to dig out of a trap brought a grim smile.

Abruptly, he stopped smiling. A sound like a door creaking. A single step. Silence.

Stranahan felt for the pepper spray on his hip. It wasn't there. He only vaguely remembered falling and realized the spray must have slipped out of his hand when he was hit. He relaxed his jaws. The LED light he'd been gripping in his teeth went out. He listened to himself breathe. Then, a scraping noise, like chalk on a blackboard. Incrementally, a rectangle of indistinct light, thin as string, revealed the outline of the trapdoor. Someone had moved the desk covering it.

Now Stranahan could hear another person breathing besides himself. The sound was muted by the floorboards, but he thought he could hear a crying sob after each inhalation. Something, instinct, kept him from speaking. A feeling of dread swept over him. He could sense anxiety through the floor, as if the person was reaching a breaking point.

He felt the weight of the big Newhouse. Placing the trap on the floor and using nearly all his strength, he pressed down the heavy springs, hoping devoutly that they were oiled. He set the toggle sear by feel. Gingerly, he lifted the trap. The jaws didn't snap shut, as he feared they might. Setting his feet down so as not to make a sound, and carrying the trap as gingerly as if he were carrying a land mine, he placed it on the bottom step below the trapdoor. It would be in shadow if the door was opened. He figured there was a fifty-fifty chance of someone descending stepping onto the pan. That is, if they didn't first shine a light, in which case the trap could be easily avoided. A slim defense, but better than nothing.

Above him, the breathing seemed to be coming faster, thin inhalations building to a climax. Stranahan backed away from the stairs, inadvertently kicking his heel against the dirt he'd excavated with the trap. He didn't fall, but in bracing his hand against the wall shelves to right himself, several Mason jars clicked together. Instantaneously, a cracking thunder shook the room and a shaft of light, the diameter of a pencil, made a spot against the floor a foot from his left shoe.

Kicking, he scrambled to the other side of the room. Two gallon jars exploded to his right. He felt a spray against his face and began to gag, the air instantly fetid. The love potion had to be the wolf lure Monroe had mentioned, made from God knows what. A third shot kicked up a volcano of earth between Stranahan's boots. Beams from the last two shots placed quarters of light to either side of him. He grappled for the nearest jar that was still intact and hurled it against the stairs. The fourth shot was straight down through the trapdoor. Stranahan could hear Choti barking from the direction of the road.

His mind raced. He could keep trying to trick the shooter into shooting where he wasn't, but it was a small room. A bullet was going to find him. He reached around, patting the ground, trying not to cut his hand on shattered glass. His hand clasped a stick. He kneed toward the steps and tapped down. Another shot, this one behind him. The shooter was catching onto Sean's game of misdirection. He tapped again, the stick depressing the pan of the trap and tripping the jaws.

In the confined space, the sound of the trap snapping shut was a thunderclap.

"I have a gun!" Stranahan shouted. He meant to put a crazy note in his voice. He needn't have. He sounded plenty crazy, even to himself. "The next one's up through the floor. Two can play this game."

Above him, he heard a sharp intake of breath, a reedy sound. "Oh, no." A moment of silence, then quick steps. The squeak of the front door opening. Had it been a woman's voice?

Stranahan counted to thirty. His heart was hammering. *Do it, damn it.* He took the steps, pushed up the trapdoor and bolted out the open front door. A sixth sense told him the shooter had gone and wouldn't be back. But he ran anyway, ran without feeling the ground and didn't stop until he was in the dark arms of the forest. He put his hands on his knees and for a time his breath came in wheezing shudders. Slowly, he started to come back into himself. He must be near the road for he could hear Choti barking quite loudly. A motorcycle coughed to life somewhere beyond. He automatically registered that it sounded like a two-stroke. The bike popped away in drawn-out flatulence. Then, nothing.

———

When he heard the rapping against the window, he awoke with a start. He rolled it down. The sound of the Kootenai River poured in; beyond the front windshield, a pearl horizon told him the hour. Choti opened an eye from where she was curled on the passenger seat. Stranahan didn't remember either hiking to his rig or driving to the boat ramp.

Sheriff Monroe's head loomed in the window. Then it pulled back sharply.

"What in the hell is that smell?"

Stranahan had to think a second.

"Love Potion Twenty-nine," he said.

CHAPTER NINE

Bloody Mary Eyes

Stranahan's inheritance upon the passing of his father, who'd been killed in a car accident when Sean was fifteen, was meager from a monetary perspective. Besides tools—his dad was an auto mechanic—the inheritance consisted of two handcrafted bamboo fly rods and a milling machine his dad had constructed to cut the bamboo strips, an original Remington Bullet knife from the 1930s, a Hardy Perfect fly reel and a Meerschaum pipe with a handsome burl figure. His father had smoked that pipe during fishing trips to the Deerfield River, outings that were among the most vivid recollections of Sean's childhood. Twenty-five years later he could close his eyes and still see the cherry circles come and go in the night, could hear the whistle of his dad's fly line and the hollow thumping of a brown trout coming to net. It was only in the past few months, after Martinique had departed for veterinary school, leaving Sean more lonely than he'd been in years, that he found himself filling a bowl for any other reason than to keep mosquitoes at bay. That evening when he returned to Bridger was one of those times, and as he drew the pipe out of his shirt pocket and started to fill it, Martha Ettinger reached out a hand and took it from him.

Stranahan arched an eyebrow.

"As you were saying," Martha said.

"What? Are you my mother?"

"Apparently you need one. Did I ever tell you about Burt, my second husband?"

"The cattle auctioneer."

"You know why he isn't one now?"

"No, but I think you're going to tell me."

"He got oral cancer from chewing Skoal. Burt doesn't have a lower jaw. You don't sell a lot of heifers when you have to talk out of a hole in your throat." She knocked the tobacco out of the pipe and handed it back to him. "Wake up. Haven't you seen the ads on TV?"

Sean swirled his hand in the air. "I live in a tipi, Martha. I don't have electricity. And, I should mention that when the host cleans his pipe, it's an indication that the visit is over. Old Indian custom."

"Fuck custom. I'm serious. And I guarantee you, no woman's going to want to kiss you once you strike a match to that corncob.

"Meerschaum."

"Same smoke."

Stranahan put his palms up. "I surrender. But for the record, I don't inhale."

"You don't have to. Now as you were saying—"

"I was saying, I'm not sure it was Nanika Martinelli."

"But you said it was a woman's voice, and the figure you saw had long hair. That fits."

"It does, but you weren't the one in the cellar. I can't be sure. And why would she want to kill me? Look, I'm guessing here, but what I think happened is this person was startled when I knocked on the front door, hid herself/himself and then knocked me down into the cellar. Time passes, I don't know how long, but long enough for me to rub my hands raw digging with the trap, then that person or another person comes back, this time with a gun. From what I've heard about this girl—"

"Woman," Martha corrected.

"Woman. There's no history of violence."

"So if it wasn't Martinelli, who do you think?"

Stranahan had been anticipating the question ever since he'd called Ettinger from a pay phone on the drive back. Now they were sitting across the fire ring from each other on folded buffalo blankets. Sean added a stick to the coals, the night setting in cold, and studied the wisp of smoke snaking toward the vent. He stood to adjust the flap poles and spoke without facing her.

"I think it could be the girl who was with the motorcycle guy, the one who came looking for Martinelli."

"Because you heard a motorcycle."

"It was a two-stroke. A lot of dirt bikes are two-stroke. The fly shop owner said the guy was riding an off-road bike."

"You told me the girl had short black hair. That doesn't sound like a Medusa."

"I could be wrong about the shadow."

"You could be wrong about the motorcycle, too."

"No, bikes I know."

"Since when?"

"My dad restored an Indian 741 Scout, the model used in World War II. There's about ten years after he died that I was lucky to live through. That Indian was only one of the risks I ran."

"Ah, those lost years. We all have a few."

"I was lost. I remember the years well enough, the good parts, anyway."

"That's the difference between us. You're an optimist." Her hand crept up to her jaw and they sat in comfortable silence. She stroked her throat. "Well, okay," she said slowly. "If you think it could be the girl, then that seems like a valid line of investigation. Frankly, I've got my hands full with the wrangler your buddy Sam beat up. I told you he stepped in a trap, didn't I? A wolf trap. Probably not much different than the one you set off in that cellar." She shook her head. "As if someone with an antler through his gut isn't enough to keep a story in headlines."

"Strange coincidence, me digging with a trap, the wrangler getting caught in one."

"A wolf runs through it." Ettinger nodded her head. "Where's your bathroom?"

"It's back in the woods. You take a path from that rock I told you about where I get my mail."

"I'll hold it." She rolled her eyes. "That path is reason number two no self-respecting woman wants to kiss you. So, how is . . . Mar-tin-ique?" She didn't want to hear Sean Stranahan talk about his girl-friend any more than she wanted to hear Harold Little Feather talk about his ex-wife, but she couldn't help herself. Why didn't either of the men who made her feel like a woman realize there was a heart under the badge. *I'm right here*, she wanted to say.

"I haven't spoken with her since coming back from B.C.," Strana-han said.

"Is there a problem?"

"I don't know. I thought this business of working as a bikini barista would be over once she went to vet school, and it is over, but now she's got a second cell phone she uses to seduce men, like a nine hun-dred number. She's up front with me about it, says the phone can't be traced and it's easy money."

"So you aren't the only one she talks dirty to."

"That's the thing. She never did. She's"—he searched for a word—"bashful."

"Are you two still . . . together?"

"I think so. But I'll tell you the truth. I'm worried. This guy who runs the phone service, his name is Red. A Cajun guy named Red who plays the ponies, a professional gambler. He gave her a phone name, calls her Caramel Candy. She says she's going to work only until the holiday break, that she'll be too busy next semester and one of the men she's been talking to is beginning to creep her out. Now what do you think the chances are of a graceful exit from this busi-ness when you work for a guy named Red?"

"Right now," Martha stifled a yawn, "I think about the same as me making the connection between a missing person case and a body in Doc Hanson's cooler. I'm going to hit the hay. I can't imagine how tired you are, so get some sleep. Tomorrow I'd like you to come with me to the Culpepper Ranch, meet a cousin of mine."

"I didn't know you had a cousin in the valley."

"Our ranch was up out of White Sulfur. I have kin from Great Falls to Pocatello. We'll have a look at where this happened. Can you sit a horse?"

Stranahan's nod was unemphatic.

"I repeat the question."

"You climb on from the left. Right?"

Ettinger sighed. "We'll put you on one that's pawing at the door to the glue factory. I'll pick you up at seven."

"Just knock on the flap. I don't have a watch."

"You don't have a cell phone. You don't have a watch. Your mailbox is under a rock and you smell like a dead cat. Oh, and the toilet is down a path. Seems to me you're entering another one of those lost years. Yet I hear myself asking for your help."

"Sorry about the wolf lure," Stranahan said. "I guess to a wolf, dead cat smells like nectar."

After she'd left, he made up his bed, which amounted to unzipping the sleeping bag on his cot. He pumped up his lantern and opened the book he'd found in the cabin. He leafed to the index. Asena, he read, was a she-wolf that figured in Turkish mythology. According to fable, the wolf had a sky-blue mane and rescued a Mongol boy who was the only survivor of an invasion by Chinese soldiers. The wolf nursed the boy back to health, became his lover and bore him ten half-wolf, half-human children, one of whom became the first khan.

A wolf runs through it, Ettinger had said.

Shutting the book, Stranahan turned off the lantern and watched the color slowly drain from the mantles.

CHAPTER TEN

The Smiling Man

"So I'm to stay in the background and observe."

"No, you're to stand beside me and observe. What did I tell you?"

"Okay, Martha. It just seems . . . I don't know. Why the cloak and dagger? Who am I, by the way? How do you introduce me?"

"You're a tracker contracted by the department. You're going to ride up to the scene and see if you can find anything Harold missed. I have a lot of faith that you can. Can you do that?"

"I can act the part. I can't see myself finding anything Harold missed."

"I know damned well you won't, but I want Bucky to think you might. There's a card I'm going to play. You don't need to know anything more than that."

They turned under the yoke-style gate. It was a blue-sky morning, the big solar panels on the Culpepper mansion's south-facing roof hauling in the wattage. Ettinger turned onto a road that wound past the guest cabins. The ranch manager's house was tucked back into an aspen stand with a half-ton Silverado in front, but no one answered Ettinger's knock. She led Stranahan around the house to a barn. He wasn't there, either. She tried the sliding door. A gutted mule deer buck hung from a block and tackle attached to a rafter beam. Nothing else but hay.

"Bucky's a bow hunter," Ettinger said. She examined the arrows on the quiver mounted to a recurve bow that was hanging from a nail. They heard the staccato roar of an ATV coming up from the manor.

As they shut the barn door and walked back to the house, Ettinger spoke out of the side of her mouth. "Wasn't all that long ago cowboys rode horses."

In the ringing silence after he'd shut off the quad, Bucky Anderson helloed and strode toward them, listing slightly to the side and rubbing at his stomach. He tilted his straw Stetson back in a form of salute. He was a big man with a very broad face, clean shaven. His Carhartt jacket was barely soiled. Stranahan noticed a C-shaped scar on his right cheek.

Despite meaty hands burned to a deep ochre color, Anderson's initial grip was tentative. Then, as Stranahan began to withdraw his hand, the bone crusher. *So, one of those.* It told him more about the man than he would have gleaned rifling his medicine cabinet.

"I was just telling Sean," Ettinger said, "the irony of the new Montana, where the only hay-eating horses are on dude ranches. You go to a ranch that runs cattle, all the horses are under the hood."

"Isn't that a fact?" Anderson said. He had a high-pitched voice that seemed incongruous with the brute strength his body betrayed.

"Bucky's ranch manager here," Martha said unnecessarily. "Going to marry the widow Culpepper, have his initials on the branding iron next summer."

"We tie the knot June twenty-one. I'll admit I'm a little nervous." He had a smile. Stranahan guessed he was one of those men who always had a smile. He recognized something else he couldn't put his finger on, but made the muscles tighten in his abdomen.

"If the little woman will still have me after what happened Tuesday," Anderson said.

Ettinger turned to Stranahan. "She's out on the coast, whiling away the 'R' months with Pilates and Pinot Gris." It seemed a harsh assessment. Stranahan wondered if she was trying to provoke Anderson.

His expression didn't change. "Now Martha, that's not fair. But you're right. Much as I'd like to have her here, I'm glad she missed out on our high-country drama." There was the smile again.

"Where are you going to get married?" Stranahan continued the string of pleasantries, feeling a little absurd.

Anderson spread his hands like a preacher. "You're looking at it."

Below them, the aspens gave ground to grasslands that rolled away toward the ribbon of the Madison River. Stranahan could see the West Fork bridge, but the island downstream, where two years earlier a drowning victim had caught up under a pile of driftwood and one of Sam's clients had accidentally hooked the body with a trout fly, was obscured by bankside pines. For a moment Stranahan thought about the arc his life had taken since then. *I'm right where I should be*, he thought. Maybe the lost years really were over.

He looked at Ettinger, who had her hands on her hips and was bringing Anderson up to date on the search or, rather, what was left of it. They were eighty-six hours in, down from a hundred ground pounders on day two to less than half that number, hopes beginning to die. They'd keep the plane in the air another day or two, go through the motions while the cadaver dogs worked their noses. But the fact was at this point in the search, the most prominent member of SAR was no longer the incident commander. It was the Reverend Marcus Miles, the county chaplain, whose job was to act as a liaison between the grieving family and the sheriff's department. He was the one who would gain the family's trust simply by being there, by listening to all the words and saying the right ones himself, who was the shoulder for women and strong men alike to cry on. Ettinger and Anderson were talking about the family now, the sister, Asena, whom Nicki had provided a phone number for and was listed as next of kin on her application to the ranch.

"So she hasn't called back?" Bucky asked.

Ettinger said, "I got in touch last night and gave her my personal number, but no, not yet. She was still on the other side of the border, so I suppose she could show any time, depending on how hard she's pressing the pedal. I told her the ranch had set aside a guest cabin for her, free of charge."

Anderson nodded. "It's the least we can do. When do you think you'll start wrapping it up?"

"So things can get back to normal?"

"No, I don't mean it that way."

"How did you mean it?"

Anderson shrugged.

Ettinger shrugged back at him. "Sometimes what happens after our funding dries up is the family hires out privately to continue the search, but in this case the sister's the only relative and I don't know what her resources are. To my knowledge, she isn't married. She may have no pocket to pick but her own."

"Jason Kent told me she was older," Anderson said. He'd taken off his hat. Stranahan saw that his hair was thinning in front, twin bays of pink scalp intruding upon a spit of hair that would soon become an island.

"That's my understanding," Ettinger said. "It wasn't a long conversation."

Stranahan put his hands in his jeans pockets and leaned back on his heels. Despite the big-dog handshake, Bucky Anderson seemed to be just who he portrayed himself to be, a concerned ranch manager wanting to help, shaking his head at the tragedy that had unfolded on property he was responsible for.

"We did find something interesting yesterday," Ettinger said. "A couple things."

"Oh, what was that?" Anderson's mouth was smiling, but his eyes had drawn into folds of flesh.

"Our tracker found a hat under the headwall, a few hundred yards above the elk kill. It's a straw cowboy with some trout flies stuck in it and we're pretty sure it's hers. Good chance she was bucked by her horse."

"What else did you find?"

"An arrow. About a third of a mile from the carcass. The biologist who examined the elk found a nick in the rear ribs consistent with the wound made by a broadhead. So what it looks like is whoever shot the elk hit it too far back for a clean kill and either didn't follow up the blood trail or lost it. Then the wolves finished the elk off. Or it died and the wolves scavenged the carcass, one or the other."

So this is the card, Stranahan thought.

"How do you know it's the same arrow that killed the elk?" Sean said. The words were out before he realized and he saw Ettinger bite on her lower lip. She'd told him not to interfere.

"Yes," Anderson echoed the doubt. "There must be quite a few arrows lost during bow season."

"Well, the arrow has elk blood on it and the blood's about five days old, according to our forensic analyst. Pretty strong circumstantial." Ettinger scratched her chin with the backs of her fingernails. "You're a traditional archer, aren't you, Bucky? Somebody told me you shoot a recurve, fletch your own arrows. What do you use for shafts, Sitka spruce? Harold, one of our deputies, that's what he uses."

"I use different kinds of wood."

"Harold, he puts his own sign on the arrows, three slashes on the diagonal. Do you put your initials on your arrows?"

Stranahan saw color come into Anderson's neck, then flush up across his cheeks, the half moon scar standing out whitely. Anderson turned his head and Stranahan saw the cauliflowering of the right ear. The man had been a fighter, the scar from a broken beer bottle, Sean would bet on it. The smile on Anderson's face had become a grimace.

"Did you shoot a bull elk last week, Bucky? I want you to think about the consequences of lying to an officer of the law and hindering an investigation before you answer."

"I didn't know this was an investigation."

Martha didn't comment. She'd let him squirm. She was good at it.

"What do you want me to say?" Anderson's hands spread apart; he turned his palms up in supplication. It was nearly the same gesture he'd used before to encompass the richness of the land that would become his kingdom. Except now his face was red and there was menace, a submerged fury that radiated like heat from his body. Stranahan's instinct was to step back. Ettinger took one step closer, looked unblinkingly into the broad face.

"You haven't changed, have you? Not really."

"I haven't had a drink in six years. I'm a different man now. You want me to say 'Yes, I shot an elk.' Yes, I shot an elk. It's bow season. It's legal. He lurched when I released and I didn't double lung him like I'd intended. I tracked him until dark. I went back the next morning and couldn't pick up his trail." He shrugged. "I lost him."

"Why didn't you tell me the night we found the body?"

"What difference does it make? I didn't have anything to do with that poor boy's death."

"You knew we found a body pinned on the antlers of an elk you shot and didn't think to tell me. It makes me feel like you have something to hide."

"I wasn't even sure it was the same elk. I mean I shot a bull, yes, but this bull, another bull. A lot of elk pass through Papoose Basin."

"Not a lot of them that big."

"Look." His hands weren't so far apart now, but straight out from the elbows at midtorso, palms facing each other. A politician's posture. *Let's be reasonable men.* "Martha, I'm sorry. I should have said something. But you have to understand my position. The Culpeppers, let's just say the brothers aren't so wild about me marrying in. I cut into the pie, so that's a threat. Evelyn's stood up for me from the start, she's a rock, but if this comes out, that I'm involved even though I had nothing to do with what happened up there. . . . You see what I'm saying? People are wanting me to slip up, anything to change her mind. I'm walking on eggshells here."

"Is there anything else you want to tell us? The truth's going to come out, that I can guarantee you."

"You've had it in for me ever since—"

"Ever since when? Since the first guy you put in the hospital. Or maybe that college kid who had to have his face reconstructed and bags groceries at Town and Country because he can't add up numbers to run a cash register. What one was he—five, or six?"

"He started that."

Ettinger's eyes never left Anderson's face. "You see," she was speaking for Stranahan's benefit, "they were the ones who always started it. Bucky would come into the bar all smiling like he is now, find some guy with a girl and step in between them, tell her how pretty she was, keep looking over at the guy, the bigger the guy the better the chance he'd take the bait, keep it up until the poor sap had to call him out to save face. Then he'd beat the crap out of him in the alley. Picked on ranch hands, didn't you Bucky, 'cause you knew they'd cowboy up and not press charges? Smile the whole goddamned time you turned their faces into hamburger."

Anderson's cheeks had become the color of vein blood. For a moment Stranahan thought he was going to hit her and stepped forward, measuring him, knowing Anderson had him by forty pounds and he'd have to rely on his speed, see how much rust was in his hands. *Too much*, he thought. But then, unexpectedly, the moment passed. Anderson took a step back. He replaced his hat and pinched the brim with two fingers.

"I'm sorry we've met under these circumstances," he said, looking at Sean. "And Martha, I'm sorry you still harbor such resentment. But I can't change the past." He opened his hands. "I can only do what I'm doing, keep trying to make myself a better person."

"Spoken like a man in therapy."

"I am in therapy. It helps."

Ettinger's face stayed stony. "We'll need your statement. I want to know everything that happened, starting with waking up on the morning you shot that elk. I'll send someone around."

Anderson nodded. "There's nobody wants to have the disappearance of this young woman cleared up more than I do. The poor thing, she'd just started here at the ranch. None of us had time to know her, but she was well thought of. I just feel like hell about it."

They left him standing on his porch, feeling like hell about it, and drove away toward the trailhead. Stranahan sat Big Mike competently enough that in little more than an hour they had reached the timberline on the headwall of the basin. Ettinger dismounted and pointed out the timber a quarter mile down the basin, where she'd discovered the wrangler's body. Except for a muttered "asshole" when they were in the Jeep, she had uttered not a word about the encounter with Bucky Anderson.

Stranahan rubbed his butt with balled fists.

"Saddle sore?"

He looked at the ground, a field of scarlet paintbrush, their stalks broken by a high altitude hailstorm. "Before we hike down there," he said. "I'd appreciate you telling me what the hell that was all about?"

"Bucky?" She chewed on her lip. "That was about getting him to admit to something I had no evidence to accuse him of."

She twirled her Resistol on her forefinger and resettled it on her head. "We did find an arrow, but it had an aluminum shaft; it wasn't Bucky's. But I had a good idea he'd stuck that bull. Everybody on the staff said he made the morning's schedule so he could hunt till ten a.m. or so. One of the ranch hands told me about the arrows with his initials. I confirmed it when we went into the barn. My hunch is Bucky found the elk the day after he wounded it; maybe he heard wolves on the kill. Then he set the trap and that kid stepped onto it by accident when he was looking for the Martinelli woman."

"Isn't it illegal to trap wolves?"

"No. But the trapping season starts December one, so it's out of season."

"What good would setting a trap do? The pack had already ruined the meat."

"Ranchers like Bucky hate wolves as much as they hate Democrats. Just the opportunity to kill one would be reason enough, take my word for it."

With the snow melted, the only lingering evidence of the tragedy was the smell. Blood that has seeped into the earth has a dark, organic scent that works on an atavistic level, causing the small hairs to stand up on the forearms.

Stranahan flared his nostrils. "Glad I'm not an undertaker," he said.

His eyes had been immediately drawn to a raw wound in the earth, twin furrows about five feet long. They would have been covered by snow when Little Feather examined the ground.

"If I hadn't been trapped in that cellar, I wouldn't know what made that," he said.

Martha grunted. "It looks like the work of a mountain vole to me."

"I don't think so."

"Are you going to tell me or do I have to ask? I'd remind you I'm the sheriff." Her mood had improved. An hour on a horse always improved her mood.

"It's the drag chain on the trap. The hooks on the end dig in when the animal tries to drag away the trap. You can see in some places it digs in more? That's where the wolf would have jerked the chain."

"But we're not talking about a wolf. We're talking about a human being. The wrangler could just reach down and lift the chain."

"No, it was dark. For a second he wouldn't know what happened. His instinct would be to lunge away. He'd be dragging the chain. This is where the elk was, right? Where the earth is stained darker."

Ettinger nodded.

"So let's reconstruct. Grady Cole's horse bucks when it smells the blood. He bails, stumbles into the opening here, sees the dead elk. He's advancing toward it." Stranahan clapped his hands. "He lunges forward, dragging the trap. Trips over the elk. Impales himself. You said just falling onto the antlers wouldn't have driven the tine all the way through . . ."

"Our CSI's not in the habit of making mistakes."

"So do you think when Bucky went out looking for Martinelli, he found the kid caught in the trap and pushed him onto the antlers? What had the kid ever done to him?"

Ettinger took off her riding gloves and tucked them into a back pocket. "Bucky stands to become co-owner of the largest ranch in the Madison Valley. If it came to light that he'd set a trap for a wolf out of season and caught one of his own employees, he might not get that *A* on the branding iron, especially if the kid brought charges. And there's something I haven't told you. Evelyn Culpepper's an animal lover. She supported wolf reintroduction, contributes to environmental causes, she's a heavy hitter in the movement. She's even funding a scat analyst who's doing his thesis on predator-prey relationships, hoping to prove that wolves aren't the big livestock killers they're made out to be. Her engagement to Bucky's hard to fathom, with the two of them being at opposite ends of the politics. I don't think it would take much bad behavior on his part to tip the apple cart."

"And you see him killing someone over this?"

She shrugged. "I've seen people kill people over fifty pounds of venison, who put his tag on a dead deer first."

"So, Martinelli, you think she arrives at the scene before Cole is killed, or after?"

"She was in the basin first, so before makes more sense. But if she was hobbling or disoriented, you could make a case for after, too."

Ettinger looked at her watch. "Let's go see your buddy Meslik. You say he's been avoiding you?"

"No, I said I hadn't been able to get ahold of him 'til this morning. He told me he was going to hang with the boys at the Liars and Fly Tiers clubhouse. They made him an honorary member. He's stepping up in the world."

"Right. More likely he's bringing them down to his level."

CHAPTER ELEVEN

Dead Man's Fancy

For the third week of September it was an unusual sight—three bare-chested men gathered on the porch of a remodeled homestead cabin, sitting on folding chairs around a card table littered with feathers. Sam Meslik and Kenneth Winston, a hairstylist from Biloxi, Mississippi, whose card read Hot Hands, were bent over portable fly-tying vises. Patrick Willoughby, the president of the Liars and Fly Tiers, stood to peer over Sam's shoulder and offer instruction. As Meslik worked his fingers, the fly rod in the grip of the Mickey Mouse tattooed on his massive left biceps waved back and forth, while the rainbow trout hooked to Mickey's fly appeared to leap and fall back. Sam glanced up as Stranahan and Ettinger drove up. He grinned, showing the grooves in his teeth.

Willoughby, whose thick-lensed glasses gave him the visage of an owl, shook hands with the newcomers.

"Sam's trying to convince us that the mind breathes when the skin is exposed to the sun. But if I'd known we would be hosting a woman," he offered a kindly smile to Ettinger, "I would have had the decorum to wear a shirt. I do hope you're planning to stay for dinner."

Ettinger began to protest.

"No, we simply won't hear of it. The nylgai loin Kenneth has defrosted is quite ample to feed the five of us, and a short trip to the wine cellar will satisfy our need of libations. Now if you'll excuse me, I'd like to make myself more presentable."

"How does he do that?" Martha said as Willoughby left.

Stranahan smiled. "One of the members told me he was a hostage negotiator for three presidential administrations. He still has his hand in as a terrorist profiler, something of that nature, it's all a bit mysterious. But he's very good about getting people to agree with him."

"Since when do we have a wine cellar?" Winston posed the question as he rose from his chair. "I guess Patrick must mean that cardboard box in the hall closet. Sean, you haven't introduced our guest." He offered his slim brown hand to Ettinger. The diamond stud in his earlobe caught the light as he bowed and kissed Ettinger's hand. She blushed.

Sean said, "I didn't think you were coming back this fall."

"I didn't, either. But when Patrick called last week to say he was swinging through, I decided to join him. With Polly's passing, he's about the best friend I have. Plus I can bluff him out of one of his divided-wings Hendricksons any time I draw a bad hand."

"I've told you we play poker for flies instead of money," Stranahan said.

Ettinger mm-hmmed.

"Why don't you join us tonight?" It was Sam, his eyes still trained on his vise. The fly he was palmering with grizzly hackle was the size of a mosquito.

"I don't tie flies," Martha said.

"I'll stake you some of mine. When you run out, you can put your duds into the pot. I've always wondered if you're as much of a man underneath your khakis as you act on the outside."

"Keep wondering, Meslik. And cover up. You look like a wolf with a bad case of mange."

Ettinger's radio crackled. She excused herself and walked a few yards away.

"Yeah, Jason, what is it?" She listened, bringing her fingers up to worry the soft skin under the corner of her jaw. "Tell her as soon as possible." Then: "You're right, she's going to be tired. How about we meet at nine?" She holstered the radio and crooked a finger at Stranahan.

"The sister will be pulling in around midnight. We're going to meet with her tomorrow morning. What I'll do is make a call to have a neighbor look in on my animals and then book us a couple motel rooms in Ennis. There's no sense driving back to Bridger just to turn right back around."

"I can stay here at the clubhouse," Sean said.

She nodded. "Look," she kept her voice low, "I want to talk to Meslik, but I want him to want to talk to me. I think he's holding back, but if he drinks enough wine, he'll come around. I'll adjust my attitude, become Martha from Portland. Somebody who waters plants and talks about her feelings. I don't know. Something."

Stranahan's expression was skeptical.

"I'm just telling you this so you'll understand if I start acting a little, say, chummy."

"Sure, if that's the way you want to play it. He *is* my best friend. If he's hiding something, it will come out sooner or later."

"We don't have time for later."

"Then let's drink some wine."

By the time they'd pulled half a dozen corks and polished off the loin of Indian antelope, Meslik and Ettinger were nearly as close as the two fingers they held together for comparison. The "attitude adjustment" amounted to a simple kissing up on Martha's part, apologizing for any bad feelings she might have engendered when she'd questioned Sam at his shop, and Sam being a pushover for the attentions of an attractive woman, especially one who wore a gun. His acerbic comments to the contrary, the tension between the two had dissolved noticeably when, several hands into the game, Sam called Ettinger's bet with a Sex Dungeon, a monstrous double-hooked streamer fly created by Kelly Galloup, then raised her by adding a bottle of Fly-Agra Dry Fly Floatant to the pot.

"Wait a gol-darned minute," Martha said, and turned the bottle over to read the label warning: "If your fly stays up for more than four hours, consult your local fly shop."

"I suppose you spray it directly on your pecker when the fishing gets a little slow," she mused.

"Depends on the woman in the bow of the boat," Sam said. "If it was you, I think I could risk leaving it at home."

"*Humpff.*" Ettinger called and won the hand.

But it was the gun that cemented their relationship. Holding a ten-high garbage hand, Martha made a show of unholstering her Glock, which she was packing instead of her customary .357. She checked the empty chamber and slapped the handle butt to extract the stacked magazine. Then she casually placed the piece on the table.

"I'm in," she said. "Anybody want to fold?" She picked up the semi-auto and itched behind her ear with the front sight. "Sam?"

Sam peered at his cards and tossed them facedown onto the table. "I don't know whether you're bluffing me or not, but you sure know how to give a man a hard-on. I'm drilling a hole into the bottom of this table right now."

"I'm going to imagine I didn't hear that," Martha said.

Another glass of wine and they were comparing the forefingers. Martha shook her head.

"How the hell do you tie size 20 flies with those . . . zucchinis?"

Sam ran his tongue over his lips.

"No, don't tell me," Martha said.

"If you were to let my zucchini—"

Ettinger put her fingers in her ears and started to hum.

Sam turned his hands palms up.

Martha lowered hers.

"Truce?" Sam said.

"Truce."

They reached across the table to shake hands. Then Sam stood up with a screeching of his chair and came around the table and put an arm around her, not the Mickey Mouse arm but the one with a tattoo of Sylvester the Cat eyeing a brown trout in a goldfish bowl. He bent down to kiss her cheek. "You're such a MILF, you know that. And to think I used to take you for a bitch."

Martha felt heat in her cheeks. "And to think," she mimicked Sam's voice, "I just thought you were an asshole."

From there the night deteriorated steadily in Martha's favor. By the time Stranahan rose from the table to follow Willoughby and Kenneth Winston into the bunkhouse, Sam's eyes were at half mast. The dead soldiers on the table stood at nine.

Ettinger studied the fly she'd won from Stranahan in the last hand. It was a steelhead pattern with a dubbed red body, a turn of Gadwall at the collar and an overwing of black magpie, with jungle cock nails on the cheeks and golden pheasant crest for the tail. She thought it quite handsome, which made her reflect on its maker's dark good looks. She shook her head at her momentary lapse into melancholy.

"Sam, what does Stranny call this fly?"

Sam opened his eyes and peered. "Hell if I know. But you won it. That gives you the right to name it."

"Is that a tradition?"

"Club policy."

"Really?"

"No, I just made it up." He touched his glass to hers. "From now on I think I'll call you 'the woman.'"

"Like Sherlock Holmes called Irene Adler? I didn't know you read."

"I saw the movie."

Martha held the fly in the palm of her hand. They studied it seriously, Martha two sheets to Sam's three to the wind.

"Nicki had hair that color," Sam said seriously. "A little more red in it."

She made a silent "hmm," pursing her mouth. "Then I'll call it Dead Man's Fancy." She nodded. "We need to talk about her. Okay if we take this round to the porch?"

"Sure. But you know what I always say, a man remembers better with his shirt off." He gave her an appraising glance. "So does 'the woman.'" He wasn't as drunk as she'd thought he was.

You sly bastard, she thought. But she'd already brought a hand up to finger the second button of her khaki shirt. She unbuttoned it and drew her middle fingernail down her cleavage to the third button.

"Don't you wish?" she said.

CHAPTER TWELVE

Unrequited Love

Sam Meslik told Ettinger that he'd first met Nanika Martinelli at a Trout Unlimited banquet the previous winter, having caught her eye during a bidding war for a box of sculpin patterns tied by the late Al Troth. It had been one of those across-a-crowded-room glances where the eyes linger longer than needed to acknowledge a shared interest, for they both wanted the box, though she'd fallen out of the bidding early on. Spurred by the scent of the chase—this was during one of Sam's hiatuses from Darcy, his on-again, off-again—the burly fishing guide found the hand holding his paddle raised once and once more against his better judgment. He was some two hundred dollars poorer when he lumbered over to the woman's table and ceremoniously presented her with the fly box. "I had just enough left over to buy you a drink," he said, handing her a plastic cup of single malt. In fact he'd poured the whiskey from the flask hidden in his sport coat, which he'd worn for the express purpose. The tattered houndstooth, a gift from an Irish client, was the only presentable garment Sam had in a wardrobe consisting mainly of T-shirts; that night's sartorial selection perversely read "Whitefish Can't Jump— Trout Can't Either if You Hit Them on the Head."

Sam said the woman reminded him of a tawny lioness. She had laughed when he showed her the shirt and shaken her mane of hair, which later that night Sam found dragging across his chest in the cramped bedroom of his trailer. He'd roared like the king of the jungle himself, and when he woke up she was gone. Drinking his hair of the dog, his bleary eyes found the note she'd left on the Formica tabletop. "Thank you kind stranger." Nothing more. He realized he didn't even know her name.

"Wham bam thank you, Sam," was the way he summarized the night to Martha. It was about a month later that he opened his subscription copy of *Fly Angler* and saw a photo of her with the caption: "Fly Fishing Venus Hooks Anglers on Kootenai River."

Ettinger asked if Martinelli had said why she was in Bridger that night, Libby being in the northwest corner of the state, a solid seven-hour drive away. Sam sipped from his glass. "If she did, I don't recall. I'd had a little whiskey." He pinched his fingers. "Just a wee sip."

When was the next time he'd seen her? Not until she'd come to his shop this summer. He was sorry for lying earlier, saying it was the first time they'd met. He'd been afraid if he admitted the truth, that they'd known each other, however fleetingly, Ettinger might think that Martinelli had sought Sam out to establish herself in the valley and that . . . well, he didn't know, but it might implicate her some way in the wrangler's death.

Suddenly he hurled his glass against the wall of the clubhouse. It shattered with enough force that in a few moments Stranahan appeared at the door. He was shining the Carnivore tracking light he'd won from Ettinger with the only good hand he'd drawn all night.

"Turn that goddamned thing off," Sam said.

"I thought maybe you two were killing each other and I'd have to follow a blood trail. Martha, you don't have a shirt on."

Ettinger peered down at her bra. She remembered *thinking* about taking the shirt off, just to take Sam's dare, but she didn't remember actually *doing* it. Who'd drunk who under the table was no longer clear.

She sought to preserve what dignity remained. "I'm getting a moon tan," she said. "Why don't you take off your pajamas and join us? Sam's going to tell us what made him so upset."

"I don't know what got into me," Sam said. He dropped his chin onto the mat of hair sprouting from his collarbone. When he raised his head it was silhouetted against the moon's pale halo, a man in the moon, or—Ettinger squinted at the image—the Wolfman. *I must be very drunk*, she thought.

"I was in love with her," Sam said. His voice was barely audible. "I thought I'd get over it. I'd been trying for weeks to get over it, and I figured once she went to the ranch it would be easier. And then that dude came into the Dollar, wanting to fight me for her honor, and it wasn't over."

"How's that?" Ettinger had shrugged back into her shirt and was buttoning up, her fingers casual while she inwardly cringed at her inexcusable behavior.

"I wanted to hit him so hard his head would explode."

Martha and Sean exchanged a quick glance. Martha leaned forward. Her tone was empathetic, her Martha-from-Portland-with-feelings voice. "What happened on Papoose Mountain? Was it an accident? Just tell us. You'll feel a lot better."

"You don't believe . . . You can't . . . *Nothing* happened. I was never up there, I'll take a polygraph if you want. I told you the truth the first time. I felt bad after I hit him. He was just another poor sap who fell for her and couldn't think straight. I'm sure she's left a trail of us. You had to know her, she was like a mythical creature. You know how most guides have a foam patch on the boat they keep their working flies on, the patterns you tie onto your client's tippet most often? She had them hooked to her shirt. Like she was the river and the flies were the hatch. She'd reach down and select one, back the hook out, let's just say some men had a hard time keeping their mind on the fishin.' And her hair, these little wavelike things that floated around on it, I don't know what you call them—"

"Ringlets," Martha said.

"Yeah, I guess. Ethereal, man, like they say about mayflies. All the way down to her butt."

"But it wasn't just her looks."

"No." He shook his head. "She glowed from the inside. She just glowed." He set his wineglass on the porch railing. The careful hand of a man who's been drinking. "It's weird, though."

"What's weird?" Martha was leaning forward. Her mind had become quite clear.

"That night at the banquet, she seemed like a woman who was sure of herself, a very put-together lady. I had to screw up my courage to talk to her. And, uh, in bed, she was in charge, said we needed a safe word in case things got crazy. I said, 'How about *no*?' She says, '*No* means yes.' 'What about *don't*?' 'No, *don't* means do.' So we agreed on *Red Serendipity*, in honor of her hair. Like the fly pattern," he added for Ettinger's benefit.

"I know what a Serendipity is. But wouldn't that be a little hard to remember in the heat of the moment?"

"I think that was the point." Sam fell silent, thinking back to that night. He turned to Stranahan. "I felt a bit used, my brother."

"So you're saying she changed?" Ettinger prompted. "This . . . put-together lady."

"Yeah, I mean, she knew what she wanted, which was a job and a place to stay, and she let me know she was willing to sleep with me to get it, but it was like a front. She wasn't as sure of herself as she acted. Our first time, I mean our second but our first at my new place, she made me turn out the lights. It's like you meet people and they come across this one way, and then when you get to know them they're not what you expected. The first Nicki, the one from the TU banquet, she was a fellow traveler, but the second Nicki"—Sam sat back in the chair and stared for a time at the heavens—"I fell for that Nicki."

He said that she'd been clingy at first, would reach out and take his hand, look at him with a shy smile that came at unexpected moments and was a more intimate gesture, somehow, than sex. He couldn't believe that this angelic person had made him the center of her world, and he was falling for her even as the river dropped into shape and she began to assert herself as a guide. Sam felt her leaving the security he offered to bask in her own confidence, in time, to regard him more as a brother than as a lover. And there was something else. A wistfulness came over her; he could hear a note of loss in her voice. It was as if she'd somehow aged ten years in two months, and had lost something that could never be regained. But then, quite abruptly, the confidence was gone and she returned to Sam's bed. But just for a couple nights. A week later she told him that she'd been offered a job as a naturalist and fishing guide at the dude ranch.

"You know how I felt, Kimosabe?" He turned to Stranahan. "I felt like I did when I raised that mallard duckling after Killer killed the hen. You get all invested and then you open your hand and it flies away. No good-bye. Gone. Unrequited love, man. It's a bastard."

"Sam, look at me," Martha said.

He did and said, "You put your shirt on. I didn't want to embarrass you before, but what I said about you being a man under your clothes, it isn't true. You're all woman. That big Indian you were going around with—he doesn't know what he's missing. I'm just saying—"

"Sam, listen to me. We're trying to find Nicki. Was there anything about her, an interest of hers, anyone she met, that might help us do that?"

"You don't think I've been asking myself the same question? The truth is I didn't know her as well as you think. She told me about growing up in B.C. a little, how her dad was a trapper and she rebelled against that, but she got close to him at the end. It meant a lot to her that she was his daughter again."

"Did she ever say why she came down here from Libby?"

"No, I thought maybe she just wanted to wipe the slate clean after he passed."

"Did she mention her sister?" Stranahan said. He'd been following the conversation but unlike Ettinger, who had her second wind, he was asleep on his feet. The question was thrown out only because she hadn't asked it.

"No, man. I didn't know she had a sister. She had a sister?"

"She'll be here tomorrow morning."

Sam shook his head. He looked up as a shooting star fell from the heavens, trailing a path of silver glitter.

"Stars every fuckin' where you look. God, there must be a million of them."

They were silent a few minutes until he spoke again. "A man would have to be a goddamned fool to leave Montana, you know it, Stranny?"

———

At eight in the morning, Martha Ettinger listened to the motor of the Cherokee ping down after the thirty-mile drive from the motel. She laid her head on the steering wheel and didn't raise it until she heard the clubhouse door open and saw Stranahan standing on the porch, holding a cup of steaming coffee. "Breakfast's on the table," he called out.

Martha blew out a long breath. She tilted the rearview. "I can't believe I took off my shirt," she said to the image that stared back at her. She shook her head. "Get a grip, Martha. What in the hell is happening to you?"

Kenneth Winston had made bacon, eggs and cinnamon toast. Patrick Willoughby fussed over her. Everybody had clothes on and she cheered up a little. Mercifully, Sam Meslik was still asleep. Maybe he'd been so drunk he wouldn't remember.

She heard a toilet flush. Sam appeared at the door of the

bunkhouse. He had on boxers and scratched at the hair on his chest, a Neanderthal hunter waking up to a Starbucks morning. He offered a gap-toothed grin, having taken his bridgework out before hitting the feathers.

"Hey there, thirty-six C," he said.

Martha felt the color run right up into her roots.

CHAPTER THIRTEEN

The Figure of a Woman

Four young men who'd been part of the initial hasty team search were gathered around a map spread on the hood of Jason Kent's diesel 4 x 4. A type—waists like carpenter ants', rock climbers' arms, a certain way of holding the body. Been-there-done-that men. Kent made the introductions. They were going to climb over the crest of the Madison Range to drop into the Hilgard Lakes Basin. It was off the search grid, but if the missing woman was trying to get as far from the source of her fright as she could, if in fact she'd been frightened but uninjured, the pass the men were taking was a natural line of retreat. Kent was driving them to the trailhead, and as the men threw their backpacks into the bed of the pickup and vaulted in, he turned to Martha and said the sister had been briefed on the search and was waiting for them at the corral. She wanted to ride the trail Nicki had taken as soon as possible.

"I don't think the fact of the matter has registered," he said. "Usually by the third day they just want to scream. Or cry. Or sleep, finally." Or even have sex, he had discovered. Even a man as plain as Jason Kent had found himself the subject of uneasy attention when a single mother began to give up her son for dead. "But this sister," he shook his head, "we're five days in and she seems to be locked in the initial phase of denial."

"Any impression of her?"

His face was impassive. Kent was always hard to read. "Nothing you won't see for yourself," he said.

From fifty feet, Asena Martinelli was a broad shouldered, trim figure under a Stetson, sitting tall in the saddle. She dismounted the bay quarter horse when Sean and Martha drove up and handed the lead to the assistant wrangler who'd helped her with the tack. Turning, she placed her hands on her iliac crests and regarded them with a cool expression.

Martha felt her abdomen press against her belt. Too much worry, too little exercise, too many pieces of MacKenzie River Pizza. She spoke out of the side of her mouth.

"That woman couldn't give birth to a well-fed gerbil."

"Now Martha," Stranahan said. "She still might have a harelip."

She did not have a harelip. Rather, her lips were perfectly even, with commas of smile lines in her cheeks that deepened as she approached. Later, Sean would believe that she was one of the most beautiful women he'd ever seen, but it was the eyes that registered first. They were a pale, cold green, a color he associated with frozen waterfalls. The eyes flashed from Martha to Sean and back again to Martha.

"Hello." She shook Martha's hand. "I'm Nadina."

"We'd heard it was Asena," Stranahan said.

"It's both." Her handshake was firm. "My sister and I were named for mountains where we grew up, the Nadina and Nanika peaks."

"What should we call you?"

"Nicki started calling me Asena when we were kids. It's stuck." Her head tilted a fraction. Something in Stranahan's face or voice seemed to have surprised her.

Sean, who was never conscious of his appearance, was conscious of his appearance.

"I'm sorry for staring, but you remind me of someone. I usually don't forget a face." Her voice had a slight French Canadian accent, with the rising inflections that turned a declaration into a question.

And to Ettinger: "I got here as fast as I could."

Martha, having done the math, let it pass. Had the woman left for Bridger even twenty-four hours after the department tracked her down, she should have been here two days ago.

"I'd like to see where this happened," she said, her tone assertive.

"And we'll take you there," Martha said, "but you have to understand . . ." She began to give the talk, the talk you gave to the husband, to the wife, to the sister, to the one who couldn't envision life without the person who'd gone missing and so refused to admit it could happen.

Stranahan used the opportunity to study the woman. Only once had he met Nicki Martinelli, at a boat launch—she was taking out, he was putting in—an encounter of a few minutes, but vivid in his mind. Like everyone else he'd been struck by her beauty, by her bubbly, playful personality, shy and bold at the same time, and, of course, her hair. The woman standing before him was obviously older, at least she acted older and her face seemed to have weathered more of life, but the physical resemblance was striking. Martha had been dead wrong. Asena Martinelli exuded fertility and shared the same body with her sister, if not the same posture. Where Nicki was comfortable in the ripeness of her flesh and did not show it off as much as not care how it was shown, that was part of her allure, this woman stood the way ranch women stand who have worn Stetsons with rain protectors and shown horses half their lives—mannishly upright, bandana knotted just so, a careful presentation of themselves to the world, with much held in reserve. If there was a noticeable difference in the faces, beyond the severity of expression, it was that this woman's skin looked thinner, stretched to reveal the sculpture of the bones. The hair was the same autumn flame, but cropped short under the shade of the wide-brimmed hat.

As Stranahan observed her, she took her hands off her hips and folded them defiantly across her chest. She'd undoubtedly heard the same talk from Jason Kent that she was hearing from Ettinger.

Stranahan took the lead from Martha and discussed the most likely scenarios, the possibility of injury, the odds of her having walked off the search grid—lost-person behavior was a science, and a woman of Nicki's age and physical fitness might travel quite far when gripped by panic, farther than they would if they were much younger or somewhat older. Was there a chance, Stranahan wanted to know, that for whatever reason she had disappeared on purpose or found her way out of the wilderness and not reported the incident?

No, that wasn't possible.

"This is grizzly country, this close to Yellowstone, isn't it." The woman made it a statement. "And wolves. One of the people I talked to this morning, Mr. Anderson, told me that wolves were in the wilderness where my sister disappeared."

"The odds of attack are very slim," Ettinger said.

"But it's a possibility." Again, a statement.

"It has to be considered."

———

In a search, relatives of the missing got in the way. They wanted to help, which meant if you couldn't dissuade them from going into the forest you had to take someone off the search to act as a bodyguard. One person missing was bad enough, let a city slicker have his head and you had two. Asena Martinelli was no city slicker, but it was clear she wasn't to be denied looking for her sister. Ettinger, letting exasperation show in her voice, went off to saddle Petal and Big Mike. She'd taken up Bucky Anderson's offer to stable them at the ranch until the search effort was over.

"I'll help you," Stranahan said, waiting for her cue.

"Nah, Big Mike will just barrel his chest if you try to put a sternum strap on him. He knows better than to try that foolishness with me." Meaning, I want you to stay with her and report your impressions later.

Martinelli turned an appraising eye on Stranahan, her gaze level and very cool, and said, "What exactly is it you do, Mr. Stranahan? You don't look very . . . official."

"I used to be a private detective," he said. "Now I consider myself a Renaissance man. I guide during the trout season, I write for the fishing magazines a bit, and paint in the winter; actually I paint whenever I get a commission."

"So you're an investigator for the department, like a freelancer," she said.

"More like a helper-outer. I'm another set of eyes on the ground when there aren't enough to see around the corners."

"I see," she said cautiously. It was clear she didn't. She offered a brief smile. "You have a funny way of talking," she said. Then the resolution he'd read in her face seemed to crack to reveal her vulnerability. The eyes that were the color of waterfalls warmed somewhat; they deepened to a green that reminded Stranahan of storm waves in the sea.

"I suppose you think I'm crazy, thinking I can find her when all of you can't. But I have to. She's my little sister. She's all I have."

"We appreciate your help," Sean said. "You know her better than we do, how she might act in a stressful situation. Knowing her tendencies can help give us direction."

"You aren't just saying that?" Her tone was hopeful, but as they saw Ettinger come around the stable leading the horses, bitterness crept in. "Your sheriff thinks the time's past when we have any chance to find her. She didn't say that, but I could tell. That big man I talked to this morning, Mr. Kent, he made it pretty clear."

"I find it's best to try not to think too much, but just keep at it. If she's out there, we'll find her."

"That's easy for you to say." She turned her back and walked to her mount, swinging effortlessly into the saddle. The wrangler who'd been holding the lead for her cocked his hat and walked away with his hands in his back pockets, trying to look like a cowboy for the pretty woman.

———

She'd obviously spent time in the stirrups. Stranahan, in line behind her as the horses reached the timberline, eyed the rhythmic motion of her buttocks not with lust but envy; his own butt, still sore from the ride the other day, bounced hard off the saddle with every step.

Ettinger reined Petal to a stop. "That copse of whitebark pine," she pointed to the clump of trees about a quarter mile downslope, "that's where we found the wrangler's body. Her hat was found on a line between those trees and where we are now. We figure she got bucked. Maybe the horse smelled the wolves."

"It's big country," Martinelli said. "But not as big as B.C. Nicki wouldn't be intimidated by a few trees."

Martha turned a sober face to the slide rock at the timberline. *What are we doing up here?* Her "Let's go look at the scene" lacked conviction.

The scene told them nothing it hadn't already, but had a pronounced affect on Asena Martinelli. She became silent and for a time appeared oblivious to Stranahan's and Ettinger's presence, wiping almost angrily at two tears that ran crookedly down the planes of her left cheek.

"Do you think he suffered?"

Ettinger nodded for Stranahan to answer.

"The medical examiner said he bled to death. He said it was quick."

"I was told it was an accident. Is that the truth?"

Ettinger swallowed. "We don't know."

"Do you think my sister saw . . . this?"

"We think she was here, but we don't know what she saw. It snowed that night. The tracks were covered and hard to read."

The hopelessness of the situation seemed to befall her at once. "I don't know what to do," she said in a small voice. "Tell me what to do."

"Miss Martinelli," Ettinger said, "I'm terribly sorry about this. You think I don't care because I didn't want to ride up here and you're half right. I didn't want to come here because I don't think it will get us any closer to finding your sister. But you're wrong that I don't care. Just because the physical search has a time limit doesn't mean I do. I'll find your sister, I promise."

It was midafternoon by the time they returned to the corral. Stranahan went to get the Jeep while the two women brushed down the horses. Martha had wanted a little time with her alone.

"So what's your impression?" he said, when Ettinger climbed into the passenger seat.

"I told her someone from the department searched her father's cabin, didn't say it was you. Didn't mention any shooting. I meant to, but I sat on it and I don't know why. Maybe because it would be a distraction. But she deserved to know we were looking other places than the mountain. My impression? It struck me as odd that she seemed more concerned about Grady Cole's fate than the disappearance of her sister."

"Oh, I didn't pick up on that."

"You don't have the antennae I do."

"I did notice you told her you were going to find Nicki. The Martha I know doesn't build false hope."

"I was sorry as soon as I said it. It's a part of the job I could do better. But we will find her. It fell below freezing that night. She's either dead of hypothermia three days ago, dead of hypothermia two days ago, or dead of hypothermia yesterday. The dogs will find her. Or else she deliberately disappeared, in which case I'll find her just so I can strangle her."

"Aren't you the pessimist?" Stranahan said. "Comes with the badge, huh?"

Ettinger grunted. "More like with two divorces."

CHAPTER FOURTEEN

A Separate Line of Enquiry

Among Plains Indians, it was customary for a man approaching another's lodge to announce himself if the front flap was closed. Stranahan had just secured the flap of his eighteen-pole, Sioux-design tipi when headlights veered into his drive. For a brief moment, the interior of the lodge was illuminated, the way countryside is brilliantly lit by a bolt of lightning. Near his head the shadow of a daddy longlegs was thrown as big as a Halloween spider against the canvas, then the lights swept past and the engine shut off. As the son of a mechanic, Sean was tuned in to the distinctive grumblings of the cars driven by his friends, but this one he couldn't place. He pumped up the Coleman and began to split sticks to build a fire. He knelt down to splash water onto his face from the basin beside the fire ring.

"Hello, the tipi," a woman's voice called. "May I come in?"

"Asena? Asena Martinelli?"

"I'm very sorry for the intrusion, but I really must speak to you."

Sean brought the forester's ax he'd been splitting kindling with up to his face. The polished blade was the closest thing he had to a mirror. He peered at the distorted image staring back at him and pushed back the comma of hair that had fallen over his left eye.

"If you're busy—"

"I'm not."

She ducked in when he removed the sticks, placing a hand on the crown of her hat to keep it from falling. Stranahan took his place behind the fire ring and sat cross-legged. As the head of the household, he faced the front of the lodge. He indicated that she enter to the left and sit to his right on a folded buffalo blanket. This also was in accordance with custom. Had it been a man entering, he would have sat to Stranahan's left.

"Are you Native American?" she asked. "You look it a little."

"No, but my friend who gave me this tipi taught me lodge etiquette. I've found I enjoy the formality. It's respectful without being arrogant. Would you like a biscuit or coffee?" He reached for the enamelware pot sitting next to the makings for his fire. "I'll have it hot in a minute."

"No thank you."

She arranged herself on the blanket.

"Now if we were adhering strictly to tradition, you'd sit with your legs folded to the side, not crossed."

When she began to move he waved a hand for her to stop. "We're not that formal in my lodge." *I've preened and now I'm rattling on,* Stranahan thought. Men were such predictable animals in the company of attractive women.

"How did you find me?"

"I talked to Sam Meslik. The sheriff said he was close to my sister."

"You know about his fight with the wrangler?"

She nodded. "He's a bit of a brute."

"He told me he was in love with her. I believe he was."

"I'll come right to the point, Mr. Stranahan. I think my sister was kidnapped. I'd like to hire you to find her."

Stranahan struck a match and held it to a bird's nest of tinder tucked under the kindling.

"Why didn't you mention that this morning?" He watched sparks zigzag toward the vent and let the silence stretch.

"It's . . . not for certain. But your sheriff, frankly, I got the impression she was tolerating me, despite her little speech. I thought you might have . . . better energy. Sam said you were a man who stepped in shit even if there was only one cow in the pasture."

Stranahan had to smile.

"Did he? Well, you're wrong about Ettinger. The search is winding down because the odds of finding a person missing in the wilderness, alive, is dwindling. The possibility that she was kidnapped is completely different, and the sheriff would pursue it, I guarantee you. Give her a lead and she'll start digging."

"I would rather have you pursue this . . . line of enquiry. How much do you charge?" Her voice had become businesslike.

He told her and watched her head move reflexively back from the fire.

"That's a lot of money," she said.

Stranahan had no intention of taking her money, but was curious to see how far she'd go. The more she was willing to part with, the more credible her suspicions. Money was a very accurate measure of confidence.

"That is acceptable," she said at length.

"Asena, I take what you are telling me very seriously. But I can't work for you because it would be a conflict of interest. I'm already being paid to find your sister. My obligation is to the county."

"For how much longer?"

The promptness of her response told Stranahan that she'd thought this aspect through. It was a damned good question. Once the county search ground to a halt, Ettinger would have a hard time justifying his continued involvement.

"I don't know," he said honestly.

Asena's shoulders visibly dropped. Stranahan found that he wanted to help her, but more than that, to help her sister, if she was alive. He noticed the way the flames patterned the tipi walls and came to a decision.

"I said I can't take your case because I'm already contractually obligated. I didn't say I wasn't interested." He removed the boiling kettle from the fire. "Why don't you tell me what you came to say, and we can go from there."

"Will you have to report anything I . . . divulge?"

"This is an active investigation. I'd be lying if I told you I wouldn't talk to the sheriff if something you told me sounded relevant."

"I need to think about this."

"If there's a chance your sister's alive, we need to act quickly."

"I don't mean sleep on it. I mean just walk around. I'm not like Nicki. Nicki does what she feels in the moment, and I'm afraid that has cost her. I have to think things through. I've spent a great deal of my life thinking things through. For both of us."

Stranahan undid the flap and stepped outside with her, noting that the motor he'd heard belonged to a boxy SUV with a short wheel base, an old Bronco.

"I'd rather be by myself. I won't be long."

Ever since he'd heard her voice, he'd known that his life was about to turn. It had happened before, when a Mississippi riverboat siren knocked on the door of his art studio and hired him to do a little innocent fishing for her, which turned out to be not so innocent. And it had happened last year when a search dog found bodies buried on Sphinx Mountain. Life went along—he guided, he mixed paints on his palette, he shot pool with Sam—and then it turned. Turned in a way that made you feel your heart beat. It was turning now, as he heard Asena's footsteps approach.

"You're back soon."

She stood inside the entrance. The flames between them licked up the length of her legs so that it appeared she'd caught fire. It was an extraordinary image.

"How much do you know about wolves?" she said.

"It's hard to live here without knowing about wolves . . . Asena." Stranahan emphasized the name. When she didn't speak, he said,

"I know enough about wolves to know Asena is a wolf in Turkish mythology."

"Yes, well, I told you, it isn't my real name. My sister got it from a book. She was into all that stuff—myths, spirit animals. I'm like my father, more practical minded, but Nicki was subject to flights of fancy. A cloud chaser. When I asked you if you knew about wolves, I meant the politics."

"It's a volatile issue," Stranahan said. "Most of the state was against the reintroduction. They believe the feds rammed it down their throats. Ranchers hate them. A lot of hunters think wolves are taking a lion's share of elk they want for their freezers."

"What about the other side, not the environmentalists who want them on the endangered species list but the fringe element, people who regard wolves as spirit brothers or hold them up as gods?"

"Harold Little Feather, the Blackfeet Indian who gave me the tipi, in his culture wolves are brothers who travel with the tribe. But you mean white people. I know demonstrators have protested wolf hunting at the capitol. They've hacked into computer lists of hunters who bought wolf tags and sent threatening e-mails, hassled them over the phone. Trap lines have been sabotaged. There are people willing to stand in front of a gun barrel to save a wolf from being shot."

Asena sat down on the blanket and faced him. "What you need to know about my sister is, she's one of those people who would take the bullet."

"And you believe that has something to do with her disappearance?"

"In a way. It's a story that is hard for me to tell. Could you make some of that coffee, please?"

CHAPTER FIFTEEN

The Venus of Botticelli Creek

Until the night a pressure ridge formed on the ice covering Two Loon Lake, life in the house in the pines on the bank of the Morice River had been idyllic, if selectively remembered. The girls' mother, Elizabeth Conner, had traveled to British Columbia by way of Aberdeen, Scotland, trading one bad weather for another, but leaving one bad man for one much better. The better man also was an immigrant, from that mountainous corner of southeastern France called Hautes-Alpes that is Italy in all but language.

A fourth generation sheepherder, Alfonso Martinelli grew up in a household so destitute that his mother shopped a block of moldy cheese from one window to another as a way of saving face, so that passersby might think they had something to eat. The boy grew up with a pair of shears in one hand and a shotgun in the other, for his duties, in addition to returning strays and righting sheep that tipped onto their backs and were in danger of suffocating, consisted of protecting the herd from predators—bears, in the spring, but wolves on a year-round basis. Like many boys of peasant heritage, he became enamored of the American Western, a black-and-white promise of freedom by six-gun, on a landscape with a quality of wildness denied him by the very age and settlement of the country where he was born—a quality that, ironically, clung to those French Alps in the form of the very wolves that were his job to eradicate. It is a common story that men drawn to wildness destroy that which makes a place wild, then move to find it elsewhere. Alfonso's quest, fueled by nothing so much as a sense of adventure, led him from France to Nova

Scotia, where he met the Scottish schoolteacher who would become his wife, from there to Polson, Montana, where sheepherding had not yet disappeared as a way of life, and finally to British Columbia, to the house in the pines on the bank of the Morice River.

At a gun show of the Historical Collector Arms Society in Terrace, Alfonso reached into his pocket for the one romantic purchase of his life—an antique Colt .45 handgun with ivory bone grips, the Peacemaker model he'd seen in Westerns growing up. He collected the traps and other tools necessary to become a fur trapper, which he'd wanted to be ever since seeing Charlton Heston in a movie about mountain men in the Rockies. In time he also would work as a commercial salmon and halibut fisherman, and as a rigger for a logging outfit—not an atypical résumé for immigrants with hard muscles and dubious English in that part of Canada.

Elizabeth found employment in a one-room schoolhouse downriver near the town of Houston. The girls, arriving two years apart and inheriting their mother's features and her hair, which Alfonso called "mountain maple leaves in the fall," were expert at constructing pocket sets with conibear traps before they had mastered their multiplication tables. Nicki, with knife flashing, had won a skinning contest in the junior division at the winter fair, skinning ten muskrats in just over seventeen minutes, with only one demerit for a slip of the blade that punctured the skin. She was ten when her father hung her blue ribbon on the mantel. Haunted by its color, she took the ribbon down and buried it in a Mason jar under the porch. It had brought back the nightmares that started a few winters before, when one of the family's two snowmobiles found the weakest part of the pressure ridge on Two Loon Lake, and the sisters had witnessed their mother drown. Asena remembered seeing a surprised expression on her mother's lips, as if she was saying "Oh," then her face rolled under and the last the girl ever saw of her was the hair that was the color of mountain maple leaves in the fall.

The family had taken both machines that day to fish for lake trout, the girls riding with their mother, Alfonso following on a Sno-Cat laden with ice fishing gear. When the ice cracked, both girls had followed their mother into the freezing water and were it not for Alfonso's quick thinking, they, too, would have drowned. He'd witnessed the accident while still on shore, had pulled the starter cord of the chainsaw bungeed to the Cat, cut a sapling and crawled across the ice until he could extend it over the hole. Little Nicki had stayed afloat by clinging to the blue coat Asena was wearing, and after Asena grabbed ahold of the branch, Alfonso had dragged them both back onto the ice.

"Dad thought Mother must have hit her head on the machine before going in, that's why she drowned so quickly. The only reason I stayed up was because my coat was so big it trapped the air; it was sewn out of a seal skin that Mother got trading with the Indians. She'd dyed it blue and made it so I had room to grow into it. It had been my Christmas present." Her voice was matter of fact. Stranahan realized it must be the only way that she could get the words out, to recite it as an impersonal history.

He said, "I'm very sorry for your tragedy. Is that why your sister called you Asena, because the wolf in the fable has blue fur and you wore a blue fur coat?"

"Yes, in some ways Nicki substituted me for our mother after that. She had to. After Mother's death, Daddy went days without even speaking."

Six years after building a monument of river stones to commemorate their mother's death, the family moved into a farmhouse with a barn on the outskirts of Kamloops. Alfonso's long experience trapping wolves had garnered him a government job as a predator control agent in the regional office. As his job would take him away parts of the winter, he had tried to coax Elizabeth's sister to undertake the rearing of the girls, who were now twelve and fourteen years of age.

But she lived in Scotland and was unwilling to travel to the middle of nowhere for a brother-in-law she'd not seen in twenty years. And so the girls became latchkey kids with the nearest neighbor a mile down a dirt road and no outsider the wiser about their living situation. As Asena was older and naturally a responsible person, she took on the duties of supervision, of which her sister was in need.

It wasn't boy trouble. That would come later. Rather, it was rebellion against the absent father and a young-adult book titled *Lobo, My Brother* that Nicki had checked out of the school library, about a boy in the Northwest Territories who is raised by a pack of wolves when his parents drown in the Great Slave Lake. The book was fiction and she knew this, but the highly anthropomorphized depictions of the wolf family coupled with the coincidence of her own mother's drowning moved the young girl to identify with the boy. Her response was two-pronged—first, to lash out at her father for killing these magnificent creatures and second, to begin a gradual withdrawal into a fantasy world in which she allied herself with animals, both real and mythical, and dreamed of becoming their savior by exacting revenge on their persecutors.

When her father scoffed at the vitriol of her pronouncements regarding his livelihood, telling her she'd grow out of such fanciful notions and asking her to pass the ketchup, she responded by squirting it all over her face, to show what happens to wolves when they break their teeth trying to chew their way out of leghold traps. She then left the table and ran to the barn where Alfonso kept the tools of his trade. There she depressed the toothy jaws of the biggest trap she could find, set the toggle sear and stepped onto the pan with her bare right foot. Her howls brought both father and sister running. What they saw in the diffused light of the barn was young Nanika with an otherworldly blandness of expression, tears streaming down her cheeks, ketchup staining her mouth, standing in a steadily expanding pool of blood. While Asena ran forward to free her from the trap, her father averted his eyes, for his young daughter, in the first blushes of puberty, was completely naked.

"I don't mean to interrupt you," Stranahan said at this point in the narrative, "but why do you think Nicki was naked?"

Asena raised her coffee cup and, seeing it was empty, set it down. "I think it was because of the book. The boy was naked when the wolves found him and grew up free and uninhibited. Later on, when he returns to civilization, he feels shame and is forced to cover himself. He eventually conforms to society, but then in the end he hears his brother wolves calling to him and runs to join them in the wilderness, shedding his clothes as he goes. Nicki saw herself as that boy."

Stranahan reached for the pot of coffee to pour some into her cup, and as he set the pot down she caught his forearm with her right hand.

"I'm not making a mistake telling you this, am I?"

As she had not yet told him anything that touched upon the mystery of her sister's disappearance, Stranahan was unsure of his response. He pressed her hand and gently extricated himself.

"I need to be sure," she said. "My sister's not going to walk off the mountain on her own. There will be a price."

Stranahan nodded at the cryptic remark, but she was already reeling back through the years to the second defining moment in her sister's life, which occurred during her high school years. By then, Nicki had not only blossomed physically but also was starting to exhibit the combination of innocence and joie de vivre that would form her adult personality. Fellow misfits found themselves drawn to her, if not to her interests. But she bent them to her specific sympathies through the sheer force of her charisma, attracting a cadre of willing cohorts to aid her quest to bring to light the atrocities man committed against wildlife.

The north fork of the Thompson River, near where the Martinellis lived, was home to British Columbia's most famous sockeye salmon run. The run peaked every fourth summer, drawing thousands of visitors to a boardwalk viewing area, from which they could witness the spectacle of a river literally running red with fish. As Nicki's junior year coincided with the fourth year of the cycle, it was her idea to draw attention to the plight of salmon that suffered from unsustainable commercial fishing practices by having her followers strip naked and lie down among the fish, feigning the death that is the inevitable conclusion of the salmon's spawning ritual.

The day arrived, but only two of Nicki's compadres met her at the appointed spot. With the boardwalk thronging with camera-carrying tourists, it might have been predicted that modesty would prevail. In the end, only Nicki took off her clothes, and after folding them neatly on a rock, walked out into the river, her hair only a shade lighter than the salmon that swam about her. Reclining in a stretch of shallow, boulder-strewn water with her head to the current and her hands folded over the joining of her legs, relatively little could actually be seen, for the sunlight bounced off the water in glittering coins and her hair flowed in ripples across her upper body, obscuring her breasts. But that was more than enough to draw a photographer from the *Kamloops Daily Reader*, and the paper, with the headline "Venus Swims with Salmon," sold out at newsstands the next morning. The word *Venus* was not an inspiration of the copywriter's, but an obvious choice, for a feeder stream called Botticelli Creek was only a stone's throw from the spawning grounds. Nanika Martinelli became known as the Venus of Botticelli Creek; she came up with the moniker Fly Fishing Venus several years later.

CHAPTER SIXTEEN

The Clan of the Three-Clawed Wolf

Swimming with salmon wasn't the only protest Nicki staged. She also organized a sit-in to protest the cutting of old-growth pines in the Cariboo Mountains, where she climbed two hundred feet to sit in the topmost branches of a tree that blocked the logging road being cut by the dozers. She'd stayed aloft for five days without food and finally had to be forcibly evacuated by a man who descended on a ladder lowered from the belly of a helicopter. After he'd buckled her into a safety strap and given the thumbs up for the pilot to pull them aloft, she kissed him on the cheek, a moment caught by the long lens of the camera belonging to the same photographer who'd snapped her with the salmon. This time his dramatic photo could be printed without editing.

Both demonstrations had the intended result of infuriating Alfonso's superiors, and when Nicki stole a wolf pelt from the barn, spray painted it red and donned it in front of the district office, the best wolfer in the predator control program found himself out of a job. Had this happened five years earlier, Alfonso Martinelli would have traveled back north to trap, but his firing coincided with the population surge of wolves in Montana, after the reintroduction program that started in Yellowstone National Park in 1995. With sport hunting outlawed until the species met federal recovery goals, the only wolves that found themselves at the end of a legal gun barrel were those that killed livestock. Suddenly, Montana found itself in need of men with Alfonso Martinelli's particular set of skills. And so the geography changed, with Nicki gaining dual citizenship in the bargain, though her sentiments remained the same.

Her old group, the misfits and the outcasts, were persuadable kids of a kind you might find anywhere, guilty of nothing but civil misconduct. To a person, the primary motivation was a desperate, ringing loneliness. All they really wanted, Asena told Stranahan, was a group to belong to and a flame to gather around; Nicki was that flame.

But now she was a flame that burned alone, without her older sister to contain the fire. Two years out of high school, Asena had enrolled in an up-province college, hoping to become a guidance counselor. Having lived so long without parental supervision herself, she wanted to work in the school system with children who had similar holes in their lives.

"I wanted Nicki to live with me, but Daddy had the law on his side. He didn't want to be alone, and I can't blame him for that. The idea was that she would join me in B.C. after her high school graduation and she did, she and Daddy visited me every winter, but that first year in Montana was hard on her. Libby wasn't Kamloops."

Stranahan made a sound between a grunt and a laugh.

"This isn't funny."

"You're right, it isn't. It's just I know what you're talking about. I wasn't there two hours before I got shot at."

"But—"

She stopped, and a perplexed look came into her face. "Wait. It was you who went to Libby to look for Nicki? The sheriff just said 'somebody.' Somebody checked the cabin. I assumed 'somebody' was some deputy. I wasn't told about any shots."

"Last Thursday night," Stranahan said. "I should have told you, I am telling you. Look, this isn't what you think. We're not trying to hold back information."

"Not trying to hold back information," she said, her voice striking a sarcastic note. "Of course not." Then, in a dead, flat tone: "I want you to tell me everything that happened there. All of it."

He didn't omit anything. The lantern had extinguished and with only the convex contours of her face illuminated by the fire, it was difficult to gauge Asena's reaction. When Stranahan finished, he handed her the wolf book.

"Is that Nicki's?"

"I . . . don't know. It could be. It's her kind of book."

"Because if it was her in the cabin that night," Stranahan went on, "then it means she's alive and we're looking in the wrong place."

"Yes, I see that." Again, a slow and measured tone.

"If she was in hiding, I can understand her lashing out at who she believed was an intruder. But what I can't understand is why she'd go away and then come back later and fire shots at me."

"No, I don't understand that, either. That . . . doesn't sound like her." She paused. "This man on the motorcycle who was with the girl with the orange eyes, up there in Libby, did he have strange eyes, too?"

"The fly shop owner didn't mention anything."

She was silent for a long time. "Still, it's him," she said, as if she were speaking to herself. "It has to be him. He takes out the contact lenses when he doesn't want to attract attention. He's followed her here. He's the one who's taken her away."

"Who is he?"

"He calls himself Amorak."

"Was he her boyfriend?"

"No. He was a monster."

———

Asena told Stranahan that Nicki met the man called Amorak during the spring of her senior year. By then a new group had formed around her: the Clan of the Three-Clawed Wolf. She had designed T-shirts for the members with bloody paw prints encircling the chest. Twice that winter, the clan had been disbanded for demonstrating against the vermiculite mine, and though the offenses were not particularly egregious, during the same time period the county experienced a spike in after-hours break-ins, with thefts that included electronics as well as cash. Two members were caught and charged, which made Nicki a pariah in the eyes of the city's arch-conservative fathers, though she wasn't implicated in the burglaries. It was on a day in May that a man had approached her. He'd seen her wearing the T-shirt and without preamble told her she was the alpha he'd been looking for, that she should come with him and they would lead the pack together. Nicki later told Asena that she'd tried to run, but had found she couldn't move. The man had red eyes that seemed to vibrate. It was as if he looked right through to her soul.

Amorak—Nicki never knew his full name, or even if the name was real—was on the surface one of those drifters who hover in the satellite systems surrounding schools, handing out reefer and roofies for a dollar here, a favor there, a tentacle of the drug trade that stains all rural communities where kids complain of having nowhere to go and nothing to do.

"My sister had never really had a relationship," Asena said, her voice dropping into a lower register. "Guys trailed around, but real boyfriends?" She shook her head. "I'm sure she was a virgin. This . . . Amorak. I've done research on cult leaders, how they project an aura of elitism and bend people to their obsessions. One day Nicki and her clan were planning their little sit-ins. The next day they were members of a cult, doing what one person told them to do. He," her voice cracked, "he made her do things."

Stranahan waited.

"Nicki had an outfitter tent that our dad used to use on his trapline. Amorak would have the clan sit in a circle inside the tent while the two of them . . . did it. In a wolf pack, only the alpha male and alpha female can have sex. Nicki was the alpha female, he was the alpha male and the rest were subordinates. He gave them all contact lenses. The alphas wore red lenses. The betas had orange ones and the lowly omegas had yellow. That's how he established the pecking order, by eye color. Imagine a half dozen people with orange and yellow eyes howling at you while you're . . . intimate. And there were other things. I think she was part of something awful. I don't know what, but it haunted her. I could hear it in her voice on the phone."

It was quiet in the tipi. The fire had died down; the only light came from the bed of coals, a gray, red-rimmed pool. Stranahan could barely make out her silhouette.

"What happened to Amorak?"

"He came in and out of her life. She'd know when he pulled up to the cabin because he drove a motorcycle. He tried to flatter our father, but Daddy saw right through him. But there wasn't anything he could do. Amorak would show up and she'd put in her contact lenses and fall right back under his spell. She didn't have her group then, they'd disbanded and she was on her own, working at the fly shop and the grocery store. Then one day about two years ago he left and never returned. Daddy had gotten sick and Nicki had that to deal with. It was easy to treat Amorak as if he'd been a bad dream. But now with him looking for her in Libby—I know my sister and I can't see her getting lost in the woods—I can't help but think he's taken her. He used to tell her that he couldn't live without her, that he'd kill them both rather than let her go—"

Stranahan stopped her. "There's another possibility, one you might not want to hear."

"I know what you're going to say, that she's gone off with him."

"He had such a hold on her before . . ."

"You're right, of course, but that's what I want you to find out. Everybody's looking for her. But maybe the way to find her is to look for him."

"I'll talk it over with Ettinger," Stranahan said. "If she isn't convinced it's a good use of the county coffers, then I'll be free to work on your behalf. How can I find you, say tomorrow around noon?"

"I'm driving back to the ranch tonight. Your search-and-rescue people want to brief me on their progress tomorrow, but I don't see how you can call it progress when there's almost no one left looking for her."

Stranahan put a hand on her wrist as she reached for the coffeepot. "You don't want coffee at this hour. Why don't you stay here? Use my cot. I'll sleep in the Land Cruiser."

"I wouldn't want to impose."

"No, it's fine. I enjoy sleeping in the back of a car—Cadillac camping we used to call it. In the morning we'll both go down to the ranch. I'd like to check in with Jason Kent myself."

He showed her how to fasten the front flap from the inside and went out to his rig. He was back within a minute.

"Your sister, why did she call her group the Clan of the Three-Clawed Wolf?"

He could hear her pumping up the lantern. There was a hissing pop as the mantles caught from a match, then a soft glow, and the tipi, under the stars that peppered the sky, became a molten gold.

"When we were little girls," she said presently, "our father trapped a wolf that lost two of its toes. The toes were in the trap, and he brought them home and strung them on elkskin laces to make necklaces, one for each of us. He said it would instill us with the wolf's courage. A lot of people wouldn't understand that coming from a trapper, but he was a complicated man, he loved wolves in his own way. Here, I'll show you."

She removed the sticks and beckoned him inside. She undid a button of her shirt and pulled the talisman out. The claw was mahogany colored with a translucent tip that showed the bloodline in the lantern light.

"I never take it off. I have all these little white scars where it's scratched my chest, but I don't care."

Stranahan felt awkward standing so close to her but she made it easy, just reached out and hugged him to her. Her hat tipped back and he felt her hair, silky on the side of his face.

"I'm so happy you didn't get shot," she said, her arms squeezing him tight. "I'm so relieved." She disengaged and there was another awkward moment, and then Stranahan said goodnight and walked to his rig.

———

He'd been asleep awhile before the Bronco started up. He decided against trying to stop her. *It will only drive her away,* he thought, an ironic choice of words that weren't lost on him as the engine rumble faded. He rolled over and tried to get back to sleep, but couldn't quiet his mind. It was on toward dawn when he heard a rapping on the window. He hadn't heard a car drive up so he must have been asleep after all. He rolled down the window to regard Martha Ettinger's tight-lipped smile.

"That's the second time in a week a Montana sheriff has interrupted my beauty rest," he said.

"Get up." It was cold enough to see her breath. "There's someplace you and I need to be."

Not another word passed between them until they were in the Cherokee, driving through Bridger on their way to the Madison Valley. Ettinger had pulled over to a coffee kiosk and they were waiting.

"Do I ask why you're sleeping in your rig?" she said.

"Asena Martinelli came over last night. I said she could sleep in the tipi, but she got up and drove away in the middle of the night. She told me an interesting story." He reached for his wallet and began to tell her the story.

"What is it with you?" Ettinger said. "You meet a woman and can't go a day before she jumps into your bed." She looked at the five-dollar bill he proffered as if it carried a smell. He folded it away.

"You saw where I spent the night and it wasn't my bed. Are you going to let me talk?"

She sipped her coffee and let him talk as the Cherokee wound through the Beartrap Canyon, the junipers blackened from a forest fire, the rusted needles fallen away to leave gnarled, grasping silhouettes patterned against the hillsides. They began the climb over the Norris Pass.

"So what do you think?" Stranahan said.

"It's an interesting theory." She tapped her fingers distractedly against the steering wheel.

"What's wrong with it?"

"Nothing. It's just that it doesn't look like this Amorak or anyone else may have been the cause of her disappearance. Why I dragged you out of your lair this morning—there's no delicate way to put this—but Nicki Martinelli, she may have been eaten."

CHAPTER SEVENTEEN

The Scatman

Harold Little Feather was waiting at the boat launch, leaning back against his pickup, his arms crossed over his chest. He chewed a stem of grass and looked up. Fall skies were the deepest blue. Why was that?

A thin line of dust showed to the east, up on the bench at the highway turnoff. He spat out the grass. "'Bout time."

It was a short trip in his canoe. The Palisades of the Madison, a half-mile-long series of cliffs over which the Shoshone had herded buffalo to bone-cracking death, stood sentinel over the west bank of the river. By noon hawks and eagles would soar above it, riding thermals. About a quarter mile downriver from where Harold launched the canoe, opposite the Wolf Creek Campground, an old johnboat was pulled up on the bank. A game path, worn deep by the hooves of elk, followed a rift in the cliffs from the river to the escarpment, allowing the winter herds to pass back and forth across the river. Other animals used it as well—bear, deer, lion, wolves.

Martha Ettinger hopped out of the canoe and stood with her hands on her hips. The scat analyst who had rowed the johnboat across at dawn motioned them to follow. They climbed to the top of the cliffs, Stranahan feeling the sweat pop out on his forehead from lack of sleep, Little Feather with his eyes on the ground out of long habit.

The scat analyst pointed with a stick.

"I see it," Martha said. "You found this when exactly?"

"About seven this morning," the man answered. His name was Jake Thorn and he looked about twenty, the same age as Martha's youngest son, David. Looked like David a little, brown hair, David's serious plain face, but not his eyes, which were blue like hers. It had been six months since she'd seen her son.

"I check a few dozen signposts on a rotating basis," Thorn said. "Record hair samples—I string barbed wire at bear crossings to snag the hair. It gives us an idea of their movements. And—"

Martha interrupted. "What's a signpost? Back up."

"Lions and especially wolves, the alphas, will deposit in a prominent place, it's like their calling card. It's a warning to other males that they're intruding on their territory. Any place that's used regularly, we call it a signpost. Most of what I do is wolf scat analysis because Fish, Wildlife and Parks is trying to get a handle on diet. We know they take down deer and elk all winter, but in the summer and fall the data points to smaller prey—gophers, marmots, trout, anything they can catch. They even eat berries. I check this post every week because the break in the cliffs is a natural funnel. A lot of game comes through. Ergo"—he smiled—"mucho shit."

He said it in a way that made Martha shake her head. Crude. *A guy like any other*, she thought. *Reptiles. Shake a stick and they coil up like snakes.*

She'd heard enough and squatted down by the curl of segmented poop. It was about ten inches long and had been deposited on a small rock shelf.

"So wolf, huh?"

He nodded.

"Have you found wolf poop here before?"

"I've found it half a dozen times since I started working out of the ranch last April."

Ettinger grunted. She shot some photos of the scat and then asked

Stranahan for his Swiss Army knife. Hers had lost the little tweezers. She gently tugged at a strand of reddish hair, but it wouldn't come free and she didn't want to break it.

"Wound tighter than a hair in a biscuit," she said. "It's human?"

Jake Thorn said, "That's why I called. I knew you were looking for that girl. I'm no expert on human hair, but I've seen a lot of hair in a lot of scat and nothing like this before. Could be a cocker spaniel. But you look at the way its wound around the stool. I've never seen a dog hair this long."

"Did you know her, Nicki Martinelli?"

"One of the deputies talked to me about her when she went missing. They talked to everybody at the ranch."

"I asked if you knew her."

"Sure."

"Then why did you call her 'that girl?'"

"I don't know." The timber of his voice had changed.

"She was an attractive young woman," Ettinger said. "Did you go out with her, spend any time?"

"She was seeing the head wrangler."

"That's not an answer."

"No. I mean, she's pretty, and she was really nice. I wish . . ."

"It's okay to have been attracted to her. She's young, you're young." She was giving him an out.

He smiled, shrugged, frowned all at once. "Nicki was a ten. Everybody had the hots for her. Even Bucky, who's got to be like twenty years older."

"Bucky Anderson, the ranch manager?"

"Yeah, he flirted with her in the game room, just attention, you know. Put his hand over hers, bent over her teaching her how to hold a pool cue."

"No, I don't know."

"Hey, I don't want to cause any trouble. I know he's getting hitched to the missus."

"This is just between you and me."

"No, really, there was nothing. All the guys hit on her."

"How's that? She'd only worked at the ranch a couple weeks."

"I . . . it was nothing, really."

"What was nothing?"

"I asked her if she'd like to check scat with me, run the loop I make up in the basin. She was really into wolves."

"So the two of you, up on that mountain . . ."

He looked sheepish. "Hey, she brushed me off. She wanted to be"— he made quote marks with his fingers—"friends."

"And that didn't sit too well."

"No, no. I respected it. Getting your rocks off at the ranch isn't too hard, you get a lot of cougars. It wasn't like I was desperate."

Martha shook her head. "Did you take her here, too?"

He swallowed his Adam's apple. "I wanted her to see wolf scat, and we didn't find any up at Papoose. So yeah."

"Did you find some?"

"Not that day, but . . ." He stopped.

"What were you going to say?"

"Nothing, just, when we got here, she seemed nervous. Like something about this place haunted her."

"What haunted her?"

"I don't know. It was just a feeling I got."

"Why didn't you tell me any of this twenty minutes ago?"

"I . . . I just thought, if you thought I liked her, maybe you'd think something happened, that I was involved in this. Her disappearing and all. Really, I hardly knew her."

"Okay, I believe you. You did the right thing, calling this in. Let's move on. Where do you do the scat analysis?"

"At the ranch. Mrs. Culpepper set up a place for me, wrote me a check. I've got a microscope, a mass spectrometer. Anything I'm not sure of I send to Julie McGregor at the FWP lab in Bridger."

"I know her." Ettinger straightened up. "No offense, Jake, but I'll take the sample to her when we're done here." She caught Harold's eye. "We'll back out and let you do your thing." She beckoned to Stranahan and Thorn, and they followed her down the steep path to the riverbank. Thorn shrugged off his backpack and put it in the johnboat.

"How old do you figure that sign is up there?" Ettinger asked him.

"It's pretty dried out. I'd say three or four days." His voice hadn't changed, but his body posture betrayed his discouragement, now that it was clear he was being forced out of the picture.

"Help me with something, Jake. How many people know about this spot?"

"The signpost?"

She nodded.

"Julie does. I e-mail her a report each week—depositor species, GPS coordinates of the samples, measurement, analysis of content. It's pretty detailed."

"Who besides Julie?"

"There's my blog."

"So your data's online?"

"Sure. The more people who are interested in our work, the more funding we get."

"I thought you worked for Mrs. Culpepper and FWP."

"It's a joint program with a consortium of environmental groups, her nonprofit's just one. Sierra Club, Montana Wilderness Association, Greater Yellowstone Coalition—there's about fifteen altogether. The study is funded by the consortium, so it's partly through membership fees, but people can donate directly to my work. That's why I write the blog."

"I see. And the coordinates of the samples are in the blog?"

"No, the blog's more general. I take people through my day, discuss the merits of the work, what it can teach us about predators, that kind of thing. I've mentioned this river crossing before as a grizzly corridor. We have a collared bear that uses this path every September. He comes down out of Bobcat Creek on the game range after dark, fords the river and scarfs apples from an old homestead orchard up Wolf Creek."

Ettinger nodded. "But you've never blogged about this specific signpost for wolves."

"No." He was shifting his weight from one foot to another and Martha caught it.

"Ever show this place to anyone besides Nicki Martinelli?"

He shook his head. "Maybe I've said something in casual conversation, but I've never actually taken anyone up there."

"Is there something else you want to tell us, or do you just have to pee?"

"I got to bleed my lizard."

"You do that."

She looked at his back and muttered "reptile" under her breath. "Confirms my theory."

"What's that, Martha?" Sean smiled at her.

"Nothing." She took off her hat and scratched her scalp. She turned to see a thin line of dust where a motorcycle was leaving the campground, the guttural pops dying in the distance. "So what do you think, Sean? You saw what I did. If that's human hair, it kind of blows the sister's story out of the water. I'm trying to keep an open mind. But a long red hair in wolf scat only a few miles from Papoose Mountain, the right time frame, wolves in the basin the night she went missing. We'll wait for the lab, but . . ." She shook her head. "You said you were going to meet the sister this afternoon?"

"A few hours from now. At the ranch."

"Don't tell her about this. I want to make sure first."

Stranahan nodded. "Why were you so interested in the blog? Do you think there's a possibility this is a hoax?"

"I'm just trying to find any reason not to jump to the logical conclusion. Wolves don't kill people. Not in the lower forty-eight they don't. Not on my watch."

CHAPTER EIGHTEEN

You Are What You Eat

The biology lab was a new addition to the Montana Fish, Wildlife & Parks complex. Julie McGregor, dressed in scrubs under a camo jacket, led Martha Ettinger through the Quonset hut past a row of confiscated game animals hanging from the rafters, their heavy odor coloring the air. McGregor spoke as she walked, sketching the story of the animals as they passed by.

"Spike bull. Hunter said he saw a brow tine. Funny how eyesight goes to hell when an elk's in range. Mule deer, uh-oh, wrong side of the fence. Landowner turned him in. Whitetail, guy told an interesting story. Said he was hunting from a tree stand. Drew on a buck and followed the blood trail to two dead deer. Near as he could figure, the arrow passed through the buck, must have glanced off the ground and nailed the doe, which he never saw 'til after."

"Do you believe him?"

"Actually I know him. He's an ethical hunter and didn't have to turn himself in. He could have just kept packing venison and no one would have been the wiser. So yeah, I do."

"You get many illegally shot wolves?"

"Not in archery season. Rifle season, a few."

Inside the lab, Ettinger shrugged off her jacket and hung her utility belt from a hook.

"What are you packing, if you don't mind my asking?" the game biologist said. She was eyeing the handle of the revolver.

"Ruger Redhawk .357 magnum."

"I have the LCR version."

"I didn't think biologists carried sidearms."

"It's up to us. I carry it in the field, not that I'm really afraid of anyone but it gives me gravity. Otherwise the hunters would just think here's some bitty girl who looks like a boy. Most guys think I'm a lesbian anyway. My hair, you know." She ruffled her mannish-looking mop of dirty blond hair.

Ettinger nodded sympathetically. As a woman in a man's world, she knew only too well that authority came at a cost. She looked beyond McGregor to the woman sitting before the steel specimen table, arranging tools in a neat line. This time she was determined to get off on the right foot.

"Thanks for coming, Georgeanne," she said.

The CSI turned and waved. Her eyes were like saucers behind her glasses. "Is it in there?"

Ettinger nodded. "It's just the one stool. I was hoping our tracker would find more, but this was all."

"Oooh, goody." A conspiratorial whisper: "Let's have a look."

I'll get used to her, Martha thought.

Ettinger gave Wilkerson the sealed evidence bag, noticing how small her hands were. Wilkerson teased the sample onto an examining plate while McGregor took photos and started a stool sample entry in her computer.

"Looks like a skinny yam," Wilkerson said. "I've never seen wolf scat before." She flipped the switch to her professional voice. "Julie, what are we looking at, besides the hair, which I'll tell you right now is human?"

"We have elk hair and some fish bones, probably trout. I'll have to dissect the stool to find out what else he's eaten."

"Can you get the hair out intact?" Ettinger said.

McGregor shook her head. "The way a wolf's digestive system

works, it wraps animal hair around the bone chunks the wolf swallows, so the sharp edges can't cut the intestinal lining. Pretty cool when you think about it."

"Well, do the best you can."

The next time McGregor looked up, nearly an hour had passed on the laboratory clock. She stretched her arms over her head. "People tell me I look at too much poop," she said.

Wilkerson had sealed the human hairs that McGregor had isolated in an uncontaminated evidence bag. There were ten strands, one nearly a foot in length and four with intact follicles, probably enough for a nuclear DNA workup, Wilkerson thought. The stool on the examining plate was now in a dozen sections, several sections showing pink pieces of elk bone. What was of interest, McGregor addressed her comment to Ettinger, was what wasn't in the stool, which were any bone chips that looked human.

"Now if we had the actual wolf," she said, "we could analyze the carcass. I could take a piece of wolf bone, trace the elements that compose it, which are derived from the protein of its prey, and I could tell you the exact makeup of the wolf's diet over the course of its life. What percent elk, what percent deer, what percent bird, human, you name it."

"It's called stable isotope analysis," Wilkerson added. "You are what you eat."

"Fascinating." Ettinger massaged her face with her right hand. "Let me ask you something. Can you tell me with absolute certainty that these human hairs passed through the gut system of a wolf? Wouldn't there be a measurement of decomposition you could use, or am I exhibiting my ignorance?"

McGregor shook her head. "That would be hard. What determines if you can digest food is whether or not you have a gut system that contains the specific enzymes necessary to digest that food. Hair is composed of keratin, same as hooves and toenails. Wolves don't have the proper enzymes, so it passes through the system undigested. Of course that's a good thing for mister wolf. If he digested the hair, then he wouldn't have anything to wrap around the bone chips to protect his intestines."

Ettinger pursed her lips.

Wilkerson spoke up. "What you're asking is if someone could have planted the hairs in the stool."

Ettinger nodded. "I have to eliminate the possibility."

"To answer your question, the way Julie knows that the hairs were ingested by a wolf is the physical evidence conveyed by the stool. You noticed how intricately the human hairs were woven through all the elk hair. There's no way a person could have done that."

Ettinger *tich-tich*ed out of the corner of her mouth. This was going to cause an uproar in the press. The wolf haters would have a field day. They were going to start forming posses.

"Thanks for making my day so much easier," she said to the two women.

CHAPTER NINETEEN

Blue Ribbon Watercolors and Private Investigations

Sean Stranahan picked up the *Bridger Mountain Star* that was rolled up in his cubby hole at the office of the cultural center and carried it up the flight of stairs to his studio. He plugged in an electric tea kettle and sat down at his fly-tying table. The story was front-page banner, above the fold.

Wolf Suspected in Missing Woman Case

by Gail Stocker/Star Reporter

The Region Three Montana Fish, Wildlife & Parks laboratory has confirmed finding human hair in wolf scat discovered yesterday near the Palisades boat launch and campground on the Madison River. The ledges where the scat was deposited are about five miles from Papoose Basin, where Nanika Martinelli, 25, disappeared during a trail ride from the Culpepper Guest Ranch September 14th.

Sheriff Martha Ettinger said the hair will be analyzed by the state crime lab to determine if it came from the missing woman.

"It's too early to conclude a connection to Miss Martinelli," Ettinger said.

Martinelli disappeared the same night that Grady Cole, 23, a wrangler at the Culpepper Ranch was found dead in the backcountry, impaled on an elk antler. The coroner's office is holding an inquest to determine if it was an accident.

A signpost, said Jacob Thorn, the University of Montana graduate student who discovered the scat during a routine. . . .

Stranahan's desk phone rang.

"You still want to fish the Kootenai?" It was Carter Monroe, the Lincoln County sheriff.

"I do." Stranahan poured hot water over some loose leaf Darjeeling second flush, one of his few indulgences. "Next time I promise not to smell like Love Potion Twenty-nine," he said.

Monroe laughed. "I sent you a package yesterday. Did you get it?"

"Not yet, but I haven't gone down for the mail. It usually doesn't come until about ten o'clock."

"I went through Martinelli's desk at the cabin. There was a hidden drawer with some of the old man's journals. They're written in French. Maybe you can find someone to translate. Of course this may be moot now that you have the hair. What's the background on that?"

They talked a few minutes about the discovery at the Palisades. Stranahan hesitated when the conversation wound down, then briefly sketched his meeting with Asena Martinelli. He didn't want to betray her confidence, but wondered how much Monroe knew about Nicki's involvement in the Clan of the Three-Clawed Wolf and whether mention of its charismatic leader had reached his ears.

The singing silence in the line was palpable.

"It's interesting you brought this up," Monroe said at length. "We did look at a man for the letter writing. One of my deputies questioned him, but he was never brought into the office and there would have been nothing to hold him on. But there's something else—"

"What letters?"

"The sister didn't tell you? Some game rangers, elk outfitters, hunting guides, other people involved in the wolf controversy—there were about twenty in all—received threatening letters. Old man Martinelli got one. Nothing ever stemmed from the letters, but they were ominous in tone. I can't remember the exact wording. The reason they were brought to my attention is they were written in blood. It was human blood."

"No, I hadn't heard."

"Well, like I said, nothing came of them. They were postmarked in Missoula, so that means they could have been sent from anywhere in the western part of the state. Not much help. A town drunk copped to it after it was in the newspaper, but he's copped to half the crimes in the county. Would you like me to see if we still have one filed away?"

"Yes." Stranahan wondered why Asena hadn't brought up the topic of the letters, but then she'd stayed in Canada. Unless Nicki told her, she'd never have known.

"If I find one, I'll scan it and attach it to an e-mail. What's your address?"

"I don't have one."

"You don't own a computer?"

"Yes, it has a satellite connection for the Internet, but it doesn't work half the time."

"Do you have a smart phone?"

"I had a flip phone, but I threw it in the lake."

"I guess you must be one of those retro detectives. Gun in a shoulder holster, bottle in the desk drawer."

"I don't own a gun, but I do have a fifth of The Famous Grouse and you're spot-on about the desk drawer. Lower right hand. Can I still be a detective?"

"I like it," Monroe said. "Shades of Phillip Marlowe. But I don't see how you get anything done."

Stranahan gave Monroe Ettinger's personal e-mail address to send the letter to, in case he found one to scan.

"The other reason I called," Monroe said, "well, two reasons. We found pillowcases on a clothesline in the backyard. They had blood-stains but had been washed, probably in the creek, so the DNA is degraded. Big thing was we dug the slugs out of the cellar—.45 caliber pistol bullets. We found five. You're a lucky man."

"I know I am."

"Since they're evidence of a homicide attempt, I can't send them to you without an official transfer request."

"I understand. I still think it was a woman's voice I heard that night."

Monroe's "possibly" was unencouraging. "Like I said, I don't know if this helps."

Stranahan thanked him and was putting down the receiver when a question occurred to him, but Monroe had hung up. He dialed him back.

"What was the guy's real name? Asena Martinelli said Nicki called him Amorak. Or that was what the man told her to call him."

Stranahan could hear the air escaping Monroe's lungs.

"I was afraid that might be the question. I looked back through the log and we dropped the ball. The deputy who questioned him about the letters asked for his ID and he said it was in the tent where he was staying, at a campground on Lake Koocanusa. He said his name was F-something, Fencer or Fercer, something like that. F-something Amorak. That's what the deputy recalls. He was busy and the guy said he'd stop by the office with his driver's license. He didn't, and we didn't follow up because the drunk copped to the letters and the deputy was new and didn't know the drunk's history. But that's no excuse."

They promised to fish the Kootenai soon and Stranahan replaced the receiver on the phone. His tea was cold. He drank it and pondered what to do with the day. The only reason he'd driven into

Bridger was to keep an appointment with Asena Martinelli, whom he'd met at the ranch yesterday after his visit to the Palisades. By the time he got there, Ettinger had already called him to confirm that the hair was human. Asena had greeted him at her cabin with her arms folded and listened impassively as he related the story of finding it in the wolf scat. She'd erected a wall around herself; it had been there from hello and he didn't know what to make of it. It wasn't exactly denial, but rather as if she were the victim of personal injustice. It didn't seem to be so much about her sister.

Then she'd done something odd. They'd been talking on the porch of the cabin when, midsentence, she had turned a circle on the heel of her cowboy boot. It was spontaneous, something a young girl might do to flare out her skirt. When she was facing him again, a different facet of her personality emerged. The vulnerable person he'd seen only glimpses of was standing before him, trembling with emotion. Her eyes were bright and her words tumbled out in a rush.

"I have to think she's alive, I just have to." She took his right hand with both of hers and brought it to her chest, squeezing it so hard that the blood ran to his fingertips. "In here. I can feel it. We were so close, I would know it if she was dead and I don't, I don't know that. When I close my eyes I can still see her, I can hear her in my head, I can feel her in my heart. Will you help me? Oh, you must help me."

"There now," Stranahan said, and immediately regretted the remark. It was something you'd say to a child, and the woman pressing his hand against the soft swell of her breast was far from a child. But when she stepped away from him, a crispness came back into her voice. "I want to hire you." The girl who'd wheeled on her heel was no longer before him. She'd been replaced by a woman with both feet on the ground. "I checked my bank statements and I can hire you for a week, once you're free from your obligation to the county."

"Why don't we wait until the hair is matched to your sister's, if it's matched? There's no sense throwing your money away."

"I don't believe I would be doing that. This Amorak, if he's back and he's taken her, I don't know what he'll do with her. I think he'd kill her if she resisted him. As you told me yesterday, time isn't on her side." Stranahan had reluctantly agreed to acept her as a client and they were to meet at his office at ten this morning.

It was ten.

Stranahan went down the stairs to retrieve his mail and found the package Monroe had sent. He carried it up to his office, and she was standing outside his door. She must have come in from the south entrance. He saw her looking at the lettering etched into the glass.

BLUE RIBBON WATERCOLORS
Private Investigations

"I keep meaning to have that last bit removed," Stranahan said.

"Are you a licensed detective?"

"As of this year I'm officially licensed as a private investigator in the Treasure State. Much to the dismay of Sheriff Ettinger, I'm afraid."

"Do you two have a thing going on? I sensed something."

"Define 'thing.'" He opened the door and ushered her in. "I'll have you sign a standard contract, but only because you insist. I won't charge you a dime if it's proven that your sister was killed by a wolf."

She opened her purse and produced a wad of bills wrapped in a rubber band. "That's for the week and there's another thousand for expenses. I actually do make money, even if it's Canadian money. I want your full attention. Are you still working for the county?"

"As of this morning, no. The focus of the investigation has shifted to the wolf. There will be a hunt now, but it won't be a manhunt."

"Yes, I understand that."

She shifted her attention from him to take in the studio, her eyes stopping on a nude study in muted shades of gray that looked out of place among the angling art.

"The subject was a woman I did a job for in Boston," Stranahan said. "The client who bought it traded it back to me for a watercolor. He said his wife told him he could stare at all the fish he wanted, but she didn't like him looking at another woman's body every day. The strange thing about being an artist is you sell your children and never see more than a few of them ever again. I was glad to get this one back."

"You're a very good artist."

"A critic once called me the 'poor man's Ogden Pleissner.'"

"Don't sell yourself short," Asena said seriously. "When this is over, when we get Nicki back, I'd like you to paint her. She's so beautiful and . . ." Her voice broke. "And I have so little to . . ."

She came into his arms and he held her, feeling the whole front of her press up against him.

"I'm okay," she said. "I'm so sorry." Her lashes brushed his cheek, but when she stepped back her eyes were dry and didn't seem to be able to focus. It was the second time she'd sought the security of his embrace. In the tipi, when she'd said how relieved she was he hadn't been shot, her arms reaching for him had seemed the most natural thing in the world. And when she'd brought his hand to her chest at the ranch, the yielding push of her breast against his skin, he had not read anything sexual into the gesture. But this felt like a seduction. She'd pressed against him as a woman presses against a man, not as someone grieving for a loved one.

He glanced over her shoulder at the package on the desk. He'd meant to open it in her presence; now that he puzzled over her motives, he was hesitant. He forestalled his decision by asking when she was heading back to British Columbia.

"I packed up my things from the ranch. But I'm not going home until we find her. They can get someone to fill in for a couple weeks where I work. Your friend Sam offered to let me stay in his barn, the room where Nicki lived. It's a way of being close to her."

Stranahan remembered the letters, the ones signed in blood, and wondered again if she had known about them. He decided to wait and see if Monroe sent one before broaching the subject.

"I'm not leaving this room until I see you put the money into your safe," she said.

Without a word, Stranahan took the stack of bills to the squat black safe in the corner of the room. He'd picked it up at a garage sale and the combination was three-zero-zero-six, like the popular rifle cartridge called the thirty-aught-six. It was the first combination any thief in the state would try.

"What's this?" Asena said, picking up the package on Stranahan's fly-tying table and making at least that decision easy for him.

"I was hoping you might tell me," he said.

CHAPTER TWENTY

Shoot, Shovel and Shut Up

"I'm next up," Martha Ettinger said. She picked up her jacket to make room for Stranahan to sit on a metal chair. He nodded to Julie McGregor sitting on the other side of Ettinger, then to Katie Sparrow, who was dressed in her park ranger uniform. Sparrow cocked her forefinger at him, tapped her chest and pointed toward the back of the room.

"Now?"

She shook her head and mouthed "Later."

Stranahan took off his hat and sat down. "Any progress on the hair?" he asked Martha.

"Wilkerson says she'll do a spectral analysis tomorrow. The techs found usable DNA in Martinelli's cabin, feminine pads with menstrual blood and a toothbrush, so there's a good chance for a match. You'll know when I know. Tell me you got a cell phone."

"I got a cell phone."

"Really?"

"No."

Martha's cheek reflexively tightened as she side-eyed him, one of her "You disappoint me" gestures, and looked down at her notes.

The last time Stranahan had been in the convention hall of the Holiday Inn, for a Trout Unlimited Banquet, the space was crowded with trust-fund trout fishermen, women sporting sculpted calves and spaghetti strap dresses, fishing guides who were the negative images of raccoons, with sun-blackened faces and ovals of fair skin where their sunglasses would normally rest, and there had been a lot of money in the room. There was a lot of money in the room tonight, but it was ranch capital, tied up in land.

Walking in, he'd passed by a banner that read "Emergency Meeting of the Ranchers and Hunters for Taking the Wolf Out of Montana." A woman wearing a Wapiti Unlimited baseball cap was hawking bumper stickers carrying the image of a wolf in the crosshairs of a rifle scope. Her competition, a man dressed in a buckskin jacket with fringe, sold rifle cartridges with the bullets drilled out and filled with silver for twenty-five dollars a pop. "The Werewolves Are Coming. Be Prepared!" read his placard.

The ink on the newspaper article was less than a day dry.

"What have I missed?" Stranahan whispered.

"Ranchers pissed at wolves. Hunters pissed at wolves. Everyone pissed at me. Sshh now, we got to stay quiet for the celebrity."

The featured speaker was Clive "Buster" Black, the treasurer of the Hyalite chapter of the Stockgrowers Association and a cowboy poet on the side, a side that had gotten him as far as a guest spot on the *Tonight Show*. Hence his Tony Lama snakeskins, hence the Johnny Cash register of his voice, hence the Magnum P.I. mustache with down-turned tips.

"What happened in the Madison Valley last week was a shame," he began, "a crying shame." He looked directly into the eye of the television camera set up in the center aisle. "All of you sittin' here saw it comin', and all of you sittin' here knew it could have been prevented. We didn't ask for the lobo; the lobo was forced on us by the U.S. of A. government, which I guess took more stock in the crying of a bunch of vegetarians from Massachusetts than the reasonable voices of the people who have to make a living in Montana." He paused, and there was murmuring assent from the crowd.

"Now that very second," he went on, "that very instant the first wolf was released into Yellowstone Park in nineteen and ninety five, why it doesn't take an Einstein to know it would only be a blink of the eye before our stock wound up in their stomachs. Just last month, the Diamond L Ranch out of Dillon lost a hundred eighteen Rambouillet bucks—that's purebred sheep to you folks don't know. Livestock loss like that, wanton killing, was why we got rid of the lobo in the first place. For every fifty heifer I raise to twelve hundred pounds, I lose one, sometimes two, to those bloodthirsty bastards."

Ettinger rolled her eyes. She whispered to Stranahan. "That man hasn't seen life from the saddle of a horse in thirty years. All he does is parcel off inherited land to Californians."

Clive Black was rolling. "Now those bastard dogs are eating into our wild meat as well, and I don't have to tell anyone here how much revenue a healthy elk herd brings. A six-point bull's one hell of a valuable commodity at the end of a gun barrel—we're talking up to ten thousand dollars by the time you add up license cost and outfitter fees—but he ain't worth a bucket of glue in the gullet of a wolf. But now they aren't content to limit their diet to our beef cattle and wild game. The reason we're here tonight is we've got ourselves a pack of wolves that have turned man killer, and the loss of human life is something you can't put a price on. Sure, it's ironic that young Nanika Martinelli was a wolf lover herself, but did she deserve the fate that awaited her in Papoose Basin? No, sir, she didn't."

He again paused to let the crowd express its sympathies. As the voices died down one young woman stood to shout. "It's the dog that's the bastard of the wolf, not the other way around, you dumb shit."

"And you can take your bleeding heart back to wherever you hail from," Black said evenly. "Please don't dishonor our memory of this woman with your political agenda."

"As if you don't have one? What are you going to do, write a poem about her? Sell it to her crying parents?"

Martha Ettinger stood up. "Gentlemen, ladies. Please. There will be a time for comments after the last speaker."

"Thank you, Sheriff Ettinger," Black said.

Ettinger sat down and muttered, "I hate standing up for that self-satisfied asshole."

Black seemed unfazed by the interruption.

"They told us"—he held up his fingers to put quotes around the word *they*—"they being the *federales* that permitted this travesty. They said that wolves wouldn't bother our livestock and compromise our livelihood, and they were wrong. They said that wolves wouldn't damage elk herds outside the park, and they were wrong. They assured us we had nothing to fear from wolves because there had never been a fatal attack on a human by a wolf in North America. Well, gentlemen, *they* were wrong about that, too."

He waved a sheet of paper.

"November 8, 2005. Kenton Joel Carnegie, twenty-two, a geological engineering student working in the Athabasca Basin in Saskatchewan went for a walk where co-workers had reported seeing wolves. He was attacked and consumed by a predator. A judicial inquest carried out by the provincial government concluded wolves were the culprits."

He raised his eyes to the room, then bent to the paper and ran thumb and forefinger along the points of his mustache.

"March 8, 2010. Candice Berner, thirty-two, a schoolteacher, went jogging near Chignik Lake, Alaska. Snowmobilers found her mutilated body among wolf tracks. Wolf DNA was found on her clothing. She had been eaten. The Alaska state medical examiner ruled her death was caused by wolves."

Again, he paused to let the information sink in.

"I won't go on with what's happened in other countries," Black said, and then did, reporting the hundreds of people who had been chased down in horse-driven sleighs or killed in their fields in medieval Europe, the thousands of Russian peasants who'd met similar fates in the teeth of wolves and as recently as the 1960s, the nearly one hundred villagers in the Indian state of Assam who had been dragged from their huts and eaten by wolves.

"Now the naysayers will tell you those were different wolves. Last time I looked they was all *Canis lupus,* each and ever' one, what biologists call the gray wolf and what most of us see as the devil incarnate. They may be scrawnier in India or fluffier in Siberia, but they all got the same blood and they all got the same color heart. Black. We assembled here tonight to find out what if anything's being done to track down and kill the monsters that snatched Miss Martinelli from the prime of her young life, but that ain't the end of the story. No, sir, not by a long shot. We want to know, we demand to know, what's going to be done about the other eight hundred and fifty wolves roamin' Montana, and we're sick and tired of settling for halfway measures like the limited hunting season we got now. The only way we're going to control these sons of bitches is by declaring war. We want to trap them year round, we want to use electronic game calls to bring them in range of our rifles and we need our FWP to shoot them from the air like they do in Alaska."

"Here, here," came a shout from behind Stranahan. He turned to see a heavyset man with a very red face pound the butt of a square blade shovel against the floor. A ringing thud echoed around the room. The man raised the shovel and brought the butt down again. "Shoot," he said, and banged the shovel. "Shovel," he said, and down came the shovel. "Shut up," he said, and once more the thud of his shovel. The chant was taken up by someone else in the same row and in a few moments half the room was chanting "Shoot, shovel, shut up! Shoot, shovel, shut up!" Metal rang off linoleum. Stranahan saw Ettinger close her eyes and blow out her breath.

"I knew I should have put Walt at the entrance," she said. She rose from her chair while shaking her head and deliberately strode to the lectern. She snapped her fingers and held up her hand.

"I'm not finished, Sheriff," Black said, the microphone held casually at his side.

"Yes, you are." She looked at him levelly. "The camera's on you, Clive.

Do you really want to create a scene here?" Ignoring her hand, he placed the mike in its cradle on the lectern, and, walking off, accepted a shovel from a woman in the front row and brought it down with a resounding thud. Then to applause, he brandished it over his head.

Ettinger waited for the angry murmur to subside.

"Stand down!" shouted a man from the back of the room. "I think we all want to hear what the sheriff has to say."

It was Sam Meslik's gravelly baritone. Stranahan swiveled his head. He'd first met the burly fishing guide in this very room two summers ago, but he knew that Sam, as a rule, avoided public meetings, gatherings of any kind for that matter, unless maybe a keg was involved. Was he here to support Martha?

Sean turned as Ettinger began to speak.

"I understand your frustration," she said. She paused for half a dozen dissenting voices to pipe down. "Thank you. First, I'd like to bring you up to date. The hair in the wolf scat collected at the Palisades is in fact human hair. The last newspaper article made it sound as if it has been linked to Nanika Martinelli. It has not. The hair has been transferred to the state crime lab for analysis and the results will be made public as soon as they are available."

"That's not good enough!" It was the first man who'd pounded a shovel.

"It's what we have," Ettinger said. "But rest assured, we're acting on the supposition that a wolf or wolves have either killed or scavenged the remains of a human being. FWP personnel along with officers from my department are actively trying to kill the animals responsible. We're also bringing in a wolfer from Hamilton who has as much experience hunting problem predators as anyone in the Rockies. The pack we heard in Papoose Basin the night Martinelli went missing is our first priority. Julie McGregor of FWP will speak to this subject more fully in a few minutes . . . No, Julie, why don't you come up now?"

The game biologist glanced at Stranahan. "Talk about being thrown to the wolves," she whispered. She gave him a "here goes nothing" look, exhaled with pursed lips and ascended the steps to the lectern.

"I'm Julie McGregor, the Region Three elk and wolf biologist," she said.

"Speak up," somebody shouted.

She flicked the mike with the backs of her fingers, which brought a shriek from the amplifying system. She raised it closer to her mouth. She repeated her position and began to talk wolves, her expertise having made her the center of aggressive attention at many public meetings over the past several years, while the federal courts waffled back and forth on removing the animals from the endangered species list. Only two years earlier, an act of Congress had overridden the judiciary and permitted wolf hunting, as long as the population was not brought below the number of breeding pairs federally mandated.

"As most of you know," McGregor said, "our department has had its hands tied in the past with regard to public wolf hunting. However, we have always been able to eliminate wolves that kill livestock through a cooperative effort with Wildlife Services, which is a branch of the U.S. Department of Agriculture, and with Animal Damage Control, another federal agency. That includes aerial hunting. So we have a system in place to eliminate problem predators. Usually it works very well because we try to capture and radio collar at least one wolf from every pack whose range overlaps areas where cattle and sheep ranchers have grazing rights. That way, if the pack is determined to have killed livestock, we can track them down. The problem we're running into with this pack is that none of them are collared."

"Why the hell not?" The question came from the back of the room.

"Here's the situation," McGregor went on. "The wolves that frequent the southern Madison Range are called the Bald Ridge Pack, because they were first spotted together up there on Baldy. In the last aerial survey, which was in March, the pack consisted of two wolves that broke away from the Black Butte Pack before that pack was destroyed for killing cattle, and two subadult females driven out of the Snowcrest Seven Pack that occupied the southern Gravelly Range. In addition, there's a black wolf that joined the group last winter. He's the alpha male of the Bald Ridge Pack and the female from the Black Butte Pack is the alpha female."

A high-pitched whistle pierced the room. A tall man dressed head-to-toe cowboy removed his fingers from his mouth and said, "Aren't we missing the point? We shoot all the wolves we'll get the one ate this girl. No sense wasting time looking for just one, or just one pack for the love of Christ."

"That's right," said the man seated next to him. He had a cane and didn't stand. "Kill 'em, let God sort 'em."

"We *are* targeting all the wolves in the area," McGregor continued. "But the only member of this pack fitted with a radio collar was the female omega from the Snowcrest Seven group and she was shot in April, probably by a spring bear hunter. We found her remains in the Papoose drainage. So this bear hunter or whoever he was that shot this wolf, illegally I might add"—she swept the rows with her light gray eyes—"destroyed our ability to locate the pack through radio telemetry. Instead of being able to zero in on their location, we have to search for them through thousands of acres of rugged country."

"If you won't kill them, we will!"

Ettinger beckoned McGregor by curling her fingers and took the microphone.

"Who said that? Jerry, was that you?"

A man dressed in muddy Carhartts stood up and said, "Hell yes, it was me."

"And just how do you propose to do that?" Ettinger said. A note of exasperation crept into her voice. When he didn't respond, she added, "You're still outfitting out of the Douglass place, aren't you?"

"I am." He paused. "For what elk are left. Our hunter success rate dropped to eighteen percent last season and this one isn't going to be any better. Not unless we kill these damned wolves."

"Look," Ettinger bubbled her exhalation, which the mike caught and exaggerated. She pulled her head back a few inches. "I know we got a wolf debate going on in this state. And I know what side most of you come down on. Jerry, I'm pretty sure where you stand."

At last, smiles from a few of the faces she could see, though not from Jerry's.

"I'm Montanan just like you are," she said. "I grew up hunting, branding, pulling calves. I'm not the enemy here. Rest assured that we are not targeting just one wolf. What I'm asking you to do, all of you, is to help me. Not by pounding your shovels. All the shovel pounding in the world isn't going to bring that woman back to life, and it sure as hell isn't going to kill any wolves. If our wolf hunting seasons these past three years have taught us anything, it's how difficult wolves can be to kill. Last year we sold twenty-four thousand wolf licenses for a six-month-long hunting season and we couldn't meet the quota set by FWP, which was two hundred twenty wolves. If a bunch of people with rifles take to the hills, those wolves will disappear pronto. So I'm asking you, Jerry, I'm asking all of you to go back to your homes and let us get on with our job. You got your work to do, I got mine. Thank you. Now if you have any questions, Julie and I will do our level best to answer them."

———

Stranahan had about as much patience for public gatherings as Sam Meslik did. When it became clear that the rest of the meeting was going to be more about venting than having a productive discourse on the wolf situation, he caught Sparrow's eye and met her at the buffet table at the back of the room. He noticed the empty chair where Sam Meslik had been sitting. It wasn't like Sam to leave without talking to Sean, but then, Sean thought, it wasn't like Sam to have attended in the first place.

"You want a cup, Katie?" He was pouring coffee for himself.

The diminutive dog handler, who had worked with Stranahan on several search operations in the past, shook her head.

"Not unless you want to stay up all night with me and bake dog biscuits. I can guarantee you they taste better than one of those cookies. Whatcha think?" She rolled her eyes at the Keebler assortment on a silver cookie tray. "They could have at least had some Pepperidge Farm."

"Is that really what you're doing tonight, baking dog biscuits?"

She shrugged. "I live in West Yellowstone. What else is there to do on a Tuesday night?"

"You keep teasing me like this, someday I'm going to say yes."

"Promises," she said.

He'd almost kissed her once, when they were talking about her nickname, Dog Breath, which had been pinned on her by the search-and-rescue team for her habit of eating dog biscuits when working a trail. "I say if you really want to find out, all you have to do is kiss me," she'd said. They'd been standing on a mountain where bodies had been unearthed and Sean had been involved with Martinique, or he would have bent down—the difference in their heights was almost a foot—and rendered his opinion.

A smile brightened her face; she peered at him with her head cocked expectantly, like an inquisitive wren. "You know it's going to happen, you and me. You're going to get past this long-distance relationship you're trying to float and find out what you're missing is a woman who knows her way around a male animal."

"You mean Lothar."

"I think you know who I mean."

"Is that why you met me back here, to talk about baking dog biscuits?"

Stranahan tried to keep his tone light. He liked Katie; he enjoyed flirting with her and seeing her smile. She'd pulled through a dark time and still wore a locket with a photograph of the young man she was going to marry, before he drowned in an avalanche. Now she was facing life with an upturned face and laugh lines that were just going to deepen. And God knows, Sean thought, I need what she's offering. But he wasn't ready to give up on Martinique, even if he'd begun thinking of her more in the past tense than the present. And how would Ettinger take it? They were more to each other than either would admit. Martha was always in the back of his mind. A maybe, a someday; they were ships in the night.

"No, I wanted to ask you if you knew about the woman we fished out of the hot pot this summer. The Jane Doe."

"Back in August, right? I read she was in a coma."

"Friday the thirteenth. She'd filled out the register at a trailhead in Gibbon Meadows, wrote that she was going on a day hike, a bad idea 'cause it's bear-y in there, but folks put a pepper spray on their hip and think they're invincible."

"If she filled out the register, then she must have put down a name."

"Well, it's not for sure it was her who signed the register. Somebody did who didn't put down a name, which happens all the time. Everybody else who signed that day we've accounted for."

"Is the park holding something back?"

Katie lowered her voice. "I shouldn't be telling you, but Martha, she was talking to me before the meeting, she talks to me now you know, I think she's got a self-confidence issue. I know that doesn't sound like the woman you and I know—anyway, we were talking and she told me what happened to you up in Libby."

"Tell me about this woman you found."

"Well, that's just it, there isn't much to go on. Who she is and how she got up there are big black holes right now."

"I don't see what this has to do with Nicki Martinelli."

"It doesn't directly, except that Martha said a guy on a motorcycle was looking for her, that you'd spoken to some fly shop owner on the Kootenai. And the Kootenai guy said the guy had a girl with him who had red eyes."

Stranahan paused with his coffee cup halfway to his lips. "Orange eyes."

"So what I'm saying is, this girl had 'em. She'd managed to crawl part way out of the pot and she had the eyes."

"How tall was she?" The Hook & Hackle owner had called the woman he'd seen a "bitty thing."

Katie indicated the top of her head, which was a hair more than five feet above the convention room floor. "Short black hair with some dyed blond streaks. She had a nose stud, a tongue stud, a bunch a tats—you know, a Goth."

"You saw her?"

"Oh, yeah. I got the call and went in there with the geyser watcher who'd found her. She looked like something out of a horror movie. Her eyes were like a branding iron just before you—" she jabbed with her fist. "*Psssss.* Turns out they were contacts. Her real eyes are pale green. So I thought if you're interested, I could take you in there. Not that you'd find anything with this much time passed, but I've read about you detective types and know how you are about seeing the scene. Now that everybody's looking for a wolf, the county doesn't need me for the missing person and I'm off park patrol for the next couple days."

Stranahan heard himself say "What time?" He'd spent the afternoon with Asena, taking notes while she translated the journals. The journals were a fascinating account of a trapper's life among the mountains whose names Alfonso Martinelli had co-opted for his daughters, and had provided Sean with two possible leads. But that could wait. The girl was a start toward finding Amorak—if, that is, she was the same person who'd been with him earlier in the summer. *Don't get your hopes up,* he told himself. But how many women could there be with eyes the color of a branding iron?

CHAPTER TWENTY-ONE

The Cobalt Necropolis

Katie Sparrow lived in a Forest Service cabin on Cougar Creek, a few miles north of West Yellowstone. The cabin was on federal land, and the National Park Service had taken over the hundred-year lease, as there was a housing shortage inside the park. A summer place, uninsulated, but Katie had replaced the barrel stove with an efficient woodstove and routed vents to the bathroom and bedroom. They drank coffee and ate some kind of a venison hash Katie reheated and cracked a couple eggs over, not Stranahan's idea of breakfast, but better than the dog biscuit of hers he'd sampled last summer. Her manner was direct and friendly, but the underlying flirtation was absent and Stranahan felt relieved. It was one thing to tease each other in a public meeting room; standing under her roof, the same conversation might have been awkward.

They were going to take Katie's park vehicle, so Stranahan got his daypack out of the Land Cruiser and climbed into the shotgun seat alongside Lothar. At the park's west gate, Katie took the lane reserved for official vehicles and kept up a mile-by-mile commentary as they headed for Madison Junction.

"You look to the left there across the river, that knob with the burned lodgepoles on it? Guy last year was parasailing and landed in a tree. Naked as a jaybird, waving it like a flag. I cited him for a trespass violation *and* indecent exposure. He blamed the wind for blowing him the wrong way."

They drove a few minutes, crossed a bridge, now the Madison was on their right. At a bend in the road past the Mount Haines overlook,

Katie pointed to a roadside rock. "Remember that camper at Madison Junction last summer who got hit by the car? Everybody wondered what he was doing five miles away walking at night. Turns out he was dressed in a suit made out of craft fur and was jumping into headlights from behind this rock, trying to create a Bigfoot sighting. They took him to the clinic in West. I cited him for being a road hazard while he was lying on the gurney with a broken hip. Darwin Award. You can't make this shit up."

At Madison Junction, Katie took a left and they began to climb along the Gibbon River. Traffic had been light, but here the cars were backed up. "It's a critter fuck," Katie said, and pulled to the side.

"What do you think it is?"

"Wolf. There's been three spotted here the last couple days, worrying the bones of a bull elk."

"I've never seen a wolf," Stranahan said.

"Here's your chance."

But it was not to be. By the time Katie and Sean drew up to the cluster of bystanders, some of whom were carrying cameras with lenses the size of Montana zucchinis, the wolf had moved into the pines. Sean got a glimpse of one long rear leg and a grizzled gray tail. They walked back to the car and didn't stop again until they reached the trailhead in Gibbon Meadows.

————

"The thing about this girl," Katie said as they began to hike, "is that I might have seen her before the accident. I'm not sure, but I think so. I was on patrol up in the Lamar Valley. This would have been June, when the elk were calving. That's when you get your wolf wackos showing up. They dress like wolves, dance around, howl even though they're not supposed to. Mostly they're just looking with spotting scopes, but sometimes I have to shoo away people who've hiked too close to a kill. Two of the groups are professional outfits that bring tourists in vans. The khaki brigade I call them, all these people who wear safari clothes—you get your dreadlocks and Tilley hats side by side."

"Can you remember who she was with?"

"You're thinking that guy on the motorcycle, but no, I'm not even certain the Lamar is where I saw her. But we could go up there after. There might be someone who remembers her better."

A mixed herd of bison, twenty or so, which had appeared as black slugs on a tan hillside when they started hiking, were close enough now that Stranahan could see the flies buzzing around their nostrils. Two of the bulls, thin flanked with all their weight in the forequarters, had squared off and were short charging, disappearing in a swirl of dust each time the massive, wooly heads butted together. Stranahan heard them roaring. They sounded more like lions than buffalo.

"We'll give them a little room," Katie said, swinging off the path. "This is the tail end of the rut. You get too much testosterone in a herd, bad things can happen. Same with folks."

They rejoined the trail in the trees and then, coming out of the trees, entered what appeared to Stranahan as moonscape, a slope pockmarked by miniature eruptions of ocher mud, the ground hot underfoot, steam issuing from cracks in the earth. The Talking Cluster included half a dozen murmuring hot pots, a mud volcano named the Spitting Toad and connecting sheets of thin, clear, moving water pinpointed with algae and with banks limned in a fantastic tapestry of lemon- and green–tinted swirls. The Jane Doe had fallen into the aptly named Cobalt Necropolis, a nearly circular hot pot with a rim painted gold, tan shallows abruptly plunging into two blue underwater pools that, each being approximately six feet long and as wide as a man's shoulders, did indeed resemble resting quarters for the dead.

"Lothar, heel," Katie commanded. She explained to Sean that most tourists who died in the park's hot pots had plunged in to rescue dogs. "You can see why the press release mentioned the Talking

Cluster but not the Cobalt Necropolis. That would be just too . . . I'm looking for a word."

"Macabre," Stranahan said.

"Yeah, that's it. Isn't he smart, Lothar? I wish I was that smart." She bent down to put an arm around the neck of the shepherd. Pointing, she said, "The girl's body was right about there, before the watcher fished her out. He said her legs were still in the pot. There were some marks in the marl where she'd tried to claw her way out. Of course there aren't any tracks now, but the first time I was here it looked like she'd marched right down to the edge. Not running, but more weight on the toes, moving pretty fast. It's like she went into the pool on purpose. The only other tracks were the watcher's." She shook her head. "Why don't you put your thinking cap on and stay here while I hike into the woods. I drank too much coffee this morning."

When she and Lothar had gone, Stranahan stared into the pool, its two-hundred-and-thirty-degree depths hinted at only by the thinnest layer of steam. Had the woman been attracted by something in the pool and approached too closely, or was she retreating? If so, what had scared her? Or had it been, as the tracks hinted, a suicide attempt? The face of the water gave him nothing and he half heard, half sensed movement behind him. Turning, he saw a man approaching in a halting gait, a walking stick tapping in front of him. A folding chair was lashed with a bungee cord to his backpack.

"I didn't know I'd be having company this morning," he said pleasantly.

"I'm here with the park ranger who investigated the accident."

"Oh, who's that?" He nodded. "I know Katie. I'm the one who found the poor thing." He was on the lee side of fifty, Stranahan decided, and a veritable giant. He offered a hand the size of a bear paw. Like Bucky Anderson, he seemed to have been born with a smile, but unlike the manager of the Culpepper Ranch, the giant's handshake was tentative, as if he knew his power and was careful exercising it. The eyes behind the smile held the saddest look Stranahan had ever seen.

"I'm Robert Knudson, but everybody calls me Geyser Bob."

He inserted a stick of chewing gum into his mouth and offered Stranahan the pack. Stranahan declined.

Chewing, Knudson told him how he'd been visiting the Talking Cluster and found the body. He'd been planning to sit by the Cobalt Necropolis, which erupted only a half dozen times each year. It had been thirty-two days since the last eruption and he was hoping to be the first person to record the activity on a high-definition camcorder. He explained that geyser watchers were mostly retired people who did the Park Service a favor by cataloging geyser activity—this much Stranahan knew. It was about nine a.m. when he'd found the girl. He described her position, also nothing Katie hadn't already told him.

"I feel like I'm the responsible party. Perhaps if I'd come earlier, we would have spoken and her moment of crisis would have passed."

"What makes you think she tried to commit suicide?"

"It's hard to fall into one of these things by accident."

Stranahan asked him how long he was planning to stay. He said until about six o'clock. It wasn't a good idea to walk out after dark.

"Must get lonely sometimes."

"Oh, I'm never bored. I sit here and write my memoir. It's called 'The Madman of Minnetonka.' Minnetonka is in Minnesota."

"You don't strike me as a madman."

"It was my ring name. I'm a retired mathematics teacher, but I used to be a professional wrestler. I'm thinking the subtitle will be 'Always the Heel, Never the Face.' My signature move was the pancake. I'd get the other wrestler in a bear hug and fall on him. I broke two of Gorilla Monsoon's ribs doing that. He was a sweet giant, almost as big as Andre." He lifted his chin, looking past Stranahan with his sad eyes.

Katie was walking out of a copse of aspen, trailed by Lothar. The gold leaves, the cobalt sky, the even deeper hue of the pool, it was hard to believe this had been a scene of tragedy.

"Hi, Bob. Come to keep her company again, have you?" Katie accepted the stick of gum he offered and sat on the ground with her arms hugging her knees. "There's an elk wallow just over that rise. It's all tracked up by a grizzly. A boar by the size of the prints."

Knudson nodded soberly. "I'll be careful."

He gazed into the depths of the Cobalt Necropolis. "It looked like the poor girl just walked right in. A person would have to be desperate."

He shook his head as he unfolded his chair and pulled out a black bound journal. Sticking two sharpened pencils behind the stub of a battle-scarred ear, he settled his bulk into the chair, the straps creaking from the abuse. "I just cannot understand it."

———

On the way back, Katie squatted by the trail as they waited for the herd of bison they'd seen earlier to mosey a safe distance away. "Imagine spending your life waiting for geysers to erupt that almost never erupt," she said. "It would be like marrying a man who can't get it up unless you catch him on the lunar eclipse."

"Yet he seemed like a very solid fellow." Stranahan lowered his binoculars. "He might be the first person I've met since moving here who speaks in complete, thoughtful, grammatically correct sentences."

"Uh-huh." Katie ran a chapstick across her lips. "I haven't met a geyser watcher yet who wasn't a sparkplug short of a slant six."

"That sounds like something Martha would say."

"Where do you think I got it?" She stood and dusted her pants. "Come on, let's get on up to the Lamar."

———

The Lamar Valley is America's Serengeti—a vast sea of grasses that bleach tan under the summer sun and roll like wheat with the autumn wind. From the sapphire ribbon of the river, the eye stretches nearly a mile to the slopes that flank Specimen Ridge. In the valley and on the slopes and on the benches above roam great herds of bison. Here, too, Stranahan knew, ranges the famous Yellowstone elk herd, trampling ground where the blood seeps deepest in June, when the cows give birth and the wolf packs pour out of the hills to run down their prey, enacting a dance of death that continued uninterrupted into the early twentieth century, when wolves were eradicated by gun and cyanide stick, only to begin again with their reintroduction. It was not so very different from the spectacle of the Tanzanian plains, which Stranahan longed to visit, where lion prides stalked migrating wildebeest and the crocodiles polished their teeth at the river crossings.

On this September afternoon, the people gathered for a glimpse of the ancient struggle would have looked at home in either venue.

"Yep," Katie said, as they swerved into a pullout behind a blue van with Simpson Wildlife Tours painted on the side, "it's the khaki brigade. If that girl hung out here looking for wolves, these folks will know about it."

A slim man bent to a spotting scope spoke without moving from the eyepiece. "I'll be with you in a second. Let me get this in focus and . . . okay, we got, yes, I think so, the beta female and the omega male, he's a shade darker. They're lying down just below that burned patch on the hillside. Everybody have a look. Be careful not to touch the focus."

The man turned a foxlike face to Katie. Certainly he remembered a punk-looking woman with orange eyes. He'd seen her on several occasions, back in June during the calving season, and yes, she was in the company of a man riding a motorcycle. "Those damned two-strokes that make all the racket." He shook his head. "They ought to be outlawed, just like the two-stroke snowmobiles. This is a place of worship. Even prayers should be whispered here."

When Katie asked what the man looked like, an expression of distaste crossed his face.

"He wore contact lenses that made him look like a vampire. Paraded around like he owned the valley. The way the girl kowtowed to him was sickening." He cocked his head so that they would follow him out of earshot of his clients. "He'd walk up behind her when she was bent to the scope, pump his pelvis up against her rear, not making a show of it but casually, like a dog lifting his leg. I told him this was not the place for that kind of behavior, that he was upsetting my clients. He just stared with those red eyes and shrugged. I complained to the Park Service but nothing came of it. I lost repeat clients because of that man; it was very off-putting."

No, he didn't know the man's name.

"When was the last time you saw him?" Katie said.

"Together with that woman? Probably not since early July. It was the morning the female alpha ran down a cow elk by the bend there opposite the cottonwoods. It's the last kill sighting we had for a while. Look, I really should get back."

"You said 'with that woman.' Have you seen this man with anyone else this summer?"

"No, but I left after the Fourth to set up a whale-watching tour in the San Juans."

Stranahan looked at the lettering on the van. "How long has Simpson Wildlife Tours been bringing clients to the Lamar Valley?" he said.

"Since the reintroduction. My partner and I bought the operation from the original owners four years ago."

"Then you may have seen this man in past years?" he prompted.

"A couple summers ago, and the summer before that. I don't recall seeing him at all last year."

"Okay, thinking back a couple years, did you see him in the company of a woman who had long red hair?"

"I saw him with two or three young women, but you're talking about Nicki."

Stranahan and Katie exchanged glances.

"How come I know her name and not the others? She wasn't like the rest. She was outgoing, very charming. Nicki's the only person I've ever seen who could draw your eye away from a wolf. One of my clients who's a children's book author said her hair was like spun gold that was struck with a match. Why?"

"She's missing," Katie said. She gave him the short version. "It's been in the papers. You haven't heard?"

"I never knew her last name," he said.

Katie handed the tour guide one of her cards. "If you see this man, whether he's alone, whatever, I want you to call me. Not after he's left, but as soon as you see him. It's important."

"There isn't any reception here."

"Then make an excuse and drive to the Yellowstone Institute. It can't be more than three miles. They'll contact me by radio."

A woman wearing a perfectly knotted red neckerchief was striding over. "The beta just stood up," she announced.

CHAPTER TWENTY-TWO

Feeding Time

After Stranahan picked up his rig at Katie's house—it had been a long day and their good-byes were perfunctory—he drove into West Yellowstone and ducked into Eagles, hoping for a chocolate malt. The soda fountain was closed for the season. Stranahan asked a cashier if he could borrow her phone.

"Ettinger."

"Did you get the DNA test back?"

"Say 'Did you get the DNA test back, please.'"

Silence. Then the sound of Martha Ettinger clearing her throat.

"Please," Stranahan said.

"It's a positive match for Nanika Martinelli. I'm sorry if I sounded flippant. I'll read a statement for the cameras tomorrow afternoon."

"You don't seem as concerned as I thought you'd be."

"I am and I'm not. I'm worried because I don't know how the wolf Nazis are going to react, and I'm not because it's closure. We're no longer failing at finding a missing woman because there's no woman to be found. Now all I have to do is kill some wolves hiding out in a mountain range the size of Rhode Island and find out how a man got himself impaled on the antlers of an elk, which has sort of got lost in the shuffle."

"You still like Bucky for that?"

"Setting aside my prejudice, he's the only one with both the opportunity and a possible motive. It could be that the wrangler's misfortune has nothing to do with the woman disappearing. I'm coming around to the possibility."

"The reason I'm calling—"

"I know, the girl with the contact lenses."

"I didn't know you were psychic, Martha."

"I just got off the phone with Katie."

"Well, if she told you about her, then she told you about the Lamar and the guy she was there with. It has to be the same man Asena Martinelli suspects of kidnapping her sister."

"This isn't your concern, Sean."

"Actually it is. I'm being paid to make it my concern."

"Let me rephrase. It isn't your business because the park is federal property. Katie will alert the proper authorities of any suspicions she has and they'll take it from there. But surely you can't still think that Nicki is alive. You don't come out the back end of a wolf alive. My advice is give the sister her money back and help us find the wolf pack."

"That's the Martha I know."

"What's that supposed to mean?"

"Good luck wolf hunting," Stranahan said, and hung up.

———

Stranahan opened the south-facing door of Eagles and felt the warmth of the sun. He noticed the big sign to the Paws of Yellowstone Wildlife Center across the street. All he knew about it was what Katie had told him, that it was a glorified zoo where problem bears trapped in the wild and unwanted show business wolves were sent to entertain Yellowstone tourists, most of whom slept in too late to have much hope of a predator sighting in the park. So far, Stranahan wasn't doing much better, his wolf sightings consisting of one rear leg and the two wolves the tour guide had centered in his spotting scope, which he and Katie had observed before they left the Lamar. Magnified thirty times, they were miniature, shimmering figures that gave you a headache if you looked very long.

Stranahan unfolded a ten from his money clip and bought a day pass. The ticket taker told him that the wolves had their second feeding in twenty minutes. She was clearly bored behind her smile and went back to the fantasy novel she'd been reading. A slow day, a calm before the storm. He had a feeling the center would do gangbuster business tomorrow, after Ettinger's press conference.

Outside the back door of the building, Stranahan followed paw prints set in cement, the path winding between cyclone fences with bears to his right, wolves to his left, and ravens perched everywhere. The one bear in the enclosure was lying with the back of his head on the ground, his nose pointing to heaven. He looked as bored as the ticket taker. Two wolves on a hillock were also lying down, their heads resting on crossed paws. Besides being nearly all white, they didn't look much different than German shepherds, just with broader heads and longer legs. The larger of the two half opened its eyes to regard Stranahan, then both wolves abruptly swung around and bounded off. They poured themselves into a small doorway in a stucco building, and Sean heard the door clang shut.

Stranahan entered the public side of the building, which had a large Plexiglas window overlooking the paddock. A man wearing Wellington boots entered from a side door, rubbing a fist into one eye. He introduced himself to the gathered tourists as James, said he was the caretaker and apologized because the naturalist was sick. He said he'd do his best to answer their questions. They were in luck today, he said. It was fish day. Stranahan glanced at the others who shared his luck, a broad-beamed father with two teenage sons who were his spitting image and his wife, who wore overalls over a Hoosiers sweatshirt and would have been equally at home as her husband anchoring an offensive line.

James led them to the big window, on the other side of which wound a manmade stream complete with riffles, pools and boulders. He said that the trout swimming in the stream were donated brood stock from the hatchery outside Bridger. He lectured them a few minutes about wolf hierarchy and told them to keep their eye on the alpha female with the grizzled ruff that was half the size of the other wolves but much more adept at catching trout. He left by the same door he'd entered and a few seconds later Stranahan heard a clang. Six wolves bounded into the paddock and set upon the trout, splashing, plunging their heads, chopping the water into a froth and pouring over and under one another in a liquid ballet. Within a few seconds the little female caught a trout, dropped it flopping on the bank, went back and caught another, then another, not bothering to eat or even to kill them.

The man returned to explain that the wolves had been fed and weren't hungry, so even though they would eventually polish off the trout on the bank, the fishing was more of a game than anything else. Stranahan asked what the wolves had been fed and was surprised to hear that it was elk, and that their diets consisted almost entirely of game meat donated by hunters.

James was wrapping his hair into a ponytail with a rubber band. "Either they bring it here or we drive out to meet them in the field. In the winter, we'll haul whole elk carcasses into the enclosure so they can eat the way they would on a natural kill, but we can't do that until the grizzly bears have denned up. The smell would attract them into town."

"Do you really think a wolf could have eaten that girl?" It was the woman in overalls. "When we heard it on the radio, some man said it would be the first person killed by a wolf in the United States. It's just horrible to think of, isn't it? But then a wolf has to eat, too. Nature's just cruel, that's all there is to it." Her eyes were bright.

"You'll have to forgive my wife," the man said. "Kathy's an . . . overly sensitive type."

"Oh, I can't help it, you know that." Now she was dabbing with a tissue. "Look at me. It's just the way the Lord made me."

James the caretaker blinked his spider-veined eyes.

"Stories of man-eating wolves have been passed down by Native Americans for hundreds of years"—his voice had assumed a professorial tone—"but when they got guns the killing stopped. Wolves are very intelligent and know when man poses a danger and when he's fair game. The reason you read more about man-eating wolves in Europe is because the people had pens to write about it but not the guns to stop it, and so the history of wolves preying upon people overseas lasted much longer than it did here, into the early twentieth century. In the park where they are protected, the wolves are again losing their fear of humans."

"But don't they hunt them in Montana?" the woman asked. "And use those awful leghold traps?"

"Yes, but the park acts as a reservoir and wolves are continually migrating outside the borders, so there is a transfusion of fearlessness. And it's justice, isn't it? We kill them. Why shouldn't they avenge their persecution?"

James said he had to go clean the bear paddock and told them to stay as long as they wanted to observe the wolves. When he'd gone, the woman brought her nose up to the window.

"They're so beautiful," she said. "Oh, I just can't think about it."

Stranahan thought about it, though. He thought about it as he walked back into town and he thought about it while he nursed a beer at the Wild West Pizzeria. By the time he entered the Book Peddler to order a coffee for the road he was thinking about something else. It was an hour and a half drive back to Bridger, but Katie's place on Cougar Creek was just eight miles up 191. He could stop there and offer to help bake dog biscuits. See where it led. He knew where it would lead.

Stranahan was a one-woman man. He'd never cheated on his wife, even after it became clear the marriage would fail. He'd not once thought about straying while under the spell of Vareda Beaudreux, and during the seven months he had lived with Martinique, right up until she left for veterinary school last February, well, he may have had the occasion to turn his eyes to follow the walk of another woman, but he'd remained firmly and happily monogamous. But the separations, the months that passed when Martinique was a voice on the telephone, and lately much less of that as she seemed to pull away, they wore on him. He wasn't made of the stone that made a mountain, and unlike a mountain he could not endure cold forever.

"You'll regret it," he said out loud as he got behind the wheel of the Land Cruiser. "In the morning, you'll regret it."

In the morning, Katie made buckwheat pancakes.

CHAPTER TWENTY-THREE

Honey Badger Don't Care

Sam Meslik was tightening the cinch straps on Stranahan's Adirondack Guideboat, securing it to the trailer, when Stranahan pulled up to the shop. He hadn't spoken to Asena Martinelli since the hairs had been positively identified as belonging to her sister and wasn't looking forward to breaking the news, if she hadn't yet heard from Ettinger.

"Kimosabe," Sam said. "Long time no see."

"Is Asena around?"

"She's been hibernating in the barn. I told her I'd take her to Wade Lake for a boat ride, see she got some sunshine. Then I got a call for a guide float, so now I'm torn between fishing for fun and fishing for my groceries. Maybe you can help me out of my predicament?"

Stranahan nodded. "Sure. I'll take her out."

"You look a little unkempt. Hard night?" Sam smiled lasciviously.

"I stayed over in West."

Sam worked a finger through a hole in a T-shirt that read Honey Badger Don't Care. He stirred his chest hair. "Who's the unlucky lady?"

"Nobody you know. Plus it's not what you think."

"Martinique know about this nobody I know."

"Martinique seems to be working her way out of the picture. Her choice, not mine."

Sam grunted sympathetically. "She was the one, buddy. Don't let her get away." He turned toward the barn door. "I'll rouse Sleeping

Beauty. She's a half decent fly caster if you can get her to pick up a rod. Nothing like the Venus, but the woman can fish some."

———

"Sam told me there was a story behind this boat, that you'd tell it better than he could."

She was sitting in the stern, facing Stranahan as he swept the oars, the tapering blades flexing, adding impetus to the stroke. The lake was capped with froth-edged wavelets that the sleek craft cut like a knife, the pine bank where they had launched pulling away, the eagle they had been watching in a tree diminishing until all they could see was the white dot of its head. Stranahan was, had been, always would be a river fisherman, but he had come to appreciate the gifts of lake fishing. The gentle rocking of the boat acted as a soothing balm. You could feel your heart rate go down.

He cocked a forefinger.

"That hole under the gunwale is where a bullet went through. About a foot to the left and we wouldn't be having this discussion." He began to relive the night on Quake Lake the summer before last, when two brothers had died and he had nearly joined them, losing four pints of blood when the blade of a custom-made hunting knife severed an artery in his shoulder. The story took them to the shoals at the far end of the lake.

"How did you come to own the boat?" Asena asked.

"Because it had been used in the commission of a crime, it became county property. The department held an auction of confiscated goods and I was high bidder."

"Isn't it like reliving the nightmare every time you take it out?"

"On the contrary. It reminds me how precious life is. That's why I never got around to patching the hole." He hesitated. "Asena, I hate to be the one who tells you—"

"You aren't. The sheriff called this morning, before she went on TV."

"I'm sorry."

He busied himself rigging a fluorocarbon leader onto a smoke-colored fly line. "When we get back to Sam's, I'm returning your money," he said, speaking around the olive damselfly nymph pattern pinched between his lips. He tied the nymph to the tippet and handed Asena the fly rod. "You don't have to do this, go fishing, you know."

"What should I be doing? Tell me what I should be doing."

Stranahan had no answer.

"I didn't think this was the season for damselflies," she said.

"It isn't. My hunch is the trout take it for a leech. Whatever they take it for, they take it."

Stranahan had only to see Asena roll the line off the water and double haul once to know that it was an injustice for Sam to have called her a "half decent" caster. She was an excellent caster and quickly picked up the retrieve that imitates the undulating pulse and pause swimming motion of a damsel nymph.

"I didn't hire you just to find my sister. I hired you to find the man who hurt her, who made her . . . damaged goods. Did you find him?"

"Don't do this to yourself, Asena. Let it go."

She cast again. There was steel in her voice. "I asked, 'Did you find him?'"

"It won't bring her back."

A trout cruising like a missile over the marl bottom took the fly and ran to the backing knot before Asena coaxed it to the net. Stranahan released it and turned to her.

"You're right, you're entitled to know."

She put the rod down while Stranahan told her about his trip with Katie to the Lamar. Her body became rigid when she heard about the tour guide's history with the man who'd been seen with her sister the summer before last. He watched her pull back into herself and look away at something only she could see, or perhaps at nothing. When he was finished, she spoke, her voice flat, her face expressionless.

"I want you to find him," she said. "I don't need you to believe that my sister is alive. It's enough that I believe it, and I don't care if that makes me look naive or unwilling to face reality. I have to know. A couple weeks salary is a small price to pay to know. Do you understand?"

For half an hour clouds had been building and Sean pointed them out. Though Adirondack Guideboats were stable craft—hunters used them to haul moose as far back as the late 1800s—Wade Lake was no place to be when the wind came up. Asena asked if she could row back and Stranahan was not surprised that she was as adept on the oars as she was with his six-weight. He relaxed while the guideboat bisected the waves over the graded depths, the water shading from green to deep blue that went black when the clouds covered the sun.

"This lake looks really deep," she said.

"It is. But Cliff Lake, the one we saw driving down the hill, is deeper—one hundred twenty feet right off the boat ramp. The state record rainbow trout was caught there back in 1952. Twenty pounds."

She whistled. Today's hat was an old fedora Sean had hung on a nail at Sam's fly shop as a wall decoration; it was pinned with rusty trout flies and she'd lined it with a bandana so it wouldn't fall off.

She caught him looking and apologized for not asking if was okay to wear it.

"I'm not looking at the hat," he said. "I'm looking at the woman under the hat. I suppose you have to get used to people staring."

She took the comment seriously.

"I never understood why men looked at me. It embarrassed me. Nicki had to tell me. My little sister, she was more worldly in that way, it was maybe the only way she was."

Stranahan said. "I'm only looking at you because you cast a tight fly line."

She dipped her head so that the hat obscured her face.

He reached over and lifted her chin with his forefinger. "Made you smile, didn't I?"

———

Sam was firing up the charcoal when they pulled up to the fly shack. A marinated loin of Kobe beef sweated blood on a platter on the side wing of the grill. He said it had been a tip from the client he'd fished that morning, squeezed Stranahan's shoulder by way of greeting, then removed the fedora Asena was wearing and kissed her on the top of the head. She put the hat back on and tilted the brim down, but not before Sean caught a glimpse of coppery hair. It was the first time he'd seen her without a hat and she looked younger and more vulnerable than the woman who'd fished from his boat. She excused herself to wash up. Killer jumped off the porch to follow her into the barn.

"Woman seems to have stolen my dog," Sam said. "They've become damned near inseparable in, what's it been, one week? Lord help the man who steps in between them or looks at her the wrong way."

He jutted his chin toward the cooler on the porch. "Beer me, Stranny."

Sean rummaged in the cooler. "Shadow Caster or Clothing Optional Pale Ale?"

CHAPTER TWENTY-FOUR

The Man with the Weatherby Kiss

When the patch of color shifted position, the cheek resting on the comb of the rifle stock inched forward. Contracting muscles drew the man's heavy eyebrows together. Sickle-moon scars shown whitely through the thicket of wiry hairs over his right eye. If there had been someone watching, and there was no one within miles, he might have said that the skin looked as if it had been cut by the rims of a dozen nickels. Without taking his eye from the scope, the man switched off the electronic game caller that had rendered the bleat of a dying rabbit, wiped his forefinger on his jeans, and then inserted it back through the trigger guard. He eased forward the two-position safety button on the Weatherby rifle.

Four hundred twenty yards across the canyon—the range finder in the scope calculated the distance to a nicety—a wolf stepped out of the pines into a small opening caused by an avalanche. It was a black wolf, fitting the description of the alpha male given to him at the FWP headquarters in Bridger. Gingerly, the man took up the slack in the trigger, which was set so light that a mouse scurrying through the trigger guard would trip the sear. Each beat of the man's heart caused the crosshairs to jump fractionally. Had his rest been perfectly steady, the man would have taken a breath, let half of it out and depressed the trigger between the pulses. But without a perfect rest, the crosshairs swam across the wolf's deep chest in unpredictable oblongs. He would have to shoot the instant they settled over the vital area, actually several inches higher to account for bullet drop. But this was not a conscious thought, nor, for that matter, did the man entertain any conscious thoughts. Rather, he had pulled down into a deep place in his being where time slowed and it was very calm and he was not cold but simply not present.

The report of the rifle echoed off the limestone walls. The man didn't hear it. Nor did he feel the recoil that jarred his shoulder. The sharp pain of the scope hitting him above his right eye, the steel rim cutting down to the bone—he felt that all right. When the sights settled back onto the opening, the wolf was gone. The man set aside the rifle and fished for a handkerchief to press over the wound. He tilted his head back and looked at a heaven he did not believe in and waited for the blood to stop flowing.

It took him twenty minutes to find a way down into the canyon and up the other side to the opening where the wolf had stood, where a spray of blood painted a dark-colored rock. The man sat down and drew out a cigarette from a pack in his shirt pocket. There had been a time in his life when he had limited himself to one cigarette a week, which he shared with his wife after making love on Saturday nights. After her death he had adopted the habit of smoking a cigarette before taking up the blood trail of any animal he shot, an odd transition of habit if he'd bothered to think about it, which he never had. He flicked a match head across his thumbnail and inhaled the sulfurous odor. He lit the cigarette. For the first time since seeing the patch of black in the trees, he permitted his mind to wander.

———

Calvin Barr had worked as a government trapper for Animal Damage Control for thirty-five years, starting during the era when trapper was a very loose definition of his job, which consisted almost entirely of using a syringe to poison horse meat with sodium fluoroacetate, known in the business as 1080, which indiscriminately killed anything that fed on the carcasses. When large-scale poisoning was banned, he learned how to set an M-44 that shot cyanide into the mouths of coyotes and foxes. He also became certified as an aerial gunner, killing coyotes from helicopters with a 12-gauge shotgun. His heaviest bags came in winter, when coyotes loitered around the herds and showed against a pelt of snow.

In the first five years of his service alone, Barr put at a rough estimate that he had accounted for some 800 foxes, 250 bobcats, 30 mountain lions, about the same number of bears and at least 3,000 coyotes, and that didn't count coyotes killed by poisoned carcasses—God knows how many there had been before the ban, the dead prairie dogs strewn across the ground like fallen bowling pins around the bait stations. It was a slaughter that jaded him, and eventually had educated him to its ineffectiveness. How many sheep and cattle had the blood on his hands actually saved? A lot, probably, in the case of coyotes, which were enemy number one in the eyes of the federal agency, though wholesale killing often missed the one or two animals that actually took their toll on the sheep, and aerial gunning was expensive, nearly always costing more money than the value of the livestock lost.

But far too often, he learned, predators were blamed for killing animals that had perished for other reasons. When the trauma that indicated the attack of a particular predator was missing—lions, for example, left fang marks in the neck and licked hair away from areas they were eating with their raspy tongues, bears turned a sheep inside out as they ate it—Barr got to the bottom of the mystery by drawing his skinning blade. Sometimes, he found that the culprit was the rancher himself, who perhaps had left dead livestock lying around for scavengers to eat, or had pressed too deeply with the branding iron, with the resulting wound becoming infected. Dehydration, disease and damnable weather took a far greater toll on livestock than talon and tooth.

Like Alfonso Martinelli, who had been his supervisor for two years back in the nineties, Barr had helped live trap several of the Canadian wolves that were released into Yellowstone Park and Idaho in the reintroduction effort. It was a job that, as the wolf population skyrocketed, came to include killing the descendants of the very wolves he'd trapped for release. The irony wasn't lost on him. More than once, he had asked himself what the point of reintroducing wolves was if all you were going to do was kill them later.

Thinking of Martinelli made Barr shake his head. He'd been shocked when his current supervisor had called to inform him that a wolf was suspected of killing a human being. He'd been shocked again to learn it was the daughter of the man he'd once worked with.

Barr dug a grave for his cigarette with the heel of his boot. He looked again at the heaven he didn't believe in, then at the rock. The blood was pink and frothy. Lung blood. The alpha would not have gone far. Barr found it dead thirty yards along the contour of the slope, lying on its unwounded side with blood on its muzzle. The bullet hole on the shoulder was red on black. Bubbles of blood formed and softly popped over the opening as gases were released from the body.

Barr knelt beside the animal and took off his wool Kromer cap. He passed his hand over the wolf's flanks and then pressed the lid of its glassy left eye until it no longer stared at nothing.

———

Barr radioed in the kill and found that he was a popular man when he drove his ATV back to the logging trace where he'd left his pickup. The group included Julie McGregor, Kellen Kirkpatrick, who was Barr's supervisor from Missoula, the county sheriff and a representative from the U.S. Fish and Wildlife Service, flown up from Denver to put the government spin on the story. Before Barr had shut down the quad, eager bodies were pressing around the wolf strapped to the utility rack, its head bent to one side with fangs bared, its tail and hindquarters hanging stiffly off the rack, the body in the early stages of rigor mortise. Barr's eyes found the biologist, whom he'd met with the day before, after driving in from his home in Darby.

"This look like the alpha from the Bald Ridge Pack to you?" he said.

McGregor bent forward to examine the back of the wolf. The alpha had been photographed twice during aerial surveys the previous winter and had a broken stripe of light gray over his spine.

"That's him," she said. "We'll autopsy his digestive tract at the lab. But it's been more than a week. My guess is if he consumed the victim, any trace will have passed by now. We'll have a better chance scraping the claws and teeth for DNA."

"How soon do you think you'll get the others?" It was the rep from Fish and Wildlife.

Barr shook his head, not trying to hide his disgust. "Wolf has a say in that. The female alpha might lead them to another part of the range after this. Might not. If the pack stays in the basin, I have snares set and ten traps baited with lure. I'll check the sets tomorrow morning."

McGregor nodded. "Let's get him loaded up."

Barr ignored the press of willing hands and hoisted the wolf onto his shoulders, so that the head lolled down against one side of his chest. He'd had a lot of practice guessing the weights of wolves he'd trapped and sedated, and put this one at about 120 pounds. An average-sized male, in his prime by the wear on his teeth.

After McGregor had hauled the wolf away in the bed of her pickup, Barr answered questions brusquely and made busy with his gear. Finally the Fish and Wildlife rep took the hint, and Barr's company dwindled to his supervisor and Sheriff Ettinger.

"Those look big enough to catch a bear," Ettinger said.

Barr finished strapping the two Brawn #9 traps to the cargo rack of his ATV.

"They aren't," he said. "But they're big for a wolf trap. I wouldn't use them if we were trapping for release. Too much chance of breaking a bone. You want to trap a wolf for release, you don't use anything bigger than a Newhouse four and a half. I mostly use number fours with button teeth I forge myself. People think teeth break legs, but it's offset jaws that break legs. Sometimes you'll mangle a toe with a toothy trap, but nothin' a vet can't fix."

Kellen Kirkpatrick had heard it all before. He interrupted to tell Barr to call him after checking his sets and left. Barr and Ettinger watched the truck out of sight.

"He knows damn well I got no way to call him here." Barr spat on the ground.

"Tell me about wolf trapping," Ettinger said.

"Well . . ." Calvin Barr was not a garrulous man, but like most men who knew their subject, he liked to put people straight. Especially with wolves, because there was no animal on earth more misunderstood. He liked that Ettinger was interested, not just working an angle.

He said, "Gotta understand a wolf's a tough critter. He's got strong bones, and he's not like a raccoon, who will chew off his toes to escape. It can happen but not usually, not if your conscientious about checking your line. Your biggest danger with a trapped wolf is overheating during transportation. I never like to set a trap in the sun. He's a dog, and a dog doesn't have sweat glands. The only way he can get rid of heat is panting. So you want to hose him down and keep him cool."

"Have you relocated a lot of wolves?"

"About a hundred and a quarter, starting before the reintroduction. Most of them I trapped weren't guilty of the crimes they were supposed to have committed. Just like the enviros calling me Killer Barr. They got it wrong. Sure, I gave the go-ahead for killing a lot of wolves before the state took over management, but only if I had irrefutable evidence of livestock depredation. The only cure for a confirmed killer is a bullet. You relocate them they just get into trouble somewhere else. But like I said, that usually wasn't the case. Killing wolves isn't something I look forward to, not at all. If I had my way, I'd never touch a trigger on one again."

"Your forehead would thank you," Ettinger said. "Looks like you got kissed by your scope."

Barr's laugh was short. "You'd think after forty years I'd have learned not to crawl a stock."

"So this wolf," Ettinger said, "do you think he killed the Martinelli girl? I didn't ask earlier because people would think I'm trying to insert doubt into a story they've shut the book on, that I'm some closet wolf lover. But now that it's just you and me, I'd value your opinion."

"You're the first person who's asked that question. All the stink and you're the first. What do I think? I think if you tell me that girl's hair was found in wolf scat, then I have to believe you. But it goes against the grain of everything I know about wolves."

"Why?" Ettinger crossed her arms.

"First off, you had a full scale manhunt for her, dogs, planes, the works, and they never found one trace—no footprint, no clothes, no scent."

"We found her hat about a thousand vertical feet above the kill. We think she was bucked from her horse, maybe became disoriented."

Barr furrowed his brow and winced. He tentatively touched the clot of blood over his right eye.

"I guess what I'm saying is, if she was killed by a wolf, I'd like to think I would have found the site. Wolf brings down a deer, that's where he eats it, where he brought it down. Now a lion, he might drag it a ways and bury what's left. Bear will do the same. Not a wolf. He leaves it where it falls. All that blood and bone, you got good men on this, they'd have their eyes to the sky looking for birds. Bird'll follow a wolf pack. Your people would see crows circling, they'd see ravens, turkey vultures. But she just disappeared into thin air. I'm not saying a wolf didn't do it, just that you'd expect to find evidence if it did."

"You said 'First off.' What else?"

"Well, the scat being found the way it was, that throws me. It seems a mite . . . convenient. Out in the open on a big rock, such an obvious signpost, right on the route that the scatman was checking? Where he was bound to look? I don't know, you tell me."

Ettinger decided to level with him. "Cal, the reason I'm asking you this is one of the men I work with has been talking to Nicki Martinelli's sister, and she's got a different idea about what happened."

He listened, interrupting only once to comment on the bottles of wolf lure in Martinelli's root cellar. "That Love Potion Twenty-nine was Alfonso's secret recipe. Had some roadkill tomcat in it if I remember correctly, you sprinkled a few drops where you buried a trap. Caught a helluva lot of wolves, that lure."

The trapper found a toothpick in his pocket that he'd whittled from the penis bone of a raccoon. He worked it as Ettinger picked up the thread and then wound down.

"So this fella," he said, "he's supposed to have somehow found out she was living in the valley and went up there in the basin and kidnapped her?"

"That's the sister's thinking."

"I'd say her story makes sense, weren't for finding that hair."

Martha steered the conversation back to the Martinellis.

"You knew her father. Did you know Nicki?"

"I met her once at a trapper rendezvous," Barr said. "Up on the Middle Fork of the Teton. Looked about sixteen, a feast for the eyes. Had a wild streak in her, no doubt. Put a coonskin cap on and just run around full of the dickens, that hair flying out. Friendliest creature you ever met. But then the next day she was more sober, seemed like a sensible young woman. Called me Mr. Barr. She reminds me why I never did understand women. You think you got 'em figured, but you don't. Even my wife before she passed." He nodded to himself, then colored, remembering it was a woman he was talking to.

"What about Asena?"

"No, her I never met. I didn't know Alfonso had another daughter. But he didn't have a lot of words—that you'd understand, I mean. Man could go on and on in French. I wouldn't have known he had Nicki if it wasn't for that rendezvous. So the sister, she's here in the valley, you say?"

Ettinger nodded. "Came down from B.C. where she works as a counselor in the schools. The girls grew up in a cabin somewhere north of nowhere. She's the one who stayed."

"You get outside Vancouver, just about all B.C., is nowhere." Barr put the toothpick back in his pocket.

"That cellar at her dad's place," he said. "You think you might talk to her, see if she minded I stopped by and helped myself to a bottle of the twenty-nine?"

CHAPTER TWENTY-FIVE

Stealing Souls

Harold Little Feather was standing in the great common room of the Lake Hotel in Yellowstone Park, looking out the windows at the vast roll of the slate-colored lake, when his phone vibrated. He'd meant to turn it off. He knew there was a cell tower disguised as a pine tree near the Old Faithful Inn. He didn't know they'd put one up here. Pretty soon there will be no place sacred, he thought. He flipped open the phone.

It was Martha Ettinger.

"What are you doing?"

"I'm looking at Yellowstone Lake, drinking tea with my pinky cocked."

"That doesn't sound like you."

"I'm a man of mystery, Martha."

Such was the manner they were back to now, easy enough in the light of day. It had taken a long time.

Harold glanced over at his sister's in-laws, who were up on vacation from Flagstaff. They were lounging on the mauve wicker furniture, listening to a woman playing a blond grand piano while waiting to be called for their dinner reservation. Harold had a hunch the lamb cutlets with the mint jelly sauce weren't going to be in his future.

"Uh-huh," he said. "No, this is the first I've heard of it." A minute later. "So I have Katie and Stranahan to thank for this. You don't see a jurisdiction problem?" He heard Ettinger say, "Not as long as you don't arrest anybody."

He closed the phone and this time remembered to turn it off. His sister, Janice, sidled up to him. He told her who'd called.

"When are you going to tell her you're a single man again?" Harold had stopped seeing his ex-wife over the summer.

"When I'm good and ready," Harold said.

"So you got to go, right? What should I tell them? They like you."

"They think I'm a novelty 'cause I look so much more like an Indian than you. It will wear off."

"You've been leaving me to do whatever since we were kids. Where to this time?"

"Up to the Lamar. Sheriff wants me to check out a man there who thinks he's a wolf."

———

At the pullout, Harold stepped out of his pickup and arched his back to get the cricks out, his long braid tracking the hollow in his back. He crossed his arms so that his biceps popped out below the cut-off sleeves of a check flannel shirt. Let them get a good look at the tattoos, the weasel tracks hunting around his left upper arm, the elk tracks hunting around the right. He could feel their eyes on him as he walked up to the rail by the interpretive sign and placed his hands on it.

"Beautiful, isn't it?" Harold spread his arms to encompass the valley of the Lamar.

The man standing a few yards away had hair as long as Harold's, tied off in a ponytail that stuck through the adjustable band of a Great Falls Dodgers baseball cap. He wore an unsnapped Harley vest over a pelt of chest hair. Tiffany blue stud earrings added a feminine touch. His eyes were very dark red, almost maroon. He was wearing the wolf pendant Ettinger had told him to look for. The woman, hardly more than a girl, had blond hair with red tips, sported a nose stud and had blazing orange eyes. A rim of baby fat blossomed between the bottom of her T-shirt and the top of her jeans, which were decorated with fake pearl beads outlining phases of the moon.

"Are you here for the wolves?" the man said. "In some Native American cultures, wolves were man's brothers. There was a Crow Indian here this summer; he told me about the myth of Running Wolf."

"Is that right?" Harold kept his hands on the railing, his eyes on the skyline.

"I'm Blackfeet," he said. "The wolf may be my brother, the Crow I'm not so fond of."

"If you stick around, you might see the Thunderer Mountain Pack. They were howling this morning like they'd made a kill." The man pointed across the valley.

The girl looked shyly at Harold, not an inconsiderable achievement for someone whose irises were the color of a fire season sunrise. "Are you full-blooded?" she said.

The presumption of some white people never ceased to amaze him. "Sure," he said. "Grew up on the rez. Mama cooked fry bread. Known seducer of white women." He watched her blush and laughed. "I'm fooling with you. I'm probably the only Native American on the eastern front can't make the claim he's seen a wolf. Thought I'd take a drive and rectify that. My wife's in-laws are staying at the Lake Hotel. Would either of you care for a beer? Pass the time while we wait."

They passed the time, the man and woman drinking the beer that Harold's sister had packed, Harold sipping at a Coke and wondering what he was doing there. Ettinger had told him to engage the couple and see if he could learn their names and where they lived. She'd tell him the whole story later.

Harold jutted his chin toward the motorcycle. "Isn't that one of the old 350 Hondas?"

"It's a '69 CB," the man said. "Somebody fried the electrical system trying to jump it with a car battery and the spark plug threads were stripped. I picked up the pieces and restored it. That red on the tank is the original paint job."

"I had a Scrambler," Harold said. "Nineteen-inch front wheel, high-set exhaust, same model the late, great Jimmy Morrison drove except his was psychedelic. Gas tank on mine was what they call candy blue. Do you mind if I take a picture? I got a brother rebuilds old bikes who'd like to see it. They made a ton of 350s but it's hard to find one hasn't been repainted or screwed with."

"Sure, what's the harm?" the man said.

Harold took photos from a couple of angles, making certain he got close-ups of the license plate.

"How about one with you two on it?" he said.

"Can we, Fen?" It was the woman, a child's pleading note in her voice.

The man looked sharply at her and then shook his head. "No, I don't think so. Got to keep the soul in the body. You understand, being Native yourself."

"Hey, no problem," Harold said. "I'm a medicine man. We still have lots of people on the rez who feel that way." Under the pretense of looking at the photos on the LCD screen, he switched the settings of the point-and-shoot to its silent operation mode.

———

Two hours later he reached Ettinger from the lobby at the hotel.

"Woman's name is Deni, short for Denise. I heard her call the man Fen. He didn't seem to like her saying it, shot her a look. They didn't offer last names and I didn't press. Deni said the contact lenses burned her eyes. At one point she wanted to remove them, but he said no. Not a mean 'no,' not a loud 'no,' just 'no.' I got the feeling she does what he tells her to."

"Did you ask why they wore them?"

"The man said it was to pay respect to the wolves. What's this about, Martha?"

"A long story." She filled him in briefly, the missing woman's sister suspecting foul play and the wolf watcher with the red eyes the prime suspect. Martha said that the guide who led wolf tours in the park had spotted the motorcycle couple that afternoon and checked in at the Yellowstone Institute as Katie Sparrow had instructed. Katie was on backcountry patrol by Electric Peak and told the ranger to relay a message to the sheriff.

Ettinger said, "People working behind my back seems to be becoming the order of the day."

"I thought the wolves ate her. I thought it was a done deal," Harold said.

"That's what the evidence suggests, but Sean's inclined to give some credence to the sister's suspicion. Let's give him the benefit of the doubt. Anyway, what were your impressions of this man? Could you buy him as a Svengali Manson type?"

"If you're asking did he look like a kidnapper, I'd say no. What he really reminded me of was the Sunday school Jesus picture my sister has in her bathroom, but anybody has serpent eyes burning out of his head is out on the small branches in my book."

"I don't suppose they told you where they lived?"

"No, when I asked he said, 'From here, man, from here.' When I asked her it was the same answer, him answering for her and her looking away. But I can give you the plate number. He wouldn't let me take their photos but I got a few when they weren't looking. Not good enough to suck the souls out of their bodies, so don't get your hopes up. I'll download them into my sister's computer when we get back to Pony and attach them for you."

"You did good, Harold. Thanks for helping me on this."

It was nine forty-five and the restaurant was still open. Harold asked for a table in the back, where he could see the black waitress with the seventies Afro who had taken his breakfast order. He looked at her name tag, then up into her golden brown eyes.

"You wouldn't happen to have any of that lamb left, would you, Alexis?"

CHAPTER TWENTY-SIX

A Piece of a Puzzle

"That's enough, Choti girl," Stranahan said. He clicked his fingers and told the sheltie to stop barking as he removed the sticks closing the flap of the tipi.

"Hey inside, it's Martha," Ettinger called out.

"I know it's you. You must have Goldie, huh?"

"Can she come in? I don't want her running around after dark. That lion's back in the canyon again. Pablo showed me its track." Pablo Mendoza was a baritone for the New York Metropolitan Opera who had a residence at the road end, a half mile up the canyon from Martha's place.

Stranahan grasped the handle of the lantern to make sure it wasn't tipped while the dogs bounded around the tipi. When they'd settled at the foot of his cot, he opened his hand to direct Martha to the folded buffalo blanket to his right.

"You might fool some people with that Indian tradition bullshit, but you don't fool the sheriff of Hyalite County," she said. But she took the seat anyway, pulling her legs up under her in a lotus position. She said, "Harold had an afternoon you'd find interesting."

Stranahan interlaced his fingers while she spoke.

"Fen," he said, his voice thoughtful. "I heard that name before."

He reached for the box underneath his cot. It contained the journals written by Alfonso Martinelli, the ones Carter Monroe had found in the cabin. There were twenty in all, one for each calendar year of the past two decades. The writing was dense, the hand precise and the letters open looped—a schoolboy's script.

"Let me see an early one." Ettinger extended her hand for the journal.

"They're mostly of the 'what I trapped today' nature," Stranahan said. "Not much personal stuff. One thing though, the old man was a list maker. Made lists of everything—catch versus escape ratios for different types of traps, gear lists for running his lines, prioritized lists of the most common reasons for livestock deaths. He had a list of what he referred to as 'Honest Abe's,' ranchers who took care of their stock and actually wanted him to find out what was killing them. He had another for ranchers who blamed wolves for any livestock fatalities, never mind that his autopsies drew different conclusions. That list was called 'Ranchers Who Cried Wolf.' It's circled in green highlighter, the only list that's marked that way."

"What's that have to do with what's his name, the guy with the red eyes?"

"I'm a Montanan now, Martha. I get to things in a circumspect way. Alfonso made a list of wolves in mythology. Actually two—one for myths about good wolves and one of myths about evil wolves." Stranahan pulled out a journal dating back four years. "Here it is," he said.

Martha scooted closer to him and together they looked at the page. Sean ran his finger halfway down and tapped his nail under the name. "Fenrir (Fen)." "It's a wolf in Norse mythology," he said. "This is the list of bad wolves."

"If you say so," Martha said. "What language is that?"

"It's mostly French words with some Italian. Martinelli grew up in the mountains north of Nice. That's where he learned to trap wolves."

"They have wolves in France?"

"In the Hautes-Alpes. Same wolf causing the same old controversy. Wolves and sheepherders are at each other's throats in France no different than they are here."

"Humpff. I would have never guessed. So you can read this?"

"No, but Asena could."

"What's it say about this Fenrir? There's words after it."

He shook his head. "I don't know. The only name I had her translate the origin of was Amorak, which is a lone wolf in Inuit legend. He's in the list of good wolves, see?" Stranahan pointed out the name. "According to the legend, Amorak killed the weak and sick caribou so the herds became healthy."

"So this guy, you figure he took the names of wolves for his first and his last names. Fenrir Amorak or Amorak Fenrir."

"One or the other," Stranahan said. "I have a book on wolf myths but I left it at my studio."

"Let's walk up to the house and boot up my computer. Bring the journals. We can research 'Fenrir' and then I want to check in with Judy. She was going to pull the DMV sheet on the license plate of that motorcycle."

"What made you change your mind about Amorak?"

"Something the wolfer told me. He killed one of the Bald Ridge Pack today. I'll fill you in on the walk up."

———

"Just set them on the stump while I make us some tea." Ettinger gestured toward the cross-sectioned trunk of an enormous Douglas fir that served as her desk. Stranahan switched on the track lighting and set down the journals.

"I didn't know you liked puzzles, Martha."

A partially completed jigsaw puzzle, acacia trees and elephants under the snow cap of Kilimanjaro, was spread across one end of the desk.

"When I'm working late, a few minutes on the puzzle helps clear my mind." *And pass the long Montana night alone*, which went unsaid.

"I guess your love life is about as active as mine," Stranahan said.

Martha poured the tea into two cups. *Yet here we are again*, she thought, standing right in front of each other. She kept her voice casual. "Did I tell you I received a 'Save the Date' from Bucky Anderson and Evelyn Culpepper. To their wedding next June. Bucky's got some nerve, huh? He wrote a PS that I ought to take you. I'm thinking I might put in an appearance just to spite him."

"Then let's go," Stranahan said. "You can look daggers at him while we dance."

"I'd rather arrest him. But maybe you're right."

"Sure. It will be fun."

Martha felt a flush of blood. She'd received the note in the morning's mail and had been filled with anxiety since, wondering how to bring it up or even if she would. Now she had a date with Sean Stranahan, even if it was half a year down the road. And he'd made it easy. She felt a release of tension as she furrowed her brow, feigning concentration.

"Fenrir, Fenrir," she muttered as the Mac booted up. "Where are you, Fenrir?" She clicked on a site titled Wolves in Myth and Astrology and read aloud.

"Fenrir, offspring of the trickster fire god, Loki . . . gave birth after eating the heart of a giantess." She read the rest of the thumbnail description.

"Fenrir was badass, no question," Stranahan said.

"Badass?"

"Sam had me watch the honey badger video."

Ettinger's expression was blank.

"You don't know about that?"

"Some of us have work to do. So . . . what? This guy takes the names of wolves in ancient mythology, the odds of this being his real name are not good. But what if he had his name changed? If he's in the system, either one of these names would stick out like a snakebit thumb."

"What makes you think he'd have a record?"

Ettinger awarded him one of her withering looks.

"Okay," Sean said. "The guy's a dirtbag, it follows."

"Remember what you said to me? That Nicki told her sister the man would disappear now and then, never said where he went. Maybe he was dealing or, I'm thinking out loud here, doing something else criminal, could be anything. Then about a year and a half ago, he disappears. Summer passes. Fall, winter, spring. At no time does he make any effort to contact Martinelli. He doesn't resurface until June, when he pulls up to the fly shop on the Kootenai, looking for Nicki."

"He was arrested," Stranahan said.

Martha nodded. "That's what I'm thinking. Or picked up on an outstanding warrant. Anyway, he goes away to a place with five-inch windows. We can narrow the records, search by age, likely period of parole, state of incarceration. It all depends on whether he went away on his given name or his wolf names . . ."

An inset message had appeared in the lower right corner of the computer screen, alerting Ettinger of incoming mail.

"Or maybe we won't have to," she said. "Let's see what Judy found."

The e-mail included an attachment, which Martha opened. It was a scanned motorcycle registration from the DMV.

Martha nodded. "J. Todd McCready. DOB 06/24/1981. Address on Shields Valley Road, Wilsall, MT." She looked up. "Why, he's just over the hill."

Stranahan felt a tingle, a chill of excitement that crawled up his arms, lifting the hairs. "He's older than I thought he'd be," he said.

"Predators are usually older than the prey."

"Maybe someone ought to drive up there and knock on the door," Stranahan said.

"Maybe someone shouldn't do anything stupid," Ettinger said.

"He wouldn't do that."

"Then maybe someone should. Frankly, I have a hard time buying that this guy kidnapped the woman, scat or no scat. But if she's alive, I do think there's a possibility she ran off with him."

"She could be there right now."

"You'll report back to me."

"Does this mean I'm back on the payroll? I have a contract with Asena through next week."

"No, it means I care what happens to you."

"I still don't have a cell phone."

The withering look.

"I amend my statement. I don't have a phone but I will by tomorrow. Is that better?"

"Call so I have your number. And leave these journals with me. I'd like to run a few more names."

Stranahan stood up. His eyes fell on the puzzle, and he spent a minute trying to fit a piece.

"There's only about seven hundred to go," Martha said. "I'll be cross-eyed until next summer."

She felt the chill air come in when Stranahan left. "Don't let the lion get you," she said after him.

She watched the beam of his headlamp bob down the road from her kitchen window, felt the pull in her heart that belied the indifference of her comment. There wasn't any real danger from a lion, was there? But then there wasn't supposed to be from a wolf, either. She poured another cup of chamomile and sat down at the puzzle. She'd completed the border and the parade of elephants crossing the plain near the center. The grass was what stumped her, hundreds of pieces of a tawny color all more or less the same. You could work from the inside out or the outside in. Working from the outside in was what she'd been doing the past week. She'd accepted the borders of the Martinelli case, the central construct that the girl had been eaten by a wolf. It naturally followed that a wolf had killed her and was somewhere in the evergreen ridges flanking Papoose Basin. Stranahan, the wolfer, Harold—they had all given her reason to suspect that she might get further working from the inside out, and that the most dangerous animal on the mountain didn't necessarily have the sharpest claws, but perhaps took on the semblance of a wolf only in the drama of his eyes. Martha did not approve of speculation without fact, and a human hair in a pile of wolf scat was fact. Still . . .

She tried the puzzle piece in the patch of grass to the right of the leading elephant, a one-tusker cow followed by a toto. It fit. She blew on her tea and picked up another.

CHAPTER TWENTY-SEVEN

Papier-Mâché Mountains

From the vantage at the turnoff, the ranch house looked to be built of Lincoln logs, with a green-colored roof and a barn with Ringling Feed and Seed painted in peeling block letters. Someone had spray painted a *W* over the *S*—Feed and Weed. The mailbox read Oddstatter. Stranahan left the motor running and got out to stretch.

The Shields Valley was the lost Montana the Madison had been thirty years ago, before the ranches got subdivided when the owners grew old and their children opted out of the life, leaving behind the fence spreader, the posthole digger and the antiquated notion that a day begins at dawn. The entrance road was potholed from summer rains and the baked ruts showed the tread of every tire that had made the turn. Stranahan did not see a motorcycle track.

He climbed into the Land Cruiser and motored back the way he'd come. At a bridge he strung his four-weight, tied on a grasshopper fly and began false casting as he hiked down to the river. Stranahan had never fished the Shields and was surprised to find it was a cutthroat stream. It took him three or four fish to get used to the way cutthroat trout rose to the fly in a lazy roll, a yellow coin turning over, as if they had all the time in the world to eat lunch. In all he took a dozen fish in two hours, none big and all within earshot of the road should a motorcycle grumble past. It didn't.

In rural Montana, you seldom get as far as knocking before a door opens, friendly and occasionally not friendly ranch dogs having made the announcement of the visitor in no uncertain terms. The

Oddstatter place was as silent as a winter night. Stranahan rapped again.

"Hold your horses."

The woman who opened the door wore a hooded UM sweatshirt tucked into overalls. Late fiftyish. Her voice came from her chest.

"You're going to ask me if you can hunt, I'm going to tell you no. It's nothing personal, it's just the way it is. If I gave every man permission they'd be parked from here to Wilsall."

"I'm not a hunter," Stranahan said.

She seemed to see him for the first time. The crow's feet grew deeper at the corners of her eyes.

"Then what are you, some kind of communist?" Her face wasn't flat so much as wide, with high cheekbones. She'd been pretty once, Stranahan realized.

He smiled at her effort at humor. "Actually, I'm looking for someone."

"There's no one here but me and the mister."

"His name is Todd, Todd McCready. He told me if I got out this way to look him up. He had a motorcycle I was interested in buying."

"When would that be?"

"Just a couple weeks ago. I met him in Yellowstone Park."

"You better come in and talk to Rayland."

The kitchen Stranahan followed her into had a long unchanged look, everything vintage from the baked enamel coffeepot on the soft-shouldered gas range to the maple kitchen table and mismatched ladderback chairs, in one of which sat a man with a haggard face not unlike a bloodhound's. He looked up so he could see Stranahan from under his heavy-rimmed glasses. Stranahan said hello, noticing a cane hooked within reach on a kitchen cabinet drawer.

"This man's asking after Todd. He wants to buy his motorcycle."

To Stranahan she said, "Todd's Rayland's sister's boy."

Stranahan felt the walls draw in, the uncomfortable silence.

"He doesn't want to talk about him," the woman said. In a louder voice, "You don't want to talk about him, do you, Rayland?"

The man's eyes swam behind the glasses' lens.

"You want to show this man your trains? I'm sure he'd like to see them."

The man reached out to hook the cane and got slowly to his feet. He was taller than Stranahan, even stooped over, spare but big boned with squared-off shoulders and a prominent Adam's apple. His hands were liver spotted and had abnormally long fingers. He shuffled toward a back room, tapping the cane.

"He'll show you his engines," she said to Stranahan. "He files them out of brass, people come from all around since they did that story in *Montana Quarterly*. Once he gets talking, you can ask him about Todd again. But he won't know any more than I do. We haven't seen that boy in at least three years. Four? Maybe four. He used to work the haying season. We took him on as a favor to Knute, that's Rayland's brother-in-law. That motorcycle you're looking to buy was a month's pay for the last summer he worked here; I know, I'm the one found it in the *Mini-Nickel*." She looked past Stranahan's shoulder. "Go on now, he's waiting on you."

He found Rayland Oddstatter in an unfinished addition to the house with taped drywall, and a full-sized Ping-Pong table minus the net, upon which was spread an elaborately detailed papier-mâché mountain range. Two HO-gauge model trains were chugging around and through the mountains, past tiny ranch houses with miniature wooden cattle in the flatlands and the figures of elk, bears and mountain goats in the high country. Stranahan recognized the odd tilting canine teeth of the papier-mâché mountains. They were the western front of the Crazies, the panorama visible from Shields Valley Road. He recognized the ranch house he was standing in.

"You ever seen anything like that before?" the man said. Oddstatter was sitting before a bench-mounted vise and had a bastard file in his fingers. The cowcatcher of an old-fashioned steam engine was emerging from a solid block of brass clamped in the vise. His voice had a rasp.

Stranahan made appreciative comments.

"That there boy," the man said with his eyes on his work, "that Todd gave my sister a heart attack with his carrying-on. We shoulda' bid him riddance after the first summer. Never done a lick of work he wasn't sitting on a tractor seat. He was good around motors, I'll give him that. But my daughter could fork more hay in an hour than he did all day. He's the one defiled my barn. I got nothing good to say about him."

But he had more to say about him, haltingly drawn forth as Oddstatter's memory searched its dusty drawers, and when Stranahan rose to leave and glanced at the wall clock, which was set inside a leather yoke strung with cobwebs, he was surprised to see that nearly an hour had passed.

The woman saw him out to the porch.

"He tell you what you want to know?" she said. Her cheek muscles drew up, but it was not the same smile he'd seen before. Her eyes were hard as obsidian. "'Cause it isn't about buying a motorcycle." When Stranahan didn't answer, she said, "He had no reason to give you this address. None."

"You're right," Stranahan said. "He didn't. I'm sorry to have bothered you, but I thought he might be traveling with a young woman, someone who is with him against her will or at least her better judgment. I found your place from the DMV log. His motorcycle registration listed your address."

"You should be ashamed of yourself."

Stranahan held her eyes. "I don't know what you know about the past few years of that man's life, but he's done worse things than spray paint a barn."

Mrs. Oddstatter—she had never offered a first name—relaxed her tightly compressed lips.

"This young woman," she said, "would she be your wife? Or your daughter? Todd likes them young. He'd take a truck into town and bring in girls on a Friday night, take them up to the barn loft. I caught him once coming out with the daughter of a woman I know. Dewy as a newborn lamb and not a lick smarter. It was statutory rape's what it was."

"The woman I'm looking for is the one who disappeared from the Culpepper Ranch in the Madison Valley."

"She was killed by wolves." She stated it as a fact.

"It's possible she wasn't."

"So what are you, some kind of environmentalist thinks wolves eat daisies, so there's got to be another explanation?"

"I work for Martha Ettinger, she's—"

"Martha. I know Martha."

It was the magic word. Stranahan could tell by the change in her voice.

"She's one of my best friends," he said, pushing the connection.

"I don't know what he told you in there," the woman said, gesturing toward the house, "but Todd called here this summer, June, maybe July. I remember the river was over its banks."

"He came here?"

"No, he called, what did I just tell you? I didn't say anything to Rayland because it would trouble him. Todd . . . has a way of getting something on you. He'd work on a person, taunt them into doing something they didn't want to. Oh he's got his country manners—yes, ma'am, no, ma'am—but underneath he's a stinker. I used to give him a few dollars once a year, for his birthday." She lifted one side of her mouth, a smile of irony. "But I hadn't heard from him for a long time. Tell you the truth I was hoping he'd left the state or crashed that bike."

"What did he want this time?"

"It was always the same thing. I never gave him more than a couple hundred."

"Why did you do it?"

"It doesn't matter one way or another."

Stranahan could see she wasn't going to be persuaded. "Look," he said, "this woman's life could be at stake. You sent this man money, he had to have provided an address."

"I wired it Western Union."

"What town?"

"West Yellowstone. But he wasn't living there. He was living in a campground, he said what one. Told me to come visit him. Imagine that," she shook her head, "me old enough to be his mother twice over. I don't remember the name, but I know where it is. I used to cook on the Armitage place and it wasn't too far from there; that's where I met Rayland."

"Do you have a map?"

"No, I have something that's just as good, though."

———

"This is where Rayland keeps his mountains."

She had led Stranahan to a horse stall in the back of the barn, which was immaculately swept and ordered, a hallmark of Scandinavian tending. A stack of four-by-eight fiberboard shelves on a roller system reached from the floor to head height. Each of the six shelves was labeled with half a Montana mountain range. Stranahan's eyes scanned from the top down: Snowcrest East, Snowcrest West, Bitterroot East, Bitterroot West, Gravelly/Madison East, Gravelly/Madison West. She drew out the shelf labeled Gravelly/Madison West. It was similar to the papier-mâché construction of the Crazy Mountains in the hobby room, but smaller scaled and missing the animal figures. Mouse droppings had collected in the valleys and creek drainages.

"Rayland makes them in halves so you can get them through the doors. Then he'd papier-mâché over the joint and paint it so you didn't notice. He has one for every place he lived. This was the first. You see how he's gotten better."

"He's quite an artist," Stranahan said.

"When I first met him, those hands of his, you'd never think he'd have a talent."

"You seem much younger than your husband."

"You mean I look sixty 'stead of seventy-five. Rayland just got . . . used up. He used to be something, though. He was the first real man I ever knew. It gets lonely when someone close to you starts pulling away. It's like living with a shadow." A flicker of smile. "I don't need to be telling you this, young man like yourself."

Stranahan was willing to listen to anything as long as she pointed her finger, which presently she did.

"These cliffs by the river," she said. "I can't remember the name."

"The Palisades," Stranahan said. He felt himself exhale. Finally, the track he'd been looking for, one that hadn't been made by a wolf.

"No word since that phone call?"

"No. And I don't hope to talk to him again."

He reached into his pocket and held out a brass carving of a coal car that the old man had given him.

"I can't take this," he said.

She took his hand and closed his fingers back over the coal car. The pads of her fingers were as coarse as sandpaper.

"Why do you think I had him show you his trains?" she said. "You kept him company. That means something. No, you take it. Just come back and visit us sometime."

CHAPTER TWENTY-EIGHT

The Blood of the Wolf

Back in Wilsall, Stranahan got a bar of reception on the phone he'd bought that morning and left a message for Ettinger, telling her where he was headed. So McCready had camped at the same fishing access where he and Martha crossed the river in Harold's canoe to meet the scat analyst. Had the analyst, what was his name, Thorn?— had he met McCready and showed him the signpost? Or told him where he could find wolf scat? For that matter, was it possible that both were involved in Nicki's disappearance?

He tried Ettinger again, and this time she picked up. She'd received his message and had news of her own.

Fifteen months earlier, a Lincoln County deputy had picked up one J. Todd McCready for distributing alcohol to minors and found he was wanted in Washington State for violating the terms of his parole. He was extradited and served ten months in the Cedar Creek Corrections Center before his release the past May.

"That's just one month before he showed back up in Libby," Stranahan said. "What was he paroled for originally?"

"Sex without consent."

"Rape?" Stranahan pulled to the side of the road.

"He had intercourse with a woman when she was passed out and she pressed charges three days later. So there were the usual questions. Was he also asleep as he claimed? Did they have carnal knowledge of each other before? Why did she wait so long? Et cetera. Evidently, the woman was the more persuasive and he served six months of a two-year sentence, was released for his stellar behavior and failed to report."

"So he's in the system under his original name."

"Yes, but with an asterisk. He filed a petition to change his name the day after his release.

"I didn't know a felon could do that."

"He can as long as he's not trying to defraud anyone or duck an outstanding violation. McCready got the court order, so as of June seventeenth he really is Fenrir Amorak."

"Then how does he have a Montana driver's license under McCready?"

"A person who's petitioned for a name change has to apply for a new driver's license within thirty days of receiving the court order. Maybe he never did that, or said he lost it and now he's got driver's licenses under both names. Now quit asking questions and listen a minute."

"Yes, ma'am."

"Judy did some digging. Parents are Knute and Margot McCready. Grew up on the family ranch near Whitefish, attended UM, bachelor's degree in zoology. Worked for two years in Pullman, Washington, at the animal research center there, I wrote down the name but now I can't read my writing. Anyway, arrested for possession with intent to sell, charges dropped. Drifted around a few years. Pops up in Bellingham, possession. Pops up in Tacoma, distributing alcohol to minors, community service. Got a job as a janitor at the Seattle Zoo and was there almost five years, maybe he straightened up. After the termination of his employment, there's a year gap before he's sent up for the rape. He goes in, he comes out, he falls right off the map. Doesn't show up in Libby until '09, when he gets a bullshit medical marijuana card from a quack. This would be about when he meets Martinelli. He's in and out of her life for about three years and manages to stay under the radar until he's picked up for the violation of parole. He goes behind bars for the second time and gets out in May and that brings us to the present."

"He worked summers on the ranch in the Shields."

"So you said in your message. It all fits. Generally speaking, when you look for monsters you find bottom feeders who deal drugs and live off girlfriends or relatives. Which as you know isn't enough to haul him in for, especially when the evidence says the person you suspect him of kidnapping was eaten by a wolf."

"Oddstatter said McCready's behavior gave his sister, McCready's mother that is, a heart attack."

"Judy's trying to reach the parents this morning. That's all I know and I gotta go. The wolfer snared another member of the pack and I got wolf lovers parading in front of Law and Justice, demanding that we let it go. Actually it's just an idiot wrapped in a coyote skin who howls when people walk by to show his pain."

"The wolf is alive?"

"For now. But it will be euthanized to check for human DNA in its digestive tract and teeth. Get this, the demonstrator's a law student from Boise State who came in by Greyhound to satisfy a class requirement. Says he's supposed to see how far he can take his protest without getting arrested. So far all he's learned is that howling at people can get you punched in the face. The wife of one of our repeat offenders dared him to open his mouth once more and she broke his nose."

"I'll let you get back to your work, then. Is it McCready, or do we call him Amorak?"

"Amorak."

"Well, the odds are he isn't at the campground anyway. It was back in June when he told Mrs. Oddstatter that's where he was staying. I doubt he's a guy who lets the grass grow under him."

Ettinger had lied to Stranahan about her schedule. There was a storm gathering over the wolves, but it was on the horizon. A delegation from the Ranchers and Hunters for Taking the Wolf Out of Montana had requested a face-to-face, but that wasn't until midafternoon. She drummed her fingers. Her eyes fell on the box of journals. She'd meant to call up some of the names Alfonso had listed in the category of "Ranchers Who Cried Wolf." Someone—Alfonso?—had circled that list. Why?

A rap on the door brought her eyes up. Erik Huntsinger, one of her junior deputies, was holding a FedEx envelope.

"What do you got for me, Hunt?"

The padded envelope was from the Lincoln County Sheriff's Department and was addressed to Sean Stranahan, care of Sheriff Martha Ettinger. Martha pulled the envelope tab. A note on department stationery:

Sean:

I located that letter. Instead of e-mailing a scan, I thought you'd get a better sense of the tenor and content if you had the original. The letter is not evidence in an open investigation, but I've found it best to preserve chain of evidence to be on the safe side. None of the recipients came to harm as a result of this letter, at least not in the weeks following the postmarked dates. It should be evident, but I would point out that the entirety of the letter is written in human blood.

See you on the Kootenai? The fishing holds up into November if you get the chance.

Tight lines,

Carter Monroe
Sheriff, Lincoln County

PS: Here's the list of men and women who reported receiving letters.

Ettinger ran her eyes down the list. Most were hunting outfitters. Two were FWP commissioners. One biologist. One local legislator. Thirty-two names and addresses. She used her penknife to open the evidence bag, pulled apart the seal and shook out a simple manila envelope. Postmarked from Missoula, Montana, it was addressed to Corwin Ackerson, Ackerson Hunting Outfitters, 33 Ruby Ridge Road, Bonner's Ferry, Montana. No return address. Ettinger used a fingernail to extract a single sheet of heavy stationery, which was impressed with a burgundy wax stamp, a howling wolf in silhouette. Below the stamp, centered on the sheet in forward slanting, rather florid script, was a poem stanza:

And the blood of the wolf will rain from the skies
And all the rivers will run red with blood
And the blood of the man who cast aspersion upon the wolf will
  flow with the river
And he will die

The dried blood was brown, but the effect was startling enough to draw a low whistle from Martha's lips. She resealed the letter in the evidence bag.

"Listen up, Hunt. I've bookmarked a page in this journal. It's got a green circle around it, a list of names of Montana residents called "Ranchers Who Cried Wolf," probably from the western half of the state. Run them through the search engines and see if anyone's been a victim of harassment or assault. Also, all the people listed on this sheet of paper." She pushed over Monroe's note. "How's your schedule?"

"I have to testify on a DWI after lunch."

"Then you better get a move on."

She paused. Something had been nagging at her ever since her conversation with Stranahan. She shooed the deputy out of her office and punched in Stranahan's cell number. Out of range. She squared her hat on her head and left word with Walter Hess as she passed the undersheriff's office.

"Aren't you going to go see the wolf that ate Little Bo Peep?" he said.

———

Driving ninety, Ettinger caught up to Stranahan's lumbering Land Cruiser outside Norris.

"Was I speeding, officer?" He stepped out and leaned back against the hood. When he'd seen the flashing lights, he'd pulled over into the drive of a business that sold handcrafted chicken coops.

"Who the hell buys these things?" Ettinger said.

"Gentlewomen farmers, I suppose."

She put her hands on her hips and drummed the butt of her revolver.

"Remember when we were looking at the wolf scat up at the Palisades? The analyst went off to 'bleed my lizard,' as he so eloquently put it."

"Vaguely," Stranahan said.

"Well, I heard a motorcycle start up in the campground across the river. I watched the line of dust as it drove toward the highway."

"You remember that?"

She cocked a finger at her temple. "It's in the hard drive. I got a memory like a bear trap."

"Was it a four-stroke? Most Honda's are four-stroke."

"It . . . was . . . a . . . motorcycle."

"So maybe he *is* there. You chased me down out of concern for my well-being, I'm touched."

"No, there's something else. We can talk in the car."

"Yours or mine."

"Mine."

"Mine's unmarked," Stranahan said.

Ettinger tossed a fly-rod tube into the backseat of the Land Cruiser, and Stranahan cocked an eye as he turned the key.

"In good time," she said. She was picking at her badge. Stranahan saw her glance at the speedometer.

"I could get there quicker on a horse."

"Relax, Martha."

"That's what both my husbands told me. Walt thinks I've got ADD, says there's a pill for it. 'Course you got to consider the source. That man talks so slow half the time I've forgotten the point before he finishes a sentence." She blew out a breath and they drove in silence, passing the turnoff to the Sphinx Mountain trailhead where last summer's drama had played out, resulting in Ettinger's fifteen minutes of fame.

"I still see that bastard in my dreams."

"Who? Crawford?"

She grunted in the affirmative. "So how do we approach Amorak?"

"You're asking me?"

"I'm asking you."

"I don't think we do. This isn't the kind of guy who's going to see your badge and pee his pants. I'd like to trail him, see if he has a job somewhere, let the string pay out until we're sure one way or the other if he's in contact with Martinelli. But it seems a hell of a coincidence that he's camped directly across the river from the cliffs where the scat analyst found the wolf poop."

"It does at that. Pull over to the side of the road. I want to show you something."

She showed Stranahan the letter. "I take it you knew about this."

"Not much. Carter told me. He said the letters were sent to—"

"I know who they were sent to. What I don't know is what this has to do with Martinelli."

"She was in her Clan of the Three-Clawed Wolf stage. Because they fancied themselves ecowarriors, the department looked at her group for being behind the letters. Amorak, specifically. There was no follow through. No arrests were made; no one who got sent a letter was hurt."

"Maybe it's nothing," Martha said. "I have someone checking the names to see if anyone's come to harm since. But if his was the blood behind the pen, then that's another reason to be careful. Anyone takes a blade to himself . . ."

"You really were worried about me."

Ettinger took off her hat. "Do you have another jacket? I don't want to look official."

———

With October on the horizon, only two of the twenty sites at Palisades Campground were occupied. No motorcycle in either. As Stranahan circled the loops, a truck pulled into the campground, stopping in front of a canvas wall tent. Two bow hunters, dressed head to toe in camo, had arrowed a raghorn bull and they had the head and one hindquarter in the bed of the pickup.

Stranahan idled the Land Cruiser as Ettinger rolled down the window.

"Where did you get lucky?" she said.

One of the men pointed across the river. His shirt, his pants cuffs, his boots and his knees were stained dark with blood. "Up Bobcat Creek. We got the rest hanging."

"You're aware a hunter was mauled there last season?" Martha said.

The hunter nodded. "The guy who got his jaw chewed off by a G-bear. It's not an image you get out of your head. We'll be careful packing meat, trust me."

Stranahan leaned across Ettinger. "We're looking for a man who was camping here. Maybe riding a motorcycle."

"Sure." The hunter nodded at his partner, who spoke for the first time. "We called him Tarzan. He had one of those outback tents you hang from a tree branch."

"Tarzan, huh?" Martha said.

"Every night he'd wade across the river and climb the cliff. Then he'd howl like a wolf. Very realistic. You could set your clock by it."

The first hunter nodded. "Nine o'clock sharp. He got wolves going a couple times, which was pretty cool. But he left a few days ago."

"More like a week," the other said.

"Did he say where he was going?"

"No. He didn't talk to us."

"Alone?"

"When we saw him he was alone."

Ettinger asked where the man had camped, and they drove to a riverside site. A rectangle of blanched grass showed the footprint of the tent. No litter, no trash in the fire ring. He'd been a clean camper.

———

The question, now what? hung in the air as they drove back through the valley, Ettinger fingering her badge, another in a long line of what she called her "new bad habits." She felt a pricking against her breast and realized the fly she'd won playing poker at the clubhouse was still in her shirt pocket. She fingered it out. It had gone through the wash, the dyed feathers leaving a reddish orange stain on the material.

"This is your fault, Sean," she said, showing him the stain.

"Biggest fish I hooked in my life took that fly," Stranahan said. "A steelhead in British Columbia, where I was commissioned for some paintings." For a moment he was back on the Kispiox River on a run called Silver Bear, two thousand miles to the north.

"Sam told me whoever won the pot got to name it. I decided Dead Man's Fancy. In honor of Grady Cole. He wouldn't be dead if he hadn't got involved with a flame-haired woman." She snapped her fingers. "Pull into the Blue Moon. Let's bat this thing around."

"Drinking on the job, huh?"

"Who's drinking on the job? I'm hungry and they got a jukebox with 'Crazy' on it. I just love Patsy Cline."

They ordered, she got change for the jukebox and waited until the song finished, then tipped her iced tea back and smacked her lips. She'd carried the fly-rod case into the bar and pulled out the rolled-up topo map that Stranahan had seen on the wall in her home office.

"Something the wolfer said got me thinking. Help me pin down this map."

Ettinger had drawn a red circle at the site of the dead elk, where the wrangler had met his fate, another on the slope farther up toward the headwall of the basin where they had found Martinelli's hat. She'd also marked the trail junction where Martinelli had left the organized saddle ride to go off on her own. The trails were marked in dotted lines.

"So what's visible from just about anywhere on this map?"

"Papoose Mountain?"

"You're warm."

"I don't know, you tell me, Martha."

"The sky, that's what's visible. And what do you see in the sky?"

"Clouds?"

"You see birds. Anybody hunts will tell you that you kill an elk, you don't have time to fill out your tag before you have ravens circling and whiskey jacks dancing on the branches. Wolves don't cover their kills. Anything they bring down draws birds."

"Okay."

"So let's back up to the afternoon Martinelli disappeared. Why did she leave the trail ride? I'm waiting for the shoe to drop."

"She saw birds?"

Ettinger nodded. Their plates had arrived, buffalo burgers and fries. Ettinger took a bite.

"That's a good burger." She wiped her mouth with her napkin.

"The birds were the trigger. She's a lobo lover, there are wolves in the basin that they've been hearing down at the ranch, she sees scavenger birds, it only makes sense they're circling a wolf kill. I'll go a step further and say it was probably the wrangler who saw them first and pointed them out."

"That's speculation."

"Then help me speculate."

"Okay, if the wrangler spotted the birds, why didn't he report it in the nine-one-one?"

"Put yourself in his position. If he says she'd gone off looking for wolves and he was the one who told her where to find them, how's it make him look? No, he keeps that part to himself. Plus, when he called he was worried, he was in a rush to get up there, he didn't have time to go into detail. My gut tells me he couldn't have stopped her from going if he'd wanted to." She nodded to herself. "All along I've been trying to figure out how the tracks of three different people ended up at the same spot on the mountain. If we assume Martinelli went to investigate what she thought was a wolf kill, and Grady Cole rode off trying to find her, it only makes sense he'd look where he'd seen the birds. That leaves the third track, and I know damned well it's Bucky's."

"Which he denies."

"Who else could have set the trap that Cole stepped into? Not Cole, not Martinelli. When you've eliminated the impossible, whatever remains, however improbable—"

"—is the truth," Stranahan finished. "You must have grown up reading Sherlock Holmes?"

"My dad gave me *The Complete Sherlock Holmes* for my tenth birthday. I aimed to become a consulting detective and that went sideways for a while. But I eventually hit pretty close to the mark, deerstalker hat notwithstanding."

"It makes sense, I guess, but why couldn't the third track belong to Amorak? He was camped only a few miles away."

"Because that *doesn't* make sense."

Ettinger held up a finger. "Number one, the Culpepper Ranch is a closed community. How would he know she was going on a trail ride, or that she would break away and ride off alone? Number two," she held up a second finger, "even if he did, how would he get there? It's a heck of a climb, and I don't see him having a horse."

"That still leaves questions about what happened up there."

"Of course it does. This isn't TV. In the real world, people lie and the truth comes out in dribs and drabs, not by divine intuition. One of the things I still don't understand is the hat. The logical conclusion is she was bucked from her horse where we found it. Maybe she was unconscious for a while, then stumbled down the hill when she saw that her horse had bolted. She would have been on a direct line to the carcass of the elk. It's possible there's another explanation. But one thing I'd bet my star on is that Bucky Anderson found Cole caught in the trap and pushed him onto the antler. He can smile all he wants, say therapy's changed him, I don't buy it. Bucky has violence in his heart." She thumped the center of her chest. "He's face to face with a man who's hurt as a result of him setting an illegal trap. For wolves, no less. That's not going to wash with the little lady. Or with her brothers, who aren't in favor of the marriage to begin with. He has to remove the trap before the searchers find it—that's probably why he was hell bent on getting a jump start and left before we arrived that night—that and to make sure Grady Cole never talked."

Stranahan ate his last french fry and reached for one of Martha's. "You're too busy talking to eat," he said.

"I'm just thinking out loud. Harold said the smaller track was a running track. What that means to me is Martinelli came on the scene after Cole was dead, saw him impaled on the antler and fled.

Possibly she witnessed Bucky killing him. Look at that night from her perspective. She's responsible for the wrangler setting out looking for her, so in her eyes she's responsible for everything that happens after that. Plus she might have witnessed a murder, or seen someone leaving the scene of one. It's a shock to the system, on top of the shock she received being thrown from the horse. The sister told you she was mentally unstable, didn't she?"

"I think the term she used was 'subject to flights of fancy.'"

"One person's 'flights of fancy' are another's old-fashioned crazy. Anyway, she panicked. I used to think the question was Where did she go? Now I'm thinking Who did she go to?"

"You're talking about Amorak. But how would she know where to find him?"

"If he was camped at the Palisades, then she might have seen him when she was guiding for Sam. Take a gander at Meslik's logbook and see how many times she floated that stretch of the river."

She pushed away the glasses that were pinning down the map and rolled it up. She rolled down the cuffs of the jean jacket Stranahan had lent her and took it off.

"I ought to get out in plain clothes more often."

CHAPTER TWENTY-NINE

Whistling in the Dark

The moon was over Sam Meslik's fly shop by the time Stranahan dropped Ettinger in Norris and made the return trip over the pass. Sam came to the door chewing a stick of jerky, working a finger into a hole in a "Master Baiter" T-shirt featuring a derelict fly fisherman digging for worms.

"You don't see me all summer except to drop the dog off and now you darken my door," he said. "What gives?"

"I'd like to look at your logbook."

"Want to know all Uncle Sam's secrets, huh? What they're bitin' on?"

"I'm trying to figure out what dates Nicki guided and where she floated."

Sam raised one eyebrow. Stranahan didn't respond.

"Yeah, yeah, police business, leave old Sam in the cold." He slapped Stranahan on the shoulder and dug his fingers in until Sean winced. "Come on. You want a brew?"

Stranahan nodded. "Where's Asena? I didn't see her Bronco."

"She goes out sometimes. I think she just drives down to the Papoose turnoff and stares at the mountain, but I learned not to ask. You know that look she gives you if you go too far? No? Well, it's the same look my sergeant gave me when we were clearing a palace in Kuwait and I had the audacity to use a gold-plated toilet."

"You were in Desert Storm? How come I don't know that?"

" 'Cause the less said the better."

"Were you a grunt?"

"I was a fucking medic. Worst thing I ever saw over there had nada to do with the war, though. One of our bomb squad guys got bit by a saw-scaled viper. It's got a poison that keeps your blood from coagulating. This guy was bleeding out his nose, out his eyes, out his pecker, *every* fuckin' orifice. I shit you not."

"And he lived?"

Sam shrugged. "He was evacced. My river log's in the shop."

He led Stranahan around a glass case displaying fly reels to the gilded cash register he'd bought at a pawn shop. He lifted out the cash drawer and produced the log. Nicki had floated from the Palisades to McAtee Bridge seven times over the summer, the last time only two days before her disappearance. It was conceivable she'd never seen the man camped on the riverbank a quarter mile below the boat launch, but she had to have seen his tent. The tent the bow hunters had described matched the description of the tent Asena said Nicki had used for gatherings of the Clan of the Three-Clawed Wolf, which Amorak had presumably appropriated. No, she could not have mistaken the tent.

"You see what you needed to see?" Sam said.

Sean's expression was noncommittal.

"Be that way. Sam's got things to do. Put it back where it belongs when you're done."

When Sean walked outside, Sam was sitting before his fly-tying vise.

"I miss the old times, bro," he said. "Shooting pool at the inn, talking cowgirls out of their paisleys and petticoats—ah man, what happened?"

"You bought this place and I got commissions that took me away from the river. I'm having a hard time recalling the petticoats."

"You really think you can outlast a Montana winter in that tipi?"

"I don't see why not. I've got fire and I've got a dog to keep me warm."

"That's the problemo, Kimosabe. You got one dog, but come December, you got three dog nights settin' in. Am I right? What do you say we have a drink? Client gave me some twenty-year-old single malt—Glen-fuckless or something."

———

At the turnoff to his property, Stranahan set the parking brake and checked his mailbox rock, stooping to retrieve a piece of paper stuck under the edge. He held the note up to the headlights.

Cell phones don't work unless you turn them on. Call Katie Sparrow.
M.E.

He got a flashlight from the tipi and decided to walk Choti the two miles down to the county road, where the canyon opened and he'd be able to pick up a bar. Give him some time to figure out how to say hello. Katie had been embarrassed when he'd left her place the last time. For more than a year she'd brazenly flirted with him, told him with her body and her eyes that he was welcome in her bed anytime, and then when he'd finally taken up the offer on the pretense of helping her bake dog biscuits, they had actually baked dog biscuits and he had wound up sleeping on the couch.

"I don't know what's wrong with me," she'd told him. "I can troll someone home from a bar, but a man I really like, how I like you, I put up a wall. It's been eight fucking years; you'd think I could get past him."

"Him" was her fiancé, Colin, the backcountry skier who'd been swallowed by an avalanche in the Bridger Mountains. It was watching the search dogs work the chute that persuaded her to become a handler.

"It's okay, Katie," Sean had said, and meant it. He'd been relieved that he wouldn't carry the guilt of cheating on Martinique, ghost that she'd become.

"No," she said, "it isn't. Goddamnit, I want a life." And he'd stayed up half the night with her, listening to a mystery radio show and talking.

Stranahan reached the end of the road and punched Katie's number.

"We ID'd the girl in the hot pot," she said without preamble. "Carrie Harding. Her old roommate came forward yesterday, and we showed her pictures. Turns out Harding was a park employee from Missouri who worked the entrance gate here in West. The reason it took so long is she'd quit the week before, so the park didn't put her down as absent. Her roommate figured it might be her from the description in the newspaper, but the roommate's boyfriend was visiting from out of state and she didn't want to spoil their time together, so she didn't call in and then she thought Carrie must have gone back to Missouri. Then I guess she finally started getting worried because she hadn't heard from her in like a month. I got the impression they weren't on the best terms."

"So it was you who talked to the roommate?"

"On the phone. I told her someone from county would be down in the morning. Martha said it would be you."

"Thanks, Katie."

"Let me get you the address." She got it. "You want company? I work afternoon shift."

Stranahan thought a moment. "No, I think maybe one person would be better."

"Yeah, you're good with the women. I'm sorry about . . . what happened." He could hear the bitterness across the line. "What should have happened and didn't, let's face it. You deserve some kind of medal."

"Hey, we talked about this. You're a beautiful woman, and this phase will pass."

"I'm not doomed to listening to mystery radio with dogs all my life?" The Katie he knew was back in her voice. "We had a good time making the biscuits. You did, didn't you?"

"I sure did. I'll see you, Katie."

Halfway back to the tipi, Choti, a few feet ahead of Sean, stiffened and growled very deep in her throat.

"You out there, lion?" Stranahan said.

He switched on his headlamp, noting the beam had dimmed since the last time he'd used it. He shone the light into the tree shadows that lay sabered across the road. He switched it off to conserve the battery and they continued forward, Choti at his side now, so close his pant leg brushed against her.

"Just a man walking his dog here," Stranahan said to the blackness. He wasn't afraid. Instead, he seemed to hover over his body, as if looking from the wings at an actor in a play. It wasn't courage. Courage was something summoned against the will. Whatever it was, it took him away for a few moments and then he again switched on the headlamp and swept the beam in a circle. Instantly, the light caught two orbs of emerald, blazing as if from out of a seam of coal.

"Good kitty." The voice wasn't exactly his. He tried again. "Good kitty cat."

The reflection of the eyes was so bright as to appear radioactive. The cat was abreast of him, thirty or forty feet to the left of the road. Stranahan took the next step, aware that stopping or, worse, bolting like a deer could trigger a response. "Stay with me, Choti," he said in a firm voice. It was the dog that worried him, or rather he worried about the dog. Another step. How far to the tipi? A quarter mile? Too late now to worry about not changing the batteries in the headlamp. Why hadn't he brought the Carnivore tracking light he'd won playing poker? It was sitting on his cot in the tipi. "Dumb," he said to himself.

A whistler all his life, Stranahan tried a note and found his mouth was dry. A hiss of air escaped his lips. He had to smile. He tried again, the theme from the old Andy Griffith show. Better. He whistled, the dog followed, Opie skipped his stone.

The light grew dimmer. He swept it and the cat was still abreast, but its eyes were dying now. Ahead, he could barely make out the pyramid of the tipi. "Almost there, Choti." The dog had been silent for a long time, but he could feel the quiver in her body when he reached his hand down to reassure her. The headlamp beam made a hazy circle at his feet. It sputtered and went out, like a candlewick in a pool of wax. He counted his steps. Fifty. Sixty. They were there. He bent to remove the sticks that secured the tipi flap. His hands were shaking. He laughed. The laugh was his. It was a story now; he could hear himself telling Sam and Martha about it.

He stepped inside and found his bear spray and the Carnivore tracking light. Switching on the light, he cast the beam in a circle outside the tipi. The lion was gone but his hands were still shaking. They were not shaking from fear. They were shaking from excitement. Something had happened a few minutes before, just as the headlamp beam died and the cat's eyes had glittered for the last time. Stranahan had envisioned another set of eyes looking at him, not an animal's eyes, but the eyes of a human. They were bloodshot eyes, irritated from wearing contact lenses. In that instant, Stranahan had flashed on the face behind those eyes.

CHAPTER THIRTY

Caffeine Courage

"**D**o you have a badge?"

The name tag on her drab green shirt said she was Marsha Siegel, from New York. Short, layered hair swept to one side, a rather horsy face, strong jaw, brown eyes with a starburst of china blue around the pupils, bosomy but solid enough under the uniform, a woman who'd stand a strong wind.

The cabin sat on the outskirts of West Yellowstone. Garbage was strewn across the front yard.

"Bear problem?" Stranahan said.

"I should have known better. Carrie used to take it out in the morning. I thought just this once I could get away with putting it out a couple nights before the collection."

"Carrie's who I want to talk to you about."

"I know, I was told to expect someone. But not without ID."

"Now you're being New York on me," he said, his smile not working. He produced his card. "Call the number on the back and ask for Martha Ettinger, she's the Hyalite County sheriff."

"No, come in. I'm just being a hardass. The woman I talked to yesterday made me feel I'd done something wrong because I waited so long before calling. I told her a story to get her off my back, but the truth is I thought Carrie had run off with that man she was seeing. Correction, I was hoping she had. Don't get me wrong. I didn't want anything bad to happen to her, but he creeped me out."

She led him into what passed for a living room: a sofa, a stuffed chair heaped with magazines, a coffee table with an ashtray and a lipstick-stained roach. Someone had made a scaffolding of plastic straws.

"Forgive the mess," she said. She scooped up the ashtray and a pair of tweezers from the table and left the room.

"I guess that's what you thought it was," she said when she returned. "One of the girls I work with brought it last night. I don't partake so I hope you aren't going to arrest me."

"I'm not, but you shouldn't leave that stuff lying around when you expect company."

"I know. It's more like something Carrie would do. She just didn't care."

"How do you mean?"

"I mean, she was just up for stuff. If someone said 'Hey, let's skinny dip in the park and get loaded and suck face,' she'd strip and pucker up. But I don't judge her, with her having no family but a grandma. She just didn't have any direction."

"How did you two meet?"

"We were both seasonal at the park. Look, I'll be straight with you, but it's got to go both ways. When I asked what happened to Carrie, I was told it looked like an accident. But if it was an accident, then why are you here? Her boyfriend, if that's what you can call him, I know that's who you think pushed her in. But I only met him like three times. He'd drive up on his motorcycle. Soon as he brought out drugs I walked right out the door."

"Did he ever threaten you?"

"No, he was more the ignoring type. But that's another form of threat, isn't it? One time he came in and I left. I walked up to the Book Peddler and got a mocha and came back in a couple hours, his motorcycle is still in the yard. I told myself, 'Hey, it's my place, too.' Caffeine courage, the city runs on it. Hah." Her voice was derisive.

"I come in and he's snorting coke off her nipples. He doesn't even look up. It's like *so* Wall Street. Carrie says you want some, it's okay. It's barely been stepped on. She buttons up, like that makes a difference. I came out here figuring *Sound of Music*, get some fresh air, maybe meet some WASP-y guy. If I wanted people on a couch doing drugs I could have stayed in Queens. I tell you, I could have fuckin' screamed."

"Did he have a name, this boyfriend?"

"Carrie called him Fen. She said she met him at the Trophy Room Lounge down in Last Chance. He told her he lived in a tent, that before that he lived in a wolf den he'd found in the park. Weird stuff. But he never said anything to me. Usually, she'd just hear the bike and be out the door. That time on the couch was the only time he was here more than a few minutes."

"Did she talk about him?"

"No." She reconsidered. "You know, I'm thirty. That's older than most park personnel. She was just a dumb kid from the sticks. One night I was up front with her. I sat her down, I said, 'Carrie, this guy is bad news.' Me telling someone else that for once. You gotta love it." She laughed. "'You got your life ahead of you,' I told her. 'You're smart, you're pretty'—okay, neither was exactly true but I'm trying here—but nothing gets through. She said the same thing Clarence Clemons said about Bruce Springsteen. 'It's like following Jesus.' And that's the strange thing. He did give off a vibe. It was like"—she shot out her arms and did a zombie walk around the sofa with her eyes half closed—"Follow me and I'll take you to the Promised Land, even if it's just a tent."

She completed the circle and stood before Stranahan. "So, are you going to arrest this guy?"

"Right now we just want to talk to him. There's no proof a crime has been committed."

"I don't know about that. Out here anyone who says 'Ouch, my aching back' can get a medical marijuana card, but I bet they draw the line at blow. Okay, I'm getting really uncomfortable here. Where did you park?"

"Out front."

"Is it a cop car?"

"No. It's an old Toyota Land Cruiser."

"Yeah, but you look like a cop. You have that bearing. You leave, I'm going to kiss you on the step, okay? I mean, if somebody's watching, you're either a cop or my boyfriend. Just in case he hears about you being here, I want anybody who's seen you to think, well, she's just hitting some guy."

"It's been more than a month since you saw this man." He waited for her to nod. "And you really think he's someone to worry about?"

"I read murder mysteries. I know I'm a loose end. That's what Carrie said once, FYI, but I'm not sure she meant him. The girl said some random things."

"Marsha, I'm not looking for this man because he might have hurt your roommate, though if he did, he'll be brought to justice. I'm here because he's a person of interest in another woman's disappearance, a tall woman with red hair."

"I never saw him with anyone but Carrie."

"I'll tell you something that wasn't in the papers. Carrie was wearing red contact lenses when she was found. Does that mean anything to you?"

She exhaled audibly. "She had contacts, but they were orange, not red. Well, yellow. Then she got the orange. She hated them because they made her eyes itch. But every time he came for her, when I was here at least, she put them in. The idea was that she would graduate to red lenses when she was fully accepted as his mate. Like the way you go through belts in judo."

She put her head down and breathed in and out. "Goddamnit. Do you have any idea how hard it is to get hired on by the park? It's just . . . I shouldn't have to go through this. Why did everything turn to shit?"

"It's okay. You're doing the right thing. What else did she say about him?"

"Nothing. I've told you what I know. Now go, please just go."

"I can call a deputy if you'd like. He can give you advice if you're really worried."

"I already know not to jump in any hot pots." A shudder ran up through her. "Do you think she's going to come out of this and be okay? I'd go see her, but it's a lot of gas to drive to Billings."

Stranahan said, "I don't know. Coma victims, sometimes they can hear people even if they can't respond. One of the reasons we couldn't ID Carrie is because no one reported her missing. I don't think she gets any visitors. It could mean a lot if you visited."

"It would be the right thing to do. A person doesn't want to go through life with regrets, that's what my mother always says. Of course that's why I'm here, 'cause I didn't want to regret never seeing the mountains, and look where that's got me."

"One more question and I promise I'll leave. Would Carrie have had any reason to hike into a remote place to see a hot pot?"

"No, but she didn't have a car and there were days off when she hitched around the park, you know, just to see the wonders. That's something a lot of us do. I don't mean stick out a thumb, but get a ride with another employee or a regular, like a bear researcher or an artist. But she never mentioned going to any hot pots. If she had, I'd have known it was her who they'd found and reported it."

On the porch, she put her arms around Stranahan's neck. She kissed the corner of his mouth. A peck.

I must not be much of a boyfriend, he thought. He started to smile and she tilted her head up and this time it was a kiss that would pass muster to anyone watching.

"One more for the road?" he said. That got the hint of a smile, but only the smile and not a kiss, and when she turned to go back inside he was watching a worried woman.

CHAPTER THIRTY-ONE

Songs of the Night

Stranahan picked up a few essentials at Cal and Jan Dunbar's grocery, drove another two blocks and found a parking spot in front of Bob Jacklin's Fly Shop. He went inside to pay his respects. Jacklin, who dressed like he was on safari and retained more enthusiasm for teaching the sport than most men half his age, represented the last of the old-time trout shop owners in West Yellowstone. A gentleman and one of the early proponents of catch-and-release fishing, he was a pivotal figure in the westward expansion of the sport.

Stranahan introduced himself and said he'd like to buy a fly. "Not a commercial tie, but one from your own fingers. I'm starting a small collection, just flies from friends and a few of the pioneers of Montana fly fishing."

"What pattern would you like?" Jacklin asked.

They traded yarns while the old master's fingers married dubbing, hackle and a slim strip of bicycle inner tube to fashion his signature stonefly nymph. Ten minutes later, Sean walked outside to a falling barometer. He placed the plastic cup that held the fly on the dash of the Land Cruiser and slid the bill Jacklin had refused to accept back into his money clip. In the distance to his left, he could see the entrance stations at Yellowstone Park's west gate, where Carrie Harding had worked. On the other side of Yellowstone Avenue, across from the fly shop and about two hundred yards away was the Paws of Yellowstone Wildlife Center. From where Stranahan stood, the motorcycle in the lot looked like a toy. He fished for his binoculars. Harold had said the gas tank was red. It was, and he traced his fingers across the spider vein cracks on the dash. *Be patient*, he told himself. *Wait the bastard out and follow him*. He glanced at his watch. It was not yet eleven. The center didn't close until six. Far too long to be sitting in a car, looking out a window.

He had the right man, didn't he? The memory of the lion's eyes was vivid. In the instant that Stranahan's headlamp flickered out and the world went black, the emerald pools had been replaced by the red eyes of the man who'd fed the wolves at the wildlife center. The steps to that conclusion had raced through Stranahan's synapses in a heartbeat—one pulse of blood and he had flashed on the girl Harold described in the Lamar Valley, the one with the itchy eyes, and then the wolf keeper, who had kept rubbing his bloodshot eyes when Stranahan visited the center. Also, the keeper had introduced himself as James, and McCready was J. Todd. J.—for James? The connection was tenuous—he could hear Martha Ettinger saying *Humpff*—but the motorcycle strengthened it. So did the trout bones found in the scat at the Palisades. Wild wolves don't catch many trout in the fall, but the wolves at the center were fed them, along with the deer and elk meat.

The one unassailable fact pointing to Nicki's demise in the teeth of the wolf had been the scat with human hairs in it—how had Martha put it, "wound tight as a hair in a biscuit"? How could Martinelli's hair pass through a wolf's gut and she still be alive? He'd been working on the answer since the moment the headlamp died.

————

With time to kill, Stranahan flashed his park pass at the gate and drove a half hour to Mule Shoe Bend on the Firehole River. He tied on two flies, a partridge and orange and a starling and herl, old-fashioned soft hackles that imitated nothing precisely, yet suggested many aquatic insects with their breathing hackle fibers, and sent them into a foamy riffle. Mule Shoe Bend was one of Stranahan's favorite escapes, a place where one wandered among intermittent geysers and steaming fissures in the earth, where an angler had to be careful not to lead trout into the trickles of near boiling water that fed the river, or he would cook his catch without ever removing it from the water.

In an hour the soft hackles underwhelmed, coaxing a few small rainbows to Stranahan's hand, along with one precocious brown trout that was scarcely as long as his middle finger. It was beginning to snow. With the first flakes, a regatta of blue-winged olive mayflies set sail on the surface, trout slashing for them as the flies were buffeted by a breeze. Stranahan switched to a dry fly, sharpened his curve cast skills and took a couple better brown trout, keeping one eye on a bull bison that was shambling down the riverbank. When the bull had closed to fifty yards, its back and humped shoulders looking like they were dusted with flour, Sean put the fly in the keeper ring and retreated up the bank. Reluctantly, he consulted his watch. Time to pencil a few quick sketches of the bison, then back to town.

He found a parking spot in front of Eagle's, where a black-and-white photo in the window showed tourists on wooden skis, standing on snowdrifts that reached the top of the store's doors. He pulled on a sweater. Maybe he wouldn't be able to survive a Montana winter in the tipi, after all. Twice he got out to wipe snow from the windshield, but then it had let up and he was hugging himself at a quarter past six when the motorcycle started up in the lot of the wildlife center.

He turned the key and . . . nothing. Not even a click. He'd been dealing with a worn ignition switch for some months, either that or there were grounding issues with the coil, but this was the first time the spark plugs had failed to fire. He glanced up to watch the motorcycle cross the intersection and head north up 191, the main drag through town. It was gone. Stranahan laughed mirthlessly. He tried again. His shoulders sagged. He took the key out, reinserted it. The engine promptly turned over and he made a right-hand turn at the corner. How much time had he lost? West Yellowstone consisted of only two real blocks, and he was through the outskirts, passing the giant Smokey the Bear with the fire danger arrow pointing to low, the needle of the Cruiser creeping up to fifty, but the motorcycle was nowhere in sight. *Damnit!*

Stranahan had assumed the driver would head for a campground. Which were the closest? Rainbow Point on Hebgen Reservoir and Baker's Hole on the Madison—he'd be coming to the turnoffs in a few miles. Stranahan pressed the pedal to the floor, his head humming. In five minutes he'd turned onto the gravel access road to Rainbow Point, an infamous campground where a man from Wisconsin had been pulled out of his sleeping bag and eaten by a grizzly bear a couple decades earlier. The only vehicle to pass since the snowfall had four tires. Stranahan made a three-point turn and continued north on the highway. He idled down to a crawl at the right turn to Baker's Hole campground. He let out a long breath. His fingers had been gripping the steering wheel so tightly he could feel the blood run out of them now that the tension eased. A snaky tire track led down the middle of the road. The hare had gone to ground.

The outback tent was pitched like a witch's hat on the riverbank. Stranahan crept around the campground loop past yawning sites and a cement outhouse; the place was deserted save for the tent. The motorcycle was parked alongside, tilted on its kickstand. A slight woman wearing an oversized check shirt was standing at the picnic table, pumping the fuel tank of a Coleman stove. She shot him a cursory glance. No sign of the man. Stranahan parked in a site farther downriver and made a show of pulling gear from the Land Cruiser. He didn't have long to wait. A man was walking back from the outhouse. It was the wolf keeper, his ponytail escaping above the adjustment band of a baseball cap. Stranahan walked to the self-registration box and filled out a permit for one night. He walked back. Now what?

Do what any fisherman would do who found himself at sunset on a trout stream. *And why not?* The fly rod is one of the world's great icebreakers. In Stranahan's experience, you got a "how's fishing?" at the very least. Often enough you were offered a beer and a chair by the fire. Occasionally, you made a friend for life. Stranahan put on his best smile as he walked past the tent, his waders squeaking. The man's nod was unencouraging. Apparently, he was not a fly fisherman. Stranahan hiked upriver and slowly worked back down with a sink-tip line and a dark spruce streamer fly. He knew that big fish were turning out of the Grayling Arm of Hebgen Reservoir every evening to ascend the Madison toward their spawning grounds. He wanted one, not for himself, but as a letter of introduction.

It could not have worked out in more timely fashion. He was passing the fly through a seam of current directly in front of the peaked tent when a heavy brown walloped the surface, jumped clear, fell back and jumped once more before bulldogging down, the head shakes labeling it a male. Stranahan led the trout into the shallows. He resisted the temptation to turn around.

"Are you going to let that fish go?"

"I was," Stranahan said. Now it was okay to turn. The man and woman were on the bank, looking down at him.

"We live pretty close to the bone," the man said.

Stranahan was not a catch-and-release purist, though he seldom kept a river trout unless it was deeply hooked and bleeding from its gills. This one was a fine male with a hooked jaw. He reached for a stone. "Sorry, old boy," he said under his breath and smacked the trout on the back of its head. He smacked it again and it quivered out straight. Using the sheathed knife on his neck lanyard, Stranahan inserted the point into the trout's vent, ran it the length of the belly, sliced open the hard V of flesh under the lower mandible, gripped it between his thumb and fingers and in one deft motion shucked the trout's gills and intestines. He ran his thumbnail to clear the blood line in the body cavity and scooped up the innards and gills and heaved them into the current, protocol in grizzly country to keep from luring bears into camp. Hooking two fingers under the gill plates, he carried the trout up the bank.

"You wouldn't have a beer, would you?" he said. He nodded toward the woman, who told him to drape the trout across two paper plates on the picnic table. The man cracked open a PBR from his cooler and handed it to Stranahan.

He said, "We sure appreciate it. I got work in town but we're trying to save money to get a place this winter. Most campgrounds shut down in October." His voice was measured and quiet, incongruous to the intensity of his expression. He seemed to be staring at Stranahan.

Stranahan said, "I live in a tipi up near Bridger. Come December, I'm not sure what I'm going to do myself. Do you have anything to go with the trout?"

The woman, or girl, she couldn't have been much over eighteen, had opened the metal bear-proof box next to the camp and carried a crate of food to the picnic table. She started pawing through it. Stranahan caught the glint of a nose stud. The scraggly tips of the straw-colored hair escaping her watch cap were dyed a dirty maroon.

"We got SpaghettiO's," she said in a voice that reminded Stranahan of a girl speaking to a kitten. There was a shy, wondrous quality about her, as if she were noticing the brightness of the world for the very first time.

"Why don't you let me make dinner?" Stranahan said. "I have

spuds and green beans. I'll bring over my lantern and we'll do up a feast."

"You seem familiar," the man said. His eyes seemed to pierce Stranahan.

"You do, too," Sean said. "Hey, aren't you the guy who feeds the wolves at the wildlife center?"

Now the man was nodding. "I knew I'd seen you. I don't forget faces." But the suspicion had gone and his eyes, close up, were green, like the cat's eyes but minus the radioactive throb.

"That was an interesting talk about the wolves. I'm Sean." Stranahan turned over his palm as if to say, "I'd shake your hand but it's covered with fish slime."

"Fen," the man said.

Stranahan looked at the woman, who had kept her head down since he'd climbed up the bank. Her irises were pale gray, the whites bloodshot.

"I'm Deni." A peek at him, the eyes glancing up and then the glance averted.

Stranahan walked to his site to shed his waders, wondering just what it was he was trying to accomplish. He'd wanted to see the man up close and now he had and, except for the expression, there seemed little remarkable about him. The animal attraction that had evidently captured the imagination of Nicki Martinelli was only hinted at, but then Stranahan wasn't the intended prey. He stacked food and a box of wine into his cook box, trapped his folding chair under his arm and hooked the handle of his lantern with a finger. He struggled back to the couple's picnic table, where he poured the wine into Dixie cups.

He raised his cup in salute and busied himself with the dinner preparations. Without looking up, he said, "So how do you like working with wolves, Fen?"

The man barked a laugh. "You mean toss them meat and carry their crap to the Dumpster. But wolves are very interesting."

"How's that?" Stranahan started slicing potatoes.

"Their family structure. Hierarchy isn't based on strength. The alpha male and female don't dominate the other members of the pack physically. Instead, it's a leadership role, based on personality and attitude. What we would call charisma. If there's enforcing to be done, it's done by a beta. The alphas stay above the fray. As in nature, as in man, or so it should be."

"What do you mean?" Stranahan chopped an onion to fry with the potatoes and set them to sizzling in a cast-iron skillet.

"I mean that leadership is an innate trait, and in an ideal society those who possess this quality should prevail. True leaders are literally born to lead. Unfortunately, we live in a culture corrupted by money. The have-nots in terms of personal magnetism can become the haves by purchasing power. Take where I work, the resident naturalist is the owner's son-in-law, even though I'm the one with the degree."

Deni, Stranahan saw out of the corner of his eye, had brought her head out of her shell and was paying her alpha rapt attention. She smiled shyly over at Stranahan, as if to say, *Isn't he wonderful?*

"That's a depressing perspective," Sean said.

Fen raised his head slightly.

"Say you're born without an abundance of either charm or money? How can you ever hope to rise through the ranks?"

"Through guile and perseverance," Fen said. "Even the lowly omega occasionally becomes an alpha if he plays a smart hand." He nodded in agreement with himself.

Stranahan instinctively recoiled from self-satisfied people, who in his experience were usually overcompensating for feelings of inferiority. But then he wasn't here to like the man, he was here to find out what had happened to Nicki Martinelli.

"I keep thinking about that woman who was eaten by the wolf," he said. "Sooner or later it was bound to happen, I guess. I remember what you said at the feeding, about wolves in the park losing their fear of people. You add in grizzly bears, it makes sleeping in a tent a mite spooky. Sometimes I wish I had a gun."

"Fen's not afraid of wolves." Deni turned to Amorak, her eyes big. "Tell him about the wolf when we met, that big black one where you found the den. He just walked right up to him like unarmed."

Fen shot her a look.

Stranahan scraped onions and potatoes onto a sheet of aluminum foil, acting as if he hadn't caught the rebuke. He dredged the trout fillets in a cornmeal and flour mix and placed them in the skillet. The flesh, colored orange from a diet of freshwater crustaceans, hissed and began to turn pale at the edges.

"But you were so—" She censored the rest of the comment. Stranahan could feel the weight of Fen's eyes on her.

"Just how does one walk up to a wolf?" Sean put nonchalance into his voice.

Amorak stared at Deni a long moment, then remembered his manners. "Remember what I said about the alphas?" he said. "They control through a projection of leadership."

"So you just have to be the bigger alpha."

"Exactly. I find that's true of everything in life. Anything you want, you can have just by looking at it, if you look at it in the right way."

"Sounds like something a man could put to good use in a singles bar." Sean smiled at Deni, who had retreated into her shell. "Or maybe to get back in the good graces of someone who left you. My girlfriend, she's gone away to vet school and I get the distinct feeling she's no longer enthralled with me."

Fen nodded. "Even if they run away, they always come back. You see, at a psychological level, you're still there. The alpha is the heroin on the table. An addict can walk out of the room, but she never locks the door behind her."

"You have anyone like that in your life?" Stranahan made the question casual as he served helpings on paper plates. It was easier to ask prying questions while your attention was on the work your hands were doing.

"You know," he added, "someone who left you, then came back?" Stranahan thought of Nicki, stumbling down the mountainside in panic, running toward the comfort of the drug Fen represented.

"You ask the wrong question." The voice had changed. It was still quiet and measured, but with a darker undercurrent. "The question isn't would she come back. The question is would I take her back. She would have to pass a test."

"What kind of test?"

"One to see if she was worthy."

Something in Fen's voice told Stranahan the subject was closed. He'd hit a nerve. "We're ready here," he said.

Deni came to small life again as they sat before the fire, the wondrous quality returning when she found that Sean was an artist. She had always wanted to paint. She thought she might have the talent. Stranahan told her to hold the thought. He found his spiral-bound sketchbook on the passenger seat of the Land Cruiser and settled on one of the pencil studies he'd done at Mule Shoe Bend earlier in the day—the Methuselah bison with his robe of snow, jets of steam issuing from his nostrils. He tore it out.

"It's for both of you," he said.

"Wow," Deni whispered. "That's good. Isn't that good, Fen?"

Fen murmured in the affirmative. He didn't like not being the center of attention.

"I know," Deni said, "let's have s'mores. I just love s'mores."

Fen took the sketch and ducked into the tent. Then he climbed down the high bank to the river, a flashlight beam marking his progress.

"He keeps his stash under a rock," Deni said.

The beam was working its way back. Amorak sat down before the fire and smiled into Stranahan's eyes as he pulled a baggie of weed from his shirt pocket. He rolled a slim joint, lit it with a butane lighter and toked. He passed it to Stranahan. Stranahan hadn't smoked for years. He pulled on the joint so that the tip went cherry red, but kept most of the smoke in his mouth. He passed the joint to Deni, who extended her hand from a blanket she'd pulled around her shoulders. Stranahan exhaled very slowly while making a show of looking at the stars. He wanted to keep his wits about him.

"Alaskan Thunderfuck," Fen said. "From the Manatuska Valley. I been there once. Valley of the fucking wolves."

The s'mores were excellent. They were maybe the best thing Stranahan had ever eaten. So much for keeping it in his mouth, he thought. He felt himself drifting; there really were a lot of stars. You could get dizzy watching them. He examined the sky in that questing way that *Australopithecus* must have, when there were no words to adequately describe it. There were still no words. He felt himself swimming upward as if the sky were a heavenly water, the stars just beyond his fingertips, and then slowly he drifted back down.

Fen was saying something about wolves. Stranahan looked across the fire to examine the man's face, dancing in the light from the flames. Two people had mentioned that his face was beatific, and for the first time Stranahan saw that, for Fen glowed as if lit by a positive life force, the way that women who are pregnant shine with health. The unwashed hippie countenance bled into the periphery to reveal the most beautiful face Stranahan had ever seen. No, not beautiful, but . . . radiant. He felt himself trembling toward it, as if being pulled by a pulsating magnet. He had enough sense to shift his eyes to Deni, to regard her as the distilled water that acts as a control in an experiment. She caught his eyes and her smile was beautiful, but it was a human beauty. She remained recognizably tethered to earth.

"Deni is attracted to you, too, Sean. Would you like to go into the tent with her?" Fen's eyes vibrated from one to the other. "You'll find her able to accommodate any position in the *Kama Sutra*. She is a compliant if inexperienced lover, aren't you, my sweet? I will be happy to stay here by the fire."

Here was the tribal chief with the camp as his kingdom, offering his woman as a gesture of hospitality. Stranahan could sense Deni stiffen in her chair. This was not part of the bargain she'd agreed to when accepting the colored contact lenses. She pulled the blanket closer.

Stranahan understood that the casual nature of the offer was not aboriginal largesse, but a display of Fen's dominance over both of them. A pounding of the chest. Suddenly, he wasn't so stoned.

"Deni is very desirable." His eyes held Fen's. "But I am committed to another. Like the alpha wolf, I'm monogamous."

Fen nodded his head. "I respect your decision, but the sentiment is misplaced. It's a fallacy to believe that wolves are faithful and that only alphas mate. Other pack members may copulate and bear the fruit of sex, but they lack the family support to successfully rear the pups. What the alphas possess is the necessary devotion of the pack to bring pups to maturity. 'It takes a village' is the expression humans use. This girlfriend—you speak of her losing her attraction to you, yet you remain faithful. In wolf society, if the female alpha strays or dies, the male wastes no time grieving his loss, but quickly replaces her with another."

He flicked the ask from the roach into the fire.

"Sean, you asked if there was a woman in my life who left and came back. In fact there was one, I will admit she enchanted me more than any other, but in her devotion she was unreliable. She was like this campfire that bows to the wind, one way and then another. A person who shows you two faces. An alpha has no time for an unsteady flame."

"What happened to her?"

"Gone. I was going to feed her to the fire, but she slipped the net. I misjudged her state of mind. It's not a mistake I'll make twice. In the meanwhile . . ." He relit the joint and pulled smoke into his lungs. He exhaled. "As you can see, I've moved on."

He stepped around the fire. Deni had retreated into the folds of her blanket, holding it pinched to her throat. She seemed to shrink away from his attention, but he caught her eyes and after a few seconds the fingers holding the blanket relaxed and the blanket fell away. Fen bent and kissed her neck, bit it lightly and tugged, so that the flesh pulled taut. He released his hold and smiled with his teeth bared in the firelight. He said, "You are quite delicious, my darling. The spirits are quiet tonight. Let's show our guest how we say goodnight to them. You would like that, wouldn't you?"

She nodded almost imperceptibly.

"Good," Fen said. He retreated to the tent and Sean looked at Deni, but she didn't meet his eyes. He was entirely sober now and saw, with a shiver of clarity, that this young woman would never ascend to the level of alpha, would never graduate to the red contact lenses and that she would be discarded in favor of another in Fen's quest to find the perfect mate.

"This man's dangerous," he wanted to say to her. "He'll discard you like the others. Come with me now and escape."

But he knew if he said anything, she would repeat it and Fen himself would disappear, and with him the chance that he would pay for his . . . what exactly? Serial humiliation of young women. A sin, if not exactly a crime. Or something much more sinister?

Fen was returning from the tent with what looked like a buffalo horn. He walked to the bank and raised the horn. The first mournful note startled Stranahan. The voice rose, held, then fell in three parts. The plaintive nightsong of wilderness, gone from Montana so many years and now returned to enrich the landscape. In the vacuum, the silence was that of the earth stopped turning. Then, far away, the first answer. They came from nowhere and from everywhere then— haunting, infinitely sad. A lament, sung in minor key.

"The Electric Peak Pack. They're hunting," Fen said.

CHAPTER THIRTY-TWO

A Perfect Crime

Except for the stale taste of smoke in Stranahan's mouth, the night might have been dreamed. By long habit, he was up in the predawn, frying bacon, flipping an egg in the grease, having his first cup of cowboy coffee sitting before a star fire. He kicked at the unburned ends of the sticks, pushing the burned ends together to encourage the flames. He had a second cup as the heavens paled. The witches' hat in the distance slumbered on.

An hour later, Stranahan saw movement in the camp. He watched Deni walk to the outhouse, her blanket dragging on the ground. Fen stepped with his back to Stranahan to the high bank, brought his hands to the front of him. His urine flow steamed. Deni walked back, her head down in the blanket. No fire, no breakfast. The motorcycle engine caught and sputtered. It fired and settled to its basso rhythm. As it passed Stranahan's camp, Fen gave him a thumbs-up. Deni had her arms wrapped tightly about him and did not look over. It did not surprise Stranahan that she had not been left behind in camp, where he might pay her a visit. Fen's moment of munificence had passed.

Stranahan waited until the sound of the engine died away before walking to the tent and untying the flap. Sleeping bags, wadded up clothes zipped in pillow covers, flashlights. A teen vampire novel on her side, a pocketbook *Kama Sutra* on his, opened to the Splitting Bamboo. A bottle of Astroglide shaped like a wave. Very little else, but then it was a motorcycle camp. He backed out of the tent and scribbled a note on a paper plate.

Great time last night. Good luck finding a place. I have to go back to
Bridger. Sean.

He slipped a card from his wallet, the one that identified him only
as a painter, and wrote his cell number on it. He pinned the card and
the paper plate to the picnic table with four bottles of Moose Drool,
then packed up his own meager camp, intending to drive into West
to verify that the motorcycle was parked at the wildlife center. On
his way, he stopped at a bear-proof garbage can and tossed in a bag of
trash. Something was sparking at the back of his mind, an association like last night's stars, just out of reach. He let out the clutch and
slowly motored toward town, passing on his left the entrance road to
the county dump. *That was it!*

———

Bob Jacklin was at the vise in his fly shop, turning out a Platte River
Special. He looked up from under his magnifying glasses.

"Bob, do you know what day they collect trash at the wildlife
center?"

"I'd assume Tuesday. Same as here."

"Thanks." He hadn't asked why, and Stranahan was grateful. He
wouldn't have known what to answer.

Martha picked up on the first ring.

"If I was to tell you there's evidence of murder or kidnapping in the
Dumpsters outside the Paws of Yellowstone Wildlife Center, how
soon do you think you could get a search warrant from Judge
Conner?"

"You better back up," she said.

Stranahan listened to the silence on the line after he finished.

"Mm-hmm." More silence. "It's certainly an interesting theory."

"It's more than a theory. This guy tears out Nicki's hair. He mixes
it into the venison at the Center, feeds it to the wolves and collects
the scat, then plants the scat at the Palisades as evidence that she

was killed by wolves. Her body is presumed eaten, people stop looking for her."

"So do you think she's alive?"

"I want to think she's alive. I think there's a good chance that she is, that he convinced her to run away with him and she consented to him pulling out her hair. But I can't dismiss the possibility that he killed her and buried the body. Either way, the hair in the scat closes the case. It's a perfect crime."

"Why do you think we'll find more hair in the Dumpster?"

"A half a dozen wolves produce a lot of scat in the course of a couple days. It makes sense he'd just collect the scat that had visual evidence of hair wound into it. The rest would be tossed into the garbage. Amorak told me he cleaned up after the wolves, and when I stopped at the garbage can at the campground and then saw the sign to the dump a couple minutes later it clicked. The next collection is tomorrow morning, though. We'd have to get the warrant today." Stranahan paused. "Another thing. My guess is if you talk to the scat analyst, he'll tell you that he told Amorak about the signpost. The guy was camping right across the river from the Palisades. It's natural they would have bumped into each other. The signpost is what gave Amorak the idea of planting the scat. He knew where to plant it so it would not only be found, but also be found by the one person who knew what he was looking at."

"Uh-huh." Stranahan could visualize Martha kneading her chin. "I'll talk to our scatman later this morning. We'll see what he says."

Stranahan could read the doubt in her voice.

"Amorak had the means, Martha. He had the opportunity, he had a motive."

"What's his motive again?"

"Nicki haunted him. He was crazy about her. And she had rejected him. Last night he told me he wouldn't take her back unless she passed a test. He was speaking hypothetically, but she's who he was talking about. If she passed the test, maybe she's alive. If she didn't, she's dead."

"What about the other girls? Does he kill them, too?"

"I don't know, but it's a pattern either way. He picks up a stray, he feeds her this wolf bullshit, and when she doesn't live up to his ideals, when she doesn't graduate to the red contact lenses, he casts her aside and finds the next. I think he could have pushed the girl into the hot pot, I don't know what he did with the rest. These are the girls in the missing posters that nobody misses."

"Humpff."

"It's your county, Martha."

"Meaning what? I should care more? I'm not like a tin star on FX. I have to follow rules."

"Do you think Crazy Conner will okay the warrant?"

"Learn your law. I don't need a warrant to go through the center's garbage. I just need them to sign off. Why refuse? It would look like they were hiding something."

"I hadn't thought of that. But if you ask and the information is passed to Amorak, he might run."

"Leave that part to me. He won't know, I promise."

"What should I do?"

"Just keep your phone on. And stay in cell range for once, damnit."

———

"**Y**ou gotta be kidding." Julie McGregor blew back an errant bang of hair. She looked from Stranahan to Martha Ettinger. "You aren't kidding."

"The two big sacks are mostly bear shit," Stranahan said, "maybe with a little wolf mixed in. It's really just the one bag."

McGregor hefted it. "Well, I'm not doing this alone."

"You won't be," Ettinger said, "Wilkerson's on her way and Stranahan's volunteering. This kind of work's right up his alley."

"Can you stay?"

"I'm the sheriff. I don't do wolf doo-doo."

When Ettinger had gone, McGregor said, "I take it this was your idea."

She heard him out and said, "Give me a real wolf any day." She told Stranahan to take a chair at the steel examining table, undid the tie on the bag, made a face and they bent to work. Wilkerson joined them straight from her shift, still wearing her lab coat.

"Better double glove," McGregor told her.

For an hour they dissected scat, the steel probes separating hair wrapped around bone chips. Most of it long, coarse and banded with tan tips—elk hair.

"Where does the center get its carcasses?" Wilkerson asked Stranahan.

"Hunters and game processors. It's all donations."

"And this guy put the girl's hair inside chunks of meat and fed it to the pack."

"That's what I'm thinking."

"How ingenious."

"Hey." Wilkerson had picked out a reddish hair from the curlicued end segment of a wolf scat. Her big eyes were swimming. "Would you look what we have here?"

By the time they had worked through the bag of wolf scat, they had isolated fourteen samples of human hair ranging from a half inch to eight inches long, most wound so intricately with the elk hair that they were not apparent until the dissection of the scats. The color was the same as the hair taken from the scat at the signpost at the Palisades, and at least six of the samples contained intact follicles.

"I better call Martha," Stranahan said.

"What do you think she'll do?" Wilkerson said.

"This tips the scales, whether you can get DNA from this hair and compare it to the samples we took from the Palisades or not.

Amorak's working at a place where they're dumping wolf scat with human hair in it. You put that together with the two of them having a prior relationship, him camping across the river from where the scat was planted, what he said to me last night—it's strong circumstantial. Martha will haul him in for questioning."

"Don't forget the girl in the hot pot," Wilkerson said. "The roommate you interviewed can ID this bastard."

"Yeah." Stranahan's voice was doubtful. "But we have nothing to tie him to the scene. I think the best chance for arrest is to build a case for murdering Nicki Martinelli. But as Martha reminds me, I don't know the law."

"The more sticks you stack, the stronger your house, but what do I know? I'm just a lowly CSI."

"No, you're Ouija Board Gigi," Stranahan said. "Someday you're going to have to tell me how you got that name."

"Can you sing?" McGregor said. "We're going to play Beatles: Rock Band at my house tonight. You should come. He should come, shouldn't he, Gigi?"

———

Stranahan didn't end up playing Beatles: Rock Band. Instead, he stood alongside Harold Little Feather, watching through a one-way window as Undersheriff Hess conducted the interview. Hess would not have been Stranahan's first choice and he said so.

"I'd do it, but he'll recognize me and turn hostile," Harold said.

"You're an Indian. You all look alike."

Harold smiled. "Don't worry about Walt. He knows what he's doing."

Hess introduced himself and finished the preliminaries. He asked the man's name.

"Fenrir Amorak."

"Like the wolf in Norse mythology."

"Fenrir is a wolf of Norse mythology. Amorak's an Inuit legend."

"Another wolf?"

"That's right."

"What's the name you were born with?"

"It no longer suits me. That person no longer exists."

"Isn't it James Todd McCready? We know . . ." Walt reiterated what Stranahan already knew from talking with Mrs. Oddstatter and later with Ettinger.

Sean felt his phone vibrate. He walked away a few feet and opened it. It was Ettinger. He listened a minute and shut the phone.

"Like I said," Amorak said when Walt had finished, "it says nothing about who I am now." He sounded bored.

"That person who no longer exists," Walt said. He looked down at the sheet of paper on the table. One by one he ticked off McCready's laundry list of misdemeanors, his sexual assault and the parole violation.

Amorak shrugged.

From behind the glass, Stranahan could see Walt lean forward and place his hands around either end of the table.

"Do you know why you're here?" he said. "I find it odd that you haven't even asked."

Most detainees brought their head back when the interrogator leaned forward. McCready only smiled. "Did someone plant weed in my panniers? That's what I figured the deputy was looking for when he date-raped my bike."

"This isn't about marijuana."

The silence was prolonged. "Whatever, it was an illegal search."

"It's because we found human hair in the Dumpster where you work. It was in wolf scat."

Again, a long pause. "Really," Amorak said. He leaned forward and spread his hands so that they were inches from Walt's, mocking him. "I wouldn't know anything about that. A lot of people work there . . . Walter."

"The hair, we believe, is from a young woman of your acquaintance, Nanika Martinelli. We'll have DNA confirmation soon."

A line of concentration drew Amorak's eyebrows into a single line. "I don't think I know that name."

"We can produce a witness who said you were looking for Miss Martinelli this spring."

"I don't think so."

From behind the glass, Harold glanced at Stranahan. "Fly shop owner on the Kootenai," Sean whispered. Harold nodded.

Amorak had pulled back into his chair. He'd given up trying to stare down Walt.

"Nan-ee-ka." Thinking about it. "Oh, you must mean Nicki. I haven't seen her in forever."

"How long is forever?"

Amorak shrugged. "Two, three years."

"Two or three?"

"Maybe two."

"Why were you looking for her?"

He flashed up his palms. "In the area. Just wanted to say hello."

"What area would that be . . . Todd?"

Now the look of worry was hard to misinterpret. Stranahan wondered how many places Amorak had searched for Nicki besides Libby. The harder he'd looked for her, the harder it would be to dismiss as just wanting to say hello.

"Up at her dad's old place on the Kootenai. I'd heard he'd passed. Wanted to see how she was holding up."

"Just neighborly concern?"

"That's right."

Walt glanced at his notes. "You want coffee. I'm going to get a cup."

"Don't touch the stuff," Amorak said. As Walt stood, he leaned forward to tower over Amorak, establishing his authority.

"You got back problems, Walter? You look like you could use some stretching exercises."

Back behind the glass, Walt shook his head. "Tough nut. Martha get back to you?"

"She just called from the road," Stranahan said. "The scat analyst admitted he talked to Amorak about the signpost. He said he didn't lead him to the rock personally, but there is only one draw up through the cliffs and it wouldn't be hard to find from the description. Martha believes his story. She doesn't think he's involved with Amorak. He's just a talkative sort and bumped into Amorak at the campground, like we figured."

"Okay." Walt dug a finger into the corner of his eye. "Right now he thinks we're putting together bits and pieces, that we don't have anything solid linking him to Martinelli's disappearance. I mention the scat analyst, he's going to feel the noose tighten. He's familiar with the system; he'll clam up before he denies something we can prove. I'm surprised he's given us as much as he has."

"He's arrogant," Harold said. "That's his Achilles."

Hess nodded. "In Chicago I had all kinds in the box—drug dealers, I'm talking big time, mobbed up politicians, gang bangers, two professional button men. There's no formula, but I look in this guy's eyes, he's telling me he did it and he's telling me to go fuck myself at the same time."

"How long can we hold him?"

"His twenty-four hours are up tomorrow afternoon. But I'm guessing he'll be cut loose first thing in the morning."

"No chance of charging him?"

Hess shook his head. "Not unless he trips up."

He didn't. But he didn't shut up, either. When pressed by Walt, he agreed that he knew Jake Thorn, had met him at the campground and, yes, they might have talked about wolf signposts. Wolves were his brothers. He was fascinated by wolves. Why wouldn't he quiz Thorn about them?

"Did you see Nanika Martinelli on the fourteenth of September, the day she disappeared in Papoose Basin?"

"No, I didn't."

"On any day since that night?"

"No, I didn't."

"On any day before that date over the past two years?"

"No, I haven't."

"Were you aware she worked at the Culpepper Ranch as a naturalist and fly-fishing guide?"

"No."

"Were you aware that prior to her employment at the ranch, she had worked for Sam Meslik's outfitting business on the Madison River?"

"I've never heard of Sam Meslik."

"Why did you have this copy of the *Bridger Mountain Star* in the panniers of your motorcycle?" Walt slid a yellowed newspaper from under his clipboard.

"There's always a few newspapers floating around in my panniers. I pick them up to start campfires with. I don't read them."

Stranahan looked at Harold. Harold flexed his cheek muscles. This was news to both of them.

"Can you read this headline? It's from July eighteenth."

"It says," Amorak peered at the paper, "'Poor Whitebark Pine Nut Season Spells Strife for Grizzly Bears.'"

"Not that one."

"'Fly Fishing Venus Catches Clients for Madison River Outfitter: Trout a Bonus.'"

"You see the photograph of her?" Walt jabbed at the paper with his forefinger. "Be hard for you to miss, your brotherly concern for her and all. The story mentions Meslik in the first paragraph."

Amorak shrugged. "Like I said, I just pick them up."

"But this paper is more than two months old. It should be ashes by now."

"Must have got lost in the shuffle. Pannier's like a belly button. Collects all kinds of shit."

Walt stood up.

"Where are you going?"

"Going to let you think if you want to change your mind about seeing this paper."

"Enlarged prostate, huh? You gotta pee again? Getting old must be hell."

Walt came around to the back of the glass and caught Stranahan's attention. "The deputy who pulled him in searched the panniers for wolf poop, not weed. But you said he possessed drugs and that was prior to the search, so either way we're on firm ground here. The search ought to stand up. I think we have enough to go to the DA, but it's not that simple. We have to present a case to him. That's not going to happen tonight. In the meantime we can't hold him. In my opinion he's a flight risk, but the law's the law."

"You think, huh?" It was Harold.

"I wouldn't be sure," Stranahan said. "You said it yourself, Harold. He's arrogant. Unless he thinks we're sitting on a card, like we have a witness who saw him with Martinelli in the time frame, he'll figure he can ride it out."

"And he'll probably be right." Walt worked his Adam's apple. "We'll let him sleep on it."

The door snicked open behind them. It was Ettinger. She walked to the glass, drummed her fingers on the butt of her Ruger.

"Give me the good news, boys."

CHAPTER THIRTY-THREE

In from the Cold

Stranahan was critically eyeing the canvas on his easel, a misty oil based on studies of the River of No Return, when the phone rang. He tucked the brush behind his right ear and groped for the receiver.

"Sean, this is Fen."

"Fen, ah . . . I'm painting." *What the hell?*

"Sorry, man, I know it's early."

"No problem, just let me finish this horizon line while the paint's still wet. It won't take a minute."

"I don't know if I can call you back."

"Then just hold the phone."

Sean cradled the old-fashioned receiver to his chest, staring off at the reverse lettering etched into the rippled glass of his studio door. He could feel his heart leaping against the receiver. He'd come into the cultural center early to pick up his mail and make a few business calls. Later, he'd planned to drive down to Sam's fly shop and tell Asena Martinelli that he'd done what she'd paid him to do, found the man she suspected of kidnapping her sister. The last thing he expected this morning was a call from that man.

"I'm back. Thanks. Where are you calling from? West?"

"No, man, I'm in Bridger. The dicks hauled me in. I spent the night as an honored guest of the facility."

"Did they charge you?"

"No. I think someone at the wildlife center tipped them that I was dealing, but they don't have shit."

"So . . . what can I do for you?"

"I need a ride. They picked me up at work and my bike's still in West."

"Does Deni know?"

"Yeah, they swung by the tent so they could turn our shit inside out and she's okay, but she can't drive the bike and I got no way of getting back. I thought they were going to hook me up with a ride, but this fucker who drilled me said it wasn't part of the service."

"So you need a lift, huh?"

"Yeah, man, I'd appreciate it. I don't know anyone else. I wouldn't have called you, but you left your card."

"Where are you?"

"Law and Justice. It's their phone."

Stranahan said he'd swing by the east door and hung up. An idea came to him. He dipped his brush in turpentine and picked the phone back up.

———

"I gotta put my John Hancock on something."

Amorak had appeared at the double doors and hollered for Stranahan to wait. Stranahan looked up and down the drive. Half the county force knew the Land Cruiser and he didn't want Amorak to catch him talking friendly to a cop. Jason Kent's half-ton diesel Chevy idled up behind him. Kent climbed out and ran the two fingers on his left hand through his crew cut. He itched at a razor scab under his short sideburn, cocked his pinkie at Stranahan and climbed the steps to the doors just as Amorak was pushing through.

"Who's the three-fingered man?" he said. He climbed into the Land Cruiser and looked hard at Stranahan.

"That's Jason Kent. He's the head of Search and Rescue. I'm a volunteer." When in doubt, go with the truth.

"How did he lose his fingers?"

"Caught in a combine. He used to ranch out of Hardin."

The answer seemed to satisfy, and Amorak settled back in the seat. "Vintage ride. How old is it?"

"Came out of the Toyota plant in seventy-six, year before I was born."

"I was conceived in the backseat of a Chevy Malibu," Amorak said, nodding at the memory. "When my mom kicked the old man out of the house, I saw her burning a blanket in the yard. It was the blanket that was in the car that night. She'd kept it all those years, but I didn't find out 'til later. Sort of sums up how she felt about having me."

They turned onto Highway 191 and headed south up the Gallatin Canyon. Most of the aspens on the mountainsides were skeletons now, white bones against the green of the pines.

"Do you think they'll come after you?" Stranahan said.

"If they do, I just might be hard to find. But I like my job and got half a mind to stay put and say fuck 'em."

"Have you made any progress finding a place to stay?"

"No, and the campground locks down on Tuesday. We could set up somewhere else, but the weather's going to chase us out sooner or later."

"Hey," Stranahan acted as if the thought had just occurred to him, "I have a friend who's got one of those forest lease cabins. She works for the Park Service and is doing an exchange where she'll be in Moab this winter. She's looking for someone to sit the place."

"How much is she asking?"

Stranahan shook his head. "I don't know. But the cabin's on Cougar Creek, it's on the way."

Lothar announced their arrival before the Land Cruiser came to a stop. Katie Sparrow opened the door wearing an untucked man's check flannel shirt, the sleeves hanging down over her hands.

"Shut up," she said to Lothar. She put her hand on the back of the shepherd's neck. He growled deep in his throat. "Quiet." The growl idled down. "Go say hi." The dog nosed Sean's crotch, looked askance at Amorak and then circled the Land Cruiser, hiking a leg at each tire.

Katie lifted a bang of hair from her right eye. She smiled, showing a darkened front tooth. "Hell, Stranny, you could have called." He hugged her and bent his head to her ear. "Don't overdo it," he whispered.

She broke away and looked Amorak up and down. "Who are you?"

"I'm Fen."

"Fen's looking for a place to stay this winter," Stranahan said. "I didn't know if you were still trying to find someone to sit the cabin."

"It would be for my girlfriend and me," Fen said.

"Do you have a job?"

"I'm a caretaker at the Wildlife Center. I work with the wolves."

"This place gets hellacious cold," she said. "And no one plows the road so you got to shoe in once the snow gets deep. But I put a blower in the woodstove and routed heat into the bedroom. I'm not going to say yes because I haven't made up my mind, but seeing that you're here you can look. Don't mind the clutter."

It wasn't the same cabin Stranahan had spent the night in. The couch where he'd slept was covered with newspapers, the coffee table strewn with the remnants of a TV dinner and an empty wine bottle. There was a cigarette stubbed out in a tea saucer. Katie didn't smoke. She must have driven into town and bought a pack after Stranahan called from his office. A book lay open, facedown. *Fifty Shades of Gray*. Stranahan smiled to himself. It was a nice touch.

"When is it you have to go to Moab?" he asked.

"Third week of October. The job runs 'til middle of April."

"How much are you asking?" Amorak said.

"You're going to have to let me think about it. I'll get back to Stranny."

Amorak nodded. "I'd have to know pretty soon."

Katie extended one arm in the down-stay gesture that Stranahan had seen her use with Lothar. "I said I'll get in touch with him, I'll get in touch with him. I got to get ready for work now. It was nice meeting you."

Back on the porch, she kissed Stranahan on the mouth. "Don't stay away so long next time."

"You tapping that?" Fen said, when they started back out the drive. "None of my business, but a woman all alone with her dog and her chick porn, tickling her clit, be a shame to let that go to waste . . . Shit, man, I hope she decides to rent."

Deni was huddled in her blanket, sitting in front of a snapping fire. When she wrapped her arms around Fen, he crooked an arm under her knees and lifted her, swung her in a circle and slowly set her down. "Everything's okay, baby girl," he said.

He looked at Stranahan. "I can't pay you, man. I got fifteen dollars 'til the next paycheck. But I can give you a smoke for the road."

"That's all right," Stranahan said. "I have a client who wants a painting of the Firehole River. I'd been thinking of coming down, anyway."

"No, man, you went out of your way. Wait here."

Amorak disappeared down the high bank. Stranahan could hear his footsteps on the gravel bar, fading as he hiked upstream.

Deni looked over shyly. "Do you think I could ever paint like you?"

"Sure," Stranahan said. "I can see that you're sensitive. That's the first requirement for being a good artist." He gestured up the river where Amorak had disappeared. "Doesn't it get lonely with him away at work all day?"

She nodded, facing him with her eyes growing large. "It's scary when I'm the only one in the campground. But I got my granddaddy's gun from the war that he took off of a dead soldier in Italy. I mean it was Fen's granddaddy, but we say it was mine 'cause of the felony and Fen can't really own a gun, not legally. He keeps it under the rock with his stash unless he's doing his business or scheduled to pick up game meat. He says he doesn't want to go into the boonies unless he's got some protection."

Stranahan nodded his agreement. "Good thing he didn't have it on him when the deputy picked him up."

He could hear Fen's footsteps coming back from upriver.

"Where are you from, Deni?"

"I'm . . . Fen doesn't. He doesn't like me to say about that."

Her face blushed as Amorak climbed up the bank.

"What have you two been talking about?" he said. His eyes were on Deni. The wolf pendant against his chest hair caught the sunlight.

"We were talking about art," Stranahan said.

Amorak stared at Deni until she dropped her head.

"Here you go, man," he said, offering Stranahan the joint. Stranahan nodded his thanks and put it in his shirt pocket as Deni came up from behind Amorak and wrapped her arms around his middle. She pushed her fingers into his jeans pockets. "Are we going to be able to stay?" she said, her voice muffled against his back.

"Yeah, we might have found a place to get out of the cold."

"I'll leave word for you at the wildlife center when I hear from Katie," Sean said. "Well, I hope they leave you alone now."

He was already thinking forty miles up the road, the clock ticking on a conversation he wasn't looking forward to having. He ignored the phone vibrating in his pocket and lifted his finger in a Montana salute, Deni still clinging to Fen like a joey kangaroo, and was back through West Yellowstone and halfway up Targhee Pass, the shortest route from West Yellowstone to the Madison Valley, when he remembered the call. He'd missed two, the second from Ettinger.

She picked up immediately. Stranahan pulled over and filled her in.

"I thought the Park Service paid for her housing."

"They do, but Amorak doesn't know that."

"So he bought Katie's coal miner's daughter routine?"

"I bought Katie's routine."

"Such an enterprising young woman," Martha said. No attempt to keep the sarcasm out of her voice.

"What is it about you and Katie?"

"Nothing. What is it about *you* and Katie?"

". . . Nothing."

"Then we're in agreement. Are you still determined to tell Asena Martinelli about finding this guy?"

"It's my contractual obligation. If she hadn't hired me, we wouldn't know Amorak's name, let alone where he worked."

"Wait a few days. Something's come up. I'd like to talk about it in person, later today if you can. It's possible he's done other crimes."

"Killed other women?"

"No, it's unrelated."

"I've waited already."

"She could screw this up by doing something stupid."

"What can she screw up? You said yourself the chances of persuading the DA to charge are slim to none. Is what's come up going to change that?"

"Probably not."

"Then I'm going to tell her. She isn't a bunch of nerve endings like Nicki. Asena's a rational person."

"Rational people make rash decisions when their loved one's are murdered."

"She might know something that would make your case."

"She's already told you what she knows."

Stranahan ran his eyes up to Lionhead Mountain. Snow dusted the ridgeline, a sprinkling on the stone mane of a cat you could only see by squinting your eyes. Stranahan squinted. *Well, maybe not.*

He heard Ettinger sigh. "Okay, but it's against my better judgment.

Damnit, I hate it when shitheads go free . . . come back with something I want to hear, okay? And keep in mind I'm holding you responsible."

"For what?"

"Anything . . . eventualities."

Stranahan saw the first call he'd missed had been from Sam. Sam's place was his next stop, but he wasn't going to drive the forty miles if Asena wasn't there.

"Kimosabe."

"I'm returning your call, buddy."

"I'm reminding you about the walk and fish tomorrow morning."

"You signed me up for a guide day?"

"Patrick Willoughby. He wants to fish the fall-run browns at Madison Junction."

"I thought he'd left and they'd shut down the clubhouse for the winter."

"They did. He's just swinging through for a day. You're to pick him up in West at the Three Bears Motel. Six a.m."

"I guess I forgot."

"Well, unforget."

Stranahan rapped his fingernails on the steering wheel. He was strung tighter than piano wire. The last thing he needed was to break momentum. But then, thinking about it, maybe it was just what he needed. He'd been crowding Amorak. If he didn't back off, he risked scaring him away. Wait a few days and then talk to him again about Katie's cabin. Stall for time.

"Is Asena there?"

"She's on the river. I got double-booked and she guided a client. She'll be taking out, ah, 'bout an hour from now."

"I didn't know you were letting her guide?"

"She insisted. Said floating the river might give some insight into

Nicki. It's like she woke up and crawled out of her shell. Ever since she went out on the lake with you and you talked about God knows what. What did you talk about?"

The answer was the man on the motorcycle in the Lamar Valley, the first hard evidence that Amorak was in the vicinity.

"Where's she taking out?" he said, avoiding the question.

"The West Madison access site, upriver from McAtee Bridge."

"I'll meet her there."

"Then I'm going to ask you to do the shuttle. Save me the gas. But what do you want to talk to her about?"

"I'd like to tell her first."

"Okay, just don't drop any bombs until she collects the tip. The client only owns half the chili joints in Texas. Chilly Billy's. You think about how much methane comes out of those bathrooms, you could fire a chimp into outer space."

———

William Weston, aka "Chilly Billy" Weston, did not look like a chili baron, or any kind of baron unless barons grew noses like Roman Polanski's and came slim as cigarillos. But he did have an accent full of West Texas twang, and the tented bills his fingers ferreted into the breast pocket of Asena's shirt had Benjamin Franklin's face on them.

"I think I've just been violated," Asena said, after Weston had disappeared in his rental Lexus. She flashed a quick smile that under other circumstances Stranahan would have been encouraged to see.

"Look, I'm just going to say it. I found Amorak. His real name's Todd McCready. Or was. He had it changed." He hesitated.

"Is this something I'm supposed to sit down for? I'm a big girl. Just tell me."

He did, the evening falling and the sound of the current coming up before he was finished. It was cold and they sat in the Land Cruiser with Stranahan cranking up the heater intermittently.

"I don't know what else to say," he said. "It's a murder investigation now, at least it will be if the DNA on the hair in the dumpster matches your sister's."

"At least he'll be arrested. It will never be enough, but he'll pay for my sister's death. What?"

Sean knew she'd seen the change in his expression.

"I'd like to tell you he will be, but I have to be honest. The evidence against him is circumstantial. There's no body and no witness who can place Fen and Nicki together within the past two years, at least not yet. DAs running for reelection don't like to prosecute cases where shitheads walk free, as the sheriff likes to say."

"So he won't pay." It was a statement.

The silence was Stranahan's answer.

"How do they get the meat?" She wasn't looking at the river but at the mountains to the east, where shadows were climbing the gold face of Papoose Peak.

"Amorak said it's donated by hunters. Sometimes he collects it in the field, sometimes it's brought to the center by the people who shot the game."

Stranahan saw her shoulders sag.

"I always knew she might be dead," she said. "I just convinced myself there was a chance she wasn't."

"There still is a chance."

"But if he kidnapped her or she was planning to run away with him, then what's he doing living with the other girl?"

"I don't know. He could be holding Nicki captive somewhere."

"That seems a stretch. No, I have to face the fact that she's gone. But how can you put something like this behind you, knowing your sister's killer is walking around free? You tell me." She sighed. When she spoke again the life had gone out of her voice. She sounded resigned. "Sooner or later I have to go back to Libby and straighten out my father's estate. I suppose that's the thing to do. Sell the house, then there's some property in B.C. up around Kamloops to dispose of. I'll go back to work. As a counselor I always tell people work is medicine for forgetting. See if it really is true."

"If you can think of anything to help us build a case . . ."

"You don't think I'd tell you if I did?"

"That's not what I meant."

"You're right, I'm sorry. It's just a lot to take in."

She was silent on the drive down the valley, except once to comment on the moon, rising over the teeth of the Gravellys to the east. "It's the Hunter's Moon," she said. "One day off, maybe. Daddy always hunted moose on the Hunter's Moon. He said it was like the ocean tides, except that it pulled blood through the veins instead of water onto land. He thought he was a better hunter for that one day of the year."

"Did he get his moose?"

"Nicki and I grew up on moose. And fish. You always know someone's from coastal B.C. because they never order salmon in a restaurant."

They were turning into Sam's drive.

"Do you want me to stay awhile?"

"No, just drop me." Her voice sounded far away. She was somewhere now where Stranahan couldn't follow. "He killed her forever," she said to herself.

The Land Cruiser's headlights lit up the shop.

Stranahan said, "If you don't mind walking, I think I'll turn around here. Sam will want to talk and I don't feel up to it."

"You either? I can't blame you. Sometimes there's nothing more to say at the end of the day. You try to be someone who knows how to cope and do what you have to to keep going."

She leaned across the space between the seats and kissed him on the cheek. Her lips were as cold as the river. Then she was gone.

CHAPTER THIRTY-FOUR

Anglers in the Age of Irony

The feather streamer Stranahan had christened the Vegas showgirl and loop-knotted to Willoughby's leader flashed its tinsel charms in a deep run of the Madison several miles below the junction pool, where the Firehole and Gibbon rivers bled together. The first rainbow came undone at the jump, the second showed its size, then bore down and suddenly pulled much harder than it should have had the muscle for. As the line arrowed toward a log sweeper, Willoughby looked at Stranahan and raised his eyes behind his thick glasses. Sean smiled as the "trout" climbed onto the log. He'd known that an otter had taken possession of the fish directly after the jump, having lost a good brown to the thief in the same pool earlier in the fall.

"What do I do?" Willoughby said. "The manual did not address this situation."

"You break him off."

Willoughby did and hobbled out of the river, his wading staff probing the streambed ahead of him. They sat on the bank and watched the otter rip orange flesh from the trout.

"If we keep fishing, he'll just follow us and take anything you hook," Stranahan said.

"You overestimate my ambition." Willoughby removed his tweed hat and examined the flies in a sheepskin patch pinned to the brim. "Sean," he said, "I have made much of my living finding the weaknesses in men's characters and in the political systems to which they profess their loyalty. I find reading a man's face is similar to reading a map, a matter of deciphering contour lines to envision a country, or if you are a naval intelligence officer as I was, to see beneath the surface of the sea. Your face tells me you're somewhere else this morning. At the risk of intrusion, might I ask where?"

"It's that obvious?"

"Quite so, I'm afraid."

"I'm not sure I can talk about an active investigation."

"We're sitting on federal soil. I assure you my clearance level in matters of state is adequate to permit our conversation, but if you feel uncomfortable talking about events that have happened outside park borders, present me with a theoretical scenario. Names are unimportant."

As Stranahan talked, clouds of steam rose about the men's heads. Willoughby's unruly eyebrows rose twice, first when Sean spoke of the girl who had been burned in the hot pot and again at his suspicion that the man responsible for that was the same person who had fed Nicki's hair to wolves.

"Are you intimating this man is a serial killer, that he seduces impressionable young women only to discard them in a fatal and quite sensational manner when they fail to meet his standard?"

"Doesn't it strike you as a possibility?"

Willoughby seriously considered the question. "Profiling is a science, Sean," he said at length. "It is a better one now than when I was more active in the field, but I do know something of these matters from a military perspective." His eyes met Stranahan's. "If I may be so bold as to offer an opinion?"

"Anything that would help put this man behind bars, I'd appreciate it."

"That I can't promise. What I will say is the person you describe runs up flags suggesting a psychopathic disorder. He is egocentric, remorseless, lacks empathy and he is a nonconformist. This wolf hierarchy he imposes on the young women is typical of psychopaths who are at heart narcissists, and who shun social and legal mores by establishing their own set of rules. And"—Willoughby raised a fore-finger pink from cold—"he can be charming when the need arises. He can put on what psychiatrists refer to as a 'mask of sanity.' These are all traits of the classic psychopath. But, and this is important"— Willoughby wagged his finger—"scratch a serial killer and you often uncover a psychopath. But scratch a psychopath—?"

"And you don't necessarily uncover a serial killer," finished Stranahan.

"You anticipate me. The defining characteristic of most serials, note that I did not say all, is their inability to form human attachments. Isolation. Serials are literally stranded in the cold. You may characterize the relationships this man has with women as control-ling, even abusive, but they *are* attachments. In the case of the woman who is missing, the attachment has become obsessive. It is entirely conceivable he killed her in order to possess her, to take that which would not be given, but if that's the case, her murder falls into a different category of crime from the majority perpetrated by seri-als, who wish to exert control over a category of people rather than an individual. Have you noticed that it's snowing? What induced me to come to Montana in such an uncivilized season?"

Stranahan was working his toes in his wading boots to keep the blood circulating. "You've given me a lot to mull over. And I think we've given the otter enough time to get bored. Let's walk upstream. If a hatch of blue-winged olives trickles off, as I think it will, we'll have some fishing."

———

Two hours and two trout later, notably a three-pound, prespawn brown that sipped in Willoughby's dry fly as delicately as a doe clip-ping a wildflower, they resumed the conversation. Willoughby had treated Sean to lunch in the bar inside the Old Faithful Inn, where they sat under a cut-glass window etched with a cartoon bear that was conducting an orchestra of cubs.

Stranahan sipped at an Irish coffee. "I noticed the look on your face when I mentioned the girl burned in the hot pot. What were you thinking, Patrick? Do you think it could have been an accident?"

"An accident? Only in that it's likely she was frightened and tripped. I'm just uncertain about the identity of the frightener. What you omitted in your recitation was of great interest." He hailed the waitress. "Would you be so kind as to bring us another round? Doctors orders. Medicine for the heart, you see."

He looked off for a moment, then the eyes snapped into focus. He tapped the faux leather covering the tabletop. "You never once mentioned that this man you are investigating exhibited uneasiness, quite the opposite. If I chased someone into boiling water and she survived, I would have a worm in my gut. What will she say when she recovers from the coma? The fact that your man has not left the area leads me to believe that he is unworried. Either there is nothing for him to worry about, or he is so confident in his authority that he believes she won't point the finger at him. I think the former more likely."

"Then who is responsible?"

"The roommate mentioned that the victim hitched around the park. Perhaps she got a ride with the hot pot watcher who is credited with finding her. Perhaps he offered to show her a secret thermal area." He let the thought hang in the air as his caterpillar eyebrows climbed into inverted Vs. "Anyone who spends his life sitting beside a pool of water and has no family to go home to. . . . Frankly, I'm surprised your sheriff hasn't looked into this man's history, but then I suppose there are jurisdictional issues."

"It's an accident as far as the Park Service is concerned. There's no evidence to suggest otherwise."

"Yes, I understand that. But the professional wrestler, this Madman from Minnetonka . . . I would think a search engine might provoke several hits on a name so distinctive."

Willoughby nodded to the waitress for the check.

"Have you ever seen an eruption of Old Faithful?"

Stranahan admitted he hadn't.

"Nor have I. I suppose such a trite display of shock and awe should be beneath us, we being anglers in the age of irony and so forth, but I rather feel a child's compulsion to stand in simple wonder of nature. Shall we?"

———

Robert Knudson, aka Geyser Bob, aka the Madman of Minnetonka, had been a featured performer in the North Country All-Star Wrestlers from 1975 through 1984, with a professional record of 27–395, including losses to such luminaries of the sport as Bruno Sammartino, Chief White Owl, and Rowdy Roddy Piper. His most memorable victory was over fellow heel George "the Animal" Steele, in what the *Milwaukee Standard*, in a retrospective of wrestling superstars, called "The Slobberfest of the Century," both men being notable for copious drooling as they stalked their opponents around the ring. The story went on to report that both Knudson and Steele had enjoyed reputations as erudite giants who had careers as high school teachers and coaches, with a notable difference. Knudson, in April 1997, had been issued a restraining order after repeated, unwanted advances on a female student. He'd lost his job as a result, although criminal charges had not been filed.

Willoughby, who was reading the story out loud in his motel room at the Three Bears, pursed his lips as he continued to search the name on his laptop.

Knudson's name popped up again in an archived story in the *Green Bay Herald* headlined "Smelt Fisherman Saves Wrestling Icon." The story was dated April 16, 1999.

> A local fisherman rescued an unconscious man he found floating naked in the icy Menominee River on Thursday night, the Green Bay County sheriff's office

reported. Andrew Larkenoff, 33, was smelt fishing when he spotted the body and waded into chest-deep water to pull the victim to shore. The fisherman said he called 911 and tried to warm the unconscious man until an ambulance arrived.

The victim was identified as Robert Knudson, 49, a former professional wrestling star known as the "Madman of Minnetonka." He was listed in fair condition at Superior Benefice Hospital.

"I used my own body warmth to try to keep him alive," said Larkenoff. "But he was so big and I was so cold myself I think he helped me more than I helped him."

The World Wrestling Almanac listed Knudson at 6′ 7″ and 330 pounds.

Capt. James Cummings of the Green Bay County Sheriff's Office said Knudson's car was found parked near the Johnsonville Bridge, about a mile upriver from where he was rescued. Cummings could not confirm that Knudson had jumped from the bridge.

Knudson's involvement with a young woman when he had been a teacher at . . .

Willoughby finished the story, which contributed no further details about the restraining order, but added that Knudson had been separated from his wife, who still lived in Minnetonka. The former wrestler had been employed in Green Bay as a construction worker and substitute high school teacher at the time of the incident.

"It's a slim thread, but a thread all the same," he said. "I hope the Park Service investigates the man."

"I'll check with a ranger friend," Stranahan said. "She'll pass the information to someone reliable."

"What will you do now?" Willoughby asked.

"I don't know. I found the man I was paid to find. Now we'll see how the judicial system responds. I'm not optimistic."

"No, I mean tonight. It's too far to drive back to Bridger. You could bunk here with me."

"Thanks, I might take you up on it. In fact I will. But I want to check the campground, make certain my buddy hasn't bailed to parts unknown."

"Is that wise? Won't he become suspicious if you keep dropping by?"

"Maybe you're right. I'll just park near the wildlife center and make sure he's on shift, then see if he drives away toward the campground afterward. I won't follow him."

"Your Land Rover—"

"Land Cruiser."

"I was going to say it's rather conspicuous. Take my rental. That way you can tail him as you see fit. I'd offer to accompany you, but the cold water seems to have played havoc on my arthritic legs."

They agreed to meet for pizza at seven. The Rocky Mountain Pizza Company was a short walk from the motel.

"If you fail to show by seven thirty, I'll call for reinforcements."

"Wait until eight, Mother," Stranahan said, closing the door behind him.

Willoughby waited until a little after nine o'clock before ringing the Hyalite County Sheriff's Department from the pizzeria.

CHAPTER THIRTY-FIVE

Hunter's Moon

Stranahan scratched at his stubble. The truck was halfway up Targhee Pass and had a cockeyed headlight that made it easy to follow. Not that it would have been difficult otherwise. The van with the howling wolf logo on the side panel was the only vehicle Stranahan had seen since the lights of West Yellowstone twinkled out in the rearview mirror. He watched the headlight flare up into the pines and then disappear over the pass into Idaho. The next fork was the right turn to Henry's Lake, which became U.S. 87 before bending north back into Montana. Which way would the van turn? A better question—why was Amorak driving it in the first place?

When Stranahan had eased Willoughby's Camry into a parking spot on Yellowstone Avenue twenty minutes earlier, it was still light enough to see the motorcycle parked in the Paws of Yellowstone lot. Six o'clock came and went, the sky grew dark, the indoor lights of the center went dark and the Honda stood on its kickstand, a horse without a rider. He paid scant attention when the van backed out of the lot and would not have suspected Amorak was behind the wheel if it hadn't turned left to pass within ten feet. Had the man seen him? No, his face stared straight ahead. Sean had waited until the van was well down the street before making a U-turn to follow.

Now the van was turning toward the lake, and again Sean's hand went to his chin. The logical explanation for the excursion was that the center had received a call from an archery hunter who wanted to donate game. Amorak would have been directed to a rendezvous site, perhaps up a logging road or at a trailhead. If so, Sean saw nothing to gain by following. The tail could make Amorak suspicious, in a worst-case scenario flush him from the area for good. But what if he wasn't meeting a hunter? What if, instead, he'd waited until the other employees had gone home and borrowed the van for a different purpose, one that had something to do with Nicki Martinelli? If he was holding her captive somewhere, perhaps Amorak was transferring her to the van to take her somewhere else. It seemed improbable, starting with the fact that Amorak was living with another woman who had assumed the mantle of his mate. But Stranahan didn't take his foot off the accelerator.

Several miles after reentering Montana and turning north on 287, the van slowed, showed its left blinker and veered onto the gravel road that crossed Three Dollar Bridge. Stranahan had a moment's unease. A few washboardy miles beyond the bridge the road forked, the right-hand turn leading to Cliff and Wade lakes, the two largest in a chain of lakes that nestled like diamonds on a string in a deep geological fault. It had been less than a week since he'd fished Wade Lake with Asena. A coincidence? Possibly, though it challenged one of Martha Ettinger's tenets of police work, that there was no such animal.

Stranahan switched off the headlights and crossed the bridge, the van far out in front, only a soft glow over the clumps of sage marking its progress. He stayed well back and reached the fork, pausing a moment before turning toward the lakes. A hunch, backed by a slight haze that may have been lifted from the gravel by the van's tires. The road dipped and climbed. Yes, there was the glow again, haunting the pines in the higher elevation with a ghostly haze. Stranahan coaxed the Camry through a crust of old snow to the pass, where the glow had vanished. Below him was Wade Lake, its deep-set eye silver in the moonlight. He pulled off the road and let the car idle, trying to envision the country below.

He remembered that the road fell toward the lakes in one long switchback, the downhill grade bending north before the road turned back on itself to complete the descent. He ought to see the van's lights coming into that last turn, and there they were, sweeping in a circle before fading out. Now he wouldn't see them again until the van approached Wade Lake. If he didn't see the lights, then the van would have turned south toward Cliff Lake; the two bodies of water were separated by a saddle in a hill. In either case there was nowhere farther Amorak could go. Both forks dead-ended at water.

Stranahan switched off the motor and walked to the edge of the ridge, where he could peer down into the fault. He should have seen the lights by now. So then, Cliff Lake. Stranahan had fished there only once, at the shoals near the boat ramp. From there the road contoured the shoreline to a campground secluded in the pines. He'd never been to that campground but recalled seeing a rope swing through his binoculars, flailing arms and legs as kids jumped in, their shouts reaching across a quarter mile of water. But that was in July. The place would be deserted now.

What was Amorak doing there?

Slowly, Stranahan motored down the grade, babying the Camry through ice in the ruts. He came to a spur leading to a Forest Service campground called Hilltop, used only when the lakeside camps filled on summer weekends. He turned into it. As expected, the loops were empty but it gave him an idea, and he parked in one of the sites. From here, the Camry would be invisible to anyone passing on the road. Cliff Lake couldn't be more than a twenty-minute hike. He'd find out what Amorak was up to without announcing his presence. He stepped out of the car feeling quite naked without his bear spray, this being grizzly country with a capital *G*. No time now to regret not packing gear from the Land Cruiser. He patted the pockets of his jacket and felt the bulk of the Carnivore tracking light. It would have to serve as his eyes.

As his boots crunched through isolated skiffs of snow, Sean felt the melancholia of men adrift in wilderness, the profound isolation that cold and darkness impose impartially and that was only partly mitigated by the assurance of the road. He smiled at his insecurity and pursed his lips to whistle, an old habit, then thought better of it.

Another half mile and the lake was before him, a pool of milk under the circle of the moon. He stopped walking. Had he heard a sound? Yes, voices. Indistinguishable words tailed in echoes as they floated across the lake. Stranahan had reached the water's edge and looked across toward the campground. No lights there, but again voices rose and now he could hear a dog barking underneath the voices, an abrupt, deep chop that carried clearly. A pause, and the air was split apart, the unmistakable crack of a gunshot. Stranahan instinctively ducked. He began to run toward the campground and went down hard, slipping on a patch of ice, his head and right side slamming against the ground. When he clambered to his feet, pain shot up the side of his body. The voices from farther up the lakeshore seemed to echo around inside his head. The dog's barking was incessant. He waited a minute to regain his equilibrium, then slowly limped toward the campground, wondering whose name the bullet had carried.

———

Stranahan stood in the shadow of a tree. Ahead, the ground was striped abstractly by moonlight filtering through scattered pines. Nothing to see but the first of the campsites. He moved forward, shadow to shadow. Ahead was the rectangular silhouette of the van. Beyond, where the ground sloped toward the lake, he could make out a boat trailer hitched to what appeared to be an SUV. The dog's bark was loud but hoarser than before, its exhalations breaking up. From the furious scratching and banging, Stranahan thought it must be locked inside the vehicle. No boat on the trailer.

One of the voices had picked back up again, a man's voice, from somewhere farther up the lake. It sounded neither angry nor conversational, but was more a murmuring like an invocation you'd hear standing outside a church service, muffled by heavy wooden doors. Stranahan skirted the vehicles, staying within the security of the pines as he worked up the shoreline. Ahead was a small clearing and as Stranahan approached, the lake came into view and he saw the vague outline of a boat pulled up in the shallows. On its near side stood a short, squat figure. No, that was an illusion. It was a man kneeling in the shallows with his head raised and hands spread as if nailed to an invisible cross. It had to be Fenrir Amorak. Now Stranahan could hear his words:

> *And the blood of the wolf will rain from the skies*
> *And all the rivers will run red with blood*
> *And the blood of man who cast aspersion upon the wolf will flow*
>   *with the river*
> *And he will die*
> *And he will die*
> *And he will die*

"Stop it. Please stop." It was Asena's voice, somewhere very near. He realized that the SUV must be Asena's Bronco and that the boat was his own Adirondack guideboat. Behind him the yelping faded as the dog lost its voice. Was it Killer?

The invocation began again. "And the blood of the wolf—"

"Stop." She couldn't be more than fifty feet away, Stranahan thought, though he still couldn't see her.

"My darling, there's nothing you can do about the deaths of the men who cried wolf." Amorak's voice was a metronome, amplified by the water. "Only I can absolve you of your sin. Come and be baptized in my arms. You know how much I love you, how it was always you and always will be you and—"

"Just stop." Asena's voice was pleading.

Now Stranahan could make out her silhouette. She was standing to Amorak's right, maybe ten feet farther up the shoreline. He could see the revolver gripped in her hands, the black barrel pointing at her feet even as Amorak beckoned from his invisible cross.

"I'll shoot again!"

"No, my darling. You won't. Feel your hands. I control them now. They are heavy, they can't move. Let your burden fall from them."

"No. Please no."

"Feel your fingers. They are on fire. Open them. I said open them!"

Stranahan heard a clatter as Asena dropped the gun. Amorak rose to his feet, water streaming down his legs, and as he lurched toward her, dragging his right foot, Stranahan saw Asena turn and grab for the gun she'd dropped. She came up with it glinting in her hand, but Amorak had reached her and wrapped his arms around her from behind. With a jerk, he wrested the gun from her. Stranahan bolted from the shadows, running low. He heard Asena scream "Killer!" and sensed, rather than heard, a rushing of air as the dog streaked past him.

Then there was the heavy report of the revolver and sharp pain as a shower of stones hit Stranahan's legs. At the next shot, the dog lurched, then in two great bounds it was on Amorak and he was down, dog, man and woman blurred as Stranahan stumbled into the melee. Amorak had Asena clenched in his embrace with Killer thrashing on top of them, his teeth tearing at the arm locked around Asena's throat. Stranahan made a lunge for the revolver in Amorak's right fist, his other hand grasping at the man's throat, his fingers tangling in the rawhide cord Amorak wore around his neck. As they wrestled, Stranahan twisting the cord in an attempt to strangle Amorak, he saw that Asena, freed from Amorak's grip, had kicked backward and was stumbling along the shore. Stranahan let go of the cord and brought both hands to bear on Amorak's hand gripping the revolver. Now they were chest to chest, Amorak's weight on top of him. He heard a click as Amorak thumbed back the hammer. Again, the revolver fired, jerking in recoil. There was a concussive sound and an eruption as the bullet struck the water only a foot away. A heartbeat, then a thin, cracking report, like the snap of a whip. Stranahan heard an echo bounce off the lake. He felt Amorak's body spasm on top of him. The man released his grip on the revolver and convulsed in a shudder. Then slowly he rose to a sitting position, his face lolling upward, silhouetted against the sky. That image froze. Then, abruptly, he fell forward onto Stranahan with the smack of a heavy stone.

Stranahan looked over to see Asena standing on the shore, her body trembling. What looked like a small pistol wavered in her hands. Killer had released his grip on Amorak's arm and was panting beside her. Stranahan felt a stabbing pain above his right hip. It occurred to him that he might have been bitten. He pushed out from under Amorak's body and got to his hands and knees, his chest heaving. His hand shook as he reached for the tracking light in his jacket pocket. He stood and played the beam over the figure in the water. Clouds of blood, lit to crimson phosphorescence by the LED bulbs, pulsed from under the surface. A river of red smoke issued from the entrance hole the bullet had made in Amorak's back.

"He's dead."

"Then it's over. He can't hurt us anymore."

Us? Stranahan was confused. Amorak had spoken to Asena as if she had been his lover, not the sister of his lover . . . but it was hard to think with the cramps that wracked the side of his body. He found he had the revolver in his hand and dropped it. He managed to cover the ten feet to Asena without falling and took the pistol from her as she collapsed in on herself. He helped her sit down on the pebbled shore. Taking the pistol, he jacked the action open to remove the chambered cartridge and ejected the stacked magazine. He walked back to collect the revolver. He pointed the barrel at a star, brought the hammer to half cock and opened the loading gate. His fingers shaking, he worked the plunger under the barrel to eject a cartridge, repeating the procedure until two loaded cartridges and four empties were ejected. They were identical to the cartridges he'd pocketed two weeks ago, a lifetime ago, in Alfonso Martinelli's cabin. It was the Colt .45, the Peacemaker her father had bought to fulfill his dream of becoming a trapper.

"What just happened?" he said, as much to himself as Asena.

"When you, when you were fighting, I saw it on the shore and got it."

"You mean this gun, the pistol? It was Amorak's?"

"Yes. I had to shoot him. Oh God, I could have killed you, too."

"Thank God it was the pistol," Stranahan said. He realized that if it had been the more powerful revolver she'd fired when Amorak was on top of him, the .45 caliber bullet would gone through Amorak's body to hit him, too.

"Well, you got him," Stranahan said.

Drained of energy, he closed his eyes. Asena's hat had fallen off, and he felt the warmth of her head where it nestled against his neck. Felt the wetness of her tears hot against his skin. He opened his eyes. She'd rolled up her jeans to her knees, to launch the boat he imagined, though that still puzzled him—*what was she doing with his boat?* Her bare shins gleamed in the moonlight. Evenly spaced white marks girded her right ankle. Stranahan touched one. It was raised, like scar tissue, and he thought about that a long minute, trying to bring something to the forefront of his mind. He looked past her to the silhouette of the guideboat. The last time he'd had a pistol fired at him, he'd been sitting in the bow. A dime of moonlight showed through the bullet hole.

"I've got to get a different boat," he said aloud.

"What?" Her voice was muffled.

"How did you find him, Asena?" Stranahan was struggling to put it together—Amorak's incantations, his declaration of love, the scars on Asena's ankle.

"I . . . I called the center. I told the woman that we'd donate meat, that my husband, he had shot an elk and we'd packed it down to the lake and were going to retrieve it with a boat. I thought he's the one they'd send. You told me that's what he did."

"Is that why you hired me? To paint a bull's-eye on him for you?"

"I had to find him. He had to pay."

"What did he have to pay for?" Stranahan realized that they were both speaking in loud voices, having been partially deafened by the gunshots.

"For what he did to us. For shooting those men. He was going to kill me, too, you have to know that."

Us? Those men?

"I heard a shot before I got to the lake. Amorak was dragging his leg. You shot him."

"I . . . I had to. He was reaching into his jacket. He had that pistol. I aimed at the water, but he stepped toward me and it hit him. It was just going to be a warning."

"Why didn't you aim for his chest and kill him? That's what you came here for."

"I . . . couldn't."

"What were you going to do with the body, Asena? Were you going to row out into the lake and dump it? You'd have capsized. Even if you managed it, he'd have washed up on shore."

She had disengaged and looked up at him. Steam rose when she spoke, her words brittle notes. "Not with forty feet of two-inch an-chor chain tied around him."

So that was it, Stranahan thought. He'd handed Amorak to her. He'd told her where to find him, he'd told her how to get him alone. He'd even told her how deep the lake was. If she had worked up the nerve to shoot him in cold blood, if the bullet that hit his leg had hit his heart, then Stranahan would have done everything but help her load the body into the boat.

"I want to get this straight. You confronted him, brandishing your father's revolver. He pulled a pistol, you shot him in the leg. Did you see the pistol?"

"Yes, I mean I think so. He dropped it when I shot. Then he . . . he talked me into dropping Daddy's gun. . . . He can do that to people."

"Yes, that part I saw."

"Killer," Stranahan heard her say.

The dog was lying down, whimpering. Stranahan shone the light. Nothing reacted with the LEDs except the blood on his left front paw, which Killer was vigorously licking. He must have been hit when Stranahan saw him lurch.

"What was Killer doing in the Bronco?"

Asena's voice was muffled. She'd buried her head back against his shoulder. "When I got here, I let him out, but he was running around and I wanted to surprise Fen. I realized taking him was a bad idea. I had the window cracked. He must have broken through or pushed it down."

"He saved your life. Probably mine, too."

Stranahan saw Asena turn her head toward the campground. Headlights were carving along the shoreline a quarter mile away. Stranahan identified the rumbling of the 5.7 liter V8 installed in the newer Jeep Cherokees. Willoughby must have reported Sean as missing, but how had Ettinger found out where he'd gone?

He said evenly, "I want you to listen carefully."

Asena had dragged Killer onto her lap and was stroking his head.

"This is important."

She nodded.

"That's a county vehicle, probably the sheriff. You're going to wait here while I talk to her. I'm going to tell her exactly what I saw, and only what I saw. Then, out of my presence, she's going to put the same questions to you. The less you say the better. You may have driven here with the intention of killing Amorak, but you can't be charged with intention. She's going to ask you about the revolver ten different ways, because you brought a gun to a word fight and there's no getting around it. Just stay on track, say you wanted to confront him about your sister, that the gun and Killer were for protection."

He paused, thinking. "The fact is an armed standoff led to a person's death. That's a problem for you. Are you listening?"

"It's a problem." She nodded.

"It's not a problem if you never brandished your revolver and you never fired that first shot. Here's what you're going to tell her. Amorak pulled his pistol. He talked you into dropping your weapon, which was holstered. His pistol fell from his hand when he tackled you, when I showed up at the scene. From that point on, everything happened exactly as we recall. There were four shots. Amorak took your revolver after you'd picked it back up and shot at Killer, who was running toward him. The first bullet missed. The second hit Killer's paw. The third was fired accidentally when I struggled with him. That's the shot that hit Amorak in the leg. The angle of the bullet might raise a question, but we were fighting, we were moving around. It's plausible. Then you picked up the pistol where Amorak had dropped it and shot him as we struggled, trying to save me. Got that?"

Stranahan shone his light onto the stones and pocketed one of the four empty cartridges he'd ejected from the .45. "Is the anchor chain in the Bronco?"

She nodded.

"If Ettinger asks about it, tell her it's there for ballast, like a sand bag."

"For ballast," she repeated. He felt her hand clamp around his forearm. Her hand was ice cold. "Why are you doing this for me?"

"You killed a very bad man in self-defense. That's the way I see it, and I can live with a lie of omission to make your life a little easier. Remember, Amorak's the one who fired the first shots. You had every reason to believe he was going to kill you. I'm an eyewitness. You'll be okay." He forced a smile. He could feel a sharp pain above his right hip. "I don't know about myself."

He heard the engine turn off and the slam of the Jeep door. He felt the wetness on his neck where her head had nestled and wiped at it. His hand came away red in the glow of the tracking light. He shone the light on the top of Asena's head, the LEDs reacting with a clot of blood the size of a fifty-cent piece.

"Were you hit?"

She reached for her hat. "I'm not hurt."

"Then why are you bleeding?"

CHAPTER THIRTY-SIX

Three Whiskeys and the Devil You Know

Martha Ettinger stepped out of the Jeep, leaving the headlights on. "This had better be good."

She put her hands on her hips, took in the Bronco, the boat trailer, the van, the rental sedan. Before Stranahan could answer, she said, "Your friend Willoughby reported you missing. I called the wildlife center. Their log lists Amorak getting a call to pick up elk quarters at Cliff Lake, I made a wild guess where that put you on the map. Enlighten me."

It was almost midnight before Doc Hanson arrived to bend over the body and mutter about being too old for this. Harold Little Feather, who had driven down from his sister's place in Pony to do the initial assessment of the scene, pulled the body to shore. Asena's first shot, from the big Peacemaker, had shattered Amorak's right shin and was through and through. The second bullet, when Asena had shot Amorak with his own pistol, had impacted the upper back, driving Amorak's wolf medallion into the ruin of his lungs, where the garnet stone eyes remained eerily intact, gleaming from the pulpy mess of the chest cavity. That puzzled Stranahan a minute. The medallion must have shifted around from Amorak's chest to his back when Stranahan was trying to strangle him with it. Doc Hanson examined the small handgun and said it was a nine millimeter Beretta, the Model 1934 with an identifying mark consisting of an etched eagle wearing a crown, to signify its manufacture for the Italian Royal Air Force. His father had brought one back from Italy at the end of the war. The pistol was undoubtedly the war relic Deni had mentioned at the campground, which left no doubt that Amorak had come to Cliff Lake armed. Stranahan knew then that unless Asena tripped up, the only punishment she'd receive would be the knowledge of committing murder in her heart, and that the one question Ettinger didn't think to ask would remain unanswered.

——

Driving on fumes to Rainbow Sam's Fly Shack two hours after Ettinger finished with him—he'd first had to return to West Yellowstone to drop off the rental and pick up his Land Cruiser, then had driven back to Bridger to collect Choti, who'd been left alone far too long—Stranahan had plenty of time to put that unasked question to himself. He reached over to the passenger seat to worry the coat of the Sheltie, who opened her brown eye, the baleful one, to regard her master.

"Who is she, Choti girl?"

"Friendliest creature you ever saw," the trapper had told him. "But then the next day she was more sober, seemed like a sensible young woman. Called me Mr. Barr." *Was he talking about Nicki or Asena?*

Amorak's words. "She was like this campfire that bows to the wind . . . a person who shows you two faces."

Then there were Asena's own statements: "I've spent a great deal of my life thinking things through. For both of us." And only a day ago—"You try to be someone who knows how to cope and do what you have to to keep going."

Now that he looked back, Stranahan saw that the clues had been there from the beginning. Asena at the Culpepper Ranch, breaking out of character to spin on her heel like a young girl. Sam talking about making love to two women in one woman's body. And the blood dried on Stranahan's neck. Amorak had presumably yanked out a considerable amount of hair to feed to the wolves. *Nicki's hair.* But it was Asena who bled.

The welts on the ankle were the clincher. It had taken Stranahan a while to recall the story, but he was sure he remembered it correctly, the girl on the verge of womanhood stripping naked to step in a wolf trap, the pool of blood spreading from her feet as her father averted his eyes. *Nicki's blood.* But the scars, they belonged to Asena.

———

Sam answered the knock saying "What the fuck, bro? It's three in the morning," and Stranahan hit him five times, right-left to the gut, then two open hand slaps to the side of his head when Sam dropped his hands, and another under the ribs when he raised them. Sam went down curled into a ball, his breath coming in stentorian gasps.

"Fuckin' Christ. What the hell'd you do that for?"

He struggled up and held out a hand. As Sean reached for it, Sam clamped his hand in a vise grip, pulled Stranahan forward and swung from the ground with his left. Stranahan dropped his arm to take the blow and hooked him twice—*thup, crack*—the fist this time, the second shot meant for the meat under Sam's ribs, but the big man ducked, taking the punch on the side of his face. He let go of Stranahan's right hand and dropped to both knees.

"Damn," Stranahan said, grasping his hand. Instantly he felt sorry. He'd almost never lost his temper in his life and now he'd hit his best friend.

Sam sat on the ground leaning back, propped on his arms. "Fuck you, man," he said. He put a finger into his mouth. "Broke my goddamned bicuspid. Ouch, Jesus that fucker's sharp." He spit out blood from where the tooth had cut his gum.

"'Ouch.' Was that what I heard you say, 'Ouch?'" Stranahan was still squeezing his hand. At least the knuckle hadn't jammed. But it would swell up for a couple days, like it always had after a match.

"Well, it hurts," Sam said. "Where the fuck did you learn how to do that? I could back you in bars and make money."

"Ah, Sam," Stranahan heaved a sigh, "you damn near got me killed.

You damn near got your dog killed. Do you have any idea how serious it is to abet someone plotting a murder?"

Sam's voice was thick. "I don't now what you're talking about."

"Start with forty feet of anchor chain. Ring a bell?"

"Anchor chain? Shit, I got piles of the stuff."

"Aren't you going to ask where Asena is?"

"Man, I told you before. I'm not her keeper. She goes off on her own."

"Yeah, well, what she went off to do tonight was wrap Amorak in chain and dump him into Cliff Lake. Using *my* boat. Don't look like you're amazed. You know who Amorak is. He's the one she wanted you to find before you told her I was a better man for the job. You know, to find the sister who was never missing because she didn't exist."

Sam hung his head.

"I had a lot of time to think about it driving here tonight, and I came to the conclusion that there was only one person she couldn't fool with her act. At least who was alive. Grady Cole she might not have convinced, but he was turning on an elk antler. It was you, Sam. You were with Nicki all summer. She couldn't come back pretending to be somebody else with you, could she?"

"What happened. Is she okay?"

"She isn't hurt, if that's what you mean. But she isn't exactly okay. Right now she's a guest of the county, sitting in a room with a desk and two chairs, drinking bad coffee. You didn't ask how I am. Your dog bit me. Is his rabies vaccination up to date?"

"I'm a responsible pet owner. Where is he?"

"He's at Svenson's Veterinary. He was shot in the paw, but it isn't serious. You can pick him up tomorrow."

Sam had struggled to his feet and was rubbing a fist into his stomach. "It's like you poked a hole through my gut."

"Just breathe shallow. It hurts more if you suck too much air."

"Man, I need a fuckin' drink."

"I'll give you one, but I want to know one thing first. Who were you in love with? Nicki or Asena?"

He shook his head. "Whoever," he said quietly. "I was in love with whoever she wanted to be."

———

It took three whiskys to get the story out of him. The first part Sean knew—how Sam had met a red-haired temptress at a Trout Unlimited banquet and taken her to bed, not knowing her name and not seeing her again until this summer, when she showed up wanting a job. What had perplexed him was that it didn't seem like the same person, the woman who'd been so sure of herself that she insisted on a safe word during sex. This woman, Nicki Martinelli, whose reputation as the Fly Fishing Venus preceded her, seemed childlike by comparison, earnest, passionate, but scattered and emotionally fragile. The child was the woman he fell in love with, only to witness her mature as the weeks passed, becoming more like the woman of the banquet and increasingly distant in the process. By the time she took the job at the ranch, they were little more than business partners. It had saddened him to discover she was having an affair with the wrangler, it had devastated him to hear she had disappeared and could be dead.

The night Sam had talked with Sean and Martha at the clubhouse, he'd been telling the truth. He had never heard anything about a sister. But at a knock the following evening, he'd opened his door to a woman who claimed she was just that. The woman had shorter hair, stood straighter, was more self-possessed than Nicki and spoke with a light French Canadian accent. She wore no makeup, and her countenance under a straw Stetson was stern. Her eyes were ice cold, green where Nicki's were gray. She told Sam she had driven from British Columbia to aid in the search for her younger sister. Her name was Asena ("Didn't Nicki ever tell you about me?").

She'd told Sam that the sheriff had given her his name, as someone who knew her sister. What could he tell her that might help?

Initially Sam had been skeptical. More than skeptical, for they were so alike and behind her eyes he could see flashes of a person that he knew, quirks of expression, a certain canting of the head, the way her nose twitched when she inhaled—nuances that seemingly couldn't be faked. It had to be Nicki. *Didn't it?*

But she'd convinced him, even if his eyebrows occasionally betrayed an involuntary reservation. For more than an hour, as she told Sam much the same story that she would repeat in the tipi to Sean later that night, Sam bought the act. Then, when setting down a cup, she'd done something catlike with her lips, touched her tongue to one corner of her mouth and half smiled. And Sam had simply reached over and unbuttoned the second button of her flannel shirt, and she had sat very still as he exposed the top swell of her right breast, where she had a small mole. Sam had always liked that mole. She'd rebuttoned the shirt without looking at him. Then she'd touched a fingertip to her eyes and taken out the contacts.

"I was going to tell you the truth, but I had to see for myself first," she said. The accent had vanished. "If I could fool you, then I knew I could fool anybody."

"Thank god you're alive," Sam said.

That's when she'd asked him to find Amorak.

———

Sam looked critically at the Mason jar holding the last finger of his whisky. He touched his lips to the blood-stained rim and winced. "I'm sorry, Kimosabe. I shoulda' never told her to look you up. I had no idea things were going to get so fucked."

Sean sipped at his cup of instant coffee. He was past being angry and simply wanted answers.

"What did she tell you about the night in Papoose Basin? What happened up there?"

"She said she wanted to check out the birds she'd seen circling and then got thrown by her horse. She figured it must have got a snootful of wolf. Knocked her cold, anyway, cut a gouge behind her ear. She was in and out of consciousness and then she heard a scream and that woke her up. When she came to, it was night. By the time she stumbled down to where the elk was, Cole was spitted like a suckling pig. Dead as a Montana Democrat. She panicked and ran off the mountain."

"She never saw Bucky Anderson?"

"She didn't see anybody but the stiff, least she never told me different."

"And she ran right into the arms of Amorak, there at the Palisades."

"She said she'd been seeing his tent there for a month. She put the blame on me for that and I deserved it."

"How's that?"

" 'Cause I couldn't keep my trap shut. I called the newspaper in Ennis about the Fly Fishing Venus. The story got picked up. He could have seen it anywhere and known where she was."

"Did she ever actually see Amorak?"

"Yeah, but that was the strange thing. She thought he'd confront her the first time she saw him. It scared the hell out of her. Mind now, I didn't know anything about this at the time. I just remember she came back from a guide day looking like she'd seen a ghost. Clung to me all night, the first time she'd let me touch her in a month."

"What did he say to her?"

"Nothing. Not one fucking word. Just stood on the bank watching when she floated by with her client. Like he was the cheese and she was the mouse. Sooner or later, she'd stick her neck in the trap. Trade the devil she didn't know for the devil she did." Sam nodded. "You know how it goes. You hit a low streak and the ex-girlfriend who was a fucking witch looks like she got hit with fairy dust. Your heart's telling you yes while your brain's saying 'Hey, wait a fucking minute.' But you don't listen to your brain 'cause it's a relief to have some-one else do the thinking."

It was Sam being Sam, but Stranahan followed well enough to get the gist.

"Sure, okay. But what happened that night? What did he do to her?"

"I don't know. I think she PTSD'd there for a day or two. Some-thing real bad. She said she got away from him and hitched a ride with an old dude who used to sell weather vanes and was so busy talking her ear off that he never noticed she was hurt. Anyway, he took her all the way to Libby and she holed up at her dad's place and licked her wounds. That's when she decided to pass herself off as the sister and get revenge on the asshole. She knew he was going to kill her; he'd told her a long time ago that if he couldn't have her no one ever would. But it was chilling, man, to see how her eyes got when she talked about him. Like a cat's eyes. I swear, though, I never thought you'd find him. You're my bro, you gotta forgive me that."

"You were in love with her, Sam. I understand how it affects IQ."

"So what's going to happen to her?"

Stranahan frowned. "Amorak wouldn't be dead if she hadn't tricked him into coming to the lake. There was an armed standoff and she's got GSR all over her hands. She admits firing the shot that killed him. So Ettinger's going to huff and puff. But unless Harold or one of the techs finds something to contradict her story, Ettinger will present the evidence to the DA with her assertion that it was self-defense. She'll recommend to not prosecute. The only thing that could trip her up is if Ettinger finds out she's Nicki in disguise."

"I'm telling you, man, there's no way. Not unless her head starts bleeding all over the floor."

"She told Ettinger she got gouged with a rock when she was strug-gling with Amorak. That's covered. I mean her documentation."

"She's a dual citizen from when her dad brought her down to the

States. She's got a U.S. driver's license as Nanika Martinelli; she's got Canuk papers as Nadina. Legally, she's two people. Or almost legally. You squint your eyes, they even have the same name. Nadina, Nanika, it's a two-letter difference. Like she told me, 'Smudge it a little, who's to notice?'"

"So were there ever two sisters, or did she just make Asena up?"

Sam shook his head. "I'm starting to think I never knew who she was."

CHAPTER THIRTY-SEVEN

Life Under Ice

He was halfway back to Bridger when something drifting around the edge of his consciousness settled long enough to pin down. It was Asena's reaction to meeting him at the Culpepper Ranch, her quizzical expression when she said he reminded her of someone. At the time it had meant nothing; now he realized that she'd recognized his voice as that of the man she'd knocked into the root cellar at her father's house. The man she'd mistaken for Fenrir Amorak. It was only *after* he'd spoken that she had quit firing through the floorboards. And when he confirmed her suspicion by telling her about his trip to Libby, the way she hugged him in the tipi, it had seemed like an overreaction. He realized now it was her relief at having not shot an innocent person. But what had happened before she hitched the ride to Libby? How had she escaped Amorak? And his incantations about the men who cried wolf? What was that about?

Stranahan thought Ettinger would hold her at least until the techs completed their work at the lakeshore, midmorning if not later. He'd meet up with her at Law and Justice, put some questions to her of his own. In the meantime, a few hours on the cot would do him a world of good. Stranahan dug his fingers into Choti's coat. "Home soon now, girl."

But in fact he did not drive directly to his tipi, but detoured to the Bridger Mountain Cultural Center, the halls five a.m. empty, his boots ringing on the travertine tiles. He let himself into his studio and booted up his computer, his brain wired on caffeine but his right-hand fingers so swollen he had to punch keys with his left.

A name search hit nothing but a spate of news stories chronicling the search for Nicki Martinelli. He sat back in his chair. Asena had told him she was seven years old when the snowmobile cracked through the ice. It was a traumatic experience and Stranahan had heard only her version, how the two girls were hurled with their mother into the freezing water. The daughters survived; their mother had died. Working backward from Asena's age—she'd told him she was twenty-seven, two years older than her sister—Stranahan isolated the probable year of the accident and finally found an account in the archives of the *Smithers Interior News*. It was dated December 29, and after he'd read the article he opened the bottom right-hand drawer, took out The Famous Grouse and poured two fingers into a water glass. While the whiskey warmed him, he read the story a second time.

Schoolteacher Drowns in Two Loon Lake

Tragedy Claims One Daughter, Leaves Second in Coma

A Houston teacher and her 7-year-old daughter died Thursday morning when their snowmobile plunged through the ice of Two Loon Lake.

The coroner's office identified the victims as Elizabeth Martinelli, 31, and her daughter Nadina.

Her younger daughter, Nanika, 5, was rescued from the icy water by her father, Alfonso Martinelli, 37, a commercial fisherman and fur trapper.

According to the sheriff's report, Mrs. Martinelli and the two girls were riding on one snowmobile across the frozen lake. Her husband was following in a second snowmobile when he heard a crack like a gunshot and saw his wife and daughters fall through the ice.

Martinelli used a chainsaw to saw a branch from a tree to attempt a rescue, but by the time he crawled to the opening in the ice, only the younger child was visible. He pulled her to safety.

The child slipped into a coma before being admitted to the Houston Community Clinic. She was listed in critical condition, suffering from hypothermic shock.

Dr. Kevin McCarthy, who related Martinelli's account of the tragedy to the *Interior News*, said the distraught man managed to convey what had happened in a mixture of French and English.

"He told me it was his fault because the daughter who drowned usually rides on his machine, but it was too laden down with ice-fishing gear that day," McCarthy said. "He kept saying, 'My life is under ice.' Either that or 'My wife is under ice.' He was babbling."

McCarthy said that even if Nanika Martinelli emerges from her coma, it could be weeks or months before the extent of her injuries are known. Depletion of oxygen can cause brain damage in hypothermic and near-drowning victims, although younger children have a better chance of recovery.

The last paragraph was a roundup of ice-related tragedies, and Stranahan glanced from the screen. So there had been two sisters and it was Nadina who died that day. The veil of fog was lifting. But what happened after Nanika came out of the coma?

Methodically, Sean searched the archives for an update on the girl's condition. Frustrated, he people searched for the doctor who had treated her. That also went nowhere. He did find a number for the clinic in Houston. A woman said in a tired voice that there was no doctor named McCarthy in personnel, but she'd only been there three years and a nurse who came on duty at seven had a longer tenure. Stranahan said he'd call back. He found himself yawning, suddenly overcome with fatigue, and lay down on the futon. Choti pushed her nose into the crook of his knees. Both were instantly asleep.

———

"Hello?"

"Dr. Kevin McCarthy?" Stranahan had slept for four hours and awakened with a dull pain behind his eyes and cramps in his side where Killer had bitten him.

"This is he. With whom am I speaking?"

Stranahan identified himself as an investigator for the Hyalite County Sheriff's Department. He said a background check on a missing woman revealed that she had once been treated by him.

"How did you find me? I haven't lived in British Columbia for twenty years."

"A nurse at the Houston Clinic told me you'd moved to Toronto. Pam Granger. I dialed every McCarthy in the white pages."

"How is Pam?"

"She sounded okay. She says to say 'hi.'"

"How can I help you, Mr. Stranahan?"

After Stranahan spoke there was silence on the line.

"Yes, I remember." The voice was careful. "I've often wondered what happened to her."

"She seems to have been confused about her identity. Sometimes she called herself by her sister's name, Nadina. Or Asena. Does that make sense to you?"

Silence.

"Dr. McCarthy?"

"I'm thinking about what you said. Unfortunately, it does make sense. The girl was comatose for several weeks, I can't recall the exact timetable of her recovery. A CAT scan showed neuropathic damage to the visual cortex, which sounds worse than it is. She had some spatial discrepancies in her nervous system, but brain function was largely unimpaired. From what I gather she had no memory of the accident except what her father told her. He may have been part of the problem. I was in the room when she spoke her first words and he called her by both her own name and the name of her sister, even in the same sentence. I think he suffered as much mental anguish as she did and carried a burden of guilt over the accident. From conversations with the girl's teachers, I gather Mr. Martinelli had been devoted to his older daughter, Nadina, the one who drowned. I was told she was very much the image of her mother. Nanika was quite an unruly child, emotional and full of undirected energy, what in my day might have been called a little dickens. I'm not a psychologist, but I would not be surprised if his calling her Nadina was an attempt to keep the memory of his older daughter alive. He might have thought that by reinforcing personality traits that reminded him of her, and indirectly of his wife, he would be better able to cope with the tragedy. But I really should not be speculating about this."

"Dr. McCarthy, we are searching for a missing person. It's hard to find someone when there's confusion about who you're looking for."

"Yes, of course. I only treated her for the initial trauma. Patient confidentiality is not an issue. I do wish to help."

But that was the note on which the extent of his help ended. He had not maintained contact with the father or his daughter and had taken a position in Ontario only a few months later. He would appreciate being informed if the woman was found. Stranahan set down the phone. On a whim he picked it back up and tapped in Martinique's number. The last time he'd called a man had picked up. Martinique had assured Sean that he was a fellow student in her study group. The phone rang six times. He set down the receiver halfway through a hello that was clearly male.

By the time he got a tetanus shot at the Bridger Health Clinic and drove to Law and Justice, Asena Martinelli, or rather the woman who had assumed the name, had been cooling her heels in the interview room some ten hours while the evidence dribbled in. Ettinger, who was in a surly mood, offered Sean a chair in her office by cocking a finger.

"I'm going to start by telling you a couple things you don't know and you're going to listen. Then we're going to get around to your shenanigans at the lake."

"I wouldn't call getting shot at and being chomped by an Airedale shenanigans."

"Humpff. Anyway, Katie's and your little extracurricular snooping in the park, the girl who got burned in the hot pot?"

"Carrie Harding. Did she come out of the coma?"

"Didn't I say listen?"

Stranahan raised a hand in acquiescence.

"No, she didn't, but the guy who found her, the professional wrestler who called himself the Madman of Minnetonka, hanged himself at a rental cabin in Gardner last night. I mean that's when they found him. He'd been swinging awhile. The suicide note said he'd given Harding a lift when she was hitchhiking and told her he'd show her the Cobalt Necropolis. All he wanted to do was touch her leg. He wrote that he felt like Frankenstein, who drowned the little child in the lake. He actually tried to save her, burned his own legs all to hell dragging her out. So our man Amorak, he's off the hook for that or would be if he still had a heartbeat."

"That doesn't come as a complete surprise," Stranahan said.

"No, but this will. Remember the list you found in old man Martinelli's journals? Ranchers Who Cried Wolf? They were some of the guys sent the anonymous poem written in blood? Sheriff Monroe over in Libby suspected Amorak, but no one on the list got hurt. Well that was then and this is now. I had one of my deputies do some digging. Turns out two of those ranchers were killed in hunting accidents well after the fact. One three years ago. One two years ago."

"So?

"So they were both hunting alone and found dead with their heads blown to hell."

"How do you get from that to Amorak?"

"You know me, I'm not the kind to leap at threads. That's your forte. But statewide we get only about one accidental shooting a year during rifle season. The odds of two men from a list of thirty-two names being the casualties of errant bullets in back-to-back years aren't so good. What I'm thinking now is Nicki Martinelli gave Amorak that list. Maybe she thought the letters would be the end of it. Scare the bad guys who hate wolves a little. Instead, her boyfriend puts bullets into a couple brain pans on opening day of the season. Maybe she knew about it, maybe she didn't."

"That would be a hard secret to live with." Stranahan thought back to Amorak's incantations at the lakeshore.

And the blood of man who cast aspersion upon the wolf will flow
    with the river
And he will die

No wonder she'd been so distraught.

Ettinger sighed. "I remember when the worst thing to happen in Montana was yearling prices fell."

"So when are you going to process her out?"

"You like that woman, don't you? Can't ever get enough of the pretty ones."

Stranahan shrugged. "She paid me to do a job."

"Uh-huh. Well, if it hadn't been for a dog breaking out a car window, you'd have got yourself dead doing it. Here's the situation. She was armed. She admits luring Amorak to the lake. She admits confronting him about her sister. She trailered a boat and there was anchor chain in her rig, which makes me think she planned to feed him to the trout. She says she didn't fire the Colt, only the pistol, but a

Colt holds six and you only extracted five cartridges, with three being empties. Where's the sixth cartridge?"

Stranahan thought about the warning shot that had hit Amorak's leg. The empty was still in his jeans' pocket. He said, "It's not unusual to carry a single-action revolver with the chamber under the hammer empty. For safety."

"I'll grant you the point. It still stinks to high heaven. But the man was scum and fired first. Thanks to you she has a witness. I told her to stay in the county until forensics comes in, but that's a formality. What are they going to find, a drop of blood from a guilty heart?" She shook her head. "To answer your question, we'll cut her loose inside the hour."

"I'll give her a lift back to Sam's. I'm sure he'll put her up as long as necessary."

Ettinger wagged her finger back and forth—"No, that's not going to happen. You were questioned at the scene, but you haven't given a formal statement. Walt will do the honors. My advice is the truth, the whole truth and nothing but. Besides, a deputy brought Martinelli's Bronco up from the lake last night. She can drive her own sweet self back to Sam's. As for you, down the hall, down the stairs, second door on the left. You know the drill."

Stranahan stood up. He'd thought of something. "Did you pick up the girl in the campground?"

Ettinger nodded. "We did an interview this morning. Denise Aldridge. Two gallons shy of a half tank. Said she'd met Amorak Monday, September 20, when she was signing the register to hike into Shoshone Lake in the park. He mentioned he knew a denning site and offered to show her a wolf—showed her a wolf. She said she'd taken a bus out here after quitting her job at the Dairy Queen in Bismarck and wanted to settle somewhere, quote, 'where there was mountains and nature and stuff,' and was looking for a sign. Amorak was the sign, but she knows next to nothing about him except that he told her he made a little money negotiating with urban entrepreneurs. That's drug dealer to you or me, but she didn't understand the word and didn't ask what it meant because she didn't want to appear dumb and jeopardize her chances of graduating to the red contact lenses. Kid's just a prey animal run out of cover where anyone can take a bite."

"What will happen to her?"

"She gave the name of an uncle in Minot who agreed to pick her up, provided the county paid his travel expenses."

"Amorak met her only a week after Martinelli went missing."

Ettinger nodded. "Makes you wonder how many others he went through. Far as I'm concerned, it's good riddance."

"You don't mean her, you mean him," Stranahan clarified.

"Right now I'm thinking just about everybody I know."

CHAPTER THIRTY-EIGHT

A Chair at the Table

In November, Stranahan drove north. Winning the lottery at the border crossing north of Sweetgrass, he leaned back against a cinderblock outbuilding while a Canadian guard searched the Land Cruiser. He took an envelope from his shirt pocket and unfolded a single sheet of stationery. The header was a two-inch-deep band of watercolor, a snow-clad mountain overlooking a river with a bankside cabin. The sign on the cabin's facing peak was made of log sections and read Martinelli's Fishing Camp. A nice piece of art, if Stranahan said so himself.

It had taken more than two weeks to track her down. Asena—it was difficult to start calling her by any other name—had once told him that she'd planned to renovate the cabin where she'd grown up and make it a fishing lodge. Though Stranahan suspected that's where she'd gone after skipping the state—by the time he'd given his statement and driven to Sam's fly shack, she'd already packed and hit the highway—he'd had no luck finding an address. He finally bought an online subscription to the *Smithers Interior News*, which he checked periodically on the off-chance her name would pop up. It did—as Nadina Martinelli—in, of all things, a team roster for a coed curling league. He'd sent a letter care of the league president, thinking it would be less threatening to her than if he'd called the man. He wrote that she had nothing to worry about, but that there had been a significant development in the lower forty-eight she'd be interested in, and to get in touch when she could.

There hadn't been a development, unless you counted an official statement from the sheriff's department to the effect that Nicki Martinelli was presumed dead. The newspapers and TV had had a field day with the story about the wolfman who was suspected of feeding Martinelli's hair to captive wolves, but as Amorak was deceased, there was little hope of recovering the woman's body. The DA had accepted Ettinger's recommendation not to prosecute the distraught sister who had shot Amorak, and the only way the case could have dragged on was if one of Amorak's relatives sued her for wrongful death. But any bridges to the McCready or Oddstatter families Amorak had burned long ago. His grave was dug at the county's expense.

A week after weather chased Stranahan from his tipi for good—Sam had been right; Montana was a winter of three-dog nights, and halfway into October Sean was already two dogs short—the phone rang in his studio. He was surprised to hear her voice.

"I was hoping you'd forget about me. I'm . . . very sorry about involving you in my life, passing myself off as someone I wasn't. . . . I suppose Sam told you everything. It's hard to—"

"Asena—"

"People call me Nadina here."

"Nadina, I know what happened the day your mother and sister drowned. I know you've been confused—"

"No, you don't."

"If you ever want to talk—"

"If I did it certainly wouldn't be on a phone."

Silence. Then: "Sean?" The voice had lost its aggressive tone. "When I think about you, the position I put you in, you and Sam both, it's unforgivable. Up at my dad's house, I . . . after I knocked you into the cellar I ran away and then I came back and shot at you. I thought you were him—you don't know all the things he did to me."

"You're forgiven. But I'd like for you to clear something up about that night. I was sure I heard a motorcycle. Was that you?"

"No, all I had was my bike. I hadn't gotten Dad's Bronco rewired yet. But the neighbor up the road races motocross. His kids are out half the night sometimes, and . . ."

And so a line of communication opened. Over the next couple weeks he'd spoken with her several times. She asked after Killer. Sean said Killer was back to being Killer, except for a limp. Sam had kept the claws that had been shot off Killer's paw and if she ever came back to Montana, he wanted to give her one, to string on her necklace with the wolf claw. That made her think of the wolves in Papoose Basin. She wondered what had happened to them and was relieved to find that the surviving members of the pack had left the area and hadn't been seen since. She volunteered that she was going ahead with plans to open the fishing lodge and sent him photographs. Would he paint the letterhead? For pay, of course. He agreed. The letter was her response. She'd wanted him to see how well the stationery turned out.

> . . . I already have slots filling for next September and what I need is a boat. With the jet sled restriction, it will have to be a raft or drift boat like we used on the Madison, but the opening's a long way off and I should be able to find a good deal in Terrace. If you ever want to catch a summer-run steelhead. . . .

Stranahan refolded the letter as the crossing guard walked up and handed over his keys.

"Those your paintings in the portfolio?" He had a very round face with a lopsided smile, like a comma.

Stranahan admitted they were.

"That one of the red-haired woman, she could stop a man's heart."

"She did," Stranahan said.

———

He'd once heard a man speak of a river as being as beautiful as the day it was made. That river drained a different continent and was fished by kings. The one Stranahan found at the end of the turnoff, some thirty miles of bad road south of Houston, was such a river, lack of royalty notwithstanding. The cabin resembled the cabin in her photos, set a little farther back from the bank. No one was home. Well, he hadn't told her he was coming. He walked down to the river and watched the water awhile, the pines, a snow-clad mountain in the distance, wondering if it was the peak that had inspired her name. When he heard the Bronco's motor over the sound of the current, he didn't turn around.

She came to stand beside him, leaning slightly back with her arms crossed. Stranahan gave her a sidelong glance. The tendrils of hair escaping a waxed cotton fishing cap turned in the breeze, like the last leaves of the bankside willows.

"You need a new timing belt," he said.

"How did you find my place? The Morice is a long river."

"I'm a detective, if you haven't forgotten. I didn't do it justice, your river." He nodded to himself. "Never paint from a photograph."

"I see you trailered one of Sam's boats. I haven't spoken to him since Montana. He must hate me."

"He doesn't."

"Does Sam know you're here?"

"No. I told him I was going fishing. Hit a few rivers in B.C. Actually, I have a commission to paint the Kispiox, but I can see I'm too late for the colors."

"You should paint this river. Come earlier next time, before the leaves fall."

Their eyes met. "When I do," Stranahan said, "you'll guide me for free. I've heard you're pretty good."

She smiled. "Take a walk with me."

They walked along the river, the grasses grown up between two well-worn ruts that betrayed a bear trail, the spacing an indication of the great breadth of a grizzly's chest.

She told him then, hesitantly at first, then simply remembering, about the girl who watched her sister drown, the blue coat going down into the icy water, her mother already drowned, a nightmare from which she had mercifully been spared those first few weeks, before she'd emerged from the coma. When the veil lifted, the drownings seemed surreal and came in blue waves, pulsing like a heartbeat. She'd be asleep and wake up screaming.

"Five years old. People don't carry many memories from when they're that young. Imagine that being your first lasting memory. It was really difficult with Dad calling me Nadina, acting like I was the one who'd drowned. I actually started to believe it, not really believe, on a basic level I always knew I was Nicki, but in a visual sense. Instead of watching my sister sink in her blue coat, I saw myself drown. She was the one on the surface and I was looking up from underwater. I had always looked up to her in life and now in death I really did look up to her, and that's the image that has both haunted and saved me ever since. For the rest of my life, during my worst times I would reach up for her, the way a drowning person reaches up. She would grab hold of my hand and pull me out of the dark water. I could become her, for a while anyway. Does that make sense?"

They'd reached a widening of the valley where the pines pulled back from the bank and the path wound into chest-high grasses.

"It's easy to surprise a bear in here. A fisherman got between a sow and a cub last year and lost half his face. This is where I usually turn back."

She walked ahead of him, the words trailing in her wake. "Growing up, the teachers thought I had a split personality. Dissociative identity disorder, they called it. They wanted me to see a psychologist all the way down to Prince Rupert. Dad wouldn't have it. But they were wrong. I always knew who I was, like someone who knows who they are under a mask. All I ever did was trade places with my sister. The worst times were after we moved to Kamloops, when Dad got the job trapping wolves. I hated what he did, and he was gone a lot and I couldn't reach far enough up for Nadina to take ahold of me. By then I was calling her Asena, after the wolf. I went sort of crazy. That's when I demonstrated in front of the ministry building and took my clothes off in the river. But it was a good time, too. I'd never had friends before and people were attracted to me. It was like I exerted a sort of power; one girl, a really smart girl, told me that people looked at me like I was an ornament that shone light and spun around so fast that I radiated a magnetic pull."

"That's when you got your little group of ecoterrorists together," Sean said.

She smiled. "It was harmless. Crazy as she was, I sort of miss that girl who swam with the salmon."

They hiked in silence awhile. "Here, I want to show you something."

She led him down to the riverbank cobbles. Upstream the river made a bend, turning out of the pines to burble over submerged boulders before smoothing into a mirror below.

"Looks like good steelhead water," Sean remarked.

"That big rock with the heavy swirl over it, we called it Daddy's Rock. Every fish that comes up from the rapids rests behind that rock. The first steelhead I ever caught on a fly rod, I got here. That's back when you were allowed to kill a wild fish and I dragged it all the way back to the cabin. Daddy was real proud of me. Of course, he called me Nadina. I really did love him though."

Her voice was reflective. "When we moved to Montana, we had a few good years before he got sick. I'm so glad we had that, being father and daughter in the best way. I grew up in Libby. I could be Nicki without the craziness, without a frantic need to be everywhere at once. Today they would say I had attention deficit disorder or I was bipolar or something else you need drugs for. All I knew was that for the first time since I was little, I didn't have to take on a different identity to empower myself, just to cope, you know. That's when I got the job guiding on the Kootenai and people started calling me the Fly Fishing Venus."

She let out a long breath. She said quietly, "I know you want me to explain about Fen. It's hard because I try not to think about him. He just took me over, maybe that's the best way to put it. He was attracted to one part of me, and I turned back into being a confused little girl for him. He was a master at keeping people off balance. One minute he'd tell me how beautiful I was and then the next how much I disappointed him. He'd make me do these . . . things. I lost my self-respect. He'd be around all summer and then he'd go away, and I'd feel dirty and try to become pure again by turning into Asena. I actually do have a degree in counseling and worked the winters up here in the rural schools. I still do, for that matter. Dad came with me and it would be like rolling back the clock. I'd almost manage to forget about Fen. But then he'd show up again, either drive here or wait for me to go back to Montana in June to guide. He'd do this thing where he'd hold out a knife and tell me the difference between love and hate was balanced on the blade. If I made the knife turn like this, and he'd turn the blade over, then he'd have to do this, and he'd cut the palm of his hand and put it on top of my head. He'd wash my head with his blood, then he'd lick it and start taking my clothes off. He'd be gentle. It was . . . so confusing.

"That night in Papoose Basin, I couldn't help going back to him. 'I've got to get to the ranch,' I said that over and over like a mantra, but my legs just kept going straight down the mountain, no matter how hard I tried to stop, my legs just kept going. I don't know when I got to the river, it had to have been midnight, but he was awake, standing outside the tent like he'd been waiting for me. My head was all bloody after falling. I think that's when he got the idea of feeding my hair to the wolves. He took me in the tent and I thought he'd lick my wound and then have sex with me, that it would be like before, but he started pulling my hair out in big clumps. It hurt like you can't believe. Look at what he did to me."

She removed her hat to part her hair. Patches were missing and there was an ugly welt behind her ear where she'd hit her head falling off the horse.

"I must have screamed my head off. I don't remember, but there was nobody else in the camp, so it wouldn't have mattered anyway. He told me if I wanted him to take me back, I had to pass a test. He was going to take me to a wolf den and tie me to a tree with nothing but a CamelBak so I could suck water, and if the pack or a bear didn't kill me and I was still alive in a week, then it would be a sign that I was worthy. He tried to prop me up on the back of his motorcycle, but I was so out of it I kept falling off. Finally he carried me back into the tent and I passed out. But then the pain would keep waking me up. He'd shine a flashlight, I'd see the light behind my eyelids, but I kept my eyes closed like I was asleep. Finally I heard the motorcycle and knew he'd left. He was going to get the van from his work so he could load me into it, I know that now, at least that's what I think, but back then all that mattered was he was gone. How I got down to the river I'll never know. But I washed myself off and wrapped my head up and got to the highway, and a guy who'd sold weathervanes and scarecrows and all kinds of stuff to ranch people back in the fifties picked me up. He told me the story of his life and kept me awake all the way to Libby, bless his heart."

Seeing her wounds made Stranahan think of the letters signed in blood.

"We found something in your father's journals. . . ."

She dragged the toe of her shoe on the bank while he told her about the men who'd been shot. Stranahan watched a tear run down her windburned cheek. She blinked, but did not wipe it away.

"I gave him that list."

"Why didn't you tell someone?"

"Because I couldn't prove it was him who shot those people. Because I was protecting myself. Because I thought I was in love. Because it wouldn't have mattered." She blinked again and turned to him. "Because because. I know you must think I'm a heartless monster."

"You can't be blamed for what he made you do."

"Yes I can. Poor Grady Cole, I let him fall in love with me and look what happened to him. It's like I'm cursed."

"That wasn't your fault. I'm sorry. Maybe I shouldn't have come. I seem to bring back nothing but bad memories."

"No, I'm glad you did. It's a relief to get it out. Who else can I ever tell?" She looked off across the river.

"Is that Nadina Mountain?"

"No, it's Nanika. Nadina's farther to the west. About where the sun is. We should be getting back. Most of the time now I really am okay. You don't have to worry about me. You'll stay for dinner, won't you? You could stay over tonight, I'd like you to. I . . . want you to."

Even in sadness, the woman standing beside him exerted a force field of energy that made the colors around her brighter, the scents more intense—the world vibrated by the simple fact of her presence. Stranahan wouldn't have been a man if he wasn't tempted.

"Thanks, but I should be going."

"Is it because I almost killed you?"

"The first time or the second? No, I seem to be attracted to dangerous women." He raised his eyebrows. "Some day that's going to get me into trouble."

"Is it the sheriff? You're more than friends, aren't you?"

"Yes, but I'm not sure what that makes us. We seem to keep circling each other."

"Then maybe when you get tired of circling, you'll come back here."

"Never say never to a steelhead river with a good run of fish."

He reached over and tilted up her chin. "Made you smile, didn't I? Come on. There's something I want you to have."

The trail was wider as they neared the cabin. He came up alongside her and she laced the fingers of her right hand through his. Sean recalled how cold her hands had felt that night at Cliff Lake, and wondered if the journey that had led her to this place in this time, from the girl who'd watched the blue coat disappear to the woman who perhaps at last had come to terms with her survival, was only a matter of the gradual rewarming of her blood.

At the Land Cruiser, he opened the portfolio and withdrew a framed watercolor.

She held it out. For a long time she said nothing.

"You said you missed her," Stranahan said.

"I do. Every evening I set a place for her at dinner. I need the light she brings into the world. Any day now, I think. All I have to do is walk around the table and sit down. After all, she's just another part of me."

"Maybe it was presumptuous. It's a nude study. But it's discreet. It's the hair flowing in the water I wanted to capture."

"It's beautiful."

Stranahan started unhitching the boat trailer.

"I thought you were going to float the Kispiox."

"No, I'm a wade fisherman at heart. The drift boat's yours. You still need one, don't you?"

"I can't accept this from you."

"You aren't. It's from Sam."

"You said you didn't tell him you were going to see me."

"I lied." Stranahan set the tongue of the boat trailer on a block of wood. It was Sam's backup ClackaCraft, the one with flowing hair painted on the side.

"See," he said, "made for you."

He clasped his hands on her shoulders and kissed her once on the mouth. "That's from Sam. He said to tell you, 'Somebody has to be the Fly Fishing Venus.' Remember that timing belt now," he said, and climbed into the Land Cruiser. He didn't look back.

CHAPTER THIRTY-NINE

Guns and White Roses

The groom wore Wrangler jeans, a cream silk shirt with pearl snaps, Larry Mahan ostrich boots and a Bailey 100X beaver felt hat with a four-inch brim, the Legacy model, custom blocked by WesTrends in Norris. The clasp on his string tie was a pewter elk. The bride, with three grown sons in attendance and a husband deep-sixed under a cross up the hill, wore white.

The band set up on three acres of manicured lawn, the leaves still tender and the June sky sapphire. Only a dusting of snow on the shoulders of the Gravelly Range across the ribbon of the Madison River recalled the spring. Stranahan got to one knee and placed his own hat, a sweat-stained Justin with a crown crack, on the other knee. He took Martha Ettinger's hand, farm rough, the nails bitten to the quick.

"May I have this dance?" he said.

"Get up," she said. "There could be somebody watching."

"Who?"

"My constituency. Come on, I'm not kidding."

On the drive down he'd asked her, as she was afraid he would, why she was so insistent on attending her cousin's wedding. After all, she still held Bucky Anderson responsible for Grady Cole's death, even though there was little chance he'd ever be prosecuted. The previous answers she'd given him, ever since receiving the invitation in March—"Because I want him to think he's clear so he'll trip up," "Because I don't want to give the bastard the satisfaction"—had never seemed entirely convincing, even to her. This time, she'd looked over at Sean from the driver's seat and said simply, "Because it's the only way I'll ever get to wear my blue dress."

It wasn't the whole truth, she didn't have the nerve to tell him the whole truth, but for a long time that afternoon, it was enough. She hadn't had occasion to wear a dress or a white rose in her hair or, for that matter, anything that revealed so much of her chromosomal makeup in, well, forever. For three hours she danced. She danced with Stranahan, she danced with other men she knew, she even danced once with Bucky Anderson when he asked her, the smiling bastard had a nerve, and managed to keep her tongue in her mouth. But for the last hour, she only danced with Stranahan.

True, she covered up the woman she'd set free those hours with her Carhartt jacket for the drive back to Bridger—the evening had grown chill if an excuse was needed—had even buckled on her utility belt out of old habit, which made Stranahan laugh. And then, sitting alone with him, she was suddenly embarrassed because she'd let him know the rest of the truth without a word being said. The memory of her body gradually relaxed as the sun cast the lawn in golden light and the ground underneath them began to whirl, until she had stood on her toes with her breasts spread against his chest and their lips so close that the kiss was as inevitable as the dying notes of "Save the Last Dance for Me," the band's swan song, suddenly made her self-conscious in a way she hadn't been for years. And then after that dance, when he had held her at arm's length and said, "But what about your constituency?" she had answered by tightening her hands around the back of his neck and kissing him again. A kiss that had gone on and on and left no doubt, the truth out at last.

Oh God, Martha, she said to herself, and felt the walls begin to build and the color come into her cheeks. Thank God it was dark inside the Cherokee.

One last chance for reprieve. "Do you want me to drop you at the tipi? I imagine Choti will be dying to see you." They were turning onto Cottonwood Road, the moon full in the window as the Jeep climbed.

"Choti's at Sam's."

"Do you want to come in for a drink? I think I've got some brandy." Martha felt the artery in her throat throbbing. *Just let him say no,* she said to herself. *Please let him say no.*

In the kitchen, still wearing the utility belt over her jacket, she washed out two glasses and found the brandy, which had been collecting dust in the cupboard ever since her second divorce, more than a decade ago. The amber liquid was thick as syrup. She switched on the track lights over the stump that served as her desk and looked down at the puzzle.

"You've almost got it finished, Martha."

"Late nights worrying about work. I'm still having trouble with the flies. Too much red."

She picked up a piece and tried to fit it, Stranahan looking over her shoulder. He'd had the puzzle made for her from a photograph he'd taken in British Columbia, his fly box opened over stones on the bank of the Kispiox River, half the flies black, the others Dead Man's Fancy. His breath was warm on the nape of her neck.

"You really want to work a puzzle wearing your Carhartts and your magnum?"

He heard her exhale as she set the piece of puzzle down on the stump. She didn't turn around to face him.

"I can't live up to your standards, I can't even come close." The words came in a rush. "I'm not from the world of Martiniques. The bits and pieces aren't where they used to be. I'm okay with who I am. I love my work, I love this farmhouse. I have Goldie. I have my cats. I've been down the road with men. It never works out. I don't want to lose you as a friend. I couldn't stand that."

He kissed the skin under her ear.

"I'm too old for you."

"You're not even forty." He kissed her again.

"It will change everything. I don't do anything casually. Tonight, what happened at the reception, we can put that behind us. If we stop right now . . ."

"I don't want to stop."

"But . . ."

He kissed her again. "Stop circling," he said. "Take off your gun."

Crazy Mountain Kiss

A Sean Stranahan Mystery

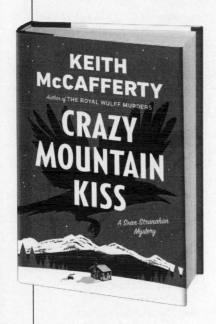

A clogged chimney flue in a Montana cabin reveals the body of a missing teenager, Cinderella "Cindy" Huntington, a rising rodeo star and the daughter of a locally infamous horse breeder. Suspects include a self-proclaimed mountain man, and among the clues is a Santa hat the victim was wearing. It's up to P.I. Sean Stranahan to learn who had the most to hide by killing Cinderella, who may have been about to expose a shameful secret.

VIKING

AVAILABLE FROM PENGUIN

The Gray Ghost Murders

"A truly wonderful read. . . . Keith [McCafferty] has created characters fresh, quirky and yet utterly believable, then stirred them into a mystery that unfolds with grace and humor against a setting of stunning beauty and danger."

—Nevada Barr, New York Times *bestselling author of the Anna Pigeon Mysteries*

The bear-scavenged remains of two gray-haired men buried in wilderness graves send Sean Stranahan searching the Montana mountains for tracks—and straight into the path of a murderous psychopath.

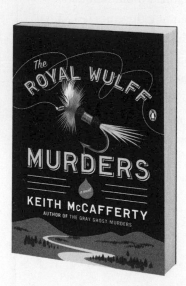

The Royal Wulff Murders

"A compelling Montana-based novel that will please both mystery readers and discerning fly-fishers. A terrific debut that rings with authenticity and style."

—C.J. Box, New York Times *bestselling author of* Stone Cold

Montanan Sean Stranahan, fly-fisher, painter, and has-been private detective, is hired to find a sultry siren's missing brother.

PENGUIN BOOKS